The

# Devil's Lance

the Devilstone Chronicles

book II

Richard Anderton

First Published in 2016 by JBA Books
An imprint of Jenny Brown Associates
Copyright © 2016 Richard Anderton
All rights reserved.
ISBN-13: 978-0-9933730-2-2
www.thedevilstonechronicles.com

For Mary, Jenny, Herries, James and Susie

# 1

## SOUTHERN GERMANY SPRING 1526

Thomas Devilstone heard the roar of angry voices and looked over the battlements.

In the fading light, he could see a rising tide of men running up the steep hill towards The Hornberg and the sight produced a murmur of unease from the other men on the castle's ramparts. Though their imposing fortress boasted high walls, tall towers and strong gates, the attackers carried siege ladders as well as a battering ram fashioned from the trunk of a tree. They also outnumbered the defenders by at least ten to one.

Though he stood shoulder to shoulder with the *landsknecht* mercenaries preparing to defend The Hornberg, Thomas wasn't dressed in the elaborate slashed doublet, colourful breeches and striped hose favoured by German soldiers of fortune.

In complete contrast to the other men on the wall, the Englishman wore the black woollen habit of a Benedictine friar and, though he was no priest, many of the defenders looked to him for guidance. In answer to their unspoken prayers, Thomas drew his sword and pointed its tip at their enemies.

"The mighty bull doesn't fear the ants, however many they may be, so light your matchcords, draw your blades and put your trust in the Devil!" Thomas cried and he had every reason to be confident.

Though the mutinous serfs advancing on The Hornberg were indeed numerous, they were armed with nothing more lethal than sharpened farm tools and ancient crossbows. By contrast, the battle-hardened veterans defending the castle were equipped with swords, halberds and the latest handguns. Moreover, the rebels' leader was nothing but a disgruntled ostler with little experience of war, whilst the defenders were led by the infamous robber baron Goetz von Berlichingen.

Though he was short, fat and nearly fifty, with a beard as white as a Templar's tunic, the Lord of The Hornberg lived for the thrill of battle and when he spoke, his voice echoed around his castle like Gabriel's trumpet.

"Listen to me, you miserable spawn of Satan! Your sins are so many and so heinous not even Almighty God can forgive you. I'm your only hope of salvation, so serve me well and live, but if any man amongst you allows just one of these ungrateful swineherds to set foot inside my walls I'll cut off his balls and stuff them up his arse!" Goetz bellowed and he called for his squires to fetch his favourite sword and sallet.

Moments later, two youths came stumbling into the courtyard and climbed the steps to the battlements. One brought Goetz's helmet, the other carried an enormous Swiss longsword, but instead of girding the heavy weapon around his master's waist, the squire fastened its hilt to Goetz's false hand.

The Lord of The Hornberg's original right arm had been carried off by a culverin ball twenty years earlier but its steel replacement boasted an ingenious array of gears and levers that allowed the mechanical fingers to grip anything from a hand of cards to a lance.

With his sword fixed firmly in his metal fist, 'Goetz of the Iron Hand' joined his men in hurling crude insults at the advancing rebels but, as soon as the peasant army came within range, the *landsknechts'* torrent of foul oaths and curses was replaced by a flesh-shredding hail of lead.

At Goetz's order, half a hundred muzzles flashed and the horde of battle-crazed farmers disappeared behind a choking fog of gun smoke. A chorus of agonised shrieks declared that the defenders' aim had been true but the rebels didn't waver.

Although a score of ploughboys now lay motionless below The Hornberg's walls, the deaths of their comrades had enraged the survivors and the peasant army continued its reckless charge with renewed vigour. Under his breath, Thomas cursed Goetz's lack of cannon but, out loud, he mocked the rebels' unimaginative siege-craft.

"Take a castle? These goat shaggers couldn't take a crap if you fed them nothing but rancid figs!" he cried but, as he said these words, the mob divided itself into two unequal groups. The larger force, which carried the battering ram, continued with their advance towards the castle's bailey but the smaller column wheeled right and ran towards The Hornberg's keep.

The castle's upper ward was surrounded by a sheer rock face twenty feet high but the lower ward had no such protection. Thinking his citadel was impregnable Goetz had placed his professional *landsknechts* in the more vulnerable bailey and left the defence of The Hornberg's keep to his domestic servants but, for once, he'd underestimated his enemy. As soon as the rebel's 'forlorn hope' had reached the base of the cliff they began raising their ladders.

"Thomas, take a score of men and knock over those ninepins," Goetz bellowed angrily but, before his captain could obey, a shower of crossbow bolts forced all the defenders to duck behind the battlements.

The bolts clattered harmlessly off the stonework but the poorly aimed volley allowed the rebels with the battering ram to reach a postern in the bailey's wall. The rhythmic thumping of the tree trunk against the gate's oak planks sounded like muffled drums at an execution but Goetz ignored the danger and repeated his order.

"What are you waiting for, you English jackanapes? I'll deal with these dogs scratching to be let in, you go and crush the fleas trying to bite my arse!" Goetz barked and he waved his good arm at the siege ladders being erected against the walls of the upper ward.

"I'm yours to command, My Lord!" Thomas replied and he ordered twenty of the castle's best arquebusiers and swordsmen to follow him.

The detachment reached the castle's upper ward quickly, and though there was no sign of the cowardly servants who were supposed to be defending the walls, the braziers used to kindle the handgunners' slow matches had been lit. Thomas barked an order and as his men primed the touch holes of their arquebuses, the tops of three siege ladders appeared between the battlements.

Shouting their defiance, the *landsknechts* prepared to repel the expected assault but, instead of attacking, the rebels called for the defenders to throw their English captain off the walls.

"You men on the ramparts are low-born like us, so open the gates and be saved. For, as St Paul said unto the Galatians, we're all united in Christ!" cried one of the peasants, who seemed to know his Bible better than most, but Thomas urged his men to ignore the preacher.

"You can't believe anything these murderous bastards say. Remember, they've all sworn to avenge their defeats at Frankenhausen and Würzburg by killing every *landsknecht* in the Holy Roman Empire, so let's blow these helots back to their pigsties!" Thomas cried but his men held their fire. Sensing that the notoriously fickle mercenaries were about to turn their coats, the peasants pressed their advantage by proclaiming that the defenders' current misfortunes were entirely the fault of the foreign wizard in their midst.

"There's no need to die in the service of the arrogant lords and dishonest bishops who hold you and your brethren in bondage, just give us the English sorcerer and you'll be spared," a rebel yelled.

"Once the vile witch is burned, the *Odenwald* will be cleansed of evil and you'll be free of your oaths to Satan," shouted another and some of the *landsknechts* began to look at Thomas with deep suspicion.

Their English captain was blessed with the tall, athletic frame and handsome features that could charm women or inspire confidence in men, yet his vigour, shock of unkempt black hair and steel grey eyes had suddenly lost their power to bewitch those on the wall.

The expression in the mercenaries' eyes told Thomas that they were on the point of throwing him to the rebels and, even though he looked as sinister as Savonarola when dressed in his monk's habit, he knew that he'd need more than fear to retain their loyalty.

Cursing the inconstancy of the ungrateful, Thomas reminded his men that he'd been at the Battle of Pavia, with the legendary mercenary colonel Georg von Frundsberg, where he'd helped the *Father of Landsknechts* crush the gilded lilies of French chivalry under his steel-shod foot.

"Have you sons of whores forgotten that I led the Devil's Band through that glorious slaughter to victory? And my men followed me because they knew that I can't be killed by a bullet, a blade or even a hangman's noose!" Thomas cried and he tore the monk's cowl off his head to reveal the rope burn around his throat.

The sight of the cruel scar produced an instantaneous effect on Thomas' men. The still livid weal reminded the superstitious *landsknechts* that their immortal souls would be damned for all eternity if they disobeyed a man who'd cheated death, so they blew on their matches and touched the glowing ends to their guns' breaches. The priming powder in the touch holes fizzed and twenty arquebuses spoke with one voice.

The peasants crowded around the base of each ladder were packed together so tightly every shot found its mark. Yet, whilst a dozen rebels fell to the ground clutching their bloodied faces and punctured guts, there were plenty of other swineherds and ditch diggers eager to be the first over the wall. Before the defenders could push the ladders away, the rungs were filled with more angry peasants, so Thomas ordered half his men to reload and half to cut down any farmer who reached the battlements.

Ten of the *landsknechts* dutifully drew their short katzbalger swords and when the first faces appeared at the top of the ladders, Thomas found himself facing the rebel preacher who'd demanded his death. Besides God's Word, this man had armed himself with a sickle tied to a long pole and, as he brandished the crude weapon, he screamed more verses from the bible.

"In Our Lord's name, I command ye, be ye repentant, and be ye converted, that all your sins be done away!" the preacher shouted but the godless sorcerer had no desire to be saved.

"And in the name of Lucifer I command you to kiss your arse goodbye!" Thomas replied and he launched a brutal, two-handed stroke that whistled through the air like an Irish banshee. The preacher tried to parry the blow with his extended sickle, but its long handle became entangled in the ladder's top and before the man could call on God to protect him, his skull was cleaved in two.

The preacher's corpse fell forty feet to the ground, accompanied by great gouts of blood and slices of butchered brain.

The other peasants howled with outrage but, before they could avenge the death of their pastor, the defenders' arquebuses roared again. Like ripe apples blown off a tree, more rebels fell from the ladders and, as their screams split the air, a large woman, with a red face and arms like hams, appeared on the walkway behind Thomas. The woman crossed herself when the hooded figure turned to face her and, lowering her head, she announced that Goetz had sent a gift.

"Lord Goetz trusts you'll use it wisely," said the woman and she pointed to half a dozen servant girls who were struggling to carry three large barrels up the flight of stone steps. The kegs were filled with lamp oil and, though there was no time to heat the liquid, Thomas knew exactly what to do. Taking his sword, he broached each of the casks and told the sweating scullery maids to tip their contents over the wall.

The attackers climbing the ladders were quickly drenched in foul-smelling fish oil but this did nothing to slow their ascent so Thomas ordered his men to empty the braziers of glowing coals over the battlements.

The slightest touch of the red-hot embers was enough to ignite the peasants' oil-soaked clothes and, in the space of a heartbeat, every man on the ladders had been transformed into a blazing pillar of fire. Shrieking with the pain of their unimaginable suffering, the burning men fell off the ladders and tumbled through the air like human fireflies.

The horrific sight finally weakened their comrades' resolve and a steady stream of defeated peasants began to flee down the hill, yet it was a different story in the castle's lower ward. Before Goetz could empty his kegs of oil over the rebels battering the postern, the little gate flew open and the triumphant peasant army flooded into The Hornberg.

The *landsknechts* defending the bailey ran for their lives but they were barely halfway along the ramp that led to the castle's upper ward when the portly Goetz stumbled. Within seconds, a dozen men had formed a rearguard to protect their stricken lord, however their courage and loyalty was their doom.

Whilst their comrades hauled Goetz to his feet, the rearguard fired into the mob and, as soon as they'd discharged their guns, they began using the empty weapons as clubs. The arquebuses' hardwood stocks shattered the jaws and limbs of a dozen peasants but the desperate defenders were soon overwhelmed and hacked to pieces.

Ignoring the butchery, Goetz led the rest of his men towards the castle's upper ward and the peasants realised too late that their enemy was about to elude them. With a great cry of anguish the enraged serfs started to give chase but the castle's inner gates were slammed shut before the vengeful mob could reach them.

Another volley of gunfire persuaded the rebels to retreat out of range and, once Goetz was safely inside the upper ward, the Lord of the Hornberg summoned Thomas to his side. The Englishman dutifully obeyed but, instead of congratulating him on quelling a mutiny and successfully defending the citadel, Goetz unleashed a fresh storm of fury.

"By all the hairs in the beard of Judas Iscariot, we were betrayed. I saw one of my own squires opening the postern, yet all your star charts and crystal balls failed to warn me that there was a traitor in our midst. Confess that you're a vile charlatan or I'll have the rack drag the truth from your filthy, bleeding body, you conniving English bastard!" Goetz cried and though Thomas was surprised by the vehemence of these insults, he refused to accept the blame for his employer's defeat.

"You dare doubt my powers? I'm the magus who raised the water dragon of Metz to devour my enemies and at my command the demon king Sabnock opened the gates of London's unconquerable Tower," he hissed.

The impudence of his sorcerer turned Goetz purple with rage but, before he could reply, he was interrupted by a loud cheer. For the time being, the Lord of the Hornberg forgot his quarrel with Thomas and led the surviving defenders to the wall that overlooked the bailey.

In the courtyard below, a thousand ecstatic peasants were celebrating their victory. Some brandished pikes decorated with the severed heads of the *landsknechts* killed in the battle for the lower ward whilst others carried poles to which unlaced shoes had been tied as symbols of their rebellion. The triumphant serfs were howling like savages but as soon as they saw Goetz and Thomas on the ramparts they fell silent.

The eerie quiet continued until the leader of the peasants' rebellion, holding a flag of truce, made his way to the front of the mob and called out that the Brethren of the *Bundschuh* wished to parley. Despite the oversized, captured helmet worn by this new Spartacus, Goetz recognised him as the groom he'd recently dismissed for drunkenness.

Seeing his disloyal former servant reignited Goetz's sense of outrage but he promised to make the man's end quick if he surrendered immediately. Ignoring the threat, the peasant chief replied with remarkable politeness.

"We of the *Bundschuh* have no quarrel with you, Lord Goetz. We remember the great victories you gave us before the disaster of Würzburg, and we know that you only abandoned our cause because you were bewitched by the fiend who stands at your side, so I'm here to offer you a way back to God. If you hand over the foreign sorcerer, you, your men and your castle will be spared but, if you refuse, we'll take The Hornberg apart, stone by stone, until we find him," said the peasant chief.

The rebel's words wove their own spell and Thomas felt the dying embers of his good fortune grow cold as the light of revelation reached the darkest corners of Goetz's soul.

"I accepted you into my service because you promised me weapons of war that would humble the Hapsburg Emperor and give me victory over my enemies but you've taken my gold and given me nothing in return. Whether you're a fraud or a witch is a matter for God to decide but, in either case, you must burn here on earth as well as in Hell for your crimes!" Goetz hissed, and he ordered his men to seize the sorcerer, but Thomas was not a man to surrender without a fight.

"Be still!" Thomas snapped and the superstitious soldiers thought it wiser to obey the man who claimed he could cheat death and command dragons. With his persecutors seemingly frozen in time, Thomas turned his attention to Goetz and declared his employer to be the worst of duplicitous poltroons.

"By the great hairy balls of St Boniface, are you the same Goetz who once told an archbishop to kiss his arse? That man would've hanged every rebel between here and the Elbe rather than bow to the mob. You're no longer Goetz of the Iron Hand, you're Goetz of the loose bowels and you shall be cursed for all time!" Thomas cried. Goetz opened his mouth to protest at his astrologer's impudence but wrath strangled the words in his throat and before the Lord of the Hornberg could speak, Thomas had begun to chant the words of a spell:

*I call upon,*
*MARQUIS ANDRAS,*
*Great Marquis of Hell,*
*Sower of discord among men,*
*To loosen the bonds wrought by Satan.*
*And release the Firedrake,*
*And I call upon EARL RÄUM,*
*Loyal servant of Lucifer,*
*Ruler of thirty legions of demons,*
*To rise up and smite my enemies,*
*O, foul demons, hear my words of power and obey!*
*ATOR AREPO*
*TENET OPERA*
*ROTAS*

Without his *grimoire*, Thomas couldn't remember the exact formula for summoning demons. He'd even borrowed the words of a Latin puzzle for the final lines of his incantation but his credulous audience were none the wiser. Moreover, Fate chose to add veracity to his words because, as soon as Thomas had spoken, a wolf howled in the distance and a dozen large, black crows settled on the castle's battlements.

Though these portentous creatures had been attracted by the smell of roasted flesh, everyone knew that Marquis Andras adopted the guise of a wolf when roaming the earth, whilst Earl *Räum* and his demon army took the form of crows.

The men of The Hornberg's garrison feared nothing that walked on the face of the earth, yet they knew that steel and shot had no power over a wizard and his legions of devils. The mercenaries' hesitancy sent their paymaster into further paroxysms of rage but, despite Goetz's repeated threats, his men refused to lay hands on the English sorcerer.

"Idiots! Don't fear this charlatan, seize him or you'll face the Holy Inquisition in his stead!" Goetz howled, as his men fell to their knees and began begging God for salvation. By the time Goetz had convinced them that demons weren't laying siege to The Hornberg, Thomas had vanished.

Whilst Goetz was cursing his men for their foolishness, Thomas had fled inside the castle's keep and barred the door. He was now in The Hornberg's great hall, a cavernous room with ancient tapestries hanging from the walls, but here fortune deserted him. Four grizzled servants armed with halberds blocked his exit but Thomas still had fear for an ally. Snatching a burning torch from its iron sconce, he began to trace a large circle on the floor and, as he did so, he called upon the demon lord *Abaddon the Destroyer* to smite his enemies:

*Hear me O ABADDON,*
*Sixth President of Satan's Kingdom,*
*I command thee to open the gates of Hell,*
*And drag all who serve the traitor Goetz of the Iron Hand,*
*Into the fiery pit so that they may answer for their treachery!*

As Thomas spoke, the tinder-dry rushes became a ring of fire and the simple-minded stewards howled in terror as they watched a portal to The Inferno open before their eyes. Seconds later, sparks from the burning rushes ignited the hall's desiccated wall hangings and the sight of a demonic monk surrounded by curtains of flame persuaded the servants to flee.

Like a huge, bloodsucking bat, Thomas pursued the shrieking dullards out of the hall and into the darkened corridor beyond but, though the stewards disappeared into the castle's kitchens, Thomas kept running until he'd reached the end of the passageway. Here, an arched door studded with nails led to The Hornberg's highest tower and though it was shut fast, Thomas had the key.

The bittersweet smell of smoke was beginning to fill the passageway as Thomas locked the tower's door behind him, and by the time he'd reached the last of the two hundred stone steps to his chamber the muscles of his legs were screaming in pain, but there was no time to rest. He barred his chamber's door and, pausing only to shed his monk's robes, he began to collect the few things he'd need outside The Hornberg.

Besides his sword, Thomas tied a dagger and a purse full of golden florins and guilders to his belt before hurriedly wrapping himself in his warmest riding coat. Once he was dressed for his journey, he removed a loose brick in the wall by the room's only window and retrieved his most precious possession: *The Munich Handbook of Demonic Magic*.

In spite of the fact that Thomas no longer put much faith in such superstitious gestures, he made the sign of the cross as he wrapped the surprisingly small spell book in a long piece of oiled cloth and tied the bundle securely around his waist.

Though he took the greatest of care to ensure his *grimoire* would survive the perils of its forthcoming journey, *The Munich Handbook* wasn't particularly rare or valuable. Most students of Natural Philosophy had a copy of the work in their libraries, yet what gave Thomas' edition its unique value was the fact that it had once belonged to Leonardo da Vinci.

Five years ago, Thomas had abandoned his studies with the great magus Heinrich Cornelius Agrippa and travelled to France with the express intention of stealing this book, or at least learning its secrets. However, he hadn't risked his life to obtain the *grimoire's* fanciful love spells and complex charms to locate a lost horse. What Thomas had wanted were the designs for the fantastic weapons of war that da Vinci had sketched in the spell book's margins.

Once he'd stolen this treasure, Thomas had planned to return to London, and make his fortune building these machines for the English King Henry VIII, but though he'd easily secured a position as the Tudor monarch's astrologer, jealous rivals had conspired against him. These men had accused Thomas of practising witchcraft and he'd been forced to flee abroad to escape execution.

Once safely across The Channel, Thomas had found sanctuary with several ambitious warlords before taking service with Goetz von Berlichingen. However, his arrival at The Hornberg had been especially timely. Though Thomas had failed to foresee the dangers ahead, shortly after appointing the Englishman as his court astrologer, Goetz had been forced to take sides in the Great Peasants' War.

Thousands of noblemen and their families had been slaughtered in the violent uprising that had left the whole of Southern Germany awash with blood but, seeing an opportunity to settle old scores with aristocratic enemies, the high-born Goetz had taken command of the same peasant army that was now besieging his castle. However Goetz was not a man who believed in dying for a cause, unless it was his own.

The notoriously fickle Goetz had swapped sides after his rebel ploughmen had been cut to pieces trying to storm the city of Würzburg and, though he'd known his former allies would never forgive such a betrayal, the speed with which retribution had come surprised both the Hornberg's Lord and his astrologer. The vengeful peasants had appeared before Goetz's castle without warning and the one machine that Thomas had built was of little use against a besieging army.

The faint sound of an explosion shook Thomas from his memories and he cursed Lady Fortune as he heard men in armour clattering up the stairs. His guess that Goetz had re-joined the rebels, and used gunpowder to blast his way inside his own tower, was confirmed once his former employer began hammering on the chamber's door. When Thomas failed to respond, Goetz ordered his men to fetch more gunpowder and be quick about it.

"We don't want Beelzebub's cup bearer flying back to his master so we'll blast our way inside this sorcerer's lair!" Goetz cried but his quarry had already climbed the ladder in the corner of the chamber and was scrambling through the trapdoor that led to the tower's roof.

Emerging into the cold air, Thomas bolted the trapdoor shut before turning to examine the strange machine that was waiting patiently for its maker. The sun had now set and the eerie shadows cast by the moonlight made this device look like a giant dragon released by one of *The Munich Handbook's* spells, yet Thomas hadn't used sorcery to summon this beast.

Instead of charms and incantations, Thomas' had followed one of Leonardo's designs and created his dragon from linen, leather and poplar wood. After building a wooden skeleton, he'd strengthened its joints with strips of cow hide soaked in a glue made from boiled holly bark, before covering the exposed spars with sheets of linen. Finally, he'd sealed the fabric with a paste made from flour and water.

Though the finished structure measured more than twenty feet across, it was light enough for one person to lift and strong enough to carry a man through the air. At least, that's what Thomas hoped because he'd yet to summon the courage to test it. The flying machine had actually been finished several weeks ago but he'd kept its existence secret out of fear that Goetz would insist on a practical demonstration.

Now, with the Lord of the Hornberg hard on his heels, Thomas had little choice but to make his maiden flight, so he peered over the parapet and let the wind cool the febrile sweat on his face. Though the breeze wasn't as strong as he'd hoped, it was at least blowing from the right direction, so he crawled inside the machine's frame and began fastening the straps that would hold him securely beneath its wings.

As his trembling fingers fumbled with the uncooperative buckles, Daedalus' Heir prayed to Aeolus, ancient God of Winds, to save him from being dashed to pieces on the rocky hillside below but the scornful deity mocked his prayer by showing him a new danger.

A sudden gust sent a shower of sparks swirling past the tower's parapet and as the tiny points of light disappeared into the darkness, Thomas realised that the fire he'd started in the great hall must have taken hold. Any sane individual would've hurried to fight the blaze but a loud bang, followed by the sound of the chamber's door splintering, proved that Goetz would rather watch his castle burn to the ground than let a man who'd failed him go unpunished.

Cursing the persistence of his former patron, Thomas braced his shoulders against the flying machine's frame and raised the whole structure a few inches off the flat roof. As he did so, another gust of wind lifted one of the wingtips. This at least was a good omen, the machine actually seemed keen to fly, but Thomas still lacked the nerve to defy God and nature.

Like a butterfly newly emerged from its chrysalis, he rested his wings on the edge of the parapet and imagined himself gliding serenely to the flat ground beyond the castle's eastern walls. Once he was safely back on terra firma he could disappear into the forest before anyone knew what was happening but, though he was sure his plan couldn't fail, Thomas' legs steadfastly refused to launch his trembling body into space.

As if to make the artificial wings soar by the sheer force of his will, Thomas closed his eyes and imagined autumn leaves whirling upwards in a gentle zephyr whilst eagles soared above mountains on rising currents of air. Unfortunately the trick failed and he remained rooted to the spot. Opening his eyes, Thomas looked over his shoulder to see if there was another avenue of escape but all he saw was an iron fist punch its way through the planks of the trapdoor.

"By the shit-stained cheeks of my mother's arse, what foul witchcraft is this?" Goetz bellowed as his grizzled head emerged through the jagged hole.

Like a metal chicken crawling from its egg, the Lord of the Hornberg tried to clamber through the shattered remains of the trapdoor but his mechanical arm became entangled in the splintered frame and this few seconds' grace spurred Thomas into action.

"Open your eyes and believe! I'm the sorcerer who once summoned the *Graoully* of Metz and now I've raised the *Firedrake*, the sulphurous dragon of The North, to burn The Hornberg to the ground!" Thomas yelled and he leapt off the parapet.

For several, heart-stopping seconds, the flying machine plummeted towards the earth, and Thomas couldn't stop himself from screaming, but with a nerve-shredding groan, the wings' rigging tightened and the lumbering artificial bird swooped skyward. An east wind was blowing steadily against The Hornberg's walls and the solid masonry was forcing the air into a strong upward draught.

For a brief moment, this powerful current of air held the flying machine motionless in space but the craft's weight inched it slowly towards the plume of choking smoke billowing from the great hall. Before Thomas could alter course, he found himself in the middle of this black cloud and the new Icarus felt panic rise in his gorge.

The heat from the burning hall could melt the flying machine's glue, or a rogue spark could set the wings alight, but the rising column of hot air merely pushed the wooden bird higher into the night sky.

As he ascended, Thomas felt the paralysing fear leave him and for a brief instant he was seized with elation. He'd become a god, soaring above even his own ambition but, at the very moment of his triumph, the machine's forward momentum carried him out of the inferno's heat.

Immediately the mechanical bird entered the cooler sky beyond the conflagration, one wingtip dipped and the machine began to turn a half-circle. With the wind now behind him, Thomas was propelled over the castle with the speed of an arrow and the men in the courtyards below screamed in terror at the sight of a gigantic, malevolent dragon swooping over The Hornberg.

Clenching his teeth, Thomas forced himself to ignore the dread gripping his bowels, and shifted his weight in the harness in a desperate attempt to stabilise the machine, but the wooden bird was as stubborn as a persistent lie.

With agonising slowness, the wings returned to level flight but Thomas' heart was now beating fast enough to break free of his chest and his hands clung to the frame tighter than a bishop clings to God's promise of forgiveness. Scarcely able to believe he was still alive, he looked ahead and saw he was flying towards the River Neckar, which lay to the west of the castle.

Now at last there was hope. If Thomas could set the flying machine down in the grassy fields on the far bank of the river, the marshy earth would cushion his landing. Furthermore, with his enemies stuck on the eastern bank, he'd have plenty of time to disappear into the dense forest that lay beyond the open pasture.

Glancing down Thomas could see the quicksilver waters of the river glittering in the moonlight but, just as he allowed himself to believe that he might survive his meteoric descent through the aether, he became aware that he was moving too fast to land safely.

With no way of slowing the flying machine, Thomas could do nothing but watch the river and fields vanish into the darkness behind him. Ahead, there were only the ghostly forms of tree tops and he let out a long scream as the first twigs began to pluck at his flailing feet. In desperation, Thomas tried to lift his lacerated legs clear of the greedy, grasping branches but nothing could prevent the inevitable.

In the end, it was a great oak that snatched the mechanical dragon from the air.

One of the tree's gnarled boughs caught the tip of the flying machine's fragile wing and Thomas felt himself cartwheel into the forest canopy. There was an almighty crash, followed by the nightmarish sounds of snapping and tearing, before Thomas' head struck the tree's trunk and the rest was silence.

# 2

## THE ANGEL OF DEATH

It was the orange glow in the night sky that made Prometheus look to the east. At first the Nubian thought he must have fallen asleep during his watch, and dawn was now breaking over The Hornberg, but when he looked again he realised that the light was coming from the huge tongues of flame that were consuming the castle.

For almost a minute he stood transfixed by the scene, as if his brain couldn't contemplate the idea of failure, but when one of the fortress's roofs collapsed in a shower of sparks the spell was broken and he began shaking his two sleeping companions.

"By the eyes of St Maurice we may be too late, someone is attacking Goetz's castle!" Prometheus hissed. The urgency in the Nubian's voice was enough to wake Luis Quintana, who'd not slept with both eyes closed since his mother had left him in a Lisbon foundling home, but Bos de Vries continued to sleep the sleep of the righteous.

With a snort of impatience the Portugee leapt to his feet, and delivered a hefty kick to the somnolent Frisian's ribs, but Bos didn't move.

"Rouse yourself you big ox. My fifty guilders are going up in smoke whilst you're dreaming of ploughing some cow-faced Frisian whore!" Quintana shouted but Bos merely pulled his cloak around his shoulders and tried to resume his slumbers.

"Have you forgotten? The one we seek has survived his own hanging, he's therefore been blessed by the Lord God Almighty and can never die by the hand of a mortal man. If I know Thomas Devilstone, we'll find that villainous English bastard sitting in a pile of ash calmly eating his breakfast," Bos muttered but Quintana was in no mood to let Lutheran heretics sleep when there was good money to be made.

Without warning, the Portugee emptied the contents of his water canteen over the Frisian's head whilst insisting that anyone who wanted to share in the gold they'd been promised had better pull on his braies. Cursing Quintana for a poltroon, Bos sat up and began tying his few possessions into a bundle but, before the travellers could begin their journey, they heard a bloodcurdling scream.

Though the terrifying cry sounded a long way off, the three men stopped what they were doing and stared into the darkness beyond the clearing. Though Bos and the others had fought in many battles, and had survived countless other dangers, they all feared the nameless perils of the night.

"What in the name of the pope's stinking pisspot was that?" Quintana whispered and, as his hand strayed to the short, unsheathed 'cat-skinner' sword at his belt, the scream sounded again. This time the unearthly howl sounded closer than before and in the next instant the ghostly form of an enormous flying creature filled the night sky above their heads.

"It's *Samael*, the Angel of Death! He's returning to The Abyss with one of the damned clasped to his belly!" Bos cried and he pointed to a tiny figure struggling beneath the beast's monstrous wings.

Still half asleep, the Frisian imagined that he and the others were already dead and their punishment for their many sins was to spend an eternity in this Stygian nightmare of a forest, being chased by winged demons. With a cry of despair, Bos dropped to his knees and began imploring heaven for salvation but Prometheus told him to be quiet in case the monster heard him and turned back.

"That wasn't the Angel of Death, it was a dragon and I swear the beast had the English wizard in its talons," he said fearfully.

Though Quintana scoffed at such a notion, Prometheus continued to insist that Thomas must have summoned the creature to help him escape from The Hornberg and that its fiery breath has set light to the castle. This prompted Bos to announce that the long foretold apocalypse was nigh.

"The Prophet Ezekiel sayeth that I heard the sound of their wings, and it was like the sound of many waters, and like the sound of the Most High God," he babbled but Quintana remained convinced that there was a perfectly rational explanation for what they'd just seen.

"Whatever that was, it looked more like a boat than a dragon. In Cathay I saw war kites large enough to carry men and I'll wager that was something similar," he said but the others refused to believe that a man could fly.

The Nubian declared that, although he was a child of the African desert, he'd learned enough about boats to know they couldn't sail through the air, whilst Bos insisted that what had just flown over their heads was not born of this world. The men continued to squabble amongst themselves until their argument was settled by the sound of a loud crash echoing through the forest.

"There you are, demons and dragons don't crash into trees," Quintana said triumphantly and he ran towards the edge of the clearing. Against their better judgement, Bos and Prometheus drew their swords and followed.

The forest was a mix of towering oaks and tall beeches, so the three men felt as if they were running through the legs of giants as they picked their way between the moss-covered trunks. To add to their sense of foreboding, the moonlight shining through the trees' leafless branches cast strange shadows over the ground and this tangle of black lines looked like demonic webs set to catch the souls of sinners.

Fighting their fears of sinister gods and terrible monsters, the reluctant huntsmen followed a narrow track through the undergrowth. This path led them deeper and deeper into the forest, yet they'd never have found the wreckage of Thomas' flying machine had it not been for the loud groans coming from its pilot.

The ethereal sounds led Bos, Prometheus and Quintana to the tree where the artificial bird had been wrecked and when they looked up into the tangle of snapped spars, they could just make out the form of a man hanging upside down. It was Thomas and he was held fast in the body of the beast by a cat's cradle of leather straps and torn linen.

Though the Englishman had recovered his senses, he couldn't see who his rescuers were so, fearing that Goetz's men had found him after all, he began to repeat his claims that he was protected by all manner of foul demons. Bos and the others had heard Thomas' empty threats many times and they merely laughed at their friend's embarrassing discomfort.

"By the great white arse of Santa Maria, this oak bears strange acorns!" Quintana declared.

"Is this man a new Sinbad, carried off by the great roc?" Prometheus asked.

"It looks to me like he's a new Lucifer, cast out of Heaven for his pride," said Bos.

Painfully, Thomas craned his neck to stare at the inverted figures and when he finally recognised the three men standing beneath the wreckage, he cursed them for continuing with their jests instead of helping him out of his tree.

"In the name of all the drunken popes of Rome, don't just stand there like eunuchs at a Vatican orgy, either get me down or leave me alone while I wait for Goetz of the Iron Hand to come and beg my forgiveness!" Thomas shouted.

The Englishman had last seen Bos, Prometheus and Quintana in the Italian city of Verona and, though he'd never admit it, he was delighted to be reunited with his former comrades. In spite of what he'd said, he was greatly relieved that the men who'd found him weren't part of The Hornberg's garrison, or from the murderous rabble that had captured Goetz's castle, and the others were equally thankful that Thomas was still alive.

"So the gods still can't hang you for your sins, however much they try," said Quintana but, before he could begin climbing the tree to cut Thomas down, Bos stopped him.

"Wait! I want to know what manner of black magic the Englishman has employed to fly over our heads because, if he's used witchcraft to escape The Hornberg, we should leave him for the crows," he said sternly and he warned the Portugee that good Christians were commanded by the Book of Exodus not to suffer a diabolical witch to live.

At this, Quintana groaned and, for the hundredth time, he told the pious Frisian that anyone expelled from their seminary for stabbing one of their tutors was in no position to pass judgement on other men. However Prometheus, who also knew his Bible by heart, shared Bos' concerns.

"I've dwelt in the land of whirring wings where the prophet Isaiah feared to tread but I've never seen such a monstrous thing. Was it born from Solomon's bird or was it summoned from Satan's stables?" Prometheus said darkly but, as soon as Thomas heard the words, he exploded with exasperated rage.

"By the five twisted limbs of the demon *Buer*, I built this flying machine with my own hands and if I'd used witchcraft I'd be safe in the nearest tavern drinking myself stupid by now, not dangling upside down like a goose on a market stall! So, don't just stand there, cut me free," Thomas snapped and his profession of innocence finally had the desired effect.

As a sometime sailor, the wiry Quintana could clamber up the tree with the skill of a Barbary ape and though Bos and Prometheus were both over six feet tall, with shoulders as broad as those of a carthorse, they too could climb with surprising agility.

When they reached the wreckage, Quintana hacked away at the leather whilst Prometheus and Bos plucked broken spars from the branches as easily as a kitchen maid plucks feathers from a chicken.

Trussed as he was, Thomas couldn't help with the work so, whilst the others sweated and strained to free him from his bonds, he told the story of his miraculous escape from The Hornberg.

At first he tried to maintain the fiction that he'd been merely testing the machine. However, when the others scoffed at this notion, he confessed that his plan to earn a fortune building war machines for Goetz of the Iron Hand hadn't worked as well as he'd hoped.

From bitter experience, Thomas' rescuers knew that the gratitude of powerful men was as fleeting as the love of a harlot. However, whilst the story of Goetz's shameless betrayal of his English alchemist came as no surprise to them, they could scarcely believe that Thomas had fled The Hornberg in a flying machine that he'd built in secret. Even when Thomas described in detail the terror he'd felt when standing on the tower's parapet, and the sense of elation that had seized his soul as he'd soared high above his enemies, the others mocked him for his reckless stupidity.

"The ostrich knows it can't fly like the falcon so it doesn't try, yet this Englishman seems to have less brains than the bird which runs in circles to escape the lion," Prometheus chuckled as he pushed one of the flying machine's ruined wings aside.

"And a duck doesn't build its nest in a tree," said Quintana as he hacked at a particularly troublesome knot.

"You fools know nothing. Thomas isn't a bird, he's the new Adam and now he's eaten from the Tree of Knowledge, God has punished him with the Second Fall, but from an even greater height than the first!" Bos added and he burst into great peals laughter at his own joke.

In truth, the Frisian was not a natural jester, he had a saturnine temperament and his face sported a voluminous beard beneath a tousled mass of red hair that looked like a diabolical halo. He also had a temper like a wounded bear and though he'd once trained for the priesthood, his murder of a tutor, during a heated debate over Christ's true nature, had cut short his career in the Roman Catholic Church.

To escape the hangman's noose, Bos had joined the rebels fighting the Hapsburg Emperor, who'd wanted to add the sand dunes and marshes of Friesland to his sprawling Holy Roman Empire, but Bos' calling to serve God was strong and he'd soon found a new church that was more to his liking.

Once the armies of imperial *landsknechts* had crushed the Frisian Rebellion, a defeat which had led to an even greater price being placed on his head, Bos had quit his devastated homeland and fled to England.

Landing in the East Anglian port of Bishop's Lynn was, Bos believed, part of the special destiny God had chosen for his most devout servant, because it had been here that he'd first heard the teachings of Martin Luther. Like the apostles at Pentecost, Bos had been seized with evangelical zeal and he'd soon left The Fens to preach Luther's word across England. On reaching the city of London, Bos had denounced the corruption of the popish church in every market place from Tyburn to Cheapside and his harangues had soon attracted the wrath of the fiercely Catholic English King Henry VIII.

The Tudor monarch, who reputedly heard up to five masses a day, had ordered the heretic arrested and consigned to the flames so, barely a month after arriving in London, Bos had found himself chained to the wall of the Fleet Prison, awaiting his terrible death. Despite welcoming the prospect of martyrdom, the Frisian was no fool and he'd gladly accepted Thomas' help to escape his dreadful fate. Yet his piety rarely allowed Bos to show his gratitude to the English sorcerer.

"Cease your struggling or I'll slit your throat," he said as he tried to cut away a fold of linen with his dagger.

"If you do, I'll command all the demons of Hell to rise up and throw you into a lake of burning brimstone. Now make haste, for my poor aching limbs are seized with the agony of cramp!" Thomas cried but Prometheus told him to be patient.

"If you'd run or ridden from The Hornberg like any sensible person, you'd not be hanging upside down like a bat in a cave. Now cease your mewling; we're nearly done," he said. Like Bos, Prometheus was a refugee from a failed war of liberation that had devastated his homeland. However, whilst the Frisian had all the subtlety of a charging boar, the Nubian carried himself with the effortless grace of a lion.

Unlike Thomas' sorcery, or Quintana's disdain for his fellow man, Prometheus' regal bearing was not a carefully crafted conceit, because he had been born to rule. Though few people knew it, the giant African with a mop of unruly black curls and a thin straggly beard was the deposed heir to the throne of Dotawo.

Along with Alodia, Makuria and Nobatia, Dotawo had been one of the ancient Christian kingdoms of Nubia. Its monarchs had once ruled all the land between Egypt's southern border and the River Nile's Second Cataract and its people had been among the first to embrace The Gospels. At his own baptism thirty years ago, Prometheus had been christened Djoel, after his father the king of Dotawo, but, before the younger Djoel had grown his first beard, their desert realm had been conquered by an army of pagans.

The invaders, who called themselves the Funj, came from beyond the marshes that lay in the far south of Nubia and, though they'd soon abandoned their false idols, they'd also spurned the Christian faith of their conquered people.

To the utter consternation of Dotawo's bishops, their foreign overlords had converted to the Moslem religion of the Turks, who'd subjugated Egypt at the same time, so the younger Djoel had grown to manhood vowing to free his people from yoke of their heathen oppressors.

After the death of his father, the heir to Dotawo's crown had continued the fight to recover his lost throne until he'd been betrayed and captured. Like Joseph in the Old Testament, the younger Djoel had been taken into Egypt as a slave and sold to a Barbary Corsair; yet his brutal servitude, chained to the oars of a galley, had been mercifully short. After a vicious battle with a Venetian fleet, in which the pirates had been defeated, Djoel was released and taken to Venice. In gratitude he'd sworn never to use his regal name until he'd defeated the Funj and restored the Church of St Mark to Nubia.

In accordance with his vow Djoel had adopted the name Prometheus, after the Greek Titan who'd saved mankind from darkness by stealing fire from Olympus, and chosen Venice as his place of exile. He'd hope d that the Venetians, sworn enemies of the infidel Turks and their allies, would be keen to reconquer the Nile kingdoms for Christ but the Venetian Doge had shown little interest in leading a new crusade. As a Christian, Prometheus had been allowed to live on The Rialto; unfortunately, like the fabled Othello before him, his sojourn in the Most Serene Republic had not been happy.

For a while Prometheus had earned a meagre living as an apothecary, using the wisdom he'd learned whilst hiding in Nubia's desert monasteries, but too few Venetians trusted the exotic remedies he'd offered for sale. Before his creditors could have him imprisoned for debt, Prometheus had stowed away on a ship bound for England and though he'd soon found himself breathing

London's free air, the English were even less welcoming to a foreign physician than the Venetians.

The last prince of Dotawo had been reduced to eking out a living as a prizefighter in the boxing booths of Southwark and Bankside, until repeated accusations that he'd deliberately lost fights had brought his career as a pugilist to an abrupt end. Convicted of cheating those who'd wagered on his bouts, the Nubian had been sentenced to hang and imprisoned in the same dungeon where Bos and Quintana were awaiting their own executions. Prometheus too would have ended his days on the scaffold, had not Thomas secured his release.

The last of Thomas' rescuers was Luis Quintana, who was a few years older than the Englishman's twenty five summers. As a boy, the orphaned Quintana had escaped a life of poverty by running away to sea and he'd spent several years in the service of the great Portuguese navigators. Twice Quintana had sailed around the tip of Africa to the Orient but it was in the palaces of the English king that he'd faced his greatest peril.

Shortly after he'd accepted a position as a captain in Catherine of Aragon's personal guard, Quintana had become embroiled in the tortuous power games being played by the Tudor King and his Spanish Queen. Accused of seducing one of Catherine's ladies-in-waiting, the hapless Quintana had been sentenced to hang and, whilst he too had been freed by Thomas, their first meeting had been less than auspicious.

After being arrested for practising witchcraft, the Englishman had been imprisoned with the Frisian, the Nubian and the Portugee in the dungeons of the Fleet Prison. Their doom had seemed certain until Thomas had contrived to use the last of his favours, and his reputation as a powerful sorcerer, to help them all escape.

Together the four men had fled their Tudor persecutors and found sanctuary in the ranks of the Holy Roman Emperor's *landsknechts*, which was fighting the French in Italy, until jealous fate had intervened to break up their profitable partnership.

After the imperial army had won a glorious victory at Pavia, Thomas and the others had hoped to continue with their lucrative employment as mercenary captains. However, the French had been so utterly defeated, the emperor had no more need of his pike squares.

Like thousands of other soldiers, the men of the Devil's Band had been dismissed from the Hapsburg emperor's service and two months after celebrating their famous triumph, they'd found themselves wandering Northern Italy looking for a new master. It wasn't long before the last of their money had been spent and, by the time they'd reached the city of Verona, the four men were quarrelling constantly.

The end had come when the deeply pious Bos had declared that their misfortune was entirely due to God's desire to punish Thomas for his attempts to cast spells. Tormented by the pain of hunger, the others had agreed that they were all being made to suffer for the Englishman's sins and so, blinded by his own anger, Thomas had left them to wallow in their own ignorance and superstition.

After crossing The Alps, Thomas had wandered through Southern Germany in the hope of finding someone more appreciative of his talents and, after Goetz of the Iron Hand had offered him a position as his personal astrologer and alchemist, he'd all but forgotten his former companions.

Now, as he waited for rescue, he wondered what had made the others come to their senses, yet Quintana was brandishing his knife in front of Thomas' face before he could ask why they'd followed him to The Hornberg.

"Hold tight," said the Portugee, as he cut through the last of the straps that imprisoned the flying machine's pilot, but Thomas' fingers were so numb he couldn't find a handhold on the slippery wood. Cursing the perfidy of his friends, Thomas crashed through the branches and landed in a pile of soft leaves at the tree's base.

For several moments the man who claimed he could tame dragons could do nothing but lie in the rotting vegetation, nursing his cuts and bruises, but Quintana and the others were quickly by his side. Without saying a word, the Portugee thrust a leather flask full of aquavit between Thomas' lips and the fiery spirit quickly brought the fallen angel to his senses.

Though the Portugee was a little older than Thomas, and the Englishman was considerably taller than Quintana, they were each blessed with the athletic build, strong muscles and dark good looks that appealed to women. The two men were alike in many ways, such as a shared passion for gold and a deep mistrust of priests but this was hardly surprising, as they'd both been born in penury and brought up to be good God-fearing Catholics.

Yet for all their similarities, Thomas and Quintana had their differences. The Englishman was as comfortable discussing the finer points of theology with a learned professor as he was wielding a sword but the Portugee had no love of books or scholarship. Moreover, in contrast to the foundling Quintana's questionable parentage, Thomas could claim descent from a noble, if now impoverished, family.

Having been fed tales of past Devilstone glories with his mother's milk, Thomas dreamed of recovering the rich North Country estates lost by his feckless ancestors.

Quintana, on the other hand, had few ambitions and considered himself lucky if he lived long enough to enjoy his next meal. Nevertheless the Portugee had a healthy respect for Thomas' esoteric knowledge and he looked at the remains of the mechanical bird with genuine awe.

"Did you really fly all the way from The Hornberg in that heap of firewood?" Quintana asked.

"It looks like he did more falling that flying," said Bos. Prometheus also agreed that Thomas' machine bore little resemblance to a bird.

"I've seen better looking chicken coops after a bad storm," he said but Thomas insisted that he was now the equal of Daedalus.

"I flew and my mechanical bird will bring me great wealth," Thomas said proudly and, as he struggled to his feet, he declared that his invention would be hugely profitable because it would make even the smallest army invincible. Unfortunately, the others failed to share his enthusiasm. Prometheus wondered why any captain would risk putting his men into such death traps, whilst Bos thought that all such endeavours were either blasphemous or of no more use to men in battle than the prayers of a heretic pope.

In that instant, Thomas' confidence in his own genius deserted him. He'd never considered how his artificial bird could win a war and, now that the others had asked the question, it seemed ridiculous to assume that conquering the skies would lead to similar victories on earth. Angered by his own folly, Thomas stared at the litter of wood and leather scattered around the tree, and saw only the wreckage of his dreams, but he quickly changed the subject.

"After what happened in Verona I thought I'd never see your ugly faces again, so what brought you all here?"

Thomas asked but Bos put his finger to his lips.

"Quiet, someone's coming," the Frisian hissed. The four men had spent enough time together to trust one another's instincts so they hid themselves as quickly as they could. Bos and Prometheus disappeared into a thicket, whilst Thomas and Quintana squeezed into a hollow beneath a fallen beech tree.

Moments later, a line of horsemen appeared on the track which ran through the clearing. They were speaking in a language that sounded like Latin, so Thomas thought that they might be clerics on their way to the university at Heidelberg, but as the column passed into a patch of moonlight he could see that these men weren't dressed as peaceful scholars.

Each of the two dozen riders wore a tall, conical cap made of scarlet felt and decorated with three black feathers. Their long, buff coloured riding coats were worn over loose blue breeches and, as well as the sabres attached to their belts, each horseman was armed with either a lance or a bow and carried a curved shield shaped like a teardrop.

All these unusual shields were painted bright red and decorated with a picture of a dragon being strangled by its own tail. Thomas knew that no German or English nobleman used such bizarre heraldry but he recognised the strange design at once. It was the *Ouroboros*, the ancient occult symbol representing mystical unity and the endless cycle of rebirth.

"More of your sorcerer friends looking for somewhere to offer their sacrifices to Satan?" Quintana whispered but Thomas told him to be quiet or they'd all be meeting the Prince of Darkness a lot sooner than they hoped.

Whoever these riders were, they seemed unconcerned by the burning castle, which was still lighting up the night sky, and their unhurried progress through the clearing made Thomas wonder if they were either afraid of something or looking for someone. A moment later the horsemen's captain, who wore a wolf's skin tied around his shoulders as a badge of his office, confirmed Thomas' suspicions by stopping at the wreckage beneath the oak tree where the flying machine had met its end.

With a cry of triumph, the captain raised his arm to call a halt and signalled for his men to proceed on foot. Obediently, the horsemen dismounted and tied their horses' reins to the nearest sapling before spreading out through the glade.

Like beaters trying to flush game into the open, the riders started slashing at the undergrowth with their sabres and, inch by inch, two of the horsemen drew closer to the thicket where Prometheus and Bos had taken refuge. Thomas and Quintana could only watch in horror as the riders thrust their blades deep into every bush; but, just when it seemed certain that their companions would be sliced like ripe cucumbers, the two giants leapt from their hiding place with their swords in their hands and blood curdling battle cries on their lips.

The appearance of a huge African, as black as belladonna and twice as deadly, accompanied by a bellowing red bearded ogre, threw the two riders into confusion and they stumbled backwards in fright. Before they could recover, two blades had flashed in the moonlight and the riders' severed heads dropped to the ground with a soft thud.

Leaping over the decapitated bodies, Bos and Prometheus ran to the nearest pair of tethered horses and untied the reins, but the surprised ponies refused to let the strange riders climb into their saddles. Whinnying with terror, the frightened horses kept turning in circles whilst Bos and Prometheus hopped about, each with one foot in the stirrups.

The sight of the two thieves struggling with the unforgiving ponies spurred the other riders into action, and they began to run towards the brigands, but now Thomas and Quintana entered the fray. As one of the horsemen vaulted the fallen tree where the Portugee was hiding, Quintana thrust his sword upwards and pierced the rider through his groin. The dead man somersaulted through the air and landed in a bush with the Portugee's sword still sticking out of his crotch.

Meanwhile, Thomas launched himself at a brutal looking man who sported a livid scar above his thick black moustache. However, the Englishman was still dazed from his crash and the scarred horseman easily parried each of his attacker's thrusts. The rider grinned like Attila before the gates of Rome as Thomas repeatedly tried, and failed, to break through his guard but the sound of the duel had alerted Quintana.

Before the scarred rider could sense any threat to his rear, the Portugee had delivered a vicious kick from behind that landed between the man's legs and as he fell to the ground, clutching his shattered nutmegs, Thomas drove his sword between his enemy's shoulder blades. Elated by this victory, Thomas whooped with delight but Quintana wasn't satisfied.

"Unless you want to be congratulated by St Peter, save your breath and find a horse. We're outnumbered and our only chance is to flee!" Quintana yelled and he pointed to the surviving riders who were trying to surround them.

Pausing only to wrench their bloodied blades from the bodies of the dead riders, Thomas and Quintana, ran towards the string of horses tied to the trees. They reached their goal just as Bos and Prometheus managed to swing themselves into their beasts' saddles and they wasted no time in mounting two more horses.

Screaming all manner of apocalyptic oaths, the four horse thieves dug their heels into their beasts' flanks, burst through the cordon of men on foot and vanished into the darkness. The riders with bows loosed a storm of arrows at the fleeing figures whilst those with lances quickly mounted their own steeds and set off in pursuit.

"By the foul smelling dung of the Behemoth, they'll turn us all into porcupines unless we lose them in the forest!" Thomas yelled as one of the hastily loosed shafts whistled past his head. Lashing the rump of his horse with the reins, Thomas quickly overtook the others and once he was leading the headlong charge through the darkened trees, he shouted for everyone to follow him.

Neither the Englishman nor his companions were expert horsemen but they had one important advantage. As a guest of Goetz von Berlichingen, Thomas had often hunted in the Neckar Valley and he knew the tracks through the forest better than he knew his catechism. At each junction, he picked the path less travelled and he thanked God that there was no frost on the frozen ground to give away his choice. His plan to double back to the river worked better than he could have hoped and by the time the fugitives reached a patch of open ground at the water's edge, there was no sign of their pursuers.

"So, who in the name of Pope Adrian's arse were those damnable servants of Lucifer?" Bos asked as he and the others reined in their sweating beasts and dismounted.

Though Thomas understood the symbolic meaning of the *Ouroboros* it didn't explain the riders' identity and none of the others recognised their enemies' exotic clothing or weapons. All they knew was that the forest was full of *landsknechts* and their noble masters hunting rebel peasants, whilst they had no allies except each other.

"Whoever they were, they weren't very friendly but let's see what these nags can tell us about their former owners," said Thomas, as he began to search his horses' saddlebags. However, much to the Englishman's annoyance, the crude leather pouches contained very little of interest.

Some dried horsemeat, a small sack of grain, flint and steel and a purse containing a few copper coins were the sum total of the previous rider's possessions. The other horses' saddlebags produced almost identical contents which left Thomas and the others none the wiser.

"They were probably bandits looking to prey on fat merchants or wealthy bishops and they got more than they bargained for when they tackled us," said Bos, yet Prometheus wasn't so sure and he wondered why a band of highwaymen had been so interested in the wreckage of Thomas' flying machine. Quintana, on the other hand, agreed with Bos and dismissed the Nubian's worries.

"For once the Frisian is right, those bastards were only interested in finding someone rich enough to rob or ransom and if they'd known Lord Scaliger was prepared to pay us a hundred guilders apiece to find this sorry specimen, they'd have put up a much harder fight," he said, jerking his thumb at Thomas, but at the sound of the name 'Scaliger' the Englishman burst out laughing.

"Scaliger? Julius Caesar Scaliger paid you three hundred guilders to find me!" Thomas cried in disbelief.

# 3

## MARBURG

Though he'd never met the man, Thomas knew that the famous Italian knight, courtier, philosopher, doctor and alchemist who called himself Julius Caesar Scaliger had once enjoyed an enviable reputation for his valour and learning.

This soldier-scholar had been a contemporary of Thomas' tutor, Cornelius Agrippa, and during his glittering early career he'd studied art with the German master Albrecht Dürer before serving Maximilian, the previous Holy Roman Emperor, as his personal squire. Unfortunately, Scaliger's fanatical pursuit of his family's lost wealth and titles had brought him nothing but ridicule and exile.

For years, Scaliger had claimed that he was descended from the House of La Scala, the noble family who'd once been Lords of Verona, but more than a century ago, an angry mob had driven the last of the tyrannical *Scaligeri* out of the city. By the time of Julius' birth, Verona had become a fief of the Holy Roman Empire so, in an attempt to persuade Maximilian to restore his ancestral titles, he'd joined the imperial army.

Though Scaliger's courage in battle had won him a knighthood, another seventeen years of loyal service had not produced his longed-for, ducal crown. In his frustration Scaliger had resigned his commission and entered the church, hoping that one day he'd occupy the throne of St Peter.

As pope, Scaliger could've forced the emperor to make him Lord of Verona; yet, in this too, he'd failed. After three successive Holy Fathers had refused to advance him to even the first rung on the Curial ladder, Scaliger had renounced his vows and enrolled in Bologna University to study philosophy.

Once he'd obtained his degree, Scaliger had accepted a position with the powerful Della Rovere family but, when Venice had suddenly added Verona to her empire, he'd been forced to admit that all his efforts had been in vain.

Those opposed to the growing power of the Most Serene Republic insisted that only Lucifer could intercede with the Doge. Therefore, it wasn't long before Scaliger's enemies began spreading rumours that the would-be Lord of Verona had decided to make a pact with the Devil.

"By the bloodstained rags of St Christina, have you really sunk so low as to take service with this deranged madman and what does he want with me?" Thomas scoffed but Bos immediately declared that there was no virtue in starving to death in the gutters of Verona.

"After you abandoned us, Scaliger gave us a good meal and the promise of honest work! Can you say the same of your robber baron?" said the Frisian bitterly and Prometheus gleefully reminded Thomas that accepting a position with the slippery Goetz of the Iron Hand hadn't been one of the Englishman's better decisions.

"Goetz is the bastard child of the Prince of Lies, but go back to him if you're not interested in what Scaliger has to say," he chided and Quintana added that anyone who was mad enough to offer them each a hundred guilders to find one Englishman should be courted for as long as was possible.

"Personally, I wouldn't give two kreuzers for your miserable carcase but Bos is right, there's no virtue or sanity in poverty," he said and Thomas had to admit he was impressed by his own worth. If he'd continued in his career as a mercenary captain, it would've taken him two years to earn a hundred guilders, if he'd survived that long, but such generosity also made him suspicious.

Looking at the others through narrowed eyes, Thomas asked why Scaliger was willing to pay so handsomely for the dubious privilege of meeting him. However, his erstwhile comrades just shrugged their shoulders and insisted that they had no idea of their employer's motives. Prometheus remarked that men like Scaliger never divulged their secrets until it was absolutely necessary, whilst Bos maintained that their instructions amounted to nothing more than finding Thomas and taking him to the Castle of Wewelsburg.

"Scaliger's fortress is four days 'journey to the north, and we must be there at least two weeks before Lady Day, so are you coming or not?" Quintana asked.

Still Thomas hesitated. He'd had enough of noble paymasters for the time being and whilst he hadn't considered what he was going to do after escaping from The Hornberg, he was certain that his plans did not include Julius Caesar Scaliger.

"Perhaps I have something to persuade you that we serve a man of honour," said Prometheus and he handed the Englishman a small leather bag which he'd produced from beneath his shirt. Puzzled, Thomas opened it and took out a circular medallion the size of a belt buckle.

The gold medal had a ring at the top for a ribbon, which was missing, and it was decorated with a picture of a dead sheep hanging from a strap fastened around its middle. Around the edge was an inscription in Latin:

PRETIUM LABORUM NON VILE

"No small reward for labours," Thomas said out loud. He knew that this was the motto of the Knights of the Golden Fleece and whilst the jewel on its own was worth half a year's pay, he also understood its deeper meaning. Scaliger was telling him that if he agreed to undertake whatever task he might be set, he'd be initiated into the Holy Roman Empire's most prestigious order of chivalry.

"If you're invested with The Fleece, every crowned head in Christendom will want you at their court and you can name your own price for your services," said Quintana jealously and Thomas had to agree that Lady Fortune had turned her lovely face towards him at last.

"Very well, I'll meet Scaliger, but I make no promises," he said as he slipped the jewel into his purse.

"Then we'd better get started before our benefactor regains his sanity and withdraws his offer," said Bos and he climbed into the saddle of his pony.

The road to Wewelsburg took the men through the Odenwald, a land characterised by dense forests and low mountains. In more peaceful times, these wooded peaks separated by broad valleys were pleasant and prosperous places to live; unfortunately, these were far from peaceful times. With every mile that Thomas and the others travelled, they saw more proof that the peasants had lost their disastrous war with the nobles and the victorious lords of the Swabian League had taken a terrible revenge on their mutinous serfs.

Once thriving villages had been reduced to smoke-blackened ruins and every large oak tree had become a gibbet festooned with the rotting corpses of hanged rebels. Some of the fresher corpses had already lost their eyes to crows but their grinning, sightless skulls still stared accusingly at any travellers who passed by. Other cadavers were in a more advanced state of decomposition and their once virile flesh was now a writhing mass of maggots. Worst of all was the stench of putrescence, which seemed to lie across the road like an invisible fog.

"God's Hooks, you'd have thought that the Germans would be sick of war," said Prometheus as they rode under one particularly fruitful gallows.

"It's one of the commandments of history that when Germans can't fight foreigners they must fight each other," said Quintana, holding his nose.

"Are other nations any different? In all the days since Cain killed Abel it's been man's destiny to fight his brother," said Bos, yet all through this exchange Thomas had remained strangely silent. The sight of lifeless ploughboys swinging gently in the breeze reminded him of his own brush with the hangman's noose and, though it had been more than a year since Frundsberg had tried to hang him as a French spy, the memory of that fateful day still made him shiver.

In his dreams Thomas sometimes felt the rope's coarse hemp tighten around his throat, and he'd awake drenched in his own sweat, but in the cold light of dawn he'd remember that at least the Devil and all his demons loved a hanged man.

"I wonder what possessed these simple-minded serfs to take up arms against their lords in the first place. Surely they knew they couldn't win?" Prometheus mused and at last Thomas was moved to speak.

"Would you believe that snails are at the root of all this slaughter?" Thomas said and he told the others that the war had started when the Countess of Lupfen had ordered her serfs to gather snail shells to use as spools for her thread. By the time the task had been completed, the peasants' crops had rotted in the fields and so, facing starvation, the desperate villagers had attacked their mistress's castle.

Though the peasants of Lupfen failed to capture the countess's fortress, thousands of oppressed serfs from other estates had joined the revolt. Within weeks, all of Swabia, Bavaria and Thuringia were in flames and the usually slate-grey rivers of Southern Germany were running blue with the blood of slaughtered barons and their families.

To crush the revolt, the nobles had revived their Swabian League and recruited thousands of *landsknecht* mercenaries, many of them veterans of the Italian Wars, to defend their estates. In a series of particularly vicious battles, where no quarter was asked or given, the serfs' earlier successes had been reversed by the nobles' armies and tens of thousands of poor shepherds and cowherds had been butchered like their sheep and cattle.

As they passed under another tree laden with corpses, Thomas told the others of how Goetz had fled from one of these disasters, leaving his men to be massacred beneath the walls of Würzburg. However, he also admitted that, when he'd first arrived in the *Odenwald*, he'd felt some sympathy for the starving peasantry. For decades, the nobles had been enclosing their serfs' common land and now no man was allowed to fish, hunt or chop wood without the permission of his feudal lord.

"Pigs rooting in the midden enjoy more freedom than the peasants of Germany, yet a rebellion is a fearsome thing. The mob is a dragon with a hundred thousand heads and it soon devours those who labour to feed its many mouths. Such dragons can't be tamed, they must be killed and I should know, for I am the master of all dragons," Thomas declared but Bos, who'd fought in the Frisian Uprising against an equally rapacious Hapsburg duke and his *landsknechts*, was quick to defend the rebels.

"So what if a little blood's been spilt? The pope and his puppet, the Holy Roman Emperor, are worse despots than the Pharaohs of Egypt. If Moses was blessed by God for defying Rameses, it's the duty of all good Christians to oppose tyrants wherever they may be found," he growled. This prompted Prometheus to remind the Frisian that Luther had condemned the rebels for their murder of innocent women and children so the serfs' downfall was rooted in their violent excesses.

"If their cause was just, God wouldn't have deserted them on the battlefield," he said firmly. Bos countered that the rebels had only been defeated because they'd been betrayed by their nobly born commanders like Goetz of the Iron Hand and now Quintana entered the fray. Though he'd no love for anyone born to wealth and privilege, the Portugee declared that the peasants were fools who deserved to be slaughtered for putting their faith in rusty scythes and worm-eaten crossbows.

"Remember Pavia, when the *landsknecht* arquebusiers and halberdiers cut down the flower of French chivalry? If our old comrades in the *fähnleins* could defeat fully-armoured knights they were sure to make mincemeat of a few sheep shaggers with a grudge," he said.

None of the others could fault the Portugee's logic but their talk only served to remind them that the forests were full of outlawed rebels who'd turned to brigandage after their defeat by the Swabian League. As witnessed by the attack on The Hornberg, and the fight with the mysterious riders, these highwaymen would have no love for men dressed in the colourful clothes favoured by their noble enemies' hired killers.

Though Thomas had dressed himself in the homespun clothing of a lowly groom before fleeing The Hornberg, the others were still wearing the slashed doublets, striped hose and wide brimmed hats that were the unmistakeable garb of *landsknecht* mercenaries.

"We should change our clothing as soon as we can or we risk being buried in it," said Quintana as they approached a narrow gully that was the perfect place for an ambush, yet Bos remarked that whatever they wore would put them in danger.

"If we dress like peasants we'll be hanged as rebels and if we stay clothed as we are we'll be mistaken for the catspaws of noble tyrants!" Bos said gloomily

"God's Wounds, a Greek sphinx couldn't think up such a diabolical riddle," added Prometheus but Thomas dismissed the others' fears with a stern rebuke.

"By the great white hart of St Hubert, you've all become more timid than forest deer! Yet, even as you cower like milkmaids in a thunderstorm, take courage, for we'll soon be in Marburg and I know just where we can find a warm bed for the night," he said and he set off through the gully.

The men had to ride hard if they were to reach their sanctuary before dusk but after several tortuous hours in the saddle, Marburg appeared on the horizon. This picturesque town occupied a spur cut from the hillside by a loop of the River Lahn and the summit of this conical peak was crowned by the Landgrave of Hesse's formidable castle. Beneath this brooding fortress there was an enormous, twin-spired church dedicated to St

Elizabeth of Hungary and the steep slopes between the castle and the town's walls were crowded with neat, half-timbered houses.

Entry to Marburg from the east was by way of a fortified bridge which boasted three stone arches at either end and a central wooden section that could be easily pulled down or set on fire in times of siege. The western end of this bridge was guarded by an imposing barbican, with sturdy wooden gates that the town's sentries were preparing to close, and a bell began to toll as Thomas and the others approached.

As the sound of the curfew echoed around the valley, the road became filled with anxious farmers driving their livestock towards the town and soon the four foreigners in the midst of this throng began to feel like Noah leading the way to the ark. Old women herding hordes of honking geese, warreners pushing barrows full of caged rabbits, poulterers with live chickens tied to long poles and numerous other tinkers, hawkers and pedlars all jostled each other impatiently as they hurried to reach the safety of Marburg before nightfall.

The captain of Marburg's watchmen was happy to let the local rustics pass through the gates unchallenged but he ordered the three men dressed as *landsknechts*, and their groom, to halt and state their business. Prometheus began to explain that they were on their way north, and merely passing through the *Odenwald*, but the captain declared his mistrust by spitting onto the cobbles.

"The war's over and we're not hiring any more thieving mercenary turds," said the captain and though Prometheus was taken aback by the man's insolence, he insisted that the man was mistaken.

"We don't want work, we simply want a hot meal and somewhere to sleep. Now, please let us enter your fine city," he said politely, yet the captain remained unmoved.

"Didn't you hear me? All *landsknechts* are low-born bastards who do nothing but get pissed and beat up the local doxies. So, turn your horses around and go to the Devil," sneered the captain.

This insult was too much for Prometheus and, in one swift motion, he'd leapt from his saddle, drawn his sword and was pressing its tip against the captain's throat. The sweet smell of urine filled the air as the man wet himself.

"Low-born am I? I'll have you know, my dear captain of cuckolds, I'm so high-born that a son of a whore like you would need a fifty foot ladder just to kiss my arse! Now stand aside before I cut off your balls and hang them round your miserable neck!" Prometheus hissed and he gave the terrified man a hard shove that sent him sprawling to the ground.

Lying on the floor, the petrified captain could do nothing to stop the four men from entering Marburg and they were soon lost in the maze of streets on the other side of the river.

As the sun set, Thomas led his companions across town to the top of a long, narrow street that sloped steeply towards the waterfront. The hill was so precipitous and the cobbles so slippery everyone had to dismount and lead their horses by their bridles. At the bottom of the slope there was a wooden gate, set in a high stone wall, and when the others realised that this was the street's only exit, they demanded to know why the Englishman had brought them to a dead end.

"I discovered this place some years ago. It used to be a nunnery," he said whereupon Quintana exploded with indignant rage.

"By the blistered feet of St Clare, what do we want with a nunnery? For once we've plenty of money, so why couldn't we find a decent inn with a warm fire and willing wenches?" the Portugee said angrily. Prometheus also wondered why they had to spend the night in a draughty convent, with nothing except bread, water and prayer offered to weary travellers, whilst Bos had deep theological objections to seeking refuge with nuns.

"I need no bride of Christ to pray for my soul, for it's by a man's faith alone that he shall be saved," he said, with a growl, but Thomas assured him that the convent had been abandoned by its nuns after Marburg's Lutheran prince had expelled all monastic orders from his lands.

"The nuns have gone but their bath house remains, and it's the best stew between the Thames and the Tiber, so let's partake of a little piece of paradise. I think we've earned it," he said and he pulled on a bell rope which hung next to the gate.

Immediately, a spyhole in the door opened and a wooden box on the end of a long stick shot out like the tongue of the serpent tempting Eve. From within, a voice demanded payment of a guilder for each man and without hesitation Thomas, Prometheus and Quintana reached for their purses. Though Bos protested loudly at the extortionate price of a bath in Marburg, he'd no wish to be found on the streets after curfew so he too dropped a golden coin in the box.

"As soon as the coin in the coffer rings, a soul from purgatory springs!" Quintana said gleefully as the door swung open.

Unlike the captain of the nightwatch, the gatekeeper of the bath house gave his visitors a truly warm welcome. After calling for grooms to take their horses to the stables, he ushered his guests across the ex-convent's courtyard and into a low, stone building with a steeply pitched roof.

Once inside, the gatekeeper invited the men to undress and they gratefully shed their mud encrusted clothes. The filthy garments were taken away to be laundered and, for the next hour, the travellers sweated away the dust and grime their bodies had accumulated during their many weeks on the road.

When the men had finished their hot bath, they passed into another room that boasted a deep pool of cold water at its centre. With great shrieks of delight the men dived into the pool's icy water before drying themselves and dressing in loose tunics fetched by the bath house servants. Finally they were taken along a passage to a building that had once been the convent's chapel. However, this was no longer a house of God.

The chapel's nave and chancel had been furnished to resemble an ancient Roman tavern, with couches arranged around low tables and a red silk curtain in place of the wooden rood screen that had once hidden the altar from public view. As a final insult to The Almighty, the nuns' edifying wall paintings, which chronicled the lives of saints and the Passion of Christ, had been covered over with obscene frescoes illustrating erotic episodes from Greek and Roman legends.

On one wall, nymphs entertained shepherds in manners never imagined by Homer or Virgil and on another the unnatural methods of coupling favoured by Zeus were revealed in shocking detail. Though these images would have embarrassed Caligula, the sight of such erotica reminded Thomas that he hadn't lain with a woman since he'd left Verona and that was over a year ago. In order to convince Goetz that he was a genuinely gifted astrologer, Thomas had lived the life of a celibate ascetic whilst he'd been at The Hornberg and now his loins ached with unsated lust.

When Thomas and the others had made themselves comfortable on the couches, a servant rang a little silver bell. A moment later, the silk curtain parted and a statuesque woman, who was dressed as a Roman goddess, entered. She wasn't in the first flush of youth but she'd applied paint and powder to her face with skill and her ample bosom more than compensated for her fading beauty. The woman introduced herself as Juno and she smiled when she recognised Thomas.

"Welcome noble students of the Ars Amatoria. The Daughters of Jupiter offer you a taste of Olympus," she said and at the clap of her hands, a dozen girls filed into the room.

These wenches were younger than their mistress but they were also dressed as classical goddesses and each girl carried a tray of food or a flagon of wine. When the platters had been placed on the tables in the front of each guest's couch, the girls retreated to the curtain and, using the red silk as a backdrop, they adopted a variety of lewd poses. Whilst they stood motionless, Juno carefully adjusted their clothing to display tantalising glimpses of firm female flesh and when she was satisfied she addressed her guests.

"Behold, my noble lords, I offer you your own judgement of Paris! Now, who'll be the first to choose their fairest?" Juno said and Quintana gallantly declared that no Trojan prince was ever so royally entertained. Thomas and Prometheus also voiced their appreciation of this feast of feminine pulchritude, but Bos failed to share in the others' enthusiasm.

As the Frisian finally realised where he was, he leapt to his feet and, looking like Samson about to destroy the Philistines' temple, he began to berate the others for their brazen pursuit of pleasure.

"You lied, Englishman! This isn't a bath house, it's a brothel and I'll not be tempted by the sins of the flesh. You may stay and send your souls to perdition but I'll eat what I paid for elsewhere," he roared and, pausing only to pick up the largest flagon of wine and biggest leg of mutton, he left the others to their debauchery. If Bos hoped his example would persuade his comrades to repent, he was disappointed, because only Juno was concerned by the Frisian's departure.

"It's a shame that your friend has left, for many of my best girls have recently exchanged the cloister for my Temple of Venus and they're all eager to make up for lost time. I do think it's so unnatural for beautiful women to become Brides of Christ, when they could be transported to heaven in the arms of such fine gladiators as yourselves," she cooed and she invited Thomas to make his selection.

"Indeed, the true sin is not to take pleasure in such God-given beauty," he said wistfully and he pointed to a blue-eyed, blonde haired girl with firm, high breasts and a slender waist. The girl smiled sweetly and joined Thomas on his couch.

"You've excellent taste but I prefer my women to have a fuller figure," said Quintana, eyeing a buxom, raven haired harlot who was dressed in imitation of the divine huntress Diana.

"I agree with the Portugee, a woman should be soft like a ripe peach, not hard like Jacob's pillow," said Prometheus and he asked a particularly well-proportioned trollop to join him.

The girl sighed happily as she began massaging the African's broad, well-muscled shoulders, yet her lover was more concerned with the food laid out on the table. In fact, all the men were so ravenously hungry, they hardly knew which sinful appetite to satisfy first. Finally, gluttony won over lust and, whilst the men ate and drank, the girls contented themselves with boasting of their extraordinary skills.

"I'm Aphrodite and I know all the secret arts of love. What's your name my brave Trojan hero," whispered the hussy with Thomas.

"I'm no Trojan, I'm Lancelot, the bravest of Arthur's knights and there's no man in England who can best me with a sword or with a woman," Thomas replied and he let his hand stray to the soft curve of the girl's breast. The contrasting feel of crisp linen and soft, female skin turned Thomas' mouth dry with desire and all he wanted was to ride this harlot harder than any whore had ever been ridden before. The girls with Quintana and Prometheus had already taken their paramours through the silk curtains at the far end of the room, yet his girl seemed to be in no hurry.

"You're an Englishman? How did you learn to speak German so well?" Aphrodite asked but Thomas was no longer interested in her idle chatter.

"Enough talk," he said and he took the girl by the hand. Aphrodite understood and with a coquettish smile she took Thomas through the silk curtains and along another passage which led to the former convent's dormitory. The Poor Clares who'd previously occupied the building had enjoyed individual cells, where they could meditate in private, but now their little rooms were being used for less holy pursuits. Already, Thomas could hear Prometheus and Quintana surrendering to the pleasures of the flesh and he could barely contain his own desires as his girl opened the door to her chamber.

The cell must have once belonged to a senior nun as it boasted such luxuries as a small window above the bed and a fireplace. Thomas was gratified to see that the bed's mattress was filled with goose down instead of straw, whilst his freshly laundered clothes and other belongings, including the oilskin wallet containing the precious *Munich Handbook*, had been placed on a wooden chair by the fire. The girl gave a little sigh of expectation as she closed the door behind her; yet, before Thomas could claim his prize, she held up her hand and begged him to be patient.

"I crave your indulgence, My Lord, for I want you to see what your gold has bought," she said teasingly as she took a spill from the fire to light a candle. Once the wick had flared, she placed the candlestick on the window's narrow sill, then turned to let the light shine through her diaphanous costume. The combination of light and linen revealed the tantalising shadows of the girl's curves and, as Thomas drank in the sight greedily, he thanked God for his gift of lovely women.

"Such beauty as yours is worth any price," he said and, pulling her close with one hand, he untied the bows of her Grecian dress with the other. Once the ribbons were undone the linen shift slipped to the ground with a whisper, and at last Thomas could feast his eyes on the girl's naked body, but the first thing he noticed was the silver pendant around her neck.

"Show me that necklace," he said suspiciously but Aphrodite immediately grasped the pendant with her long, delicate fingers. In Thomas' mind this was an admission of guilt, so he seized the girl's wrist and repeated his demand, but the girl steadfastly refused to let go of the trinket.

"You're hurting me! Stop or I'll call Klaus and he'll cut off your tiny English cock and feed it to the pigs with the other rotten carrots!" Aphrodite wailed and she began to squirm like a young rabbit caught in a snare.

Ignoring the girl's threat, Thomas jerked Aphrodite's arm backwards, which snapped the pendant's chain, but this did nothing to loosen her grip on the seemingly worthless jewel.

Still struggling to free herself from the Englishman's clutches, Aphrodite spat full in her tormentor's face. This insult exhausted Thomas' patience so he pushed the girl onto the bed and snatched up his sword from the chair. As he wiped the spittle from his cheeks, he pointed the tip of his cat-skinner at Aphrodite's heart and demanded that she hand over the necklace or face the consequences.

"Give me that bauble or I'll take it from your cold, dead hand," Thomas said menacingly and Aphrodite knew she was beaten. Trembling with fear, she dropped the pendant into Thomas' outstretched palm and a quick glance at the medallion confirmed that it was engraved with the same *Ouroboros* symbol that the riders in the forest had displayed on their shields.

"Who paid you to betray me to the dragon men? And don't try to deny it. You were to wear this sign of the strangled dragon so the assassins would spare you!" Thomas growled as he held up the pendant in one hand and pressed the point of his sword a little deeper into Aphrodite's soft, white flesh with the other.

The girl flinched but she talked.

"Juno told us that whoever was chosen by the Englishman had to bring him to the old Mother Superior's room and place a lighted candle in the window. That's all I know, I swear it on my sainted mother's life!" Aphrodite wailed and there was something in the girl's voice that made Thomas believe her.

Cursing his own foolishness at being duped by such a simple artifice, Thomas pulled on his breeches, slipped the oilskin wallet inside his shirt and ran from the room.

He began to run down the passageway that led back to the chapel but, after hearing low moans coming from one of the cells, he stopped and kicked open the door. The female occupant screamed in terror when she saw the angry Englishman, sword in hand, standing in the doorway and Prometheus spluttered with outrage at the unwarranted interruption.

"Get out! I've had men flayed alive for less!" he yelled but Thomas shouted that they'd all been betrayed.

"Let go of her and grab your sword. These harlots are in the pay of the dragon men!" Thomas cried and, as proof of his claim, he tossed the amulet he'd taken from Aphrodite onto the bed. Prometheus looked at it and damned every duplicitous daughter of Eve to hell.

"You go and look for Bos whilst I warn Quintana," said Prometheus, leaping from the bed, but the Frisian had already made his way to the dormitory and was standing at the end of the passage, roaring like the breath of God.

"I warned you that death was the wages of sin, now there are dragon men swarming all over the courtyard!" he bellowed as the half-dressed Quintana emerged from one of the other cells with his cat-skinner at the ready.

"Where's that lying bitch Juno? Surely she can show us another way out?" said the Portugee but Bos shook his head despondently.

"She's probably counting her thirty pieces of silver but, I've already told you, it's too late. The dragon men have the whole place surrounded!"

# 4
## WEWELSBURG

With their minds clouded by unsated lust, neither Thomas nor his companions could think rationally and their only thought was to head back along the passageway that led to the bath house.

There was a slim chance that they could escape by clambering over the convent's outer wall but, as the four men entered the steam room, they saw half a dozen ghostly forms advancing towards them through the broiling mist. There was no mistaking their enemies' long riding coats and tall feathered caps, so Thomas and the others hastily retraced their steps.

"What do we do now?" Quintana hissed as they retreated to the bath house's cold room. The others looked at each other in bewilderment but before the others could speak, the Portugee's question was answered by a shrill female scream.

"The bastards are slaughtering those poor girls. We should go back and help," said Thomas, forgetting that at least one of the harlots had been quite prepared to betray him to his enemies.

"It's too late and unless we wish to share their fate, we

must cut our way out of this snare," growled Prometheus and he drew his sword just as six sweating figures emerged from the steam room.

As the others also unsheathed their blades, the rasp of metal against leather cast a strange spell over the assassins. Instead of advancing on their victims, the riders stood motionless on the far side of the cold room's pool.

"Don't stand there like a flock of frightened sheep, advance and be slaughtered!" Bos bellowed, in an attempt to goad their opponents into action, yet only one of the dragon riders stepped forward.

"Give us the *Hexe Teufel Stein* and go free. Resist and die," said the dragon rider in a voice which sounded like the coldest winter wind whispering through a forest of dead trees. He spoke in faltering German but Thomas and the others had no difficulty in understanding his words. *Hexe Teufel Stein* meant the Witch Devil Stone.

"We'll give you nothing but cold steel!" Bos replied, whereupon the dragon riders shouted their own unintelligible battle cries and charged. The six howling assassins were met by the promised storm of flashing blades and the clash of metal echoed around the tiled walls of the bath house like St Peter's trumpet in a tomb.

"You stinking spawn of diseased dung-beetles, feel the claws of a Nubian lion!" Prometheus cried as he swung his sword in a series of wide arcs. However, the rider facing him countered every stroke with surprising strength and skill.

"I shall smite thee as Joshua smote the Amalekites on the plain before Rephidim!" Bos roared but his opponent was also an accomplished swordsman. The dragon rider's expertly wielded blade turned each of the Frisian's bone-crushing blows and Bos' ruddy face began to flush even redder with exertion.

Meanwhile, on the other side of the pool, Thomas launched a flurry of swingeing cuts at a hulking brute with cold grey eyes, whilst Quintana engaged a man whose great black moustache was so long it coiled around his cheeks like an enormous caterpillar.

"Let me shave that ugly bush from your face," spat Quintana as he slashed at his enemy's head. Ignoring the insult, his opponent parried the lunge and aimed his own powerful thrust at the Portugee's groin. Fortunately the moustachioed man's cut was poorly timed, and Quintana easily sidestepped the attack, but his rage made him careless. As he delivered his counterstroke, the Portugee's worn shoes slipped on the wet floor and he fell headlong into the pool with a cry of dismay.

The loud splash distracted Thomas' opponent just long enough for the Englishman to run the assassin through but, there was no time to celebrate, because Quintana was having to fight both Aquarius and his hirsute opponent standing at the edge of the pool. Each time the foundering Portugee's head appeared above the water, the moustachioed rider's sabre whistled through the air, and though the cuts missed the top of the Portugee's skull by the breadth of a hair, Quintana was forced to seek sanctuary in the water's depths.

Fearing that his comrade would soon drown, or be sliced open like a boiled goose egg, Thomas sprang to the rescue but, at the last moment, the dragon rider spotted the danger. The assassin turned on his heel and blocked the cut with his sabre yet nothing could stop Thomas' charge. The Englishman smashed into the dragon rider with the force of a blacksmith's hammer and the two men joined Quintana in the pool.

The water was barely deep enough to cover a man's head but the sudden chill snatched the breath from

Thomas' body and the weight of his waterlogged clothes became an anchor pinning him to the bottom. Fighting the panic rising in his gorge, Thomas kicked off his boots and clawed his way back to the surface. However, as he sucked air into his burning lungs, he felt the arms of the dragon rider wrap around his neck.

Whether the assassin was attacking him, or hoping to be saved from drowning, Thomas didn't know but he was in no mood to be merciful. Smashing the hilt of his sword into the side of his enemy's skull, he knocked the man senseless and struggled to the edge of the pool. This second victory finally turned the tide of battle in favour of the fugitives; in quick succession Prometheus cut down a third dragon rider whilst Bos dispatched the man who'd demanded their surrender.

The last stroke from the Frisian's sword ripped a gash in the chief assassin's neck and the screaming man toppled forward to join his lifeless comrade in the pool. The great red stain, spreading through the water like the first of the plagues Moses visited on Egypt, convinced the two remaining riders that the battle was lost and they ran for their lives.

With their foes vanquished, an eerie silence filled the room but this tranquillity was shattered by the screams of Quintana, who erupted from the pool as if the water had suddenly turned to vitriol. In cries loud enough to wake the Leviathan, the Portugee shrieked that he'd been poisoned with foul, heathen blood and though Bos helped the sopping wet Portugee out of the pool, he urged him to be silent.

"These murderous assassins may die easily but they're bound to have friends, so let's leave whilst we still have God's blessing," he said grimly whereupon Thomas began to complain that they couldn't leave until they'd retrieved his boots from the bottom of the pool. Ignoring the Englishman's protests, the others set off through the doorway that led to the courtyard and Thomas had little choice except to follow.

The four men emerged into the cold night air, hoping that darkness would hide their sprint for the convent's gate but, to their utter consternation, the courtyard was ablaze with light.

Thirty dragon riders carrying burning torches, and as many more armed with their characteristic short Eastern bows, barred their way to freedom. Like worshippers at an ancient temple, the dragon riders had arranged themselves in a semi-circle facing their sacrificial victims and each archer had an arrow nocked to his bowstring.

"Are we to be shot to death like St Sebastian?" Prometheus growled. This prompted Bos to remind the Nubian that the saint had survived being used for archery practice and his tormentors had to beat him to death.

"What does it matter how some smug-faced martyr met his end? In five minutes we'll all be lying face down in Satan's shit pit unless our sorcerer can do something," Quintana hissed. However, before the Portugee had finished speaking, Thomas was addressing their enemies in a voice that sounded like Leonidas goading the Persians at Thermopylae.

"Hear me, you sons of whores, I'm the *Hexe Teufel Stein* and I can summon a legion of demons to drag you all to Hell!" Thomas cried and he began to chant a spell from *The Munich Handbook* which promised to summon an army of devils:

*Oh USYR, SALAUL, SILITOR, DEMOR, ZANNO, SYRTROY, RISBEL, CUTROY, LYTAY, ONOR, MOLOY, PUMOTOR, TAMI, OOR and YM!*

*Ye squire spirits,*
*Whose function it is to bear arms and deceive human senses,*
*I, Thomas Devilstone, Do conjure and exorcise and invoke you,*
*That, indissolubly bound to my power,*
*You should come to me without delay,*
*In a form that will not frighten me,*
*Yet will confound mine enemies,*
*And subject and prepared to do,*
*And reveal for me all that I wish,*
*And to do this willingly,*

*By all things that are in heaven and on earth,*
*I do command thee!*

After his impromptu bath, Thomas was still barefoot and bareheaded, just as *The Munich Handbook* insisted the successful spell caster must be, but he was not in some secret place outside of town, nor was this the tenth day of the moon. He'd also neglected to bring the milk and honey, which the spell required to be sprinkled on the ground, so no one was more surprised than Thomas when the air was filled with a cacophony of demonic horses' hooves clattering over Marburg's cobblestones.

The sound of Satan's horsemen grew louder and louder until it became a hellish, apocalyptic bang. Fearing the wrath of the Dark Lord, the dragon riders scattered, yet the thunderclap hadn't been caused by Thomas's spell or Lucifer's Legions.

A large cart packed with heavy stones had hurtled down the steep, cobbled street and smashed into the convent's gateway. As well as reducing the gate's oak planks to firewood, the cart tore a huge hole in the masonry surrounding the entrance before crashing into the more solid walls of the bath house.

As the runaway tumbrel died in a cloud of splinters and choking dust, a phalanx of men armed with long halberds charged through the hole in the wall and spread out across the courtyard. The halberdiers wore outdated Italian barbute helmets and coats of chain mail under red tunics decorated with the badge of a silver ladder. These men were no more hellish than the wrath of a shrewish wife but, to the dragon riders, they looked like the legion of demons Thomas had promised to release from Hades.

The extra reach provided by their weapons' eight foot shafts gave the halberdiers the advantage and their opponents' riding coats were no defence against a halberd's combined axe, hook and spike. Realising they were beaten, most of the dragon riders fled by scaling the ivy that covered the convent wall but several of their wounded were left behind. The halberdiers' showed their stricken enemies no mercy and savagely butchered the dying dragon riders, splattering their victims' blood over the cobblestones until the courtyard looked like it had been pelted with ripe tomatoes. Soon the only people left alive who weren't wearing scarlet tunics were Thomas, Bos, Prometheus and Quintana.

The four men had found shelter in the wreckage of the convent's gate. However, whilst they'd been happy to remain neutral during the battle, when a tall, thin man stepped out of the shadows, the others carefully avoided Thomas' puzzled look. The new arrival was aged about forty, though his long white beard and rheumy eyes made him look older. He wore the knee length, black robes and square cap of a scholar but, though he walked with the aid of a stick, he carried himself like a soldier. An order, barked in Italian, brought the halberdiers to the bearded man's side and, when he addressed the men hiding in the piles of broken stones, he spoke in good English.

"Come, Thomas, it's undignified for a magus of your power to be cowering under a pile of bricks like a beetle. Stand up and follow me if you wish to know your destiny," he said. Astonished at hearing his name, Thomas rose slowly to his feet and brushed the dust from his damp clothes.

"If you know who I am, perhaps you'd be so good as to tell me who you are," said Thomas and though the man looked insulted by this remark, he replied politely.

"I'm Julius Caesar Scaliger and whilst I'm disappointed that you don't recognise me, I'm even more disappointed in your friends. They were well paid to find you, and keep you safe, yet it appears that I have had to perform these simple tasks myself," said Scaliger in a shrill, petulant voice. His tone seemed calculated to annoy the others and as they emerged from their hiding places, Bos insisted they could have handled the dragon riders without any help, whilst Prometheus demanded that Scaliger apologise for his impudence. Quintana, however, simply held out his hand.

"Well, as you're here, you can pay up. Our agreement was bring the Englishman to you safely. Here he is, so you owe us a hundred guilders each," Quintana demanded, whereupon Scaliger glared at the Portugee.

"If I keep a cat, I don't expect to have to kill my own rats! Our agreement was for you to bring the English sorcerer to the Castle of Wewelsburg and that's still a day's ride from here. If I were to hold you to the letter of our contract, I'd have every right to declare it void and withhold all payment," he snapped.

"I knew he'd try and wriggle out of it. Better to make a bargain with Lucifer than with a man of letters," groaned Quintana. However, Scaliger suddenly put aside his anger and insisted that he'd every intention of honouring their agreement if they all accompanied him to Wewelsburg. Still the men hesitated, and Bos asked why the nightwatch hadn't been summoned, but Scaliger explained that he'd bribed the captain of the city guard to look the other way.

"All will be well if we leave at once," he said and he ordered his men to fetch horses, dry clothes and new boots for his guests.

This was enough to convince Thomas and the others to go with Scaliger, so they mounted their steeds and set off for the town's northern gate. Just as their benefactor had promised, no one tried to prevent them from leaving and within the hour they'd left Marburg far behind.

Though Thomas managed to hold his tongue until the town's tallest spire had vanished below the horizon, eventually he could bare the silence no longer. He insisted on being told something about the assassins who wore the badge of the dragon swallowing its own tail and demanded to know why these riders were chasing him through the forests of Germany.

"And don't tell me you know nothing about these dragon riders. Your men fought them like Montagues brawling with Capulets, so speak up," he said firmly. Scaliger thought for a moment and decided that Thomas ought to know something of the perils that he and his companions faced.

"Your enemies belong to the Order of the Dragon. They call themselves Draconists and their Grand Master is a disgraced Wallachian prince named Lord Dracul. He claims to be a Christian and a crusader, whose only enemy is the Turkish Sultan Suleiman, but he lies. Make no mistake, Thomas, Lord Dracul is a man who was sired by a devil and suckled by a she-dragon and he serves only his own evil ambition," Scaliger replied, yet Thomas wasn't satisfied.

"You're still speaking in riddles Scaliger. I've no quarrel with anyone called Dracul and I've never heard of the Order of the Dragon or a place called Wallachia," he said irritably.

The ignorance of Englishmen caused Scaliger to shake his head in sadness, yet with the patience of a priest teaching the mysteries of The Trinity to a child, he told Thomas that Wallachia was a Christian principality that lay between the Catholic kingdom of Hungary and the Moslem Empire of the Ottoman Turks. For generations, these two great powers had fought for control of Wallachia's fertile plain, which stretched from the northern bank of the River Danube to the southern slopes of the Carpathian Mountains, yet the Wallachians had always managed to maintain their independence.

"No game of chess was ever more complicated than the struggle for the throne of Wallachia," said Scaliger grimly and he described how, a century ago, the principality's ruling House of *Basarab* had split into two competing branches, the *Dăneşti* and the *Drăculeşti*.

After this bitter schism, successive princes from these rival clans had fought innumerable civil wars but each faction could only hold power with either Hungarian or Turkish help. In hushed tones, Scaliger also stated that both sides hadn't hesitated to murder their rivals or betray their allies whenever the situation suited them.

"It's this unholy synthesis of diplomacy and duplicity that has preserved Wallachia's illusion of freedom," Scaliger insisted, whereupon Thomas remarked that such fratricidal struggles weren't unique to the East. He proudly declared that both his grandfather and great-grandfather had fought in the long war between the English royal houses of Lancaster and York. Unfortunately this information failed to impress his host.

Instead of asking to hear more about the exploits of Thomas' heroic ancestors, Scaliger began to explain how the *Drăculeşti* had come by their strange name.

"In the tongue of the Wallachians, *Drăculeşti* can mean both 'dragon' and 'devil', so this hellish clan took their name to commemorate their investiture in the Order of the Dragon," Scaliger said sternly

Whilst the column plodded slowly along the muddy road, Scaliger told Thomas that the first two *Drăculeşti* princes had taken the Draconist oath in Nuremberg's ancient Chapel of The Holy Spirit, which was the official seat of The Order. Unfortunately this explanation left Thomas none the wiser so, as the miles passed, Scaliger laboriously described how the Order of the Dragon had been founded by the Holy Roman Emperor, Sigismund, at a time when the English King Henry V had been fighting the Battle of Agincourt.

The deeply pious Emperor Sigismund, who was also King of Hungary, had wanted to save Christian Constantinople from the encircling empire of the Moslem Turks, so he'd invited all the crowned heads of Europe, including Henry V, to join him in his new crusade. As Wallachia lay in the path of Sigismund's planned attack on the Turks, the ruler of this remote principality, Vlad II, together with his heir, Vlad III, had been among first men initiated into The Order of the Dragon.

"They've been known as the *Drăculeşti* ever since and by custom the head of the clan is always called Dracul, The Dragon, whilst his heir is Dracula, Son of the Dragon," Scaliger added. He also revealed that Sigismund's alliance of western kings and eastern warlords had been no more successful in defending Christendom than the disgraced Templars or moribund Hospitallers. The rulers of France, Spain and England had been too busy invading each other to send men to the Balkans and the Draconist Order had been disbanded once Constantinople had finally fallen to the Turks.

"Nor did membership save the *Drăculeşti*. The Wallachians had become so sickened by the merciless cruelty of Vlad III Dracula, who'd skewered thousands of his own people, as well as his enemies, on sharpened stakes, they rebelled and forced him into exile. The man who now calls himself Lord Dracul is the grandson of this murderous fiend and it's he who has revived the Order of the Dragon. The Draconists have become Dracul's private army of assassins, sworn to restore their Grand Master to his lost throne and, if such a thing comes to pass, the whole world is doomed!" Scaliger cried. This was too much for Thomas and he dismissed his host's fears with a scornful wave of his hand.

"It seems to me that the crazed loon of which you speak is just one more deposed tyrant trying to avoid the wrath of his own people," he said but Scaliger warned Thomas not to underestimate their enemy. Though fearless in battle, and blessed with many princely virtues, Scaliger maintained that the last of the *Drăculeşti* was also an evil wizard in league with the Powers of Darkness.

"Like the Templars, Lord Dracul prays to Baphomet, the goat-headed demon who demands human sacrifice and, like his grandfather, he loves to see men suffer," Scaliger whispered.

If Thomas needed further convincing of Dracul's debauchery, his host told him lurid tales about his grandsire's fondness for eating his meals surrounded by the rotting corpses of his impaled enemies. Thomas listened patiently to these grisly stories but he failed to understand why the grandson of 'The Impaler' was pursuing him across Germany.

"Forgive me for saying so, My Lord, but if the depraved princes of far-off lands wish to slaughter each other in amusing ways, that's hardly my concern," he said. This prompted Thomas' host to insist that the future of Wallachia was of grave importance to everyone who feared Satan's power.

"I've vowed to stop the Draconists from betraying the world to the Prince of Darkness, and I'll not rest until all the lands of the Danube have been secured for the one true God, but Dracul has learned of my plans and he'll stop at nothing to frustrate me. To defeat this evil monster, I need a necromancer of greater power. In other words I need you, Master Thomas, for you are the one man in Europe who's proved he can tame dragons," said Scaliger earnestly.

Under his breath, Thomas cursed the reputation he'd spent years cultivating but he knew better than to contradict a madman who called himself Julius Caesar. For the time being, all he could do was protest that the stories told about him were greatly exaggerated, yet this feigned modesty did nothing to quench Scaliger's enthusiasm for the Englishman's powers.

"Your humility does you credit, Thomas, but there can be no doubt that the famous sorcerer who raised the *Graoully* of Metz from the waters of the Moselle and rode the *Firedrake* from the highest tower of The Hornberg has the power to defeat Lord Dracul," said Scaliger.

Whatever the truth of his claims, about himself and Lord Dracul, at least Scaliger travelled with an escort worthy of a noble Lord of Verona. No fewer than sixty armed horsemen rode behind their master and they all wore the *Scaligeri* badge of a silver scaling ladder on their scarlet surcoats.

This small army was more than sufficient to deter any

attacks from Draconists, *landsknechts*, rebels or bandits. However, even though they were practically invulnerable to their enemies, Scaliger insisted that they rode through the night. It was a gruelling journey, for both horses and men, but eighteen hours after defeating the Draconists in the battle of the bath house, the victors saw a white tower rising above the green ocean of the Teutoburg Forest like a rocky island.

The Castle of Wewelsburg stood on a triangular shaped spur of land formed by a meander of the River Alme. Two sides of this high cliff were steep and densely wooded but the land to the east of the castle sloped away gently. It was here that Wewelsburg's wretched serfs had built a hamlet of crude wooden shacks and though Scaliger's guests should have felt relieved that they were nearing the end of their journey, they each sensed something was wrong.

"There's not a soul here," whispered Prometheus to the others as they rode along the deserted muddy street that ran through the centre of the hamlet.

"It's as if God himself has turned his back on this place," said Bos, looking at the abandoned hovels.

"This is indeed the home of something profoundly evil," added Quintana.

"You're all imagining things. The peasants have merely fled the war or the nobles' revenge," said Thomas but, he too, felt unnerved by the eerie silence. Wewelsburg's Castle seemed to brood over the deserted village, as if it were guarding some terrible secret, and his fear that he might be a prisoner rather than a guest increased when Scaliger began apologising for the crude accommodation offered by the fortress.

"This was never meant to be the home of a great lord, it's nothing more than a refuge of last resort for the

Bishops of Paderborn and now the recent war against the serfs has ended it's been leased to me," he said and Thomas soon found out that Scaliger hadn't understated the lack of luxury.

A drawbridge spanned the broad, dry moat that separated the spur on which the castle stood from the rest of the hillside. Thomas thought that the sharpened stakes at the bottom of this ditch, and the stench of rotting garbage, would be enough to deter all but the most determined attack. Nevertheless, Paderborn's bishops had felt that three towers linked by stone walls and crenellated walkways were also required. The two towers guarding the entrance to the castle were little more than square blockhouses, yet the round watchtower overlooking the valley was tall and graceful.

Once inside the ramparts, Thomas and the others began to wonder why Scaliger had brought them to this unremarkable castle in a forgotten corner of the Hapsburg's Holy Roman Empire. However, before they could ask any questions, their host dismissed his guests from his presence.

"I've no need of you for the moment, so one of my men will show you to your quarters. You may refresh yourselves and sleep until I send for you," said Scaliger and without another word he disappeared through a small wooden door in the base of the round tower.

As soon as Scaliger had departed, a sergeant-at-arms took Thomas and the others to a large room on the upper floor of the nearest square tower. The room must have once served as a barracks and mess for Wewelsburg's garrison, as there were weapon racks along one wall and a row of a dozen cots against the other. In the middle were a single, wooden mess table and two crude benches, while the only windows were three archers' loopholes in each wall. There was no glass, only wooden shutters, to keep out the draughts but the room was kept warm and snug by a huge log fire burning in the grate.

"There's bread, beer and sausage on the table. Eat and rest until Lord Scaliger summons you," said the sergeant.

By the way he spoke, Thomas guessed that the man wasn't German, or even Italian, but this proved nothing. Though their host claimed to be Veronese, every nobleman worthy of his title kept a polyglot retinue of mercenary men-at-arms recruited from all over Christendom.

"So what do we do until Scaliger has need of us?" Bos asked as he stared at the food like a half-starved mastiff.

"Let Lucifer take tomorrow! Today I wish nothing more than to rest my aching backside. Those nags were the boniest I've ever ridden," said Quintana as he lay down on a cot.

"What about that whore in Lodi? She was bonier than a barrel full of sardines, yet you rode her happily enough," said Prometheus. The Portugee was too busy enjoying the relative luxury of a mattress to reply but Thomas insisted that they forget about whoring and home comforts.

"We should find out whether we're guests or prisoners, so let's see what happens if we try to leave," he said and he strode purposefully to the door, which obediently swung open when he tugged on the handle. This was an encouraging sign but any further progress was barred by Scaliger's sergeant-at-arms and he politely refused the Englishman's request to take a stroll around the castle.

"I'm sorry gentlemen. Lord Scaliger says you must all remain in this room until he sends for you. If you need anything, please ask and one of my men shall fetch it," said the sergeant, whereupon Quintana immediately called for a dozen trollops and three dozen bottles of wine.

"After we were so rudely interrupted in Marburg we've unfinished business with the servants of Venus, so be quick about it," he added but the sergeant shook his head.

"Again, I must offer my apologies, for the wine cellars here are empty and there are no women in the castle. In this barbarous country we must satisfy our appetites with beer, bread and sausage. If I'd been nobly born, things in this fortress would be different, yet God made Lord Scaliger the master and decreed that I should serve him. That's the way of things," the sergeant said sadly and he closed the door.

"By all the matted hairs in Onan's beard is this Scaliger a man or a monk?" Quintana moaned and Prometheus replied that he feared their host was the latter. Bos declared that he didn't care if Scaliger was the Chief Abbot of Cluny, he had to eat and he helped himself to the largest of the sausages in the dish on the table. With nothing else to do, the others joined the Frisian and in between mouthfuls of beer, bratwurst and bread they tried to make sense of their host.

"Scaliger told me he wants to reconquer the east for God but he needs a powerful sorcerer to defeat the dragon men, who are led by a devil-worshipping fiend named Lord Dracul," said Thomas. The others listened patiently as the Englishman repeated what he'd been told about the Order of the Dragon, but Quintana thought that the exiled Lord of Verona might have more selfish reasons for seeking out Thomas.

"My guess is he wants you to summon a dragon to help him take back his lost city and then he'll kill us all to avoid paying what he owes," he said, spitting crumbs across the table.

"More likely he wants to teach a low-born peasant like you some manners," said Prometheus brushing half-chewed bread from his doublet.

"Whatever Scaliger wants, if he employs the Dark Arts to get it, he'll condemn all of our souls to eternal damnation," Bos warned. However, Thomas had already decided to ignore his earlier misgivings and play Scaliger's game, at least for the time being.

"You're too gloomy, Frisian, Scaliger must need us as his allies or why else would he come to our aid in Marburg? So, I say we should eat and drink our fill, for who knows when we may eat again?" Thomas said and he reminded the others that they'd thrown in their lot with Scaliger several months ago.

"The Englishman's right. Scaliger may yet prove to be a man of honour and pay us what he owes, so whilst we wait let's enjoy his hospitality," said Prometheus. Even Bos had to agree there was nothing wrong with their host's food and to end the discussion Quintana produced his dog-eared pack of playing cards.

"So that's settled. Now, whilst we wait, what about a little game of primero? I'm feeling rather lucky," he said and the men settled down to a game. It was a good thing they had some means of passing the time, because it was almost a week before they received the promised summons from Scaliger.

# 5

## THE NEMETON

It was the evening of the sixth day after their arrival at Wewelsburg when the sergeant returned to the room and informed the men that their host required their presence in the Nemeton at once. Thomas and the others looked at each other in confusion and Quintana, fearing the worst, demanded to know what a Nemeton was.

The sergeant replied that it was a chamber beneath the round watchtower but he couldn't say what it was used for as he'd never been allowed inside.

"All I know is that the Lord Scaliger is usually the only person permitted to enter and, as he doesn't like to be kept waiting, you must make haste," said the sergeant.

"Why should we hurry? He kept us waiting for a week," Bos grumbled but he followed the others out of the room.

Once in the darkened courtyard, the sergeant hurried Scaliger's guests to the entrance of the round tower, which was guarded by two halberdiers wearing tunics embroidered with the badge of the silver ladder. After giving the watchword, the sergeant instructed the four men to enter the tower and take the downward stair.

"My money had better be at the bottom or I'll flay Scaliger alive and sell his miserable hide for shoe leather," Quintana muttered before he disappeared into the tower.

The others, inspired more by curiosity than greed, followed the Portugee as he descended a long flight of spiral steps and squeezed through a small, arched door that led to an underground chamber.

The circular crypt measured sixty feet across and, though its floor was nothing but tamped earth, its walls were made of large flagstones laid in overhanging courses. Each ring of stones, which had been fitted together without mortar, was smaller than the one below so that they formed a cone twenty feet high. The corbelled stones gave the chamber the appearance of a giant beehive but there was nothing to indicate its use.

The only furnishings were five, large, wooden chests, which had been placed on the floor at the exact centre of the room. These iron-bound coffers were surrounded by an open circle of twelve intricately carved pillars, each about the height of a man and fashioned from oak, but these columns did not support the roof. Instead, polished brass bowls full of burning coals had been placed on the top of each pillar and the flickering firelight cast strange, unearthly shadows onto the stone walls.

"When I was a boy, the sailors returning from Cathay and Africa told tales of the savage tribes who offered human sacrifices to their terrible gods in temples such as this. Whilst their evil priests summoned these bloodthirsty demons, the screaming victims had their beating hearts ripped from their still living bodies, so those boxes will most likely be our coffins!" Quintana managed to croak.

"If they'd been sacrificed, how could they come back and tell you about it?" Bos queried but, before Quintana could reply, Scaliger appeared at the entrance to the crypt.

Their host had exchanged his scholar's cap and robes for the simple white habit of a Dominican friar but, around his neck, instead of the customary crucifix he wore a chain to which a small painted icon in a silver frame had been affixed. After welcoming his guests, Scaliger apologised for keeping them waiting but excused himself by saying that he'd spent the days since their arrival at the castle fasting, praying and studying the heavens for signs of God's blessing.

"This chamber has been a temple since ancient times and for centuries only the priests of the barbarian tribe that built it were permitted to enter. Even now there are evil spirits haunting this place but the stars have shown that this is the most propitious hour and the most auspicious place for our discussion," said Scaliger in a soft, reverent voice, whereupon Thomas interrupted him with a snort of irritation.

"I'm growing tired of your riddles Scaliger. My companions and I have travelled many miles to meet you, yet you keep us waiting for days and then insist on conducting our interview in an old wine cellar. I warn you, our patience is almost exhausted, so take us into your confidence or let us leave," he said firmly. However, Thomas' annoyance changed to bewilderment when Scaliger declared that God himself had brought them all to this place and, as proof of his claim, he held up the icon that hung around his neck.

The light in the chamber was poor, and the icon crudely painted, but the image was instantly recognisable to any pious Christian as it showed the final moments of the Crucifixion. The three crosses bearing their suffering occupants were shown in grisly detail and in the centre of the picture the Roman centurion Longinus was puncturing Christ's side with a long lance to prove that the 'King of the Jews' was dead.

There was nothing particularly notable about this holy picture but Scaliger's voice began to tremble with religious fervour when he pointed to the centurion's over-sized spear.

"Gentlemen, you're the most fortunate of all God's children, for it's your destiny to steal the precious Holy Lance that St Longinus used to wound the body of The Christ as he hung upon the cross and bring it to me, here in the Nemeton!" Scaliger announced triumphantly.

If their host had asked them to purloin the jewelled slippers of a Chinese emperor, Scaliger's guests couldn't have been more surprised. However, as the four men looked at each other in bewilderment, he insisted that only a relic as powerful as the Holy Lance could save the world from its rapidly approaching destruction.

Like a general rousing his men, Scaliger declared that the Roman Emperor, Constantine, and the Frankish warlord, Charles Martel, had only managed to crush their pagan enemies because they'd carried the Holy Lance into battle but the others continued to look confused. Struggling to hide his annoyance, Scaliger added that the Holy Lance had also been wielded by Charlemagne, the first Holy Roman Emperor, and it had been part of the imperial coronation regalia ever since.

"Charlemagne kept the Holy Lance in Aachen, the city where he'd been born, but when Sigismund became emperor he moved both the imperial capital and the empire's most precious treasures to Nuremberg, the city where his Order of the Dragon was to have its headquarters," said Scaliger but if he hoped that the Holy Lance's pedigree would persuade the others to join his quest he was again mistaken.

In a voice as cold as a Frisian winter, Bos repeated Luther's claims that a superstitious belief in the power of relics was a sin whilst Prometheus announced that he was a king of Nubia, not a prince of thieves. Thomas was strangely silent but Quintana declared that, whilst he had no moral objection to thievery, he'd have nothing to do with such a foolhardy endeavour.

"By all the hairs in St Nicholas' soup-stained beard, if you're asking us to storm an imperial castle and break into the emperor's most heavily guarded vault just to steal an old spear, you must be as mad as a mooncalf," he said. However, Scaliger assured him that such a daring robbery would be quite easy for men of their courage, ingenuity and daring.

"The Holy Lance may be a treasure of incalculable value but it's not locked away in a strongroom, it's kept in a monastery in the centre of Nuremberg. To be precise, it hangs over the altar of the Church of the Hospital of the Holy Spirit, which is the same chapel where those being initiated into the Order of the Dragon took their oaths," said Scaliger and he explained that Sigismund, true to his pious crusading vows, had ordered the Holy Lance and the other imperial treasures to be placed inside a specially made silver casket which was then suspended by a long chain from the church's ceiling.

"Until the madness of Luther infected the city, this casket was lowered once a year, on the fourteenth day after Good Friday, so all the imperial relics and regalia could be paraded through the streets of Nuremberg. Thousands of pilgrims came to see such treasures but, since the city's Lutheran council abolished the ceremony, the casket hasn't moved and its only watchmen are the abbey's elderly monks," said Scaliger. This prompted Prometheus to insist that a lack of guards didn't make a virtue out of stealing from a church.

"Sacrilege is the worst of crimes, for it condemns our immortal souls as well as our earthly bodies to the fire, so why would you ask us to risk an agonising death and eternal damnation by committing such a sin?" Prometheus asked, and though Scaliger had to admit that any such an enterprise was prohibited by scripture, he insisted that God would forgive them all because they'd be saving Christendom's most precious relic from those who wanted to use its power for evil.

"I've learned that Lord Dracul also plans to steal the Holy Lance, and he intends to use it to bewitch the people of the Danube into restoring him to the throne of Wallachia, but this is only the beginning of his foul ambition. Once he's regained his crown, he'll build an Empire of Darkness that will engulf the whole world and the handful of decrepit monks who guard The Lance won't be able to stop him. Yet, if the relic is hidden here, buried in this forgotten fortress, it can be kept safe from Dracul until he's finally defeated," he said. However, Thomas immediately raised an objection.

"The Lance needs no earthly protection. It belongs to God, so any man who touches it will die just as Uzzah the Israelite was struck dead when he touched the Arc of the Covenant," said Thomas and Prometheus nodded sagely.

"Even though the wretch Uzzah meant no blasphemy, he was not of the tribe of the Levites, so God sent his thunderbolt to destroy him," the Nubian added, whereupon Scaliger triumphantly proclaimed that a fear of divine retribution was exactly why Dracul had been searching the forests of Germany for England's most famous sorcerer.

"My dear Thomas, surely you understand that Dracul believes you're the only necromancer in Christendom who can cast a spell powerful enough to protect him from God's anger and that's why he'll never rest until he has you in his power," said Scaliger, yet Thomas refused to be intimidated.

"I don't care if he commands ten thousand assassins, he can't force me to cast his spells," he said but Scaliger was adamant that no mortal could resist Dracul's exquisite tortures.

"Once you see your comrades screaming in agony as sharpened stakes are hammered into their innards, you will obey him. On the other hand, if you help me save the world from this monster, I'll reward you with wealth and honours beyond your wildest dreams," said Scaliger and the mention of a reward prompted Quintana to ask why he still hadn't been paid for tasks already performed.

"I'd be more inclined to join you if I'd been paid for finding Thomas in the first place," he said. Unfortunately, Scaliger failed to appreciate being reminded of the debt.

"Forget your paltry hundred guilders, if you bring me the Holy Lance, I'll pay you each a hundred thousand!" Scaliger cried as he marched over to the wooden chests inside the circle of pillars and flung open the nearest coffer's lid. Instantly the whole Nemeton was bathed in a golden glow as the light from the braziers was reflected by the great piles of German guilders, Spanish ducats, French livres and Greek bezants inside the chests. Without a word, Scaliger picked up a handful of coins and gave them to the Portugee.

"This alone would keep a man in wine and whores until his wits were scrambled and his nutmegs shrivelled to the size of grape pips," Quintana said breathlessly and even Prometheus, who'd been born in the land that had supplied all the pharaohs of Egypt with their gold, was deeply impressed.

"With such wealth I could raise an army to drive the infidel invaders from my homeland for ever," he said but the Lutheran Bos remained unmoved. He still maintained that belief in the power of relics was a sin, so Scaliger began to argue that, in defeating Dracul, they'd be doing God's work.

"The man who calls himself Lord Dracul is the False Messiah and the restoration of the *Drăculești* will herald The Apocalypse, so will you stand by whilst this Lord of Lies places the mark of The Beast upon us all? Or will you stop the Antichrist from destroying the world by bringing the Holy Lance to the one place on earth where it will be safe?" Scaliger said earnestly. Bos thought for a moment, then he joined Prometheus and Quintana in swearing to do everything he could to defeat the enemies of Christ.

"If it's the will of Almighty God then I must obey, for those who serve The Lord are always righteous in His sight," Bos said solemnly, whereupon Scaliger clapped his hands in triumph.

"And Thomas' magic will protect you just as surely as it would've protected Dracul, perhaps even more so for our cause is just," he said, and he ordered the Englishman to begin casting the necessary spells to protect the thieves from the Holy Lance's power immediately, but the expedition's newly appointed sorcerer failed to share the others' enthusiasm.

Whilst Scaliger had been convincing the others of their quest's virtue, Thomas had suddenly realised that his host's plan for stealing the Holy Lance meant he faced a far greater peril than the displeasure of the Roman Church. Thomas had long known that there was no truth in magic and, though he'd persisted in using spurious spells and counterfeit charms to outwit his superstitious enemies, if Scaliger was asking him to defeat a crazed madman using nothing but empty rituals and nonsensical rhymes he was bound to fail.

It was also abundantly clear that Thomas' host was not a man who readily forgave failure and once his 'magic' had been exposed as a fraud, all he could expect was a painful death. His only hope was to delay Scaliger's schemes until an opportunity to escape presented itself, so Thomas tried to hide his desperation by insisting that there was no need for such haste.

"My Lord, our enemies are far away and if we have God's blessing, we'll have all the spiritual armour we need," he said but Scaliger insisted that there was more protecting the Holy Lance than the Wrath of God.

"No, Thomas, time is of the essence, because the demons that control the evil within this relic are growing more powerful and must be banished as soon as possible," he said. However, this revelation was too much for the Englishman.

"By the blessed tits of the Holy Virgin, what's this fresh talk of demons? Make up your mind Scaliger. Does this lump of iron belong to God or the Devil?" Thomas said angrily, whereupon Scaliger calmly assured him that the Holy Lance, like everything in God's Creation, had two opposing natures.

"Just as a stone can grind the miller's corn or sharpen the assassin's knife, so the Holy Lance can serve both God and Satan. All of you must understand that, although it became a force for good when it touched the flesh of Our Saviour, the metal still retains the malevolent power given to it by the heathen wizards who'd first fashioned the blade, here in this very chamber," Scaliger whispered and, in hushed tones, he revealed the pagan birth of Christendom's most sacred relic.

According to Scaliger, in the year that Caesar Augustus had become Rome's first emperor, a star had tumbled out of the sky and landed on the very spot where the Castle of Wewelsburg now stood.

This fallen star had been no bigger than a man's fist but it had been made of pure iron and the *Nemetes*, the barbarian tribe who'd lived in the Forest of Teutoburg at this time, had believed that the star had been sent by their war goddess, Nemetona. In her honour the tribe's priests had ordered a fine spearhead to be forged from its metal. The finished blade was named The Spear of Destiny and to house this sacred weapon the priests had built the stone shrine, now called the Nemeton, over the crater where the goddess's divine gift had been found.

As time passed, the *Nemetes'* priests had used the power of their sacred spear to unite all the peoples of the Rhine and bring peace to the Teutoburg. However, nine years after Christ's birth, news of this miraculous spear had reached Rome. The Emperor Augustus had become so obsessed with owning the spear, he'd sent not one but three legions, and his best general, Varus, to fetch it.

In desperation, Nemetona's priests had invested Arminius, the great warrior-king of Germania, with the spear's power and he'd won a miraculous victory. In the trackless wastes of the Teutoburg, Arminius had ambushed and annihilated Varus' legions but he'd failed to honour his enemy's dead. Thousands of Roman corpses had been left unburied and to punish this unpardonable blasphemy, Nemetona had turned her back on her worshippers.

Without the war goddess's blessing, the tribes of Germania had been powerless to prevent the Romans from avenging Varus' shameful defeat. Augustus' successor Tiberius had sent new legions, led by the aptly named Germanicus, who'd destroyed Arminius' armies and captured the Spear of Destiny. The priests of Nemetona had been taken to Rome in chains but, before being torn apart by wild beasts in the arena, they'd placed a terrible curse on their sacred spear.

To those who believed in such things, it was the priests' curse that had forced the Romans to abandon all their conquests beyond the Rhine and caused the destruction of the man who'd stolen the Spear of Destiny from the Nemeton. Shortly after returning to Rome, Germanicus had been placed in command of the imperial legions in Syria but here the man who'd come to symbolise Roman health and vitality had suddenly succumbed to a mysterious illness. The rapid demise of Germanicus was, Scaliger insisted, entirely due to the curse placed on the Spear of Destiny by the priests, yet this was not the end of his story. Scaliger was also adamant that the ill-starred Germanicus had bequeathed the *Nemetes'* sacred blade to Longinus, his most trusted centurion, and the spear's demons had punished this man by causing his sight to fail.

"The half-blind Longinus was sent to Judea where the only duty he could perform was the supervision of executions. So fate decreed that it should be the Spear of Destiny which pierced the body of Jesus but at that moment the pagan blade was transformed into the Holy Lance. As a sign of this miracle, milk and water flowed from the wound in Christ's side and God restored the sight to Longinus' eyes," said Scaliger.

At the end of his tale, Scaliger fell silent and the Nemeton was filled with a reverent hush as the others wondered if what they'd been told was truth or a lie. This uneasy silence lasted for several minutes but eventually Prometheus found his voice.

"So those who would use the Holy Lance for evil must employ magic to protect themselves from God, whilst those who would use it for good must do likewise to shield themselves from the Devil?" he said slowly and though Scaliger admitted this was indeed the case, doubt still clouded Thomas' mind.

"How did you come by this knowledge, which has eluded all other scholars?" Thomas asked. Scaliger thought for a moment and then declared that, during his years of study, he'd discovered secret texts that proved it was the conflict between the blade's twin natures that gave the Holy Lance its power.

"Now Dracul's ambition has reignited the eternal war for control of the Holy Lance and the rule of 'As Above So Below' insists that the fight against him must begin here, in the very place where the spear was made! Only when the demons which control the evil in the blade have been rendered powerless, will God grant us His blessing and allow the relic to be removed from Nuremberg," Scaliger cried and in that instant, Thomas realised that unless he could convince his host that Nemetona's curse had been lifted, he'd never leave Wewelsburg alive.

"Very well, I'll do as you ask, but the road to the Gates of Hell is long and fraught with peril, so you must permit me time to prepare," he said and the mercurial Scaliger was delighted by Thomas' sudden change of heart.

"Take as long as you need, but be ready by tonight, as the omens were never more favourable," he said and he beamed at his protégé like a bishop welcoming a new boy into his choir.

With that, the audience was over and without another word, Scaliger ushered everyone out of the chamber. Bos, Prometheus and Quintana were taken back to the room in the square tower where they'd first been lodged, and for the rest of the day they amused themselves by playing primero, but Thomas wasn't with them.

Three of Scaliger's halberdiers had escorted the English sorcerer to a small chamber at the top of the round tower above the Nemeton. Fortunately for Thomas, they'd left him alone in this room and, once his gaolers had withdrawn, he'd retrieved the oilskin wallet which he'd kept beneath his shirt ever since fleeing Marburg. The waterproof cloth contained his copy of *The Munich Handbook of Demonic Magic* and though he knew that Leonardo's inventions would be of no help in his current predicament, Thomas felt sure that he could use one of the book's spells to dupe Scaliger.

As he turned the *grimoire's* battered and musty pages, he reminded himself that if he could escape the clutches of an unhinged warlord like Goetz of the Iron Hand, it shouldn't be too difficult to outwit a loon who believed in magic spears. He quickly found a suitable spell for summoning demons and, as he memorised the words, a plan formed in his mind.

To convince his host that the blade was no longer possessed by evil spirits, Thomas decided to present Scaliger with a piece of parchment declaring that *Beleth*, the Prince of Hell who controlled the spear's dark side, had agreed to relinquish his diabolical power over the Holy Lance for ever.

Naturally, any such contract would have to look properly magical and, at first, Thomas thought he should write it in blood but on reflection he dismissed this idea. Apart from the obvious difficulties of using gore for ink, he doubted that Scaliger would be fooled by the mere opening of a vein. What he needed was some sort of occult writing, something which only appeared when a secret incantation was spoken, and he soon realised that

Leonardo had the answer after all. Seconds later, Thomas flung open the chamber's door and gave the puzzled man-at-arms outside a shopping list.

"Fetch me a wand of ash wood four feet long and sharpened at one end. I'll also need a ring fashioned from pure silver, a blank sheet of clean parchment and a fresh goose quill. All these items must be procured by midnight and, when you have them, you may tell Lord Scaliger I'll be ready to perform his ceremony," Thomas snapped.

The man-at-arms remarked that if the noble lord wished to write a letter, he'd also require some ink, but Thomas cursed the man's impertinence and insisted that what he'd asked for was all that he'd need. Confused, the man scurried away, leaving Thomas with nothing to do except wait.

It seemed to take an age for the sun to crawl below the horizon. However, once darkness had fallen, the man-at-arms returned with everything Thomas had asked for and escorted him back to the Nemeton. Scaliger and the others were waiting but, whilst their host appeared to be as excited as a new bride on her wedding night, Bos, Prometheus and Quintana looked as if they wanted to be somewhere else.

After greeting his acolytes, Thomas instructed everyone to stand at the edge of the chamber whilst he used the wand of ash wood to scratch a large triangle in the floor's bare earth. The shape was simple enough, although to convince Scaliger of its power, its execution had to be according to the accepted rules of magic. Thomas therefore began at the northern point, drew a line south, then east, then back to the north.

"It's within a magic sigil such as this that a skilled magus may summon *Beleth*, the King of Hell who has power over all other fiends. If the pagan Furies who guard the Holy Lance are to return to the Infernal Pit, it will be at this demon's order," said Thomas when he'd finished his drawing.

"Ah yes, *Beleth*, the fallen angel, the Pale Rider who was first summoned by Ham, son of Noah, to teach humanity mathematics after The Flood. He's a good choice and I approve," said Scaliger, who seemed to be well pleased with his sorcerer's plan. In reply, Thomas bowed politely and informed his host that he intended to make a diabolical contract with this demon king.

"Our bargain shall be that *Beleth's* sins will be forgiven and he may resume his place among the angels if he orders the pagan guardians of the Holy Lance to leave this world forever," he said, whereupon Scaliger clapped his hands in happiness and declared that he was eager to witness such a momentous event. Thomas, however, shook his head.

"I'm sorry, My Lord, but it will be far too dangerous for anyone but me to be present in the Nemeton during *Beleth's* visit to the Upper World, for he's a monster so hideous men go mad if they gaze upon him. Even I, as the conjuror, must wear something silver to ensure my safety," said Thomas but, as he showed everyone the ring he'd requested, Scaliger angrily declared that the Englishman's conditions were unacceptable.

"Do you think me a fool? How will I know *Beleth* has appeared if I'm not permitted to be in the Nemeton to witness it?" Scaliger said, whereupon Thomas explained that, once the spell was complete, everyone would be able to see the parchment with *Beleth's* demonic signature and, as a further protection against fraud, he announced that this document would be written without using any ink.

"The magical letters will remain invisible until a secret word has been spoken and, so there can be absolutely no possibility of deceit, the choice of this magic word will be yours, My Lord, and only you shall utter it," he said. Scaliger thought for a moment and though he looked at his sorcerer with deep suspicion, he agreed.

"Very well, I'll let you perform the rite alone, but to be sure that you've not concealed any secret inks in your clothing. I must insist that you're naked when you cast the spell," he said and though there was an unmistakeable note of glee in Scaliger's voice, Thomas accepted this condition gladly.

"As you wish, My Lord, but the bewitching hour is almost upon us, so I must disrobe and you must withdraw," he said and, after placing both the parchment and quill he intended to use in the centre of the floor's magic triangle, he began to undress. Scaliger had no shame and his eyes never left Thomas until the Englishman was as naked as a newborn babe.

Before quitting the chamber, Scaliger scrutinised every inch of the discarded garments and, though he found nothing, he insisted on taking Thomas' clothes with him when he left the Nemeton. Prometheus and Quintana followed their host without a word but, as Bos stooped to squeeze his massive frame through the crypt's narrow door, he turned to speak.

"Sometimes, I think you're the most insane of us all," he said and with a shake of his head, he climbed the stairs. Thomas was left naked and alone in the pagan temple and he shivered in spite of the heat being produced by the braziers of hot coals atop the pillars.

Though the Nemeton was underground these fires kept the temperature surprisingly comfortable. This was just as well, as Thomas needed warmth to perform an important part of his deception, but first he needed to convince any eavesdroppers that a real ritual had begun.

To this end, Thomas first implored St Barnabas to protect him during his interview with *Beleth* and then, in a voice loud enough to be heard outside, he recited the spell that would force Satan to release his most powerful demon from The Pit:

*By all things that were and are and will be,*
*By all the things that exist beneath the heavens,*
*By all the powers of heaven and earth and sea,*
*By all things that are in them,*
*By all emperors, kings, princes, counts, knights and citizens,*
*By all things that the four parts of the world contain,*
*By all the animals that exist beneath the heavens,*
*By serpents and flying things, bipeds, tripeds, quadrupeds,*
*By the eternity of all creatures,*
*By the heavenly and earthly Paradise,*
*By the five AGES and seven ÆONS of the world,*
*By the Sun and Moon and all the heavenly stars,*
*By all things which hath power to terrify and constrain you,*
*By the power which it behoves you to come*
*to those summon you,*
*By all things which hath power to bind you,*
*By your virtue and all things that have power against you,*
*I summon thee:*

### BELETH

... and as soon as he'd finished his incantation, Thomas began to scream at the top of his voice.

In the castle's courtyard, Scaliger listened to his sorcerer's strangled cries, which were magnified by the conical shape of the Nemeton and funnelled to the surface by the tower's spiral stair, and became convinced that Thomas was engaged in an apocalyptic battle with a great king of Hell.

When the screams ended abruptly, Scaliger was seized by the urge to join in the fight against the demon but Bos, Prometheus and Quintana repeated Thomas' dire warning that it would be fatal to even glimpse the monster and they all remained in the courtyard.

Back in the crypt, Thomas took a deep breath and prepared to write his strange contract but, instead of offering a new prayer to St Barnabas or St Peter he asked Ishtar, the ancient Babylonian love goddess who'd once journeyed to the Underworld and returned safely to Heaven, to aid him.

"If thou openest not the gate to let me enter, I will break the door and wrench the lock, I will smash the doorposts and force the doors, I will bring up the dead to eat the living and the dead will outnumber the living," Thomas whispered to himself as he warmed his hands by the nearest brazier.

The key to the success of Thomas' plan lay in his old tutor's advice that, in an emergency, every man could use his own seed to write an invisible message and, considering the deprivations of the last few weeks, Ishtar answered Thomas' prayers with surprising speed. However, whilst he was gratified with his own fecundity, his first emission provided only enough 'ink' to complete half of what was needed.

After resting for several minutes, Thomas' returned to his labours and, though he successfully added a few more words to the text, each time he needed to refill his pen the task became harder. Soon, his renewed screams and anguished pleas to be released from his torment became genuine but he persevered and after an hour, the demonic contract was complete. He'd just enough strength to climb the stairs and stagger into the courtyard where Scaliger and the others were waiting.

"I have it, My Lord!" Thomas managed to croak as he gave the blank piece of parchment to Scaliger, who snatched it eagerly from the sorcerer's outstretched hand.

"You look awful," said Bos as he and Prometheus helped Thomas dress himself.

"So would you, if you'd been to hell and back," Thomas replied and before the Frisian could ask how such a feat could be accomplished without resorting to forbidden witchcraft, Scaliger howled with unbridled rage.

"Thieves, frauds, swindlers! There's nothing written here at all!" he cried.

"I told you, the text will only appear when you speak the secret word," said Thomas.

"Liar! I've spoken the word a dozen times, yet the parchment remains blank," snapped Scaliger. He waved the incriminating document under his sorcerer's nose, but Thomas replied that his host had been too hasty.

"Hell doesn't give up its secrets so easily, the text will only appear if the secret word is spoken inside the Nemeton," he said quietly and he ordered everyone to return to the crypt.

Once they were all back underground, Thomas instructed Scaliger to stand in the centre of the magic triangle and warm the parchment by holding it in front of the nearest brazier. Though he was greatly puzzled by this request, Scaliger obeyed and the light from the burning coals infused the parchment with an eerie glow. For one, heart-stopping moment, it seemed as if *Beleth* had played the impudent sorcerer false but then the words of Thomas' contract with the demon began to appear:

*I Beleth, High King of the Infernal Realm,*
*As I am commanded by the power of the Lord Jesus Christ,*
*So I command my vassals Taranis, Esus and Toutatis,*

*And their queen Nemetona,*
*Who holds the power of the Holy Lance in her thrall,*
*To release this Holy Relic so it may again bring light to the*
*world, and drive the powers of darkness from the earth.*
*To this bargain, which is as unbreakable and eternal as God's*
*covenant with mankind, I affix my name:*

## *BELETH*

"Blessed Jesu, this is a most remarkable document! I can't imagine what you must have suffered to get it," said Scaliger as he read the barely legible signature at the bottom of the parchment.

"It cost the souls of ten thousand, thousand unborn children," said Thomas truthfully.

"But it was worth it! Congratulations, Master Thomas, you've taken the first step on the road that will lead to our glorious victory over the fiend Dracul," Scaliger gushed and though Thomas smiled with relief he knew that this had been the easiest part of their quest.

"Now all we have to do is break into a church and steal the holiest relic in Christendom from under the nose of the Holy Roman Emperor," he muttered to himself.

# 6
## THE ABBEY

In spite of his sorcerer's misgivings, Scaliger remained convinced that stealing Christendom's most precious relic would be easy and he confidently announced that Fate had decreed that he should be the next guardian of the Holy Lance.

"Though I wouldn't compare my own small talent to that of a celebrated magus such as Thomas Devilstone, I do have some skill as an astrologer and I've seen it in the stars that The Wewelsburg is to become the new Grail Castle, with me as its Fisher King," Scaliger said dreamily and he began to outline his plan to keep the Holy Lance safe from the diabolical Order of the Dragon and its malevolent Grand Master.

In the dim, conspiratorial light of the Nemeton's braziers, Scaliger proposed that the thieves should disguise themselves as pilgrims and travel to Nuremberg in secret. This simple subterfuge, Scaliger insisted, would enable the plotters to mingle, unnoticed, with the thronging multitudes visiting the numerous holy shrines in the imperial capital but Bos immediately raised an objection to the plan.

"You told us that Nuremberg's council has adopted the teachings of Luther and forbidden the public display of relics," he said but Scaliger assured him that, although the imperial treasures had kept from public view for nearly two years, many of the city's churches openly defied the ban so there were plenty of other sacred objects for pilgrims to venerate.

"Chief of these is St Sebald's Stone and the council allows the church where it is kept to remain open because credulous pilgrims continue to spend their money in the city. Nuremberg's venal burghers are not so stupid as to dam the river of gold that has made them all rich," said Scaliger with an ill-disguised note of contempt in his voice. Though Bos shared his host's disgust of such hypocrisy, Thomas suddenly clapped his hand to his forehead and declared that there was no need to go to Nuremberg after all.

"If Dracul can't possess the relic without my help, as long as I remain here, the Holy Lance will be quite safe," he said triumphantly and he promised not to leave the confines of the castle until Dracul was defeated. Unfortunately, Scaliger was unmoved by this observation and he insisted that the Holy Lance had to be brought to Wewelsburg as quickly as possible.

"You may be the best necromancer in all of Christendom, Master Thomas, but you're not the only one. There's Faust in Helmstadt, Paracelsus in Strasbourg and the last I heard the great magus, Heinrich Cornelius Agrippa, your own tutor, was back in Cologne. All these men have the knowledge and skills Dracul requires so, every day the Holy Lance remains in Nuremberg, it's in danger of falling into his clutches," he said but Thomas countered that the journey to the imperial capital was highly dangerous.

"Our chances of reaching our destination are slim, because it's not only Dracul's riders we must fear. The roads are also infested with bandits and rebels, so I say we wait until the Swabian League has cleansed their Augean Stables," he said, whereupon Scaliger burst out laughing.

"You make a good jest, Thomas, but I know that to wash that midden Heracles had to dam the River of Alpheus!" Scaliger cried and he explained that if the roads were fraught with peril the thieves should travel by water wherever possible.

The debate ended with an agreement that Scaliger's men would escort Thomas and the others to Münden, where they could acquire a boat, but then turn back lest their presence alert Dracul. The thieves agreed to this but they declined to disguise themselves as peasants as their patron had advised.

"If the nobles are rounding up rebel serfs and slaughtering them like so many stray dogs, dressing in the garb of pious ploughmen on a pilgrimage would be suicide," said Quintana.

"On the other hand now the war's over, no one will notice four jobless *landsknechts* looking for a new master," said Prometheus.

"Very well, but I urge you to take the greatest of care, because, whether you travel by road or river, Dracul has spies everywhere and we must not alert our enemy that we've made our first move," said Scaliger and with that he ordered the four men to retire to their chamber and rest.

At dawn the following day, which, fortuitously, was the Feast of St Phocas, the patron saint of boatmen, Scaliger's new Grail Knights left Wewelsburg and they arrived at Münden three days later. The journey had passed without incident and the thieves' luck held as they began their search for a boat to take them upstream.

The picturesque town of Münden had once been the busiest port on the River Werra, but, as many of its boatmen had been killed in the peasants' rebellion, Quintana had no difficulty in finding a suitable vessel for sale. For a paltry three guilders, he bought a neat, clinker-built skiff with two rowing benches and a small sail, but Bos looked at the little boat bobbing against the town's weed-encrusted wharf with disdain.

"How are we all going to fit in that cockleshell? By all the saints, I've seen bigger turds floating in a cesspit," he said. However, after being told that he could walk to Nuremberg through the bandit infested forests if he wished, he reluctantly took his place on the rowing bench. Prometheus was even less comfortable on water and the others roared with laughter as they watched the giant Nubian clamber aboard.

"Be silent, you scabrous sons of Japheth! In the desert, the only water I saw came from my enemies who pissed themselves with fear!" he said irritably, whereupon the others remembered the incontinent captain of Marburg's nightwatch and wisely stifled their laughter. There was no wind, so they each took turns at either the oars or the tiller, and though they were travelling against the current, they made steady progress.

Beyond the town's water gate, the Lower Werra ran sluggishly between peaceful meadows, so rowing was easy and the voyage became almost pleasant. At sunset, Quintana moored against a convenient willow overhanging the water and made a temporary shelter by stretching the skiff's sail over the unstepped mast laid along the length of the hull.

After a frugal but filling meal of mutton, black bread and ale, the four men fell asleep in the bottom of their boat and though the night air was damp and cold, they were warm enough huddled together beneath their cloaks. At sunrise, the men shook themselves awake, stretched their cramped limbs and renewed their journey.

As the spring sun rose higher in the cloudless sky, the landscape on both sides of the valley began to change. The hills became steeper as the Werra passed through a natural gap in the Rhön Mountains but, between these high, wooded spurs, the river's meanders had carved flat, open spaces.

Before the Peasants' War, most of these 'haughs' had supported a prosperous farm or a thriving village. Yet, even though the fighting had ended a year ago, every settlement Thomas and the others passed appeared to be deserted. Looking at the abandoned shacks and empty fields, the four men began to feel the same unease they'd felt on the way to Wewelsburg and their apprehension only deepened when they noticed a plume of thick, black smoke rising above the trees.

"Have the flames of the serfs' rebellion been rekindled so quickly?" Prometheus asked and though Thomas agreed that this was entirely likely, Quintana was certain that the smoke had been made by a band of foresters making charcoal.

"It makes no difference what's caused that smoke, there's no way through this part of the forest except by boat," said Bos and he pointed to the dense thickets that lined both banks of the river.

With the thick hedge of willows and alders preventing a landing, all the rowers could do was pull hard on their oars and hope that they could slip by whatever dangers lay ahead without being seen. Hardly daring to look up, the men bent to their task but they couldn't ignore the dreadful scene that confronted them around the river's next bend and the sight only confirmed their worst fears.

The column of smoke was rising from a small abbey that stood on a low, treeless bluff overlooking the river. The fields and meadows surrounding the monastery sloped gently towards several fishponds at the water's edge and though the abbey's main buildings were over a hundred yards away, the men in the boat could see that its once fine church had been reduced to a roofless, smoke-blackened shell.

"We must stop, it's our duty as good Christians to help the villagers and monks fight the fire," said Prometheus as he watched a large crowd of people thronging around the smouldering ruin.

"It doesn't look like there's much we can do and don't forget we have to be back in Wewelsburg as soon as possible," said Bos, who had no desire to save a popish church from the flames of divine retribution, but Quintana's sudden cry of alarm decided the matter.

"By all the brimstone in Satan's pisspot, those farm boys aren't fighting the flames, they're feeding them!" Quintana cried and he pointed to a second plume of smoke that was beginning to rise from an arched gateway in the abbey's wall.

The wooden gates, which had once allowed the monks access to their fishponds, had gone and in their place two naked figures were hanging by their wrists from ropes tied to the top of the arch. As the men in the boat watched, flames leapt from the fire that had been lit beneath the victims' feet and the wretches' agonised screams echoed around the valley.

"Who are these devils who persecute holy men with such cruelty?" Prometheus demanded to know and in reply Thomas pointed to one of the torturers who was brandishing a pitchfork with an old leather shoe tied to its long wooden shaft.

"The peasants who besieged The Hornberg carried a similar talisman, it's called the *Bundschuh* and it's supposed to represent the march to a new Garden of Eden that's free of cruel lords and corrupt priests," said Thomas and he added that although the badge of the unlaced shoe belonged to an earlier rebellion, it had been a popular banner with many of the peasant armies in their recent war with the nobility.

"Are these the same mutinous serfs who turned on Goetz of the Iron Hand after he deserted them?" Quintana asked but Thomas shook his head.

"We're too far from The Hornberg for these to be the same rebels but we must still be on our guard. All *Bundschuh* bands reserve their worst tortures for low-born soldiers of fortune who fight for wealthy noblemen and don't forget we chose to dress as *landsknechts*," he said grimly. The others didn't need to be reminded that, although Scaliger had advised them to dress as pilgrims, they'd chosen to keep wearing the elaborate, colourful garments that identified them as imperial mercenaries. Yet Bos refused to admit their mistake.

"Most likely these cowardly cowherds will be so terrified they'll soil themselves and run for the hills," he said confidently but, as the words left his mouth, a raft appeared from behind a clump of willows and headed towards them.

The crude vessel approaching the skiff had been fashioned from tree trunks lashed together but it was strong enough to carry six men armed with swords and crossbows. In case there was any doubt as to their allegiance, one of the men held a large, black banner, decorated with a picture of a red shoe inside a gold ring, and as the two craft neared each other, he waved his flag furiously as a signal for the strangers to halt.

"By the foul tongue of a blaspheming bishop, we're done for!" Quintana cried. Yet, even dressed as they were, Thomas felt certain they could bluff their way past the river's sentinels. He hurriedly told the others that he'd heard that some *landsknechts* who'd deserted their noble paymasters had joined the Eternal League of God. This had been one of the largest of the peasant armies and, until his capture and brutal execution, it had been led by a Utopian visionary named Müntzer.

"We must pose as veterans of Müntzer's army and swear by The Twelve Articles of Freedom that since our defeat we've spent more than a year hiding in the forest. If we're questioned further, you must say we wish nothing more than to continue the fight against the noble tyrants who've enslaved the innocent sons and daughters of the soil," he said and, whilst his companions tried to make sense of what they'd just been told, Thomas hailed the captain of the raft.

"Welcome fellow Brothers of the Untied Shoe, we're most pleased to see your friendly faces!" Thomas cried and he proudly declared that he and his companions had fought bravely for the Eternal League of God until its final destruction on the bone-strewn, blood-soaked battlefield of Frankenhausen.

The raft's commander, a slovenly brute with a patch over one eye and a scowl that would've terrified Torquemada, listened to Thomas' impassioned speech with the patience of a priest hearing confession. Yet all the while, the other men on the raft continued to look at the four foreigners in the boat with deep suspicion.

"Though you're dressed like *landsknecht* filth, if you've shed blood for the great Müntzer you've nothing to fear from Little Heinrich," said the peasants' captain and he ordered Quintana to steer his boat towards the bank.

"Who in Satan's Kingdom is Little Heinrich?" Bos whispered but Thomas had never heard of a rebel leader by that name.

Moments later, their boat grounded on a mud-flat below the burned-out abbey and the one-eyed captain ordered the four men to disembark. Fearing the worst, Thomas and the others splashed through the shallow water to the riverbank, where they were surrounded by more grim-faced serfs armed with a variety of lethal-looking agricultural implements.

Once ashore, the raft's captain demanded that the men surrender their swords and, though Thomas repeated his claims that he and his comrades had sworn to fight injustice so long as they could draw breath, the rebel captain insisted that no man could appear armed before Little Heinrich. As he collected their cat-skinners and long daggers, the captain also told Thomas that no one could be admitted into the Brotherhood of The Ring without Little Heinrich's approval.

"Our leader interviews all strangers personally and, if your hearts are pure and your sword arms strong, you'll be made welcome. On the other hand, if you're spies and traitors to the Twelve Articles, you'll spend a week praying for death before you spend an eternity in Hell praying for life," spat the captain and he ordered his men to take the four captive *landsknechts* to the abbey church.

The path from the river passed by the monastery's fishponds, which were full of red faced farmer's wives wading waist-deep through the water. These women were busily netting the plump carp once destined for the monks' table but, whilst they barely glanced at the prisoners being marched towards the abbey's gate, Thomas and the others couldn't fail to notice the two roasted corpses hanging from the stone arch.

The blackened lumps of flesh had once been an elderly man and an equally aged woman. Though death had ended their cruel torment, the peasant guarding the gate was still prodding the charred cadavers with a billhook, so the corpses turned in the fire's smoke like hams being cured for winter. The rancid smell of broiled human flesh was almost overpowering but Thomas and others managed to resist the desire to retch as they walked through the gateway.

On the other side of the hellish entrance there was a broad patch of grass, where the monks had once walked in quiet contemplation, but this Elysian Field was now crowded with tents and wagons. Washing was hanging from lines strung between the different carts and everywhere that the captives looked, they saw men, women and children gorging themselves on food and wine looted from the abbey's well-stocked larders.

The prisoners were bewildered by the rebels' apparent lack of preparation for the counterattack that was bound to follow their rape of Mother Church and when a swarm of scruffy children began pelting the newcomers with mud, Prometheus demanded that the raft's captain discipline the unruly urchins. The one-eyed peasant replied that everyone, even the young, were free to say and do as they pleased in the Brotherhood of the Ring, whereupon Thomas declared that such idealistic nonsense had led to the previous revolt's failure.

"By the ragged cloak of St Martin, you can't run a war like a wedding breakfast, so unless you accept our help to beat your ploughshares into swords you'll all end up on the gallows!" Thomas cried. Strangely, in spite of the one-eyed captain's promise of freedom of speech for all, the Englishman's outburst earned him nothing but swift and brutal retribution.

A vicious blow from the butt end of a billhook knocked the breath from Thomas' body, so he had to be helped into the abbey church by his companions, but the acrid stench of scorched wood, stale wine and vomit soon brought him back to his senses. Coughing and spluttering, Thomas looked around him and was astonished to see that this former house of prayer now resembled Caligula's favourite villa during an especially drunken orgy.

In the side chapels, a dozen brawny swineherds were using flails and hammers to smash exquisitely carved statues of saints, whilst at the far end of the choir stalls, children were throwing stones at what remained of the rose window's delicate stained glass. Such wanton destruction would have appalled even the iconoclastic Luther but far worse blasphemy was being committed at the entrance to the chancel. Here, a group of naked men and women were performing highly artistic acts of fornication whilst an orchestra of inebriated fiddlers played loud and discordant descants on tuneless viols.

A surfeit of wine and the elation of victory had driven every vestige of shame from these revellers and whilst they copulated with the fervour of *maenads* celebrating the Bacchanalia, they were applauded by a dwarf who sported a thick black beard and long greasy hair. This diminutive figure was sitting on the deposed abbot's gilded throne, which had been dragged to the top of the altar steps, and he was attended by four burly *trabant* bodyguards. In between taking huge swigs of beer from enormous wooden tankards, these former pig-gelders bellowed their own ribald words of encouragement and cheered the most imaginative displays of the erotic arts.

"I have news, *Führer*," said the captain of the raft but his attempts to announce his presence were silenced by the music which was becoming louder and more frenetic as the lovers' lewd gyrations quickened.

The prisoners and their escort could do nothing except wait at the back of the church until the lascivious spectacle had ended. However, once the strangled cries of ecstatic release had died away, Little Heinrich allowed the four captives to approach the desecrated chancel.

Under the watchful gaze of the rebel chief's piercing blue eyes, the prisoners were led slowly up the aisle like reluctant brides. After what they'd just seen, Thomas and the others had no doubt that Little Heinrich's peculiar appetites extended to pitiless cruelty, as well as perverted lust, or that a single word out of place would sign their death warrants.

"Who are these cocksucking sodomites?" Little Heinrich asked and the captain of the raft proudly announced that he'd caught four *landsknecht* spies trying to sneak upriver.

"They claim to have fought for Müntzer and say they want to join us, so, just as you instructed, *Führer*, I've brought them to you," said the one-eyed captain but Little Heinrich was too busy staring at the exotic figure of Prometheus to answer.

Though he'd never seen an African, the peasants' chief had heard tales of the dark-skinned slaves who toiled for cruel Arab masters and he'd always felt a kinship with those who laboured in bondage. With hatred in his eyes, the gnomish rebel turned to Thomas, Bos and Quintana and accused them of being willing instruments of the noble's tyranny.

"You wish to become part of The Ring, yet your clothes and ownership of a slave prove that your loyalties lie with those mother-buggering bastards who think an accident of birth gives them the right to keep their brothers in chains! Your bondsman is hereby set free but you others must answer for your crimes," he cried in a shrill, reedy voice. Despite Little Heinrich's munificence towards him, Prometheus could scarcely contain his anger and he was about to declare that he was a king, not a slave, when Thomas interrupted.

"This son of Ham is as free as the desert wind and like us he wants to continue the fight begun by the Eternal League of God. We all followed the Rainbow Banner until the disaster of Frankenhausen and we've been hunted like rats ever since the Great Müntzer was martyred," Thomas said, yet his speech failed to impress one of the harlots who been prostituting herself for Little Heinrich's pleasure. Without bothering to cover her nakedness, she pointed an accusing finger at the prisoners and declared that they must all die.

"All traitors deserve nothing but death and these men are *landsknecht* filth who have betrayed their brethren. If you don't believe me, search them. If they're telling the truth, they'll be penniless. If they're lying, their purses will be stuffed with coins stained red by the blood of the poor," the trollop hissed and Little Heinrich, nodding in agreement, ordered the prisoners to surrender the leather pouches tied to their belts.

When Quintana protested, the *trabants* drew their swords, so the four captives reluctantly emptied their purses into Little Heinrich's outstretched hands. Scaliger had given them each twenty guilders on account and though this sum was not enough to condemn the men out of hand, the last piece of gold to fall from Thomas' purse was the amulet of the Golden Fleece, which Scaliger had sent to the Englishman as evidence of his good faith. The moment the harlot saw this fabled badge of nobility, she howled in triumph and cried that the prisoners had been condemned by their own greed.

"You see! No man can earn such riches by honest labour, so these leeches must be in the pay of the nobles. For that heinous crime alone they must answer to St Peter!" the harlot screeched, yet Thomas denied her accusation with equal venom.

"Is this wench's brain as small as her tiny tits? We stole this money, and the jewel, from one of the fat merchants who travel the road to Bamberg!" Thomas cried and he was gratified to see a confused look spread over Little Heinrich's face.

Seizing his chance, Thomas hurriedly added that he'd been driven from his home by the scheming of a vengeful king and his corrupt cardinal. The others were also quick to tell their own tales of woe to provide further evidence of their impecunious virtue.

Drawing himself up to his full height, Bos declared that he'd fought with the famous Frisian rebel chieftain Great Peter against the tyrannical Hapsburg despots, whilst Prometheus conveniently forgot his royal ancestry and boasted that he'd escaped from the slave markets of the Barbary Coast in order to breathe the free air of Christendom. Finally Quintana announced, with some pride, that his mother had been the best whore in the whole of Lisbon.

Little Heinrich listened to the prisoners' biographies with interest and, though he seemed to be on the point of deciding in their favour, the harlot was not to be denied her vengeance. In a voice as cold as a cobra's stare, she demanded that the strangers' guilt or innocence be decided by The Ring.

"Have you forgotten the Twelve Articles? Unless you let all the Brethren judge these men you're no better than the tyrants who held us in bondage," she hissed and Little Heinrich was only too pleased to grant her request. He immediately ordered the entire Brotherhood of The Ring to be summoned, whereupon one of the *trabants* blew a long blast on a battered hunting horn. As the mournful notes echoed around the scorched stones of the church, the drunken congregation gave a great cry of triumph and helped the *trabants* bundle the prisoners outside.

Though Bos' threatened violent retribution unless they were all released immediately, the rebels ignored the Frisian and marched the four men to the meadow between abbey and the river. Moments later, the crowd of shouting, jeering revellers from the church were joined by hundreds more serfs and the two groups quickly formed a human amphitheatre around the accused.

The storm of abuse heaped upon the prisoners' heads was deafening but their tormentors fell silent when another blast of the hunting horn announced that Little Heinrich was ready to preside over the impromptu court.

Two of the *trabants* used their wooden clubs to force a path through the circular wall of humanity and the peasants' chief entered The Ring still seated on the abbot's gilded throne. This chair had been fitted with sockets to hold long poles, so, in more peaceful times, the monastery's abbot could travel in luxury when he collected his tithes from the local peasantry. Now it was rebel chief who was being carried, shoulder-high, through the crowd of villagers.

Once Little Heinrich was inside The Ring, he announced that he'd summoned The Brethren to judge four spies on trial for their lives and though his shrill voice made him sound like a petulant child, his followers listened intently to every word.

"Brothers and Sisters of The Ring, hear me! These men claim to have abandoned the easy ways of wickedness and want to join us on the hard road to the sunlit uplands of the New Eden, so do we admit them to our ranks or hang them as traitors to all those who must toil for their bread?" Little Heinrich cried.

"Hanging's too good for these villainous bastards, toss them into the flames like the lice they are!" shouted a voice and the air was filled with cries that all those who took up arms in return for gold must suffer death. Thomas hurriedly repeated his offer to train the rebels in the arts of war, and lead them to victory in their battles with the nobility, but his words were answered with another chorus of jeers and catcalls.

"No man shall ever lead the Brotherhood of The Ring, that's why we chose half a man to be our *Führer*!" cackled an old woman with a flagon of wine in her hand and evil in her heart.

"When Adam delved and Eve span, no one then was gentleman," yelled a second crone and soon the whole mob was bleating her slogan. Thomas' insistence that he and his companions could unlock the doors of freedom was lost in the pandemonium and the riotous chanting continued unabated until Little Heinrich held up his hand for silence.

"There's a way to settle this once and for all. Fetch one of the black crows and we'll put these men to the test," he said and whilst the prisoners wondered what diabolical instrument of torture a 'black crow' might be, the one-eyed captain of the raft and two of Little Heinrich's guards disappeared inside the ruined church. Five anxious minutes later, the captain returned with the *trabants* and they were dragging the dishevelled figure of a Benedictine monk between them.

The friar was so old there was barely enough grey hair on his head for the tonsure and, though the monk's bony face was already a mask of livid, purple bruises, the *trabants* showed him no mercy. The elderly priest was kicked and punched as he was forced to kneel in the circle's centre, yet he bore his suffering with fortitude. He didn't flinch when the captain drew his sword and simply bowed his head in prayer when his tormentor tossed the blade onto the grass in front of Thomas.

"If you wish to join us, you must prove your loyalty to the New Order by cutting off this old crow's head!" Little Heinrich shouted but Thomas didn't move a muscle.

Though he'd no qualms about killing a man in a fair fight, he was not an executioner or a murderer but the crowd took his reluctance as an admission of guilt and began to scream for the spies to be executed without any more delay. Realising their remaining time on earth was now numbered in minutes, Thomas reluctantly took the sword, whereupon the crowd fell silent in excited expectation. In the deathly hush that followed, all that could be heard was the friar's mumbled recitation of the Twenty-third Psalm. However, as Thomas took a step towards the kneeling monk, Prometheus cried out.

"Don't do it! Only a king's order may put a man to death and you'll bring the wrath of God upon us if you slaughter an innocent holy man," he cried, whereupon Little Heinrich roared with laughter and declared that the monk was neither innocent nor holy.

"This wretched sinner is a loathsome sodomite and no apple-cheeked altar boy was safe from his filthy, unnatural lust. Now kill him, or you and your friends will suffer a far more painful death than beheading!" Little Heinrich shrieked.

"I'm sorry Father, I've no choice," Thomas whispered and he was astonished to hear the friar say that he was ready to die.

"I've committed many grave sins and now I thank

God that you've been sent to deliver me from this life of pain. I forgive you, as I hope to be forgiven by Our Saviour, and all I ask is that you make my end swift," he said and he closed his eyes in anticipation of the killing blow. Marvelling at the condemned man's calmness, Thomas gripped the sword's hilt with both hands and lifted the weapon high above his head.

"In the name of Sweet Jesus, what are you doing?" Prometheus shouted but it was too late. Thomas was already swinging the sword with all his might and its keen edge sliced though the bones of the monk's neck with barely a whisper. The crowd gasped as the friar's grizzled head rolled across the grass and this distraction was all that Thomas needed.

Whilst the mob celebrated the monk's grisly death with more wild huzzas, Thomas spun on his heel and slashed at the two nearest *trabants* carrying Little Heinrich. With the weight of the portable throne resting on their shoulders, the rebel chief's bodyguards were powerless to defend themselves and Thomas' blade cut through the men's fingers and the gilded wooden poles as easily as it had the friar's spine.

Howling with agony the two *trabants* fell to their knees, the chair toppled forward and Little Heinrich was pitched onto the bloody grass. The *Führer* landed by the monk's headless torso and, before he could recover, Thomas had placed his foot on the dwarf's misshapen chest.

"All of you, drop your weapons and stay back or your leader dies. Remember, if I can kill a monk I can easily stamp on this snivelling cockroach!" Thomas yelled as he waved his sword at the mob.

"Do as he says!" Little Heinrich croaked and, after a brief pause, the serfs who were armed let their sharpened spades, pitchforks and billhooks fall to the ground.

Immediately, Bos, Quintana and Prometheus snatched up three of the discarded weapons and formed a cordon around Thomas as he hauled Little Heinrich to his feet by his long hair. The rebel chief shrieked with pain but the Englishman's steel at his throat silenced the *Führer's* cries. With Little Heinrich at his mercy, Thomas ordered the Brotherhood of the Ring to let them pass and the astonished crowd parted like the waters of the Red Sea before Moses.

Leaving the dumbfounded mob behind, the fugitives retreated to the river and, once they'd reached the water's edge, Bos set the peasant's raft adrift whilst the others bundled Little Heinrich aboard their skiff.

The river's powerful current soon swept the empty raft downstream but the fugitives were too busy rowing in the opposite direction to notice. Whilst Bos and Prometheus strained at the oars, and Quintana manned the tiller, Thomas guarded their prisoner. Unfortunately, the *Führer's* capture had done nothing to improve his temper.

"You filthy, lying, traitorous, dog-buggering bastards won't get far! Müntzer may be dead but his banner still flies in the valleys of the south. My men will send messages to the *Bundschuh* bands upstream, they'll throw ropes across the river and you'll be caught like four stinking fish," he hissed and he began to list all the imaginative tortures that Thomas and his companions would suffer once their roles were reversed.

"Keep quiet or I'll tie you to a rope and use you as an anchor," Thomas snapped, yet one glance at the riverbank proved that Little Heinrich wasn't making empty threats. Like a pack of deerhounds trailing a wounded stag, a sizeable group of peasants was already following the fugitives' boat and several of them were armed with crossbows.

The thin wooden planks of the skiff would offer no more protection from iron-tipped crossbow bolts than a bedsheet and as there was nowhere to hide in the middle of a river, Thomas reckoned that their only chance was to disappear into the forest on the opposite bank as soon as they could.

He yelled for Quintana to steer for the far shore, and urged the oarsmen to put all their strength into their rowing, but as he desperately searched for somewhere to land, he heard the unmistakeable twang of bowstrings being released.

# 7

## THE WATCHTOWER

With no other shelter available, Thomas and the others instinctively ducked below the boat's gunwale but what saved them was the width of the River Werra. The pursuers' crossbows had been designed for hunting and, as they lacked the range of military arbalests, their bolts splashed harmlessly into the water.

Though this first volley fell short of its target by several yards, those in the skiff were still far from safety because the river was beginning to narrow as it approached the rapids at the entrance to a rocky gorge. If the Brethren of The Ring could reach the open ground high above the churning water, it would be easy for their crossbowmen to pick off the boat's occupants as they battled to pass through the rapids.

Keeping one eye on Little Heinrich, Thomas continued to search the opposite bank for somewhere to land. However he couldn't see any break in the ramparts of rock and of wood guarding the far shore. The overhanging branches of the trees formed an impenetrable web and a growing number of half-submerged boulders protruded from the water, like the fins of sharks circling for the kill. All the while, the current was growing stronger and the rowers had to pull hard to keep the boat moving upstream.

When the skiff was less than two hundred yards from the flooded canyon, the peasant band suddenly disappeared behind an outcrop of rock and the once placid Werra became a series of powerful eddies that spiralled downstream like runaway cartwheels. The increasingly pugnacious river began to push the boat violently from side to side, and its passengers struggled to keep their balance, but Bos and Prometheus continued to heave on their oars whilst Quintana fought to steer a safe course through the whitening water.

"The Argonauts facing the Cyanean Rocks didn't have to row as hard as this!" Prometheus cried as a wave broke over the boat's side and drenched him from head to foot. Bos demanded to know which fool had decided that they should escape upstream instead of down. Yet, even as Quintana told the Frisian to shut up and row, Thomas spotted a small stretch of stony beach at the water's edge.

"A portage!" Thomas cried happily and he pointed to the spot where small boats were brought ashore and carried around the rapids to be relaunched in the calmer water beyond the gorge. Using all his skill, Quintana turned the skiff towards the riverbank but, thirty yards from dry land, the treacherous undertow flung the boat against something hard.

With a squealing, screeching, crash, the skiff heeled over on its side, tipping everyone off their benches, and Little Heinrich seized his chance. The *Führer's* small size allowed him to extricate himself quickly from the tangled mass of limbs in the bottom of the boat and, before Thomas could grab his captive, he'd reached the relative safety of the boat's prow.

"Hear me, you poxed sons of Judas, my men will hunt you down and, when we find you, we'll skin you alive!" he cried and, pausing only to thumb his nose at his prostrate captors, he jumped into the water. Clambering over the others, Thomas struggled to the side of the boat, and stared into the chaotic waves, but there was no sign of Little Heinrich.

"In the name of Jonah's Great Fish, why didn't you look where you were going, you blind papist poltroon?" Bos growled as he clung to the boat's gunwale.

"Save your breath for swimming, you'll need it," snapped Quintana but his words were drowned by a howl of despair from Prometheus.

"By the great fat arse of Ati, Queen of all the lands of Punt, how many times do I have to tell you ignorant heathens? I can't swim!" Prometheus wailed but he knew that nothing could save the doomed skiff. Cold, muddy water was pouring through the large hole in the boat's shattered planks, so the Nubian crossed himself and said a prayer to St Adjutor as they all prepared to swim for their lives.

"May the crusading saint, who swam all the way back to France to escape his Saracen captors, guide us to shore!" Prometheus cried, yet Thomas had a more practical solution to their predicament than praying for miracles. Drawing his sword, the Englishman swiftly cut through the ropes securing the skiff's unstepped mast and once the slender pole was free of its bonds he ordered the Nubian to grab hold.

"Hang on to this and we'll tow you to the bank," he said. Prometheus looked at the spar suspiciously but there was no time for further discussion because the weight of water inside the skiff had become so great the stricken vessel could no longer remain on its perch.

With a groan of tortured wood, the boat slid off the rock that had caused its destruction and the four men were pitched headlong into the freezing river. After splashing around like dogs chasing ducks, each man managed to grab the mast, unfortunately Prometheus' massive frame threatened to drag them all to the bottom.

"Did the Lord God Almighty make all Nubians from lead? Try and swim, you great African elephant!" Quintana spluttered and though Prometheus could only gurgle as the water surged over his head, he managed to kick his legs as he clung to the mast.

Between the half-submerged rocks, the river was a treacherous labyrinth of whirlpools and cross-currents, so the swimmers felt as if the capricious Nixe water sprites were trying to seize their flailing legs and drag them to their deaths. The cold and effort quickly sapped their energies, though fear renewed their strength and at last Thomas and the others felt solid ground under their feet.

The castaways hauled themselves onto dry land feeling as if they'd swum across the German Ocean and for several minutes they could do nothing except lie on the pebbles like stranded whales. It took a dozen crossbow bolts thudding into the trees to rouse the men and send them scurrying for the shelter of a large boulder.

"I thought we were out of range," said Prometheus but Bos pointed to a raft in the centre of the river. The raft's one-eyed captain was pointing his sword at the shipwrecked refugees and the dozen men with him were re-spanning their crossbows.

There was no time for Thomas and the others to wonder how the Brotherhood of The Ring had retrieved their vessel so quickly. In a few minutes the rebels' raft would reach the shore, so the four men dragged themselves wearily to their feet and fled into the forest.

The track from the pebble beach soon became steep and rutted, yet the fugitives didn't slow their pace. They continued to run up the wooded hillside, faster than Actaeon pursued by his hounds, but when they reached the broad clearing at the hill's summit, they found, to their horror, that they could go no further. Though the path continued to meander lazily across the open heath, it passed close to a watchtower which had been built on a rocky outcrop at the very lip of the gorge.

As this circular turret overlooked both the river and the path, the men guessed that it had been built by the abbey's monks to extract tolls from the boatmen trying to avoid the rapids below. The little fort looked deserted but the men couldn't be sure; if the tower was occupied, the garrison was bound to be unfriendly, so Thomas and the others retreated into the forest to watch and wait.

The fugitives continued to stare at the tower, looking for signs of life, until Bos announced that only deer and bandits cowered in thickets. With a snort of disgust at his own timidity, the Frisian rose to his feet and tried to make his way to the edge of the trees. However, before he could step into the clearing, Quintana stopped him. Tugging on Bos' sleeve, the Portugee pointed feverishly towards the tower's battlements and whispered that he'd just seen someone.

"Wait, you big ox, if Little Heinrich's men are in that tower, we'll be shot to death the moment we show our faces," he hissed but Bos was convinced that there was no danger.

"You're imagining things, Portugee. The Brethren of the Ring have been too busy filling their bellies with stolen wine to bother about collecting tolls," he said and Prometheus added that ignorant farm boys would never have the foresight to occupy such a strategic position.

Thomas agreed that they had little choice but to go on and he reminded everyone that the crossbowmen on the raft must have landed on their side of the river by now.

"If we delay any longer, Little Heinrich's curs will soon run us to earth," he said, yet Quintana was adamant that he'd seen someone in the tower and he refused to leave the safety of the trees.

"There's two hundred yards of killing ground in front of that watchtower and anyone trying to cross it in daylight will soon find an arrow or an arquebus ball in his gizzard," he said emphatically. The debate was ended by Thomas, who'd spotted six armed men leaving the tower.

Judging by their dress and demeanour, the Englishman reckoned that these were the dregs of Little Heinrich's rabble but this didn't make them any less dangerous. The sentries carried long billhooks that were as lethal as any *landsknecht's* halberd and they were heading straight for the thicket where the fugitives were hiding.

"So we're in for a fight," said Thomas, drawing his sword. Unfortunately, the others had lost their weapons in the river.

"Without swords we're as defenceless as new-born herring," Bos moaned but Thomas told him not to worry.

"All I need is your shoe and I'll scatter our enemies like Cadmus scattered the *Spartoi*," he said and before Bos could declare that he wanted no part of any wizardry, the others had wrestled the Frisian to the ground and snatched a badly worn boot from Bos' grimy foot. Ignoring the torrent of abuse from his recumbent comrade, Thomas tied the pungent trophy to a long stick and went to meet the advancing sentries.

In spite of Prometheus' low opinion of Little Heinrich's martial abilities, the rebel chief had had the good sense to garrison the tower. However, he'd kept his best men to defend the abbey and sent half a dozen simpletons to guard the path through the forest. These slow-witted sentries knew nothing of recent events and they believed that the men who'd appeared at the edge of the clearing were their relief. Eager to return to the drunken orgy at the abbey, they'd abandoned their posts with alacrity and it was only when Thomas greeted them in a strange accent that their suspicions were aroused.

"Stop who comes hither?" cried a horse-faced hedgelayer who'd been put in charge of the tower.

"Hail Brothers of the Untied Shoe! We've come to take over your lonely vigil and you must hasten back to the abbey. The wine is flowing and the wenches willing but such bounty can't last forever," Thomas said, and he held the stick with Bos' shoe tied to it a little higher, but the garrison's leader took one look at the stranger's sodden clothing and pointed his billhook at Thomas.

"Are you sure you're from The Ring? You're dressed like *landsknechts*, and we hang mercenary turds round here," said the hedge-layer and, before Thomas could allay the man's fears, a chorus of shouts from the trees indicated that his bluff had failed. Prometheus and Quintana, followed by the partially barefoot Bos, were sprinting towards the tower and when Thomas glanced over his shoulder he saw more of Little Heinrich's men had appeared at the edge of the clearing.

The hedge-layer had also seen the reinforcements and he lunged at Thomas with his billhook but the man's thrust was as slow as his wits and his opponent easily countered the stroke before landing a brutal cut of his own. The Englishman's blade lopped off the rebel's arm, as if it were nothing more than a stout branch of blackthorn and the sight of their leader's severed limb lying in the grass caused the other dullards to panic.

Leaving their howling commander to his fate, the pusillanimous peasants ran to join their comrades emerging from the trees. Thomas, however, headed towards the tower.

Panting hard, Thomas followed Bos, Prometheus and Quintana, who'd completed their headlong dash across the clearing and disappeared inside the now deserted fort. As he reached the short flight of steps that led to the gateway, a dozen crossbow bolts clattered against the outcrop of granite that formed the tower's foundations but, not one missile found its mark, and Thomas joined the others inside the tower.

Though the fort's original door had been battered into firewood when the Brethren of The Ring had captured the outpost, the new garrison had made a palisade as a replacement and the four fugitives wasted no time in hauling it into place. The crude hurdle didn't quite fill the gateway but the rest of the tower's defences were in a much better state of repair.

The crenellated walls were twenty feet high and just below the battlements there was a narrow walkway, reached by a wooden ladder. These ramparts enclosed a circular courtyard, with a floor of beaten earth, but the only buildings were a pair of lean-to shelters made from tree trunks covered with turf. Whilst Thomas, Prometheus and Bos secured the palisade, by jamming several sturdy wooden stakes behind one of the cross-members, Quintana investigated the nearest of these crude shelters and discovered a treasure more valuable than a priest's promise of heaven.

"At last Mistress Fortune smiles on us! There are enough guns, shot and powder in here to stop a Tartar horde. There's even flint, steel and an old hook gun but these'll do for now," he said and he held up four fine

Spanish arquebuses for the others to admire. Thomas and Prometheus nodded in appreciation but Bos wondered why the peasant sentries hadn't armed themselves with these weapons.

"Little Heinrich's men must have no more sense than the servant who buried his master's gift," he said.

"And the worthless slave was cast into the outer darkness where there was great weeping, wailing and gnashing of teeth," Prometheus added, whereupon Thomas suggested that, instead of quoting the Gospel of St Matthew, loading the guns might be a more effective use of their time.

"Scripture may save our souls but right now we need bullets, not a bible," he said and, as he spoke, a chorus of shouts from outside the tower warned its new owners that an attack was imminent.

Without wasting another moment, the four men began packing their guns with double loads of shot but, as they kindled their matchcords, Bos insisted on thanking Jehovah, the God of Battles, for giving them the means to defend themselves.

"By all the houris in Saracen heaven, I hope your shooting's as good as your praying, Frisian," said Quintana, as the men climbed the ladder to the tower's parapet and took up their firing positions, but Bos said nothing as he wound the slow burning matchcord securely around his arm and primed his gun's firing pan. Thomas and Prometheus also kept their own counsel as they made their guns ready and for a brief moment there was silence as each side offered up their unspoken prayers asking for God to bless their endeavours.

The crossbowmen from the raft had now been reinforced by more Brethren of the Ring, and at least fifty men followed the one-eyed captain as he led a charge across the heath but, if the peasants' strength was their overwhelming numbers, their weakness was their rage. Had they attacked the tower from all sides, they'd have easily crushed the defenders, but the peasants were so intent on revenge they ran towards the tower in a dense, undisciplined mob.

Scarcely able to believe their luck, Thomas and the others fired their double-shotted arquebuses into the throng and six men in the attackers' front line became a bloodied mass of mangled flesh and smashed bone.

The screams of their fallen comrades seemed to paralyse the rest of the mob and, as the attack wavered, a second volley crashed into their ranks. At such short range the defenders couldn't miss and the storm of lead ripped through more guts and splintered more skulls with the ruthless efficiency of a torturer. This new slaughter convinced most of the surviving attackers that the tower was impregnable, and they began to fall back, but three young ploughboys were determined to prove their valour and they ran towards the tower's gate.

The defenders on the walls were too busy ramming fresh powder into their arquebuses to notice the approach of this 'forlorn hope' and the ill-fitting palisade presented no obstacle to peasants who'd spent their childhood climbing trees. The first of the farmers easily clambered through the narrow gap between the top of the palisade and the gateway's stone lintel and only Thomas spotted the danger.

Though the Englishman yelled at the others to turn their guns on the gate, his warning was lost in a third crash of gunfire. As his was the only arquebus still loaded Thomas aimed at the serf, who was busy trying to remove the stakes holding the palisade in place, and fired. However, the Englishman's shot was too hurried and the bullet missed its target by several feet. Cursing his haste, Thomas dropped his gun, drew his sword and scrambled down the ladder.

Before his enemy knew what was happening, Thomas was plunging his blade into the serf's back but, as he withdrew the bloody steel, another attacker climbed over the palisade. The second man was older than the first and Thomas guessed that his foe had experienced something of real war because he stood in the proper stance, with a razor-sharp arming sword in one hand and a dagger with upturned crossguards in the other.

"You preening Swabian coxcomb, I'll turn you into a eunuch as easily as I geld my pigs," the peasant sneered and he thrust his sword towards Thomas' groin.

"Pigs don't fight back, I do!" Thomas cried as he parried the blow and launched his own attack.

Using measured, easy thrusts, Thomas tested his opponent's defences and found, to his annoyance, that the swineherd was indeed no novice. After one badly timed stroke, the peasant deftly caught Thomas's blade in the crossguard of his dagger, and twisted the knife in an attempt to wrench his opponent's sword out of his hand, but the Englishman also knew a few tricks. Turning his wrist in the same direction, Thomas slid his blade backwards out of the dagger's crossguard. However, as he did so, another man appeared at the top of the palisade.

"I'm coming Hans!" the third peasant cried, and though his shout encouraged the swineherd to redouble his efforts, it was too late. A crash of gunfire from the parapet killed the third rebel and the sound of his comrade falling dead into the mud caused the swineherd to turn his head. In that same instant Thomas swung his sword and sent the top of his opponent's skull, together with a large slice of his brain, spinning through the air.

In death, the swineherd fell against the crude shelter to the right of the gate and the impact of even an undernourished serf was too much for the fragile lean-to. The flimsy structure collapsed with a shriek of splintered wood but, as Thomas began to climb back to the parapet, he saw a frightened face peering out of the tangle of turf and shattered branches. Curious, the Englishman climbed down the ladder and returned to the courtyard. Gripping his sword a little more tightly he took a cautious step towards the ruined shelter but, as he did so, the face disappeared into the shadows.

At first, Thomas thought he'd imagined seeing anything at all, but he had to be sure that there was no one hostile lurking in the wreckage, so he dragged the bloody corpse of the swineherd to one side and began to search through the broken trusses. He expected to find a young son of one of the rebels but what he found was a girl. Her face, though filthy, was striking and though she was of marriageable age, she had the wild stare of a woman who'd not been tamed by a husband.

Despite the sudden uncovering of her hiding place, the girl remained motionless and the only sound she made was a low growl, like that of a hound about to be whipped by its master. Her demeanour and torn chemise, which revealed far more than modesty permitted, convinced Thomas that she was nothing more than a local whore who'd been thrown out of her village for making too many wives jealous.

However, when he looked again, he noticed that the girl's blonde hair had been cut short and her hands had been tied to an iron ring set in the wall with leather thongs. Realising this girl was no harlot, Thomas lifted his sword to cut her free, whereupon she howled like a whipped dog and spat in her rescuer's face.

"If you come a step closer, I'll kill you," she hissed and her eyes flashed bright with hatred. She spoke in German but with a heavy accent that Thomas couldn't place.

"Kill me, with what? Is your spittle full of venom like that of the *basilisk*?" Thomas replied as he wiped his face.

"I'll call upon God to smite you, as he did the Midianites, for the Peace and Truce of God makes it a mortal sin to lay hands on any woman in Holy Orders," the girl replied and she spoke with all the rage of Lilith in her voice.

"Is that so? But you don't look like a nun," Thomas said suspiciously. Though the girl was covered in grime and clothed in the coarse habit of the Poor Clares, it was evident that she lacked the humility normally found in Brides of Christ. Even tied to a wall, the girl carried herself with the arrogance of someone used to luxury, so Thomas wondered if she'd been immured in a nunnery against her will.

It was not uncommon for women born of noble families to be sent to convents as punishment for giving birth to bastard children, or for refusing to marry the old, but wealthy, husbands their fathers had chosen for them. Yet, whatever this girl had done, Thomas thought she was far too comely to endure life in the cloister or death in this midden.

"I may be a novice but I'm still protected by the Peace and Truce of God as well as all the laws of chivalry, if you know what they are, you low-born lackwit. God's Wounds, I've seen more nobility in the droppings of diseased dogs than in you and your villainous rebel friends," she said angrily. Thomas replied by insisting that he had no reason to love the Brethren of the Ring and as evidence of his claim he pointed to the corpses lying in the courtyard.

"Were these brigands holding you for ransom?" Thomas asked and, as the girl glanced at the peasants' dead bodies, her manner suddenly softened. She admitted that her father was rich and explained that she'd been accompanying her Mother Superior on a visit to the abbey in the valley when their party had been attacked. The men they'd hired to protect them had fled and the two nuns had been left to the mercy of the rebels who carried the banner of the unlaced shoe.

"Those fiends were led by a wicked *homunculus*, and they did unspeakable things to the abbess before they dragged her off to God knows where, but they brought me here and tied me to this wall as if I was a bitch in heat," she said bitterly.

After considering the matter for a moment, Thomas decided to believe the girl. It seemed logical that Little Heinrich would hide his richest treasure in this outpost of his miniature empire, especially as a nobly born girl would have no value if she was dishonoured in the Brethren's orgiastic revels. However, it was the memory of the roasted corpse of an elderly woman dangling from the abbey's smoke-blackened arch that finally convinced him the girl was telling the truth.

"I'm afraid your Mother Superior's dead but I'll do what I can to return you to your family, once I've dealt with the more pressing matters claiming my attention," Thomas said gallantly and he swung his sword to cut the girl's bonds.

The captive nun flinched as the polished steel blade struck the rusty iron ring but she took her rescuer's outstretched hand when he offered it and as he helped the girl to her feet, Thomas was rewarded with a glimpse of shapely breasts beneath the torn linen shift. In that instant he felt a flood of desire wash away the travails of the last few weeks but another crack of gunfire from the parapet reminded him that everyone inside the tower was still in mortal danger.

Struggling to hide his frustration, Thomas took the girl firmly by the hand and dragged her to the foot of the ladder. Whatever the truth of her story, he daren't leave her alone in the courtyard, so he told her to climb up to the parapet. The girl protested that her vows forbade her to take up arms but she did as she was told and they reached the walkway just as the attacking serfs' nerve failed them for a second time.

"Go home to your pig-faced wives!" Prometheus roared at the men running for the safety of the forest but Thomas told him to mind his tongue.

"Do you always curse like a cuckolded sailor when you're in the presence of a lady?" Thomas said.

On hearing these words of admonishment, the puzzled Nubian turned and was astonished to see the Englishman was now accompanied by a half-naked nun. However, before Thomas could offer an explanation, the girl had fallen to her knees and begun to pray.

"Praise be to Lord Jesus, who has sent St Maurice in answer to my prayers," she said reverently. This failed to satisfy the others, who insisted that Thomas tell them what he was doing in the company of a raving lunatic.

"I found her hiding in one of the shelters. She claims to be a nobly born nun being held for ransom," Thomas explained, whereupon Quintana burst out laughing.

"She belongs in Bedlam, not a convent, if she believes our princely prizefighter is St Maurice!" Quintana cried, yet the girl continued to insist that Prometheus was the reincarnation of the black-skinned Nubian centurion, who was martyred in the days of the ancient Roman Emperor, Maximian.

"My order's house is at Coburg, and the Blessed Maurice is the patron saint of that city, so this is a clear sign that God has chosen you men to escort me home. Yet, if Our Lord's blessing is not a rich enough reward, my father will give you plenty of gold for my safe return," the girl said loftily.

As Coburg was only thirty miles to the south, Thomas thought that this was an excellent opportunity to replace their money, which had been stolen by Little Heinrich. Though Bos had little time for nuns, whatever their mental state, he agreed with Prometheus that entry into Heaven was only granted to those who followed the example of the Good Samaritan. This argument did not impress Quintana, who pointed out that their plans would come to nought if the peasants stormed the tower.

"But, if this girl has value, perhaps we can give her to Little Heinrich in exchange for our lives," he added. Unfortunately, the girl didn't think much of being offered for barter like a chicken in a market and she slapped the Portugee hard across his face.

"I'm Ursula, daughter of the Royal House of *Basarab* and my father can have you put to death for merely gazing upon me!" she snapped and before Quintana could raise his hand to chastise the girl for her insolence, he was interrupted by the sound of beating drums. Scrambling to the parapet's edge, the tower's defenders looked over the battlements and saw that Little Heinrich had arrived to take charge of the battle.

The *Führer*, who seemed to be none the worse for his recent swim, was seated once more on his stolen throne and he was accompanied by the captain of the raft, who'd exchanged his black banner for a white flag of truce. As the drummers fell silent, Little Heinrich hailed the tower's defenders and declared that he was ready to parley.

"You men, listen to me! Surrender the girl and you may go free. If you continue to resist, I'll see to it that each of you takes a week to die. You have five minutes in which to throw down your weapons, after that we'll raze your refuge to the ground!" He cried in his small but powerful voice. This was no idle threat, as there were now enough Brethren to swamp the watchtower, but for the moment Little Heinrich kept his men a healthy distance from the defenders' handguns.

"By the milk-white tits of the *Lorelei*, I thought that little monster had drowned," muttered Bos.

"At least we now know the girl is speaking the truth. If Little Heinrich is willing to bargain she must have some worth," said Prometheus.

"Perhaps this trollop's his runaway daughter," said Quintana, as he nursed his bruised cheek, but the Portugee's remark earned him another hard slap across the face.

"Me, the daughter of that dung gatherer? I doubt if he could father anything but a lie!" Ursula taunted.

"If only I had a *culverin* or a *saker*, I'd blow Little Heinrich back to his abbey," Thomas said grimly and he cursed the *Führer's* cunning that kept the rebel chief just out of range.

"I hear and I obey," said Quintana with a broad grin and he told everyone to keep the rebel chief talking for as long as possible.

Ignoring his bruised face, the Portugee clambered down the ladder and ran to the shelter where he'd found the handguns. He emerged a few moments later, carrying what looked like the big brother of an arquebus and a battered leather bucket.

"By all the saints, I'd forgotten the hook gun!" Thomas cried as Quintana returned to the parapet.

"The dragon is hungry and must be fed," he said and he held up the bucket, which was full of old nails.

The hook gun was identical to the smaller handguns except that it was considerably larger than an arquebus and its barrel had been cast with an iron hook underneath so it could be braced against the ramparts of a fortress. Everyone helped load the monstrous weapon and, when the last wad had been rammed home, Thomas asked for the privilege of firing it.

"The death of that old monk will be on my conscience for all time unless I can avenge him," he said and the others were happy to indulge his request. Though the large gun was even heavier than it looked, with the hook jammed against the tower's masonry, Thomas managed to point its muzzle at the *Führer* and as he took careful aim Little Heinrich demanded an answer to his offer.

"Your time is up, so what say you? Will you give up the girl or will you face the painful consequences of your pointless defiance?" the *Führer* demanded but Thomas' only reply was to touch a slow match to the tiny hole in the hook gun's breech.

The priming powder fizzed with a sickly sulphurous smell and this was followed by an enormous bang. A heartbeat later, Little Heinrich disappeared behind a huge fountain of gore, as hundreds of rusted nails shredded him into a crimson pulp.

Both the Brethren of the Ring and the tower's defenders were rendered speechless by the lethal power of the hook gun and once the echo of the explosion had died away, the forest was held in the grip of a deathly silence. This eerie quiet lasted until it was broken by the mournful sound of a hunting horn.

"Is that more rebels coming to avenge their master?" Bos whispered but it was Ursula who answered him.

"I'd recognise that horn anywhere, it belongs to my father! He must have been searching for me and now he's heard that thunder-clap he'll hasten to my rescue," the girl said gleefully and she added that her father commanded enough men to slaughter every rebel serf between the Rhine and the Elbe.

"We must light a beacon so he can find us," said Prometheus but Ursula assured him there was no need.

"I can call him with this," she replied and she retrieved a small silver whistle that had been hidden in the folds of her skirts.

Holding the instrument to her lips, Ursula blew as hard as she could. The notes drifted away on the wind but instead of expressing their gratitude the men on the wall could only stare at the girl in utter astonishment. Ursula's whistle was shaped like a coiled dragon, with its tail wrapped around its neck, and before its shrill cry had died away, the girl found four razor sharp swords pointed at her own throat.

The speed of her rescuers' transformation into assassins took Ursula completely by surprise, so, though she protested loudly, she could do nothing to stop Prometheus snatching the whistle from her hand.

"There's no mistake, this is almost identical to that foul badge of the *Ouroboros* worn by the Order of The Dragon!" Prometheus cried, after he'd examined the bauble closely.

"By all that's unholy, you're one of those accursed Draconists who tried to kill us in Marburg!" Quintana hissed and though Ursula tried to protest that she'd never been in that town, Bos insisted that her dragon-shaped whistle proved her guilt.

"Admit that you're the handmaiden of the traitor Dracul and we'll kill you quickly," he said.

"But deny it and we'll let those peasant pig-botherers have you," added Thomas angrily but Ursula merely laughed in the Englishman's face.

"Sweet Jesu, if only your manhood was as great as your ignorance, your wife would be a much happier woman! Yes, I freely admit that I serve the Lord Mircea, also called Dracul, the Grandmaster of the Order of The Dragon, but he's no traitor. He's the rightful King of Wallachia and a fearless crusader who's given his life to defend my homeland from the infidel Turks. For this he was driven into exile by his faithless enemies, who are in league with the Ottoman Sultan, and I know this to be true because Lord Dracul is my father," she said proudly.

# 8

## LORD DRACUL

Before Thomas and the others could recover their wits, Ursula had revealed she was a granddaughter of Mihnea the Bad and a great-granddaughter of Vlad Dracula, who'd earned his soubriquet *Tepes* by impaling 20,000 Turkish prisoners on the banks of the Danube.

Through such ancestors Ursula could also claim descent from *Basarab*, founder of the ancient royal house of Wallachia, but, before she could offer more evidence of her royal pedigree, the sound of angry voices demanded the defenders' attention.

Once again, the Brethren of the Ring were advancing towards the watchtower and this time they were carrying three scaling ladders. These had been crudely fashioned by lopping off the branches from the trunks of suitable pine trees but, in spite of their simple construction, the ladders were more than capable of allowing men to climb over the watchtower's walls.

"Those shit-covered sons of the soil don't know when they're beaten," said Bos ruefully but Ursula had a more likely explanation for the Brethren of the Ring's renewed zeal for battle.

"They know my father slaughters rebel scum like cattle and their only hope is to have me as a hostage," she said, yet there was no time for further discussion.

A rattle of crossbow bolts striking the tower forced her to duck below the parapet. Bos, Quintana and Thomas also threw themselves behind the battlements but Prometheus, who was still marvelling at the girl's claim that he was St Maurice reborn, was too slow and a well-aimed bolt buried itself in his shoulder.

With a cry of pain, the Nubian took a step backwards and tumbled off the narrow walkway. He landed on the wet ground twenty feet below with a squelching thud and, before the others could rush to help their motionless comrade, Ursula had scrambled down the ladder.

"I was taught many of the healing arts at my convent, so I'll do what I can for the Blessed Maurice Reborn, but you must keep those filthy Poor Conrads at bay until my father arrives!" Ursula ordered. Thomas and the others knew that each of them would be needed to defend the tower, so, Draconist or not, they let the girl attend to the unconscious Nubian whilst they prepared for battle.

The one-eyed captain, who'd found himself back in charge after Little Heinrich's demise, had finally learned the lessons of his previous defeats and split his forces into three. He now ordered each party to attack the tower simultaneously, but from different directions.

Moreover, just as Ursula had guessed, the peasants' resolve had been strengthened by their fear of Dracul. Knowing that they'd soon face a far more terrible foe than four renegade *landsknechts*, not even another volley of arquebus fire could persuade the Brotherhood of the Ring to remain in the trees, so, before the defenders could reload, three ladders had been placed against the tower's walls.

The first of the attackers to reach the top of his ladder was a bare-chested blacksmith who had arms like the branches of an oak and a head as bald as an acorn. The burly smith was carrying an ancient wooden shield, which he'd reinforced with nails and strips of iron, and he held this antiquated pavise high above his head as Bos unleashed a storm of metal.

Though the blacksmith's shield belonged to an earlier age, it was strong enough to deflect every one of the defender's bone-crushing blows and the increasing effort that the enraged Bos put into each stroke caused him to stumble. As the Frisian struggled to regain his balance, the smith hurriedly clambered over the battlements and Bos knew that if he didn't kill this man quickly, the rest of the Brethren of the Ring would pour into the tower like water through a leaky dyke.

Cursing his enemies, Bos swung his sword with even greater fury. However, the smith's shield seemed to possess an almost mythical strength. Out of sheer frustration Bos roared at the man to surrender, but the blacksmith merely spat and questioned the marital status of his enemy's parents. Now almost blind with wrath, the Frisian released another blizzard of steel but, though its oak planks became pitted and splintered, the blacksmith's shield remained intact.

"The wall is breached!" Bos cried, as he wondered why the force of his attacks hadn't shattered the blacksmith's forearm, but the others were too busy with their own duels. Thomas was fencing furiously with a peasant on top of the second ladder, whilst Quintana was busy filleting a terrified sod-cutter who was armed with nothing but a sharpened spade.

Again, Bos cursed as he realised he had to face his enemy alone but, as the blacksmith began to shout for more of his comrades to join him, the point of a pike erupted from the man's chest. The smith screamed, dropped his battered shield, and clutched the two feet of bloody, iron-tipped wood now protruding from his ribs.

It took a split second for Bos to realise that the spear had been thrust upwards from below and, when he glanced down, he saw Ursula was holding the other end of the pike's eighteen foot shaft. The tear in the girl's chemise had grown large enough to reveal the full glory of her womanhood; yet, like Penthesilea defending the walls of Troy, she gave no heed to her nakedness as she pitched the dead blacksmith off the wall as if he were nothing more than a bale of hay.

With the skill of a practised pikeman, Ursula twisted the long spear's shaft and withdrew the weapon from the blacksmith's corpse. However, as she did so, a second peasant, a cobbler, clambered onto the parapet.

Having seen the fate of the blacksmith, the shoemaker managed to parry another of Ursula's pike thrusts, yet the sight of a beautiful, bare-breasted Amazon, with the fire of battle in her eyes, threw him into confusion. This hesitation gave Bos enough time to plunge his sword into the cobbler's face.

There was such force in the Frisian's blow, the blade emerged from the back of his enemy's head but, with a roar of triumph, and a rasp of metal against bone, Bos ripped his sword from the dead man's skull. The cobbler's corpse toppled backwards over the parapet and, as it fell, it stripped the ladder of his comrades like a woodcutter's adze lopping branches off a tree.

As soon as the makeshift ladder was empty, Bos sheathed his sword, leaned over the battlements and seized the topmost rung. With a great heave, the giant Frisian hauled the ladder up and over the tower's wall so that it fell into the courtyard, narrowly avoiding the still prostrate Prometheus and his nurse. Once his victory was complete, Bos looked around to see that Thomas and Quintana were also surrounded by limbless, eviscerated corpses. Unfortunately, their success had not ended the fight for the watchtower.

As if to signal the start of a new round in the contest, a second blast from a hunting horn heralded the imminent arrival of Lord Dracul and the sound prompted dozens of heavily armed peasants to run from the trees shouting dreadful oaths. In reply, Bos began waving his sword around his head like a Viking berserker and yelling his own battle cries.

"Come hither, you godless sons of Cain and I'll kick your filthy, flea-bitten arses all the way back to Hell!" Bos roared. Thomas, Quintana and Prometheus also prepared to sell their lives dearly but, when the peasants ran past the tower, they realised that the Brethren of the Ring were no longer attacking.

"They're being flushed from the undergrowth like a covey of partridge!" Thomas cried as he watched the frightened ploughmen and cowherds run for their lives.

Though most of the fleeing serfs disappeared into the trees on the far side of the clearing, around fifty peasants were trapped by a line of horsemen that suddenly appeared at the edge of the forest. These riders were dressed in the same feathered caps and long coats that Thomas and the others had first seen in the forest of The Hornberg and their red, tear-drop shields bore the unmistakeable badge of the *Ouroboros*.

The Draconists quickly surrounded the remnants of the rebel band and began to herd them towards the centre of the clearing. Those peasants who dallied were swiftly cut down and once the surviving Brethren of the Ring had been surrounded by a hedge of steel and horseflesh, the terrified serfs sank to their knees.

In loud, tearful voices, the defeated rebels began to pray but their guards ignored their prisoners' desperate pleas for mercy and the serfs' plaintive cries continued until a fully armoured horseman appeared at the edge of the trees. This sinister knight, who was mounted on a huge black stallion, looked as chilling as the plague and the sight of him cowed the wretched captives into silence.

The horseman's armour may have been old-fashioned and obsolete but this did nothing to allay the prisoners' fears because everything the man wore was the colour of death. His full harness of expensive steel plate had been blackened with oil and soot and his great helm was topped by a crest of a large dragon carved from priceless African ebony. The only thing about this dark rider that wasn't the colour of night was the silver badge of the *Ouroboros* embroidered on his long surcoat of black linen.

"So this is the famous Lord Dracul," muttered Quintana in a hushed voice.

"We've seen the one wearing the wolf pelt before," added Bos and he pointed to one of the Draconists who'd left the other horsemen to speak to his lord. This rider was the same weasel-faced man who'd chased Thomas and his comrades all the way to Marburg and though they couldn't hear what was being said, they guessed that Dracul's captain was asking what was to be done with the prisoners.

One look at the Order of the Dragon's Grand Master was enough to convince the tower's defenders that Lord Dracul knew nothing of mercy and, seconds later, their fears were confirmed. In a voice as chilling as a crypt, the exiled Prince of Wallachia addressed the sobbing prisoners and pronounced a death sentence on them all.

"For laying hands on the sacred person of my daughter, for the desecration of Christ's church and for the murder of his holy priests, I sentence you all to die in the manner prescribed for every infidel and blasphemer!" Dracul cried in a voice that was as pitiless as a money-lender's bargain.

The appearance of Lord Dracul had reduced the condemned men to a state of hysteria, so, even though they knew that their last hour had come, the prisoners had no power to resist as the Draconists stripped them of their clothes and bound their hands behind their backs. Once all the prisoners were naked and lying face down in the mud, Dracul sent a score of his men into the forest and the sound of chopping soon filled the clearing.

When the riders returned, they were carrying armfuls of hazel poles which were each about twelve feet long, as thick as a man's arm and sharpened at both ends. The riders piled these stakes in front of the prisoners, who began to resemble giant maggots trying to escape a fishing hook as their naked, pale bodies writhed in terror.

"My God, they can't be going to ..." gasped Thomas, but his mouth had suddenly become so dry he couldn't finish his sentence. He tried to turn away but the dreadful horror he was about to witness somehow held his gaze. The others had been similarly bewitched and they too could do nothing but watch as the Draconists seized their first victim and fastened ropes to each of his ankles. The other end of these ropes were tied to the saddle of a horse and, as the helpless, squirming captive screamed for mercy, Thomas recognised him as the same man who'd tormented the dying abbot.

Once the ropes had been tied to the horse, a hazel pole was placed between the supine victim's thighs so when the horse leapt forward, the prisoner was dragged onto the stake. Accompanied by his screams, the sharpened point slid into the man's bowels and emerged from his throat in a great gout of blood, vomit and ordure, but the shrieking wretch didn't die. Now, to increase the prisoner's suffering, the Draconists raised the stake upright and planted it in the ground.

Like a blasphemous parody of Christ's suffering at Golgotha the impaled prisoner hung from his branchless tree, writhing like a broken marionette and, moments later, this profane version of The Crucifixion was completed by the impaling of two thieves. As the ropes were tied to their ankles, these reincarnations of Dismas and Gestas loudly protested their innocence but the Draconists were deaf to their pleas.

The two footpads were impaled on either side of the original victim and this time the gods of death were more merciful. The stakes ruptured each man's heart, killing him instantly, but the fifth and sixth captives danced the same grisly galliard as the first. This greatly amused the callous torturers.

After a dozen more stakes had been erected in this way, Dracul's executioners grew bored and began to dispatch their victims in ever more imaginative ways, such as piercing them through their belly or planting the stakes upside down. Lord Dracul seemed to appreciate his executioners' extraordinary powers of invention, and he waved his black gauntlet in approval as each new stake was raised, but Thomas and the others in the tower were paralysed by their sense of revulsion.

The strangled shrieks of the victims, mingled with the harsh screech of crows gathering for the feast of carrion. These hellish birds provided the ghastly music for Dracul's Dance of Death, yet the worst thing of all was the loathsome smell. The mix of blood, excrement and urine flowing from ruptured entrails and punctured veins meant those watching from the watchtower's walls couldn't even escape the horror by closing their eyes and covering their ears.

Throughout the executions, Lord Dracul remained seated on his gigantic black horse, whilst the man in the wolf skin skipped between the stakes and taunted the groaning victims with obscene jests like an old king's fool. The other Draconists loudly applauded each new insult but this was more than the spectators in the tower could bear. Swallowing the bile rising in their throats, Thomas and the others tore themselves away from the ghastly pageant and climbed down the ladder to join the insensible Prometheus and his nurse in the courtyard.

Mercifully, the soft ground had cushioned the Nubian's fall, so he'd broken no bones, and though Ursula had spent little over a year in the convent, she'd learned enough of the physician's art to know that a bolt or arrow shouldn't be removed until the wound could be closed with stitches or a hot iron. As she could do neither in the mud of a battlefield, she'd torn strips of linen from her skirts and wrapped them around the bolt sticking out of her patient's shoulder.

These cloths had both staunched the bleeding and immobilised the bolt, so it couldn't move and cause more damage, but there was a deep gash in Prometheus' cheek so she'd wound more bandages around his face until he resembled one of the embalmed mummies of Egypt.

"Trust a king to leave others to do the fighting whilst he has a nice long nap," said Quintana, as he and the others arrived at Ursula's side, but no one laughed.

"Will he live?" Thomas asked and Ursula assured him that the Nubian had a hide as thick as that of a hippopotamus and an even thicker skull.

"If his wounds are closed quickly he'll recover. If they're left to fester, even for a day, he'll need a priest, not a nurse. You must therefore take me to my father at once and I'll see to it that your friend has the proper care," said Ursula, wiping her slender, bloodstained fingers on the remains of her nun's habit.

The three men looked at the unconscious Nubian and agreed that they couldn't leave him to die, yet Thomas begged a moment to speak to the others in private. With a shrug, Bos and Quintana followed the Englishman to the other side of the courtyard, where Thomas whispered that he couldn't go with them if they left the tower.

"I understand that if our comrade is to live, he must be taken to Dracul but I haven't forgotten that this monster wants me for his own diabolical purpose and after the horrors we've just witnessed, I don't care to enter his service. The girl has no idea who I am, so, before she learns the truth, I'll slip away," he said and, though he reminded the others that they'd be well rewarded for saving Dracul's daughter, his companions were reluctant to take their leave.

Ever since Thomas had helped them escape King Henry's hangman, his companions had regarded the Englishman as a man who bore a charmed life and, by keeping him close, they'd hoped to prolong their own time on earth. However, in their current predicament, Bos and Quintana couldn't fault the logic of their companion's argument.

"I suppose Dracul will be so overcome with joy at being reunited with his daughter, he won't notice if one of her rescuers is missing," Quintana admitted.

"But we must promise to meet again in Nuremberg, or have you also forgotten that God himself has charged us with the sacred task of saving the world from Dracul and the forces of darkness?" Bos added and, once Thomas had agreed to this condition, they returned to Ursula.

Whilst Bos and Quintana removed the palisade that blocked the watchtower's entrance, Thomas explained to Dracul's daughter that he'd watch over the Nubian whilst she returned to her father. Though Ursula had no objections to this arrangement, as soon as she and the others had left the tower, Thomas abandoned her patient and looked around for somewhere to conceal himself.

The tower's spartan interior offered very little in the way of hiding places. There was nothing inside the walls except the shelters, and one of those was in ruins, but the cliff on which the tower stood might provide a convenient ledge where he could remain unseen until dark. With no other choice, Thomas waited until a cheer from outside indicated that Ursula had been reunited with Lord Dracul before crawling out of the tower and slithering to the edge of the precipice.

Peering over the cliff's edge, the first thing Thomas saw was the white water churning through the gorge but the second thing that caught his eye was a hollow just below the edge of the turf. Provided he didn't move, someone would have to be directly above the ledge to spot him so he scrambled down and lay still. The narrow, stony shelf was barely wide enough for his frame, and Thomas had to grasp the exposed roots of a bush to stop himself from falling, but at least he was safe.

Secreted in this hiding place, Thomas couldn't see what was going on but he could hear Dracul thank God for the return of his daughter. This solemn prayer was followed by the booming sound of Bos saying 'amen' and the next person to speak was the captain who wore the wolf skin. Whilst the man's broken German was difficult to follow, no one could mistake its meaning and, slowly, the realisation dawned on Thomas that this ginning fiend was sentencing his comrades to death. As he heard these traitorous words, the Englishman's face became a mask of fury yet all he could do was listen.

"The Lord Dracul thanks you for guarding his daughter's honour so valiantly but you have gazed upon the Lady Ursula's uncovered flesh and for this you cannot be permitted to live," the Draconist captain declared.

This speech was followed by the sounds of a violent struggle, during which Bos and Quintana threatened the Draconists with all manner of torments unless they were set free. When their protests ceased abruptly, Thomas concluded that his companions had been overpowered and whilst he lay on his ledge, quivering with frustrated anger, the Draconist captain spoke again.

"Yet, in gratitude for his daughter's safe return, Lord Dracul is mindful to be merciful. He has therefore waived the usual punishment for those who commit such treason and decreed that you shall be beheaded instead of impaled," he said and this travesty of mercy finally stung Thomas into action.

Once he'd scrambled from his hiding place, the first thing Thomas saw was the bound and kneeling figures of his comrades. Behind them was a group of Draconists, with drawn swords in their hands, and in front of them stood a hooded executioner armed with a huge, curved *bardiche*. This brute was carefully honing his colossal axe's blade and the scrape of metal against the whetstone sounded like a demon's scream.

Though he only had his name with which to save his companions, Thomas didn't hesitate. Standing on the edge of the cliff like the Last Bard of Cambria cursing King Edward, he drew himself up to his full height and shouted as loudly as he could.

"Hear me, Dracul, Lord of Lies! Before you is Thomas Devilstone, the greatest necromancer in all England. I'm the man who can summon the most powerful dragons and the foulest demons to do his bidding, so release these men who've done you no harm, before I summon a monster so terrible it will devour you and all your treacherous acolytes in a single bite!" Thomas bellowed.

Incredibly, the bluff worked and Dracul, who was still seated on his horse, ordered the executions to be stopped. Slowly, the Grand Master of the Order of the Dragon removed his helmet, so Thomas could gaze upon the man who'd been searching for him across Germany. It was not a privilege that the Englishman enjoyed.

The face that stared at Thomas was noble, with fine, almost handsome, features, yet Lord Dracul's expression was utterly devoid of human warmth. He had the pitiless eyes of a caged beast and the long, black moustaches which curved under his high cheek bones gave him the look of an oriental tyrant. Whilst it was difficult to judge his exact age, Thomas reckoned that the heir to Wallachia's throne must be in his late forties; however Dracul's graceful bearing and powerful demeanour suggested that he'd retained all the strength and vigour of a much younger man.

"Are you really Thomas Devilstone, the famed Master of Dragons, for whom I've been searching for so long?" Dracul asked incredulously and though Thomas was surprised to hear that this monster spoke in soft, cultured tones, he did not moderate his reply.

"If you doubt me, I'll unleash Earl *Räum* and his thirty legions of demons, whom I've already summoned from The Abyss. See how they gather and await my orders!" Thomas cried and he pointed to the crows that were already plucking the soft eyeballs from the impaled prisoners' skulls. If everything Scaliger had told Thomas was true, Dracul would know that Earl *Räum* and his demons must take the form of crows when roaming the earth and, once again, Thomas' deception worked better than he could have hoped.

"Please, Master of Dragons, send the Great Earl back to The Pit. I meant no offence but I've sworn that my daughter shall remain undefiled until I've recovered my throne and these men have violated that sacred oath by gazing upon her naked flesh," said Dracul.

The thought of Ursula's smooth, white body undulating beneath her shredded blouse reminded Thomas that the girl was nowhere to be seen, yet he had no time to consider her fate.

"Fool! These men serve me and, if you harm them, the next throne you see will be occupied by Satan! Now release them, before I release the great and terrible Earl *Räum*!" Thomas repeated.

In his confusion, Dracul hesitated. He wasn't used to having his authority questioned, least of all by a lone Englishman wearing the costume of a German mercenary, yet the crows flocking overhead convinced him to ignore his suspicions and he ordered Bos and Quintana to be set free.

"I swear gladly, by the sacred symbol of the *Ouroboros*, that neither you nor your servants will be harmed," said Dracul. However, as his men hurried to cut Bos and Quintana's bonds, the man who wore the wolf skin began to protest.

"My Lord, none of these men have been admitted to The Order of the Dragon, so they're not worthy of an oath made on the sacred symbol of rebirth," he hissed but the Grand Master silenced his captain's protests with a wave of his hand.

"Hold your tongue, Radu. These are the men whom I seek and I dare not offend them," he replied. Thomas smiled, more with relief than triumph, and he informed Dracul that there was another member of his party, lying inside the tower, who'd been badly wounded.

On hearing Thomas' words, Dracul immediately ordered his men to fetch the third of the Dragon Master's companions. A short while later the unconscious Prometheus, his face still swathed in bandages, was lying on a litter slung between two mules and whilst this was being done, fresh horses were fetched for Thomas, Bos and Quintana. Once everyone was in the saddle, Dracul sounded his great hunting horn and the victorious column set off down the hillside.

Lord Dracul was in a jubilant mood as he led the Draconists away from the watchtower. His men shared their master's elation and the normally taciturn riders chatted happily among themselves whilst drinking copious amounts of an evil-smelling liquid they carried in goat-skin flasks tied to their belts. As Dracul's honoured guest, Thomas rode at the head of the column, so he was separated from his companions, who rode at the rear with the litter and an enclosed two-wheeled cart that carried Dracul's baggage.

The Order of the Dragon's Grand Master was overjoyed to have found both his daughter and his long sought Master of Dragons in the same place and as they rode he talked excitedly of the great things that he and Thomas would accomplish.

As the forest of stakes receded into the distance, Thomas could scarcely believe that his genial host was the same man who'd just condemned so many men to the worst of deaths and, for all his promises of future triumphs, the Grand Master wouldn't discuss his plans in detail. In answer to all of Thomas' questions, Dracul would only say that it was the Englishman's manifest destiny to join the Order of the Dragon in their great quest to save Christendom from the Turks.

After an hour of such talk, all Thomas wanted was sleep. Unfortunately, as the Grand Master was determined to reach his camp by dawn, he ordered his men to ride through the night. Strangely, the darkness only seemed to enliven Dracul, so, even though Thomas struggled to keep awake, the Grand Master continued to lecture him on the justness of the Draconist cause.

As the story unfolded, Thomas wasn't surprised to learn that Wallachia's crown had been passed around its three competing royal houses, like a bottle of wine at a feast, but Dracul insisted that only princes from the House of *Drăculești* could be Wallachia's *voivodes* and *hospodars*. Pretenders from the opposing houses of the *Dănești* and *Craiovești* were, according to his host, vile traitors who must be crushed like verminous lice and though these names meant nothing to Thomas, there was no mistaking the hatred Dracul expressed for his rivals.

"As a boy, I shared the throne with my father, Mihnea, who'd succeeded my grandfather, Vlad Dracula. Forget what lies you may have been told by our enemies. Vlad Dracula was a true patriot, and a great warrior for Christ, who after he'd driven the Turks back across the Danube, was murdered by jealous rivals in the pay of the Sultan. My father fled into exile, but he swore revenge and though the struggle took many years he did regain his throne," said Dracul and he told Thomas how his father had punished his grandfather's murderers.

The common soldiers who'd fought against the *Drăculești* were hanged or drowned but these were the lucky ones. The great *boyar* nobles who'd led the conspiracy had their noses and lips cut off, before being enslaved, and their wives fared no better.

The *boyars'* womenfolk became Mihnea's concubines, so, whilst their husbands endured a living death in the quarries of the Carpathian Mountains, the captive women were repeatedly violated until they killed themselves or died of shame. For these outrages, Mihnea was nicknamed The Bad by his enemies; yet, in spite of this brutal campaign of terror, the current Lord Dracul's father had failed to defeat his rivals.

After little more than a year on the throne, a new *boyar* revolt had driven Mihnea the Bad and his two sons into exile for a second time. The fugitive members of the House of *Drăculeşti* had taken refuge in the Transylvanian city of Sibiu, then under the protection of the Hungarian kings, but this time Mihnea would not return.

Lord Dracul's eyes narrowed into reptilian slits as he told Thomas how a paid assassin had plunged a dagger into his father's heart as he'd left Sibiu's great cathedral. Whilst the murder of a newly shriven man on the steps of God's House was an unpardonable blasphemy, worse was to befall Mihnea's youngest son who'd been buried alive.

Fortunately for the House of *Drăculeşti*, Dracul and his mother had escaped the assassins and fled to the family's strongest fortress. It was here that Dracul had learned of his brother's dreadful death, whereupon he'd vowed to revive the Order of the Dragon so it could be the instrument of his vengeance.

By what authority he'd appointed himself the order's Grand Master, Dracul wouldn't say, but he told Thomas of how he'd brought all those still loyal to the *Drăculeşti* to this secret castle and initiated them in his revived Order of the Dragon. Like the Templars and Hospitallers of old, these new crusaders had sworn to fight for Christ but they'd also learned the dark arts of the spy and assassin.

For two years, the Draconists had trained in secret and when they were ready to strike back at their enemies, Dracul had sent his best men to discover who'd ordered the deaths of his father and brother. Once his spies had learned the plotters' names, Dracul had set out to hunt them down.

"Like the Furies of Erebus, I couldn't rest until my enemies were dead and, when I found them, I strangled each of those traitorous dogs with my bare hands. I laughed as their lying tongues turned blue and, when their eyes bulged from their heads, I spat in their faces," Dracul hissed but after this confession he fell silent.

Recalling the memories of his vengeance seemed to have lulled Dracul into something that resembled sleep and he said nothing more for the last few miles of their journey. With the story unfinished, Thomas was left to wonder how Dracul had failed to recover his throne after murdering his rivals or why such a man needed the services of an English necromancer.

# 9

## THE WAGON FORT

The light of a new day roused Dracul from his torpor but there was no time for him to resume his family history as the column had arrived at a flat stretch of open ground about two hundred yards across.

A broad, though shallow, stream ran through the middle of this clearing and on its right bank was a wagon fort constructed from several dozen carts chained together in a circle. Thomas had seen scores of similar camps during his command of the Devil's Band, although this collection of tumbrels seemed to belong to a tribe of barbarian nomads rather than an army of professional *landsknecht* mercenaries.

There were no horses to draw the carts, only oxen and these sullen beasts were grazing lazily in the muddy pasture outside the circle of wagons. Inside, instead of the neat triangular, linen tents used by imperial or French armies on campaign, the space between the wagon fort's wooden walls was filled with strange, dome-shaped structures, each made of curved larch poles covered with large squares of felt. Equally unfamiliar were the clothes worn by the camp's inhabitants.

In contrast to the drab garments that, by law, German peasant women had to wear, the Draconists' wives and daughters were dressed in brightly coloured skirts. Though the men dressed more modestly, in sheepskin jerkins and cross-gartered leggings, even these seemed strange to Thomas' eyes.

It was evident that the wagons had only just arrived in the clearing because a circular animal pen to the right of the fort remained unfinished. A dozen wooden posts, each about the height of a man, had been driven into the ground to mark the boundary of this stockade but the cross-rails had yet to be fixed to the uprights, so the pen resembled a wooden version of an ancient stone ring.

Before Thomas could ask why this pinfold hadn't been completed, the column was spotted and a gaggle of old men, excited women and unruly children came running to greet the riders. The crowd cheered loudly as the two groups met, though Dracul seemed to be shamed by their cries of welcome.

"These are the families of the loyal Draconists who followed me into exile. Now, like the Israelites, we must wander in the wilderness whilst others grow fat on the land promised to our forefathers," said Dracul.

The bitterness of these words confused Thomas. Whilst he understood that the loyalty of a few peasants could never compensate for the loss of a kingdom, he found it hard to believe that the powerful secret society of spies and assassins led by Dracul and feared by Scaliger lived as beggarly nomads in a few ramshackle carts. On the other hand, living in constant fear of murder and betrayal was good reason to keep moving and Dracul's violent family history also explained why he chose to hide his daughter in a nunnery. This thought prompted Thomas to ask what would happen to Ursula.

"Now you're home, will you send your daughter back to her convent?" Thomas enquired and Dracul frowned.

"Since the impure have gazed upon her naked flesh, Ursula cannot return to a House of God until she's been cleansed of her sins. Only when she's been properly shriven, and brought back to a state of grace, can she continue with her sacred duty, which is to pray for my victory. Only when the last of my enemies have knelt before me and begged for death, may she return to the world," Dracul declared and before he could say anything more, the column passed through the wagon fort's gates.

Whilst the riders began to disperse, six handmaidens surrounded the Draconists' baggage cart and held up thick rugs so its passenger could alight in private. In spite of these precautions, the crowd caught a glimpse of the *Drăculești* princess and they cheered even more loudly to give thanks for her safe return. Ursula tried to acknowledge the crowd's good wishes but her maids quickly bundled their mistress inside a large covered cart that looked like a small cottage on wheels.

As Ursula's wagon was in a better state of repair than the others, Thomas wondered if it housed Dracul's wife as well as his daughter. However, this question remained unanswered as his host was too busy ordering the camp's elderly wise woman to use whatever physics she had to treat the unconscious Nubian.

Once Prometheus had been carried away, Dracul led Thomas, Bos and Quintana to his own cart in the centre of the fort. This wagon had the same solid wheels and sturdy frame as the others in the Draconist caravan but it was twice the width and had no sides. This unusual construction allowed one of the dome-shaped dwellings to be erected permanently on its planks and a short flight of wooden steps led to this strange tent's low entrance.

If the outside of Dracul's wheeled palace looked like a Tartar goatherd's hovel, the inside offered a glimpse of paradise. The exiled Prince of Wallachia's personal quarters were as opulent as those of any Turkish bey and his guests were astonished to see exotic carpets on the floor, damask curtains lining the walls and soft divans, covered in red silk cushions, arranged around a low table.

Such luxury reminded Thomas of the brothel in Marburg and here, too, the guests were asked to cleanse themselves. Whilst Dracul's valets hurried to dress their master in a loose robe, more servants brought scented rosewater in polished brass bowls for the guests to wash their hands and faces. Once everyone had finished their ablutions, Dracul invited Thomas and the others to make themselves comfortable whilst a steward placed a silver tray bearing a tall, brass jug and several small glasses on the ornately carved table.

"The Turks live in the darkness of the heathen but they've one redeeming habit. They never discuss business until they've shared a cup of *kahve*," said Dracul and, whilst his servants filled his guests' glasses with hot, black liquid from the jug, he explained that the followers of Mahomet would never touch wine or beer, because alcohol dulled the senses for battle. However, this drink, which was made from the dried seeds of a tree found in the mountains of Axum, had the power to banish sleep from a man's mind.

The servants served each man with a glass of *kahve* but Thomas and the others hesitated before taking a drink. The steam rising from the syrupy liquid smelled strong and bitter, like the root of the poisonous mandrake. However, when Dracul drained his glass, and glowered at his guests for their impoliteness, they each took a sip. They all found the drink surprisingly good, yet even though there was no hint of agaric or other poison, they'd never admit to liking this alien brew.

"Such a beverage can only appeal to the taste of infidels. To put fire in his belly and courage in his heart, a man needs beer," said Bos, smacking his lips. Quintana agreed but remarked that cultured men must drink wine to be considered heroes, whilst Thomas observed that Jesus hadn't turned water into *kahve*. Despite their lack of appreciation for the new drink, Dracul refused to be insulted and instead he turned their discussion to the matter of Julius Caesar Scaliger.

"My spies report that you've already pledged to serve this madman, so please don't insult my intelligence by trying to deny it. Yet I'm prepared to believe that Scaliger has bewitched you because I've seen for myself how this venomous spider hides his treachery behind a web of deceit," said Dracul. He spoke politely, like a man trying to engage a much admired cook, but Bos immediately dismissed Dracul's claims with a snort of annoyance.

"You say Scaliger's a traitor. He says he's been chosen by God to defeat Christ's enemies," he said and if he'd preached Luther's sermon to the College of Cardinals, he couldn't have provoked more anger in Dracul.

"You fool! Scaliger is the new Judas but his price is much higher than thirty pieces of silver! Twice I sent men to warn you, and each time you slaughtered them rather than hear their message, yet even now I forgive you," said Dracul and as his air of calmness returned, he told his guests that their former employer had learned to lie before he'd learned to walk.

According to Dracul, the man who called himself Julius Caesar Scaliger wasn't an Italian nobleman unjustly deprived of his birthright. In fact, Scaliger was nothing but a low-born trickster named Giulio Bordone, whose artist father, Benedetto, had been forced to enlist in the Hapsburg army to pay his debts. As the older Bordone had always imagined himself to be related to Verona's aristocratic La Scala family, his son had grown up believing he'd been cheated of his inheritance. Dracul, however, insisted that this was pure fancy.

"Two hundred years ago, the Scaligeri were Lords of Verona but they'd been driven out by a mob in the pay of the Venetians," he said, before adding that, before his death at the Battle of Ravenna, Benedetto had somehow secured a position for his son at the imperial court. However, the younger Bordone, his mind filled with dreams of nobility by his wastrel father, had wanted to be more than a mere squire.

To further his ambitions, Giulio had changed his name to Julius and repeatedly petitioned the old emperor Maximilian to make him Lord of Verona. Scaliger had fought loyally for the Hapsburgs, and though he'd distinguished himself at the same battle in which his father had died, his only reward was to be made a Knight of the Golden Spur. Disgusted at this insult, Scaliger had left the Hapsburg court and became secretary to an Italian born French bishop.

Much of this Thomas already knew; moreover, he could understand Scaliger's plight as his own father had been killed in battle and the endless wars that cursed England's Northern Marches had reduced Thomas' aristocratic ancestors to penury. The last of the once noble Devilstones could, therefore, sympathise with Scaliger's struggle and he didn't believe that Dracul's story proved the man was a traitor.

"Scaliger's already told me he's abandoned his claims to Verona and he now wishes to devote his life to God," Thomas said firmly, and he demanded that their host prove his accusations or let them go, but Dracul continued to insist that Scaliger was at the centre of a dastardly plot.

"It's perhaps the supreme irony that the Scaligeri Lords of Verona were once members of the Order of the Dragon, because the man who has usurped their name now plans to sell all of Christendom to the Turkish sultan. You see, my friends, Julius Caesar Scaliger is now the French King's spy and the price of his treachery is Verona," said Dracul triumphantly, yet once again Bos cried out in annoyance.

"By the lying eyes of a Medici pope, you make no sense! First you say Scaliger will betray us to the Turks and then you say he spies for France. Which is it?" Bos cried but Dracul remained adamant that both his statements were true.

In careful, measured tones, he explained that once Scaliger's petitions had been rejected by the emperor, it was only natural that he should turn to the Hapsburg's French and Turkish enemies for justice. Moreover, Scaliger had timed his defection perfectly because the French King, Francis, and the Turkish Sultan, Suleiman, had recently made a secret alliance.

"Scaliger serves his own ambition by conveying secret messages between Constantinople and Paris and I know this to be true, because, just a few months ago, my Draconists intercepted a party of French ambassadors travelling through the Turkish province of Bosnia. These rats were carrying a coded letter from Suleiman as well as this ring," said Dracul and, before he continued his story, he removed one of the rings he was wearing and placed it on the table.

"This trinket bears the device of a scaling ladder. In Italian the word is scala, thus the ladder is the badge of the Scaligeri," he said. Quintana replied that this proved nothing, so Dracul fetched a wooden rod and a length of white silk ribbon from a chest. Still puzzled, Bos demanded to know what an old stick and a grubby rag had to do with Scaliger's loyalty but Thomas recognised these items as the components of a *scytale*.

"The Spartan, Lysander, used such devices in his war with the Athenians and, when I was apprenticed to Agrippa, we used *scytale* to hide our communications with other scholars from the Holy Inquisition," he said and he explained how, if a message was written along a strip of cloth wound around a rod, the letters would appear to be arranged at random when the cloth was unwound. Once encrypted in this way, the message could be carried in safety because even if it was intercepted its contents would remain scrambled unless the enemy had a rod of exactly the same diameter.

"The Englishman is correct, and this seemingly innocent ring reveals the exact diameter of the rod needed to decode this particular message. Observe," said Dracul and he showed his guests how the rod fitted inside Scaliger's ring perfectly. He then reassembled the message, which was written in minuscule Greek script, and read it out loud so that all those present could know the depth of French perfidy:

*I, Khan and Sultan of the Mediterranean, Black Sea, Anatolia, Karaman, Kurdistan, Persia, Damascus, Aleppo, Egypt, Mecca and Medina, Jerusalem and all of the lands of Arabia, Yemen and all of many other countries, Son of the Bayezid, Son of the Sultan Selim, Shadow of God on Earth, SULEIMAN, To you, governor of the Franks, FRANCIS:*

*You've sent to my Porte, refuge of sovereigns, a letter by your faithful agent, and furthermore entrusted to him sundry verbal communications. You have informed me that the enemy has overrun your country and that you are at present in prison and a captive, and you have here asked aid and succour for your deliverance.*

*Take courage, then, and be not dismayed.*
*Our glorious predecessors and our illustrious ancestors (may God light up their tombs!) have never ceased to make war to repel the foe and conquer his lands. We ourselves have followed in their footsteps, and have at all times conquered provinces and citadels of great strength and difficult of approach.*
*Night and day, our horse is saddled and our sabre is girt.*

*May God on High promote righteousness!*
*May whatsoever He wills, be accomplished!*
*For the rest, question your ambassador and be informed!*

When their host had finished reading, Dracul's guests had to admit that the French King was guilty of the greatest betrayal of Christendom since his crusading ancestors had sacked Constantinople. Quintana, however, wanted to know why the 'First Daughter of the Church' would form such a treacherous alliance with the enemies of Christendom. To answer his question, Dracul went back to his chest and took out a scroll, which he unrolled on the table. Though the place names were written in another strange alphabet, everyone could see that the parchment was a map of Europe.

Using his map, Dracul showed his guests how France was surrounded by the Hapsburg Empire of Charles V, who was the grandson of the same emperor who'd rejected Scaliger's petitions. Spain, Germany, Burgundy and Italy were all ruled by Charles and even England was a brick in the Hapsburg wall by virtue of Henry VIII's marriage to the emperor's aunt, Catherine of Aragon. Moreover, the French King's latest attempt to break the Hapsburg stranglehold on France had ended in catastrophe with Francis' ignominious defeat and capture at the Battle of Pavia.

Whilst Thomas and the others remembered their own part in this battle, Dracul informed them that, during Francis' imprisonment, his mother had sent letters to Constantinople offering an alliance. Under the terms of this treaty, the French would renew the war in the west whilst Suleiman crossed the Danube and invaded the Hapsburg heartlands from the east

"Charles' empire will be crushed like apples in a cider press and, as you have heard, the Sultan readily agreed to the terms of this unholy treaty. Suleiman, who believes he's destined to rule the world, has already begun to gather his armies and soon all the lands east of the Rhine will be bound to the Turkish yoke unless I can prevent it!" Dracul cried yet, once again, Quintana scoffed at these outlandish claims.

"By the punctured backsides of the 300 Spartans, how do you intend to defeat an army of a 100,000 battle-crazed Turkish *janissaries* with a handful of horsemen?" Quintana demanded. Thomas, however, had already guessed the answer.

"It's simple. Our host wants us to steal the Holy Lance for him instead of Scaliger," Thomas said and, when the others looked at him like he was a raving madman, he explained how possession of this famous relic could alter the course of the forthcoming war.

Turning Dracul's map around, Thomas showed the others how any Turkish army wanting to invade the Hapsburg heartlands in Austria and Germany had first to pass through the Danubian kingdoms of Hungary and Wallachia. Unfortunately both these bulwarks of Christianity had been weakened by decades of civil war and would fall into the Sultan's lap like ripe fruit unless someone, or something, could end these bitter, unending blood feuds.

"So, Scaliger was telling the truth when he claimed that Lord Dracul wanted to use the Holy Lance to unite all the peoples of the east in a new crusade against the infidel Turks," said Bos thoughtfully and Thomas nodded his head in agreement.

"Even if the Holy Lance is nothing more than a lump of rusted iron, there are many who believe that it genuinely holds the power of God, so any prince who carries this relic into battle will easily find men to follow him. It also follows that the best way to ensure the success of the Turkish invasion is to prevent Dracul, or any of the Sultan's enemies, from possessing The Lance and that's why Scaliger wanted to hide the relic in his Castle of Wewelsburg," he said.

After Thomas had finished speaking, there was complete quiet in the tent as Bos and Quintana chided themselves for having been duped so easily by Scaliger.

Even Dracul fell silent, as he marvelled at how the Englishman had grasped the situation so quickly but the Grand Master soon decided that Thomas' prescience was further proof of his unique talents and he congratulated his guest on his powers.

"Truly, I was right to choose you over the fraudster Faust and the popinjay Paracelsus. With the Holy Lance in my hand, and the man who can summon dragons at my side, my enemies are doomed," he said happily, but Quintana had yet to be convinced that he'd any part to play in defeating the Turks.

"What I don't understand is, if this worm-eaten old spear is so important to the fate of the Hapsburgs, why doesn't our august Emperor Charles simply use it himself or, if he's busy fighting the French, why doesn't he let you or the King of Hungary borrow it for a few weeks?" Quintana said innocently but, though he hadn't meant to goad Lord Dracul, the Portugee's words had the same effect as the sharpest spurs pressed into the flank of the most skittish horse.

"By the sightless eyes of St Longinus, I swear that Charles of Hapsburg is as mad as his mother, whilst his spineless brother-in-law, the King of Hungary, is a beardless weakling! These usurpers are not fit to carry dung from a stable, yet they refuse to recognise me as the rightful heir of the Caesars and deny that the Holy Lance is mine! I'm the Grand Master of the Order of the Dragon and once you've become Draconists, you'll learn more of our order's secrets. Until then you must be patient!" Dracul bellowed.

Catching the strange look in his host's eye, Thomas shivered. However, before he could question his own role in Dracul's plans, Radu entered and prostrated himself before his master.

"Forgive the intrusion, My Lord, but you gave orders that you were to be informed the moment the injured man regained his wits," he said.

This news miraculously restored Dracul's good humour and he declared that the three men in the tent must be reunited with their comrade at once.

"As The Almighty has restored your companion to life, there can be no clearer sign that God wishes you to bring the Holy Lance to me instead of Scaliger, so let us welcome your comrade into our company of paladins," said Dracul imperiously and without another word he took his guests to the wise woman's tent at the edge of the wagon fort.

After dismissing the crone, who bowed low and scurried off to draw water, Dracul ushered them all inside the tent, but, once they'd stepped into the dark and filthy hovel, the men found it very hard not to vomit. The cause of their nausea was the foetid stench coming from the mix of rancid animal fat used to waterproof the tent's walls and the sooty smoke rising from the brazier of burning dung that kept the hut warm.

In spite of the foul air and squalid surroundings, Prometheus looked surprisingly well. He'd recovered his senses, the crossbow bolt in his shoulder had gone and the wound had been neatly bandaged.

The cloths around his head had also been removed, allowing the Nubian to enjoy a bowl of hot soup, and though Thomas and the others were overjoyed at seeing their friend, their delight could not match the delirium that seemed to seize Lord Dracul.

"God be praised, this man is a Nubian! Can it be that Heaven has sent Maurice of Thebes, the very saint who brought the Holy Lance to Europe, to ensure the success of our quest?" Dracul cried. Prometheus tried to protest that Heaven had done no such thing but Dracul, like his daughter, was utterly convinced that the man before him was the reborn Nubian saint who'd once possessed the Holy Lance.

The Order of the Dragon's Grand Master also insisted that this new omen meant the ceremony of initiation must begin at once and what happened next took all of Dracul's guests by surprise. Like a sower scattering seed, in one swift motion Dracul had reached into a pouch hanging from his belt and thrown a handful of grey powder into the brazier of smouldering manure. Instantly the burning grains gave off thick clouds of choking smoke and, before Thomas and the others could stop him, Dracul had fled outside.

Coughing and spluttering, the four men tried to follow their host into the fresh air but it was too late. The sweet-smelling vapours had bewitched them and, within a few seconds of drawing the noxious fumes into their lungs, Thomas and the others found that their muscles had rebelled against the tyranny of the body politic.

Though the men remained conscious, their mutinous legs refused to propel them to safety and their disobedient tongues declined to call for help. In this state of confusion, Thomas and the others were powerless to resist as a dozen Draconists, their mouths and noses covered by protective cloths, burst into the tent and dragged them all, including Prometheus, to the unfinished stockade outside the wagon fort.

The captives could only moan in protest as they were tied to stakes at the four cardinal points of the compass and their flesh began to crawl as Dracul's men placed large iron bowls in front of them. The rims of these bowls had been fashioned to represent a dragon swallowing its own tail and, though their purpose was a mystery, there could be no mistaking how the piles of wood being heaped in the centre of the circle would be used. Moments later, as if to confirm their worst suspicions, Dracul announced that all those who wish to enter the Order of the Dragon must be baptised with flame and he gave his men the signal to light the bonfire.

The pyre roared into life and, as huge tongues of fire leapt into the darkening sky, Radu emerged from the shadows. Dracul's captain was wearing his wolf skin and carrying a large box, made from polished rosewood, which he opened before presenting it to his master.

After some thought, Dracul selected four metal rods from the dozen inside, made the sign of the cross and returned the box to Radu. For a moment Thomas' febrile brain thought that these sinister looking rods, which were each the length of a man's thigh, were more *scytale* but when the Draconists began filling the iron bowls with glowing embers from the bonfire he realised that they were branding irons.

"Members of the Order of the Dragon must swear to carry the badge of the *Ouroboros* about their person at all times and the only way this can be done is to burn the sign of the eternal dragon into their flesh with hot irons. Remember that Our Lord and Saviour had to suffer worse torments before he could ascend into heaven and the pain you're about to endure is but a foretaste of the rivers of scalding brimstone that await your souls if you betray the Order of the Dragon," said Dracul.

As he spoke, Dracul made the sign of the cross and thrust one the irons into the fire bowl in front of each prisoner. In desperation Thomas tried to shout that he was the fabled Dragon Master, who'd tamed the water dragon of Metz and the fire-breathing serpent of The Hornberg, and he'd wreak a terrible revenge for this blasphemy, but no sound came from his mouth as Radu ripped open each initiate's shirt.

Despite the cold night air chilling their exposed skin, the men began to sweat, yet Dracul ignored their fear as, like a priest at a baptism, he began to explain the significance of the ritual he was about to perform.

"Sigismund, the emperor who founded our order, had different irons made to represent each of the Christian peoples to be united by the Dragon Oath. Thus the Nubian shall be marked with *Apep* the sand dragon of Egypt, whilst the Portugee shall bear *Cuco* the ghost dragon of Iberia. The Frisian shall have *Jörmungandr*, the sea-serpent that girds the earth, whilst the Englishman shall carry the golden *wyvern* of the Saxon kings. Now, hear the words of the oath and accept your dragon mark as a sign that you will abide by its rule for all time," Dracul said solemnly and he began to recite the ancient formula that bound all Draconists to Almighty God and one another:

*In company with the prelates, Lords and Princes of our kingdom whom we invite to participate with us in this society, by reason of the sign and effigy of our pure inclination and intention to crush the pernicious deeds of the same Perfidious Enemy, and the followers of pagan knights, schismatics and other nations of heretical faiths, and those envious of the Cross of Christ, and of our kingdoms, and of his holy and saving religion of faith, under the banner of the triumphant Cross of Christ.*

*We also swear to serve, in perpetuity, the true heirs and descendants of Sigismund, by the grace of God King of the Magyars and Holy Roman Emperor, as here represented by the person of the Grand Master of the Order of the Dragon, Mircea, Lord Dracul of the House of the Drăculeşti, Voivode and Hospodar of Wallachia.*

*And we the faithful Lords and Princes of his kingdom shall at all times bear and have, and do choose and agree to wear and bear, in the manner of our society, the sign or effigy of the Dragon and the effigy shall be incurved into the form of a circle, its tail winding around its neck, divided through the middle of its back along its length from the top of its head right to the tip of its tail, with its blood a Rose Cross flowing out into the interior of the cleft by a white crack, untouched by blood.*

*Just as, and in the same way, that those who fight under the banner of the glorious martyr Saint George are accustomed to bear a red cross on a white field, those who now draw near must so swear to uphold the honour and dignity of our society and keep its laws until the last drop of their blood is drained from their body,*

"To this do you all swear?" Dracul said finally.

"We so swear," said the reluctant acolytes, who'd at last found the strength to speak, but even if they'd wanted to refuse the oath, they couldn't. The prisoners' minds and bodies were entirely in thrall to the man who called himself the Grand Master of the Order of the Dragon and the drugs coursing through their veins had spoken for them.

Once he was satisfied the men had entered a state of grace, Dracul gave Radu the order to proceed and the weasel-faced man went straight to the brazier in front of Thomas. Withdrawing the *wyvern* brand, Radu held the white hot iron in front of the Englishman's face and though it was no bigger than a thumbnail, the glowing metal produced a fearful heat.

"You foreigners and heretics are not worthy to wear this mark of honour but, as My Lord Dracul commands, so I obey," Radu hissed and he pressed the brand into his prisoner's shoulder.

The nauseating smell of his own roasting flesh filled Thomas' nostrils, and in the same instant his trembling body was overwhelmed by waves of excruciating pain; yet the only sound that came from his lips was a low moan. The drug Thomas had inhaled was playing strange tricks with his mind, so he found himself almost enjoying the exquisite agony, and when Radu repeated the torture with the others they, too, did not struggle against what should've been the most unbearable torment.

The four men even began to welcome the pain and they revelled in the ecstasy known only to the flagellant, the martyr and all those who'd suffered to become at one with their God. When it was over, Dracul looked at his latest disciples with genuine pride and declared that they could, from this day forth, call themselves Draconists.

"You men have done well. On the morrow we must begin our quest to return the Holy Lance to its rightful owner, but for the moment you may sleep," he said and he instructed the four new Draconists to be released.

As if from nowhere, a gaggle of wizened old women appeared. They were led by the crone who'd treated Prometheus and she'd brought a stone jar full of a pungent smelling salve. The soothing ointment was gently applied to each man's wound and their seared flesh bound with strips of clean linen.

Once this was done, Thomas and the others were taken to one of the domed tents and left alone but sleep eluded them. All they could do was lie on their cots and listen to the rain as it started to fall on the roof of their tent. By dawn, the torrential rain had become a wild storm and the weather gods' tempestuous fury lasted for more than a week.

Though Dracul raged against the gusting winds and freezing hail that made all travel impossible, Bos, Thomas, Quintana and Prometheus were grateful for this respite. They needed time to recover their strength because they knew that, whatever the future held in store for them, they could only trust their swords, their wits and each other.

# 10
## NUREMBERG

It took several days for Thomas and the others to forgive Dracul for subjecting to them to the pain of the Draconist initiation. However, with the spring storms making it impossible for them to do anything except sit and talk, the four men soon managed to convince themselves that their fortunes were best served by remaining with Dracul.

Even though the Grand Master had promised them nothing but the gratitude of God, whilst Scaliger had offered them each a fortune in gold, they all agreed that Dracul would have to reward them with more tangible treasures if they were successful. Quintana offered the most persuasive argument, by insisting that Dracul was likely to be much more generous than the slave of a sultan, but it was Prometheus who was the most keen to abandon their previous employer.

The Nubian may have been insensible when the others had tried Scaliger *in absentia*, and found him guilty, nevertheless he was outraged at being duped by a scheming Turkish spy. Once the others had told, him about Suleiman's coded letter to the King of France, offering an unholy alliance against the Hapsburgs, Prometheus cursed Scaliger and declared that any Christian who served the Turkish sultans deserved nothing but the cruellest of all deaths.

"Those who conquered Christian Nubia are also the pet jackals of Suleiman and if Scaliger could see how my people suffer at their hands, he'd run to the scaffold and beg the executioner to strike off his lying, deceitful head! By all the seven hundred wives of Solomon, if St Maurice did once possess the Holy Lance, it should be taken back to Africa and used to help me liberate my homeland!" Prometheus said bitterly, whereupon Quintana looked at him in confusion.

"First, Scaliger tells us that the Holy Lance belonged to St Longinus in Palestine, now Dracul says it ended up in Egypt with St Maurice, who took it to Europe. Can both these stories be true?" he said but it was Bos who answered his question.

"In the seminary, we studied the lives of all the saints mentioned in The Golden Legend and we were soundly beaten if we didn't know everything about them," he growled and, as the rain hammered on the roof of their tent, he told the others what he could remember about the humble African soldier who'd become the patron saint of German emperors.

According to Bos, St Maurice had been born during the reign of Decius, the Roman Emperor who'd revived the brutal persecution of Christians, and the place of his birth had been Thebes on the banks of the River Nile. This Egyptian city had guarded the Roman Empire's border with the desert kingdom of Nubia and it was garrisoned by the Theban Legion.

Though he'd been raised as a Christian, Maurice had enlisted in the pagan Theban Legion after a vision of St

James had ordered him to join the army of Christ's persecutors. The pious Maurice had obeyed gladly, whereupon the entire legion had miraculously converted to Christianity. Safe in their remote desert outpost, the newly baptised soldiers had continued to praise Jesus until the Emperor Maximian had summoned them to Gaul to put down a rebellion of Alpine tribes.

With Maurice now in command, the Theban Legion had marched from the baking deserts of Africa to the snow-capped mountains of Gaul and dutifully crushed the revolt. However, when Maximian had ordered his men to give thanks for their victory by sacrificing to Rome's pagan gods, they'd refused.

In order to avoid any taint of idolatry, Maurice had withdrawn his men to the town of Agaunum but the mutiny had so enraged Maximian he'd ordered his loyal legions to attack the Thebans' camp. True to their faith, the rebel legionaries had offered no resistance; nevertheless, Maximian had sentenced one third of their ranks to be beheaded.

Despite the dreadful slaughter of their comrades, the remaining Thebans had remained steadfast in their refusal to sprinkle the required grains of incense on the pagan altars but their courage was to no avail. The Christians' valour had failed to impress Maximian, who'd ordered another third of the legion to be killed, and this savage inquisition had continued until all 6,666 Theban legionaries, including Maurice, lay dead.

"What's this got to do with the Holy Lance?" Quintana asked and whilst Bos had to admit that The Golden Legend didn't record how Maurice had obtained the relic in the first place, he declared that in later years a shrine to house Maurice's body, sword, spurs and lance had been built over the site of the Thebans' martyrdom.

"There's much truth in what you say, Frisian. For did not the Emperor Constantine take the Holy Lance from this shrine on his way to his victory at the Milvian Bridge? For this triumph, he honoured God by ending the persecution of Christians throughout his new empire," said Prometheus and he added that he'd heard a story in which Constantine had used the Holy Lance to scratch a line in the earth to mark the boundaries of his new capital at Constantinople.

"I thought Constantine's victory was due to his vision of the Chi-Rho," said Thomas but he agreed that Prometheus' version of the story would explain why St Maurice had become the patron saint of the Holy Roman Empire and its emperors.

The men's hagiographic discussions certainly helped pass the time but, after five days of incessant rain, Dracul's prayers were finally answered. The skies cleared, the spring sun shone brightly and the smell of wet grass filled the air as the Draconists prepared to move their camp closer to Nuremberg and the church where the Holy Lance was being kept.

On the day of their departure, scores of flustered women struggled to gather unruly children and pack away their family's meagre possessions, whilst their menfolk dismantled the camp's sodden tents and yoked stubborn, steaming oxen to the heavy wagons. Within the hour, the camp had been completely demolished, though in spite of all this activity, Ursula was still nowhere to be seen.

The girl's continued absence was no mystery as Dracul had already declared that his truant child must do penance for allowing the rebel peasants to gaze upon her unclothed flesh before she could return to her nunnery. In the light of this, Thomas guessed that Ursula would remain in the covered cart until arrangements could be made for her to be properly shriven, yet such knowledge only served to inflame the Englishman's lustful thoughts for the girl. Day by day, the worm of desire burrowed deeper into his soul until he began to believe that the only cure for his madness was to ravish this siren who'd bewitched him.

Unfortunately, he could see no way to storm the ramparts of Ursula's virtue without being caught. The sight of the grim-faced sentries, who guarded Dracul's daughter day and night, warned him that neither his reputation as a necromancer, nor his oath to serve the Order of the Dragon, would save him from being sodomised by ten feet of sharpened hazel wood were he to be discovered. This realisation soon turned his love for Ursula into a festering resentment of her father, yet there was no time to dwell on the subject of thwarted passion once the Draconists had set off for Nuremberg.

A squad of Dracul's men went ahead to scout the way and these were followed by their Grand Master, mounted on his magnificent black stallion. Thomas and his companions rode with Dracul, whilst Radu led the eight score of fully armed riders that made up the bulk of the column. The carts that carried the caravan's food, tents and families brought up the rear and as the great serpent of humanity slithered out of the clearing, Quintana joked that all they needed was some artillery and they could take the imperial capital by storm.

For seven days, the Draconists' carts jolted along the muddy roads of Franconia but on the eighth day, when the column was still a day's ride from Nuremberg, Dracul ordered his men to halt and make camp in a secluded forest clearing. The strange mounds hidden among the surrounding trees indicated that the lonely glade had once been an ancient burial ground, but this made the site ideally suited to Dracul's purpose. Though the identities of those interred in the mounds had been long forgotten, the Grand Master was certain that their ghosts would keep the superstitious locals at a distance whilst he planned the next phase of his quest in secret.

As before, Dracul ordered the carts to be formed into a circle and, whilst the dome shaped tents mushroomed behind the camp's wooden walls, Thomas slipped away to explore the mysterious mounds. The largest of these low hillocks had a forest of saplings growing from its grassy slopes, so it looked like an immense slumbering porcupine, and whilst Thomas was certain that anything of value had been looted long ago, he hadn't come to these abandoned graves in search of treasure.

What Thomas was looking for, was somewhere to hide *The Munich Handbook of Demonic Magic*. The priceless *grimoire* had already suffered a worrying amount of damage, so he'd decided to leave it in a safe place and come back for it later. The huge stone that had once blocked the mound's entrance was missing, so Thomas took a deep breath and went inside.

The walls of the tomb had been built by placing great slabs of stone on top of each other, and this made the mound's interior resemble that of the Nemeton. However, instead of a single circular chamber, there was a long passage with several square rooms on either side. Thomas chose the driest of these empty chambers and it took less than a minute to hide *The Munich Handbook* behind one of the loose cobbles in the wall.

Once the stone had been replaced, Thomas had no doubt that the spirits of the dead, aided by the oilcloth in which he'd wrapped it, would keep the book containing da Vinci's secrets safe until he returned and he set off back to camp feeling as if he'd laid down a great burden.

The sun was setting as Thomas picked his way through the trees but he hadn't travelled more than a few hundred yards before he had the strange sensation that he was being followed. He stopped, and as he pretended to retie one of the laces that secured his hose to his breeches, he heard something move in the undergrowth.

Slipping into the deep shadow cast by a large oak, Thomas placed his hand on the hilt of his sword and held his breath. Seconds later, a roe deer emerged from the thicket ten yards to his right, sniffed the night air and disappeared into the darkness. Thomas breathed a sigh of relief but, as he did so, the butt of a quarterstaff smashed into the back of his head.

The force of the impact sent the Englishman crashing to the ground and, with his senses reeling, he could do nothing as his assailant delivered a second blow to his chest that bludgeoned the breath from his lungs. The third strike of the assassin's staff landed squarely between Thomas' thighs and a great cloud of excruciating pain exploded in his brain like a Chinese firework.

Stunned, winded and crippled, Thomas lay helpless on the ground as a masked figure, dressed in the reeking garb of a charcoal burner, sat on his stomach and began to search his prostrate victim's clothing. For several seconds Thomas felt the thief's practised hands claw at his doublet and undershirt, yet the ignominy of being pawed like a drunken doxy soon stung him into action.

Feeling in the fallen leaves, Thomas' fingers closed around a hefty rock with sharp edges and he smashed this stone into the side of the bandit's skull. With a cry of anguish, the assassin went sprawling backwards into the mud and Thomas struggled painfully to his feet.

Now their roles were reversed, the stricken bandit held up his hand in surrender but Thomas wanted revenge, not a truce. Ignoring the man's plaintive cry for clemency, he drew his sword and swung his blade with all his might. There was a noise like a rotten apple hitting a pillory and the thief's severed hand went spiralling into the darkness.

Unfortunately, this effort proved to be too much for Thomas' badly bruised manhood and he sank to his knees with a noiseless sigh. By contrast, the thief howled like a whipped dog and fled into the forest, clutching the bloodied stump of his wrist. Thomas should have given chase but his nutmegs felt as if they'd been trampled by a herd of elephants, so he lay in the damp leaves, groaning, and it was almost an hour before he found the strength to walk back to camp.

"What, in the name of Beelzebub's great black balls, happened to you?" Prometheus asked when he saw the Englishman's battered figure entering their tent. Thomas' hair and face were caked in mud and blood, whilst his clothes were covered in leaves and broken twigs.

"Put up a fight, did she?" Quintana added but Thomas was in no mood for jests. By way of explanation, he tossed the thief's severed hand into the centre of the tent and the others stared at the grisly trophy, which seemed to be making some sort of obscene gesture, as Thomas recounted how he'd been ambushed. Once he'd finished his tale, Bos wanted to know what sort of thief would dare attack even a solitary *landsknecht*.

"Perhaps it was one of Little Heinrich's men out for revenge," said Prometheus, as Thomas washed the grime from his face, but Quintana declared that the Englishman's assailant had to be Scaliger's spy.

"If it was one of The Brethren they'd have slit Thomas' throat as he lay senseless. This man was obviously looking for something and if he makes it back to Wewelsburg, our previous employer will know that we've deserted him and joined his rival," he said.

This certainly seemed to be the most likely explanation but their discussion was ended by the appearance of Dracul's steward, who presented the Grand Master's compliments and announced that their attendance was required without delay. Though it was past midnight, Thomas and the others followed the servant to the wheeled palace, where, after the ritual *kahve* had been drunk, Dracul announced that he'd decided to send Ursula to Nuremberg to be cleansed of her sins.

"I've spent many hours searching for the road that will lead my daughter back to God and this very night the Holy Mother has revealed the path Ursula must follow. If she travels to Nuremberg's *Frauenkirche*, and confesses her sins before the veil and girdle of The Virgin which are kept in this church, God will forgive her and she may return to her convent. As our quest must not be endangered by ignoring God's will, I've decided that Ursula shall make this pilgrimage before anything else and three of you men shall accompany her," said Dracul.

Before the others could protest, Dracul had added that Thomas, Quintana and Bos would have the honour of acting as Ursula's guardians, whilst Prometheus would remain in the camp until he'd recovered from his wound. Being appointed Ursula's nursemaids did nothing to improve the others' humour but Dracul held up his hand for silence and revealed his second reason for sending his daughter and her chaperones to the imperial capital.

"Whilst Ursula does penance in the *Frauenkirche*, you men will go to the Church of the Holy Spirit and make careful study of the reliquary containing the Holy Lance. You must discover how it's guarded, what mechanism is used to lower it and any other information that will help us recover what we seek. Once this has been done, you will return here to make your report," said Dracul, whereupon Bos threw up his hands in despair.

"How will my soul enter Heaven if I must be a spy as well as a thief?" Bos moaned. Thomas also had concerns.

"Even if we survive such a reconnaissance, once we've stolen the spear, how will we escape? The monks are sure to notice their relic is missing and then they'll command every pious Christian in the Holy Roman Empire to look for us," he said but Dracul assured him that there was absolutely no danger.

"In the first place, no one will suspect three farm boys taking their sister to be shriven and, in the second, I've already taken steps to ensure that the theft won't be discovered. Being mindful of all dangers, I've engaged a man of rare skill to fashion an exact copy of the relic and you'll leave this counterfeit behind to cover your tracks," he said. After saying these words Dracul beamed benignly at the thieves. Yet his curious smile prompted Quintana to ask how the Grand Master intended to prove to those who doubted the *Drăculești's* right to rule that he had the genuine Holy Lance.

"If the forgery's good enough to fool the monks, how will your allies know that you have the real relic and the Hapsburgs have the fake?" he said but Dracul was growing angry.

"By all the filthy dogs in all infidel bazaar, your questions bite my ears like swarms of angry fleas! I'll say only this, once Thomas has performed the Ritual of Rebirth at the great gathering of Christian princes, whom I shall summon to my castle in the mountains, all shall know that I've been chosen to build God's Kingdom on Earth! Now go. You must depart at daybreak, because the Sultan's *janissaries* don't waste time questioning their master!" Dracul said angrily.

The ferocity of this outburst convinced Thomas and the others that their employer would not welcome any further arguments, so they obeyed Dracul's command and withdrew.

"Why do you think I'm not permitted to go with you? My wound has healed and my strength is undiminished," Prometheus said irritably as the four men made their way back to their tent. In reply, Thomas said that the Nubian was probably being kept as a hostage.

"I'm sure that Dracul doesn't trust us any more than we trust him," he added and Quintana wondered if the mysterious bandit who'd ambushed Thomas a few hours earlier could've been one of Dracul's men.

"If we're so important to Dracul's plans, perhaps he has set men to spy on us all," he said and, whilst Thomas doubted this, Bos had other concerns.

"What exactly is the Ritual of Rebirth?" Bos asked and he stared accusingly at Thomas.

"In truth, I don't know, but you heard what Scaliger said. Dracul fears the Wrath of God as much as he covets the power of the Holy Lance, so he probably believes this ritual will protect him from evil," Thomas answered. This seemed to satisfy Bos and with nothing else to say, they all retired to bed.

At dawn, servants arrived with the clothes the spies would need to disguise themselves and, as they dressed, Ursula was brought to their tent. She'd donned the habit of a novice in the Order of Poor Clares and, though her period of freedom was to be short, she was delighted to be released from her *seraglio*.

Even wearing the shapeless, woollen skirts of a nun, Ursula could make St Anthony succumb to temptation, and her chaperones eyed the girl appreciatively as they prepared to leave the camp, but their disguises worked just as Dracul intended. No one on the road to Nuremberg paid the slightest attention to the three devout farmers taking their 'sister' to her convent and their journey passed without incident.

After spending the night in an inn, the pilgrims reached Nuremberg early the following day and joined the crowd of travellers waiting to pass through the city's north gate. The queue moved slowly because the city's watchmen were searching for fugitive rebels and papist spies trying to enter the Imperial capital. However, Thomas and the others were too busy marvelling at the size of the city's ramparts to realise that their carefully planned disguises had placed them in danger.

"In the name of Pope Clement's poxed, purple prick, are you trying to smuggle a nun into a Lutheran city?" said an incredulous sentry who'd spotted Ursula's habit. Though his question dumbfounded the others, Bos answered him without a moment's hesitation.

"We've brought our sister here to find sanctuary. She's no desire to enter a convent, as our father wishes, and she wants to hear your great scholar Spengler denounce the tyranny of St Benedict's Rule," he said gruffly and despite the lack of physical resemblance between the supposed siblings, the sentry seemed happy to accept this story.

"City air makes you free, is that it? But if your sister wishes to escape the cloister, she'd better change her clothes. Monks and nuns aren't popular in Nuremberg nowadays, the Charterhouse is closed and the Poor Clares forbidden to accept novices," said the sentry and he added that Spengler spoke in the Church of St Lorenz every day in the hour before sunset.

Having done his duty, the watchman stood aside to let the party enter; though, before passing through the gate, Thomas asked if the Hospital of the Holy Spirit had also been closed as he'd been suffering from a particularly painful boil which he hoped the monks could lance. The sentry replied that the monastery's infirmary had been allowed to remain open, as it performed a useful service, but the chapel had been closed to ordinary pilgrims on the orders of the city's Lutheran council.

"What of the holy relics that were kept in the chapel, are they still there?" Thomas asked cautiously, whereupon the sentry spat onto the cobblestones.

"If you want to see those vainglorious baubles you'd best either catch the plague or marry a Hapsburg princess because only the sick and high-born guests of the Emperor are still permitted to pray in the Chapel of the Holy Spirit. Now move along before I have you flogged for being secret papists," he said and the four pilgrims thought it wise to obey.

In spite of the crowds thronging through Nuremberg's streets, it didn't take long for Thomas and the others to find suitable lodgings. An inn called The Golden Bear provided them with two attic rooms and, as it was still early in the day, the pilgrims decided to take Ursula to the *Frauenkirche* as Dracul had requested.

The House of God, where Ursula was to be absolved of her sins, stood on the opposite side of the square to The Golden Bear and this imperious church boasted a triangular west front that rose above the cobbles like an Egyptian pyramid. However, whilst the niches of this towering facade were still adorned with hundreds of gaily painted statues, the jewelled reliquaries that contained the reputed girdle and veil of the Virgin Mary had gone.

In order to comply with the city council's ordinances prohibiting popery, the relics of The Madonna had been locked away in the church's crypt, yet their absence hadn't deterred sinners from coming to the *Frauenkirche* to confess their wickedness. Scores of people were waiting outside the confessional boxes and their number surprised Quintana.

"If this is now a Protestant church, why is the Catholic sacrament of Confession still permitted?" Quintana asked, whereupon Bos cursed the Portugee for his appalling ignorance.

"Luther doesn't deny that Confession and Absolution are holy sacraments," he said but the finer points of Protestant theology didn't concern Ursula. She cleansed her soul with almost unseemly speed and then insisted on visiting St Sebald's Church to see the famous stone that had once been a cheese.

When the others asked what was so miraculous about a stale cheese, Ursula informed them that, in the time of Henry the Pious, St Sebald had come to Nuremberg to convert the pagan Franconians and having successfully accomplished his mission, he'd retreated into the forest to live as a hermit.

"One day, a peasant woman decided to ask for the saint's blessing and to ensure Sebald's favour, she decided to take him a big cheese. However, before the woman left home, she was overcome by greed and she swapped the large cheese for a smaller one. Naturally, the miserly old crone couldn't hide her avarice from a saint and as she laid the smaller cheese before Sebald, it was miraculously turned into the stone that now adorns his tomb," said Ursula and more out of curiosity than religious fervour, the men agreed to take her to the second of Nuremberg's three great houses of worship.

The church of St Sebald was another imposing edifice located near the city hall, and the tomb of Nuremberg's patron saint stood at the eastern end of the lofty, yet austere, nave. The famous petrified cheese was suspended above the saint's ornate sepulchre by a long iron chain and Thomas wondered why the city council had allowed this relic to remain on display whilst other religious treasures had to be hidden away.

"The stone represents the Covenant with God that is the guarantee of Nuremberg's prosperity and independence," Ursula explained, whereupon Bos declared that anyone who believed in the power of relics must have cheese for brains.

"If you want God's Truth instead of fairy tales, we should go to the Church of St Lorenz and listen to what the scholar Spengler has to say on the subject of relics," he said sternly and he was surprised to hear Ursula echo his sentiments.

"Oh yes, let's hear Spengler, I've heard he's wonderfully angry at the whole world! Besides, we promised the sentry and God may not be the only one watching us," she said eagerly.

With a groan, Thomas and Quintana began to complain that they'd more than enough of churches, and it was time to return to their tavern to enjoy a hearty supper. Bos, however, agreed with Ursula and insisted that there was a good chance they were being followed by one of the city's many informers.

"These are troubled times, there are spies everywhere and if the city authorities think we're agents of the pope we'll be lucky to escape with just a flogging," he said and he reminded the others that Thomas had been ambushed by an unknown assassin just a few days earlier.

"Very well, we'll play the role of pious pilgrims just a little while longer," said Thomas with a shrug.

"So, to preserve my good Catholic body, I must imperil my immortal soul by listening to Lutheran heretics denounce the Holy Father," Quintana said ruefully, yet Bos was quite certain that the Portugee was utterly beyond redemption.

"A thousand nuns praying for a thousand years couldn't save you from damnation," he said and he set off for the first of Nuremberg's churches to have embraced Luther's reforms.

The congregation who worshipped at the Church of St Lorenz counted themselves among the most ardent of Protestants and all the paraphernalia of Catholicism had been removed from their church months ago. The gold and silver incense burners had been sold for scrap and the money given to the poor. The holy pictures and painted wooden statues had been burned in a 'bonfire of the vanities', and the elaborate marble altar had been replaced by a plain wooden table.

The church's lack of adornment had done nothing to discourage those who thirsted after God's Truth and a large crowd had gathered to hear Spengler's daily denouncement of corrupt popes, priests and prelates. As the evening shadows lengthened, Ursula and her chaperones mingled with this throng and a hush descended on the church as the famous orator appeared at the entrance to the vestry.

Nuremberg's most notorious firebrand, who'd once earned his living as the city's clerk, was a good-looking man in his mid-forties with piercing blue eyes and a thin moustache but his chin lacked the beard normally worn by scholars. Ursula, who was barely able to contain her excitement, squeaked with delight when she saw him but this unseemly show of emotion prompted harsh words from Bos.

"You should be more respectful," the Frisian hissed and, having been suitably chastised, Dracul's daughter fell silent as the preacher made his way to the pulpit.

In a harangue that lasted well over two hours, Spengler argued that, because God had sent His only begotten Son into the world to teach all mankind, every abbey and convent must be turned into a school. Ursula's 'Amens' were among the loudest shouted by the congregation but her enthusiastic support for the dissolution of monasteries only served to draw attention to her nun's habit. Men began to mutter that such beauty as hers shouldn't be locked away in a nunnery whilst women whispered that those who sought Christ for a husband should be punished for the sin of pride.

As Spengler's condemnation of the cloistered life grew more hostile, even Bos agreed it was time to leave, so Thomas and the others began to shuffle surreptitiously towards the church's door. It was no easy task to make a tactical withdrawal under the disapproving stares of the entire congregation but they managed to emerge into the square with only their pride wounded. They were soon back at The Golden Bear and, whilst Ursula retired to her room to rest, the men found a quiet corner of the tavern in which to plan their next move.

"How are we going to get inside the monks' hospital if only the sick are allowed through its doors?" Bos asked but Thomas had already thought of the answer.

"A weak potion made from mandrake root can give the semblance of sickness without causing lasting harm. If one of us drinks such a potion, the monks would have to both care for him and let him give thanks for his recovery in their chapel," said Thomas. The others, however, wanted to know what sort of loon would be foolish enough to poison himself.

For once, Bos and Quintana were in complete agreement when they insisted that God forbade suicide, so Thomas suggested that the Holy Spirit should chose the victim through the drawing of lots. As this seemed fair, Quintana produced his pack of cards, and quickly turned over a nine of cups whilst Bos drew a five of swords. Thomas' card, however, was the three of coins.

"If I thought you cheating bastards had played me false, I'd turn you both into frogs," Thomas said but, as they all knew he'd no way to carry out his threat, the others simply roared with laughter. Reluctantly accepting his fate, Thomas left the inn, and went to buy the noxious root from an apothecary's shop he'd seen in the square.

Returning an hour later, Thomas found his companions enjoying a hearty meal of sausage and ale, unfortunately the knowledge that mandrake purged the bowels with ruthless efficiency had curtailed the Englishman's appetite. He declined the others' offer to join them and instead begged a jug of hot water and a small wooden bowl from the inn's kitchen. Though the rapacious innkeeper charged Thomas a penny to hire these items, at least he asked no questions.

Ignoring Bos and Quintana's cheery advice that ale was the best medicine, Thomas climbed the stairs to his garret and, with each step, he said a silent prayer to the spirits of Asclepius, Hippocrates and Galen. By the time he'd reached his room, he was fully prepared for his ordeal but he wasn't prepared for Ursula. Dracul's daughter was sitting casually on one of the beds and she was dressed in nothing but a plain linen shift which had been gathered at the waist with a sash.

The simple garment accentuated the curves of Ursula's body and Thomas felt the breath catch in his throat as he imagined what lay beneath the thin cloth. Even though the girl's hair had been cropped shorter than before, as a sign of her penance, Thomas doubted if Hero in her stone tower looked more alluring than Ursula did at that moment. However, before he could praise her beauty, she'd put a finger to her lips and urged him to be silent.

"I sent one of my maids to spy on your councils with my father, so I know that this pilgrimage is a sham to help you steal the Holy Lance. I also know that there isn't much time to save my homeland from the Turks and I want to help," she whispered, yet the nonchalance of her confession threw Thomas into confusion.

"Do all good Wallachian girls spy on their fathers?" Thomas asked as he placed his jug and bowl on the room's worm-eaten table.

"They do, if most of their kin have been murdered by their own relatives. Besides, I'm a *Drăculeşti*, not a nun, and my destiny is to fight for Christ as His warrior, not plead with Him like a beggar," Ursula snapped but, whilst Thomas felt some sympathy for her plight, he wondered why her father hadn't found a suitable husband for his wayward daughter.

"Somewhere in Christendom there must be a wealthy duke or a noble prince who could offer you a life more to your choosing. Besides, surely your father would welcome any alliance with a powerful monarch?" he said but Ursula merely scowled at such a suggestion.

"My father believes there's no stronger ally than the Lord God Almighty, so I must be a Bride of Christ," she said bitterly and without another word she threw her arms around Thomas.

For a girl who'd spent most of her life in the seclusion of the cloister or the *seraglio*, her kiss was surprisingly expert and Thomas felt his manhood stiffen as his resolved weakened. The scent of her hair and the warmth of her body were intoxicating but, when Thomas tried to return her kiss, Ursula turned away and began to rail against her fate.

"A convent is a coffin for the living and nuns are the worms who'll devour my youth! Please, Thomas, take me to England or the New World. I don't care, just so long as I'm with you and a thousand miles from any nunnery," she cried and she kissed him again with even more passion than before.

"To lie with you, I'd travel all the way to the sunless Kingdom of Hades and back," Thomas said breathlessly but, as he tried to lead Ursula to the bed, she pulled away from his embrace.

"Not yet. Once my father has the Holy Lance, he'll have no more need of me and then I can be yours. Until that time, tell me how a cracked jug and an old wooden bowl can confound the Sultan's plans to enslave us all," said Ursula and she pointed to the objects on the table.

With his mind racing, and the hot humours of lust throbbing in his loins, Thomas could do nothing but stare at the girl. She looked as beguiling as Delilah, so he explained how the first step in stealing the Holy Lance was to poison himself.

# 11

## THE CHURCH & HOSPITAL OF THE HOLY SPIRIT

Whilst Ursula watched, Thomas carefully unwrapped the mandrake plant he'd purchased from the apothecary and placed it on the table. The fleshy root, with its gnarled bifurcations, which resembled the body and limbs of a miniature man, looked no more dangerous than a bunch of small, pale carrots yet Ursula recoiled in horror at the sight.

"Mandrake! But I thought its screams sent men mad," she said but Thomas assured her that skilled necromancers knew how to harvest the poisonous vegetable in complete safety.

"To avoid being driven mad, or killed, by the plant's cries, the sorcerer ties a dog to the stem then runs away. When the loyal hound tries to follow its master, the mandrake is pulled from the ground but it's the dog that suffers the effects of the plant's screams not the sorcerer," he said and, whilst Ursula pondered the cruelty of magic, Thomas cut a piece off the enchanted root.

After placing the slice of mandrake in the bowl, Thomas crushed it into pulp with his dagger's pommel before adding the hot water from the jug. A cloud of pungent steam filled the room and, though Ursula covered her face, Thomas insisted there was no danger.

"A strong dose can kill but this weaker preparation will merely loosen the bowels. If you truly want to help, wait until the potion takes effect, then call the others," he said, as he placed the cup on the table to cool.

Reluctantly Ursula agreed to do as she was asked. However, whilst she was genuinely impressed by Thomas' devotion to her father's cause, she couldn't understand why a foreigner would risk death to help an exiled Wallachian prince regain his crown.

"Does the Draconist oath force you to drink deadly poison if my father commands it?" Ursula enquired but Thomas told her that promises of wealth, honour and titles could weave far more powerful bonds between men than mere oaths.

"Cheating the grave is the only way a landless knight can make his way in this world of kings and emperors, so I drink to *Samael*, the Angel of Death," he said and, whilst Ursula watched, wide-eyed with dismay, Thomas drained the cup.

It took no more than a minute for the potion to wreak havoc in Thomas' gut. At first he thought he'd made the potion too strong, as his insides were seized by such violent cramps he felt as if he was going to give birth to some monstrous demon, but within a few minutes the waves of intense pain had subsided.

Thanking God for this blessed relief, Thomas lay on the bed whilst Ursula mopped the sweat from his fevered brow, but soon new torments caused fresh agonies.

First his stomach tried to expel the poison by vomiting up every meal he'd ever eaten and then, when this failed, his tortured body opened another sluice. Thomas' noxious emissions quickly filled all three of the room's chamber pots, whereupon Ursula went in search of Bos and Quintana.

The three of them returned to the room to find that Thomas had been reduced to a gibbering, evil-smelling wreck of a man. The Englishman was lying on the floor, with his knees drawn up under his chin, begging for death, yet his comrades merely laughed at the sight.

"I hope you think this is worth it," Bos grinned as he watched Thomas writhe in pain.

"Physician heal thyself," Quintana added gleefully, whereupon Thomas cursed the apostle Luke and demanded that his companions take him to the hospital.

"There's plenty of potion left if you wish to try it, you heartless bastards! Otherwise, I think it's time that you conveyed me to the monks," Thomas managed to groan.

Though Bos and Quintana continued to laugh at their friend's misfortune, they did as Thomas asked and fetched two grooms from the inn's stables. For the price of three pfennigs apiece, the stable boys agreed to carry the green-faced patient to the infirmary but copper coins didn't buy a proper litter. Instead, the grooms placed Thomas on a plank and carried him, like a pauper's corpse, to the Hospital of the Holy Spirit.

It was late in the evening, and the curfew bells were ringing all over the city, when Bos, Quintana, Ursula and the stretcher bearers left the inn. Though the streets were crowded with people hurrying home, the overpowering smell emanating from the vomiting, defecating bundle on the plank cleared a wide path.

Halfway to the hospital, the grooms rebelled, dumped Thomas in the gutter and demanded more money. It was only Bos' threats of lethal violence that persuaded the profiteers to keep to their bargain.

The sprawling priory that housed the Church and Hospital of the Holy Spirit stood in the heart of Nuremberg, between two of the city's bridges over the River Pegnitz. Its walls were built of pink sandstone and the steeply pitched roofs, each pierced by rows of small skylights, were made of russet-coloured tiles. In recent years, the hospital had been extended by building a series of low arches to a small islet called *The Schutt* and these supported both a new infirmary and two pleasant courtyards where the sick could convalesce.

The monastery's church, which served as the monks' house of prayer as well as the Holy Roman Emperors' treasury, was a long, narrow building that extended for a hundred yards along the northern bank of the river. A clerestory ran from the short, slender spire over the west door to the rounded apse at the eastern end of the building, yet, compared to Nuremberg's other famous places of worship, this chapel looked very plain.

In spite of its imperial associations, the Church and Hospital of the Holy Spirit had not been adorned with a glorious Gothic façade covered with sumptuous statuary or magnificent stained glass. Instead, a single stone figure of the Archangel Raphael, the patron of healing, marked the infirmary's public entrance and the grooms deposited Thomas beneath this effigy before departing with unseemly haste. Though Bos and Quintana cursed the youths for their venality and cowardice, they fell silent when an elderly friar appeared in the infirmary's doorway.

"Dear me, what's the matter with this poor pilgrim?" the friar asked and Ursula quickly explained that, after eating too many mushrooms for his supper, her brother Johan had been taken gravely ill.

"Though I'm still a novice in the Convent of Poor Clares at Coburg, I've learned much about the use of medicinal herbs. Yet, I fear the purge I've administered has done little good. Perhaps if my other brothers and I could pray beneath your chapel's holy relics, God will be merciful and let our dear Johan live," she said tearfully but the monk shook his head.

"I'm afraid that only the sick may enter our house of prayer but you may leave your brother with us. We will ask the Blessed St Jude to intercede with The Lord on his behalf and I'll send word when, if God wills it, he has recovered," said the friar. There was nothing more that Ursula or the others could do, except bid Thomas farewell, as two lay-brothers carried the filth-covered patient into the monastery.

Once inside, it soon became clear why the new hospital had been built over the river. Thomas was taken to a marble-floored chamber that was completely empty of furniture. Here, the Englishman was stripped naked and dowsed with buckets of freezing water. The pails were replenished from the river by lowering them through one of the rooms open windows, and the effluent drained through a hole in the centre of the floor. Whilst this method of bathing was crude, it was effective, especially as the monks had the good sense to refill their buckets upstream of the drain.

When Thomas looked more like a man, and less like a turd floating in a chamber pot, he was given a physick and taken to a large dormitory which measured about a hundred feet from end to end.

Though the rows of curtained stalls, which lined the two long walls, resembled confessional boxes instead of a priest and a penitent, each of these booths contained a bed and a patient. There was a strong smell of vinegar but Thomas was too ill to pay much attention to his surroundings. He was still suffering from the agonies of cramp and he could do little more than mumble his thanks as the monks dressed him in a white linen gown and put him to bed.

It was the faint tolling of a bell that woke Thomas and though the few hours' sleep had done much to restore his system, it still took some minutes for him to remember where he was. The dormitory was so dark, he could see nothing except the outline of the curtain around his bed but as he lay in the gloom, he began to wonder if he should make his clandestine survey of the relics' security now, whilst everyone else was asleep.

Deciding that fortune favoured the brave, Thomas rose from his sickbed and tiptoed, somewhat unsteadily, to the end of the dormitory. All was quiet as he opened the door, yet, as he entered the passageway beyond, he heard the sound of chanting. The mournful plainsong announced that the monks were beginning their midnight prayers, so, until they'd finished, Thomas dare not leave the dormitory.

Cursing his missed opportunity, Thomas hurried back to his bed but as he crawled under the sheets, the door at the far end of the dormitory creaked open. The sound of footsteps on the bare, wooden floorboards drew closer and then stopped outside his stall. A moment later, the curtains were thrown open and the small space exploded with light.

In his confusion, Thomas thought the nightwatch had come to haul him off to the gallows but, as he sat bolt upright and balled his fists in anticipation of a hard fight, the friar holding the lantern urged him to stay calm.

"Have no fear, my son, I'm not Death come to claim you. I merely wanted to make sure your condition hadn't worsened and by the looks of things, you've made a remarkable recovery," said the friar as he held his candle up to his patient's face. Seeing the look of surprise in the friar's eyes, Thomas hurriedly crossed himself and declared that God was merciful.

"My deliverance is indeed a miracle, therefore I must offer my thanks to The Lord Jesus as soon as possible and so will you take me to your chapel?" Thomas said weakly and he managed to add that he had plenty of money to pay for a mass.

"Your generosity is a virtue and your rapid recovery shows you've been blessed by the Holy Spirit. At daybreak, you may come into the chapel and receive the sacraments due to the sick, in the meantime you must rest," said the friar firmly.

"You're most kind, Father and may I see the Holy Lance when I pray?" Thomas asked hopefully, yet the friar repeated what the sentry had told him on his arrival in Nuremberg.

"After the city council embraced Luther's heresies, it was decreed that only those who are of royal blood may set eyes on the Holy Lance. Therefore, the casket can only be lowered and opened in the presence of the Emperor or his kingly guests," said the friar and he left Thomas with nothing but a firm promise that he'd be back at dawn.

The friar was as good as his word and he returned at daybreak with his patient's freshly laundered clothes. Once Thomas had dressed, he followed the monk into the chapel, where he was surprised by the building's curious blend of stark simplicity and outrageous ostentation. The unembellished ribs of the chapel's vaulted ceiling were supported by plain Doric columns but, whilst the long, narrow nave was almost completely unadorned, the chancel was as richly decorated as any church in Christendom.

Filling the semi-circular apse behind the altar was a huge marble *reredos* nearly thirty feet high. This altarpiece resembled two classical temples built on top of each other. However, whilst the lower temple boasted three pairs of Roman pilasters supporting a semi-circular arch, the rounded columns of the upper temple were crowned with a triangular Greek pediment.

Besides the pastiche of ancient architecture, the *reredos* was decorated with a painting of St Christopher carrying the infant Jesus on his shoulders. This icon filled the space between the lower pillars but the upper columns framed a large fresco of a disembodied eye surrounded by the gilded rays of the sun.

From his studies, Thomas knew that this symbol had two meanings. To a theologian, it was the Eye of Providence, representing a benign God watching over Creation, but to the alchemist, it was the All-Seeing Eye signifying the wisdom of the ancients. Yet, as Thomas continued to stare at the mystical image, he realised that it was meant to be a watchful sentry, because its immutable gaze was fixed on a large reliquary that was suspended from the chapel's ceiling by a single iron chain.

This casket measured about ten feet long and its pentagonal shape reminded Thomas of a barn with a steeply pitched roof. In the weak light of the chapel's candles, he could see that the panels forming the casket's sides were made of exquisitely chased silver. However, whilst he was sure that the sacred treasures were still inside, he also began to suspect that the Holy Lance would remain forever beyond his grasp.

What dismayed Thomas was the fact that, though the reliquary was hanging more than twenty feet above the ground, there was no obvious way to return the imperial relics to earth.

No matter how hard he looked, he couldn't spot a door or a stairway that might lead to a room where a winch had been concealed and he began to wonder if the mechanism had been deliberately removed on the orders of the city's council. Thomas could understand why Nuremberg's Lutheran burghers wanted to keep the Emperor's idolatrous treasures permanently aloft but such reasoning didn't solve his problem.

If the casket couldn't be lowered, and the thieves couldn't transform themselves into birds, they'd have to construct some sort of scaffold to reach their prize. Moreover, the reliquary was certain to be locked, therefore they'd have to steal a key or force open the lid. These problems filled Thomas with anguish but the low moans that were beginning to permeate the nave didn't come from the Englishman's growing sense of despair.

In fact, the peculiar sounds were being uttered by the hospital's other patients who'd been allowed into the church to seek God's Blessing. Some of these invalids hobbled on crutches, whilst others were carried in litters, and for several minutes the only sounds to be heard were the wheezing coughs and muffled groans of the infirm. This pestilential chorus disturbed Thomas' thoughts, which irritated him greatly, but soon the gentle sounds of plainsong began to echo down the corridor that led to the monastery's dormitory.

The solemn chanting continued as the monks took their places in the chancel's choir stalls and as the whole chapel filled with ethereal music, one of the younger friars walked among the penitents with a wooden collecting box attached to a long handle. As Thomas deposited the money needed to buy God's grace, he wondered if The Almighty considered simony to be as great a sin as stealing a holy relic, but before he could ask such a question, the monk had moved on and was enthusiastically greeting a man who'd just arrived.

The latecomer wore a long, black cloak with the hood pulled over his head and he walked with a stick. Clearly, whatever ailment afflicted him had yet to be cured by the power of prayer but he still had to pay his two florins. The invalid started to grumble about the cost of redemption yet, though Thomas shared his sentiments, he gave the man no more thought. Instead, he forced himself to concentrate on how to reach a metal box floating in the void.

The mass proceeded in time-honoured tradition and, after the Gospel Reading, the monastery's stern-faced abbot entered the pulpit to deliver the Homily. In a fearsome voice, the priest informed his congregation of consumptives and cripples that sin was the cause of sickness and the only way to health was to follow the path set by the church. To emphasise his point, the abbot told the story of the angels who'd ascended to heaven by climbing Jacob's Ladder, though Thomas stopped listening when he became aware that the lame man was standing by his side. The invalid's face was still hidden by his cloak's black hood, yet Thomas felt his blood freeze when the man spoke.

"I had hoped you'd back in Wewelsburg by now, or perhaps I didn't make myself clear when I stressed the urgency of our mission," said Julius Caesar Scaliger.

To ensure the Englishman had no doubt as to the identity of his inquisitor, Scaliger threw back his cloak, to reveal a small, enamelled badge bearing the device of a silver ladder. In that moment, Thomas solved the riddle of how to reach the casket but he managed to stifle his cry of triumph. Instead, he accused his former employer of being a dastardly spy.

"I've read Suleiman's secret message to the French King and the *scytale* proves you're their cats-paw. So, unless you want to end your days in an imperial dungeon, you'd better make yourself scarce," Thomas said in a harsh whisper but, if he hoped that this revelation would force his enemy to beg for forgiveness, he was disappointed. Scaliger's reply was to admit he was in the pay of the French and he seemed delighted by the look of consternation this produced on Thomas' face.

"Only the bandit, Dracul, knows the secret of the *scytale*, so I must conclude that he has used this knowledge to bewitch you. Don't you see, Thomas? Only an alliance between the French and Turks can defeat the Order of the Dragon and it is they who are the real enemy," he said with unashamed pride, yet Thomas refused to be intimidated by Scaliger's candour.

"By all the saints, you must be as mad as the Gadarene Swine! Dracul is a landless prince with barely a hundred men to command, so why do you think it needs the might of two empires to stop him?" Thomas scoffed. Scaliger, however, remained adamant that Dracul was a greater threat to civilisation than all the barbarians who'd destroyed the first Empire of Rome.

"This monster is a brutal tyrant who was driven from Wallachia by his own people. If he seizes the Holy Lance, he'll become invincible. I've already told you of this relic's power and if it falls into the Draconists' hands they'll plunge the world into chaos," Scaliger said angrily, and he began to list all the crimes of previous *Drăculeşti*, but Thomas insisted that Dracul wasn't the only prince to cruelly torture his enemies.

"I don't deny that Dracul shares his forbears' unnatural delight in watching men suffer agonising death but is he alone? The enemies of French kings are broken on the wheel, whilst those who defy the Ottoman sultans are castrated and blinded. Are their fates any worse than those who die by Dracul's order?" Thomas countered, yet Scaliger continued to insist that the French alliance with the Turks offered the only chance of restitution for those unjustly deprived of their birthright.

"I don't blame you for believing Dracul's lies, the serpent in Eden was no less persuasive, but the only way to prevent this tyrant from conquering the earth is to bring the Holy Lance to me. If it's gold you seek, the French King will make you richer than a Borgia pope. If it's wisdom you desire, the Sultan will grant you access to all the great libraries of the east. Could there be any finer reward for a scholar?" Scaliger said.

For brief a moment, the thought of such glittering prizes dazzled Thomas but, as the monks sang the Stabat Mater, he thought of Ursula. Whatever riches Suleiman and the French King could offer, Dracul's daughter was not in their gift.

"My destiny lies not with Suleiman or Francis," he said quietly and though Scaliger's expression remained inscrutable, when he spoke, his voice had become as cold as that of Dracul.

"That's most unfortunate, Thomas, because your co-operation is essential to securing the future of men who are not as forgiving as myself. I must have the Holy Lance, and you will give me what I want, either willingly or unwillingly. If you have any remaining qualms, perhaps this will convince you that mine is the only path you must follow," he said icily.

Without another word, Scaliger reached beneath his cloak and pulled out a small wallet. He opened it and showed Thomas a scrap of paper, upon which Ursula had scrawled her name, as well as a lock of her blonde hair.

Richard Anderton

Scaliger smiled as he sensed Thomas' rage and assured him that Dracul's daughter would not be harmed, so long as the Englishman did exactly as he was told. Fighting the desire to wring Scaliger's neck, Thomas insisted that he'd agree to nothing until he knew that Ursula was still alive.

"Take me to her now or I'll throttle you with your own puke-stained beard," he hissed.

"As you wish, though I hardly need warn you that any attempt to thwart me will result in the girl's instant and painful death. Moreover, I'll see to it that Dracul learns that you were to blame," Scaliger replied. Thomas was now too angry to speak and it was all he could do to follow the other man out of the church. If the monks thought it strange that two invalids should leave a mass for the sick before being anointed with the oil that had cost them both a month's wages, they said nothing and went on with their liturgy.

Outside, Thomas was greeted by a dozen men, all dressed in red tunics emblazoned with the badge of the silver ladder. Scaliger mumbled a few words of command but no one else spoke as the party crossed the bridge that led to the southern half of the city.

They continued walking in tense silence until they reached the Church of St Lorenz where, the day before, Thomas and the others had heard Spengler denounce the wickedness of monasteries and convents. After crossing the plaza in front of this church, Scaliger halted his men by a square tower made of brown stone and capped with a roof of red tiles.

The tower was one of many built by the city's wealthy merchants to protect themselves and their money during periods of civil strife. Once, this small fortress had stood in splendid isolation but, as Nuremberg had been at peace for decades, a jumble of shops and houses now crowded against two of the tower's four walls.

A decorative oriel window had been built over the narrow, arched doorway, which was the only entrance, but the tower still boasted formidable defences. A crenellated parapet linked four roofed turrets at each of the tower's corners and these watchtowers housed sentries armed with swords and crossbows.

With ill-disguised glee, Scaliger revealed that he'd paid for this fortress in the heart of his enemy's capital with French gold. He also boasted that the city's Lutheran fathers had been too busy wondering how many angels could dance on the head of a pin to notice a scorpion building its nest in their midst.

Though he was enraged by Scaliger's crowing, Thomas had the good sense to ignore the provocation. Instead, he gritted his teeth and demanded to see Ursula at once.

"I warn you Scaliger, unless I see the girl, I'll go straight to the city watch and tell them everything I know," he said. In reply, Scaliger merely shrugged and waved his stick in the direction of the tower. Seconds later, Dracul's daughter appeared at the oriel window and, though she appeared to be unharmed, she was struggling like a wildcat.

"You see, the girl is quite safe in my care but, at any moment, the window may open and she may fall to her tragic and untimely death," Scaliger warned.

By now, Thomas' desire to punish Ursula's kidnapper for his treachery was overwhelming but Scaliger's tower looked impregnable and the Englishman had no doubt that any attempt to rescue Ursula by force of arms would result in her instant murder. For the time being, Thomas was beaten and he could do nothing except stand in voiceless rage as the sentries pulled their prisoner away from the window.

"What must I do?" Thomas hissed and he was surprised when Scaliger told him to return to his inn.

"When the time comes, you must help me defeat whatever scheme the fiend Dracul has devised to steal the Holy Lance. Until then you may go to your lodgings and wait for my word," he said.

"Don't you wish to imprison me in your tower? Aren't you afraid I'll run away?" Thomas replied.

"Where would you go? Dracul has many enemies in this city and one word from me will send you and your companions to the gallows. If, by some miracle, you managed to leave Nuremberg without my permission, I'll sell Dracul's daughter to the nearest brothel and she'll spend the rest of her days satisfying the carnal desires of fat German merchants. Now go," said Scaliger and, with a wave of his hand, he dismissed the Englishman from his presence. Thomas left the square vowing vengeance but he knew it would be almost impossible to make Scaliger pay for his villainy. So long as he and the others were disguised as peasants, they couldn't carry any weapon and this sense of impotence only increased Thomas' rage.

As he made his way back to the inn, he began to wonder how Ursula had been kidnapped so easily, because Bos and Quintana should've been more than a match for Scaliger's ruffians. By the time he'd reached The Golden Bear, Thomas' anger had fledged into a fury and he'd decided that the others had failed to protect Ursula because they'd been drunk.

Just as he'd feared, he found Bos and Quintana fast asleep in a corner of the tavern's deserted taproom. It appeared as if they'd been drinking all night, because the two men were both slumped over a table littered with empty tankards. Thomas felt the fog of battle cloud his mind and before he could stop himself, he'd hauled the slumbering Quintana to his feet and smashed his fist into the Portugee's face. Quintana staggered backwards as Thomas roared that Scaliger was in Nuremberg and had kidnapped Ursula whilst her supposed chaperones had been drinking themselves into a stupor.

"You dregs from Lucifer's own pisspot! You traitorous turds from the arse of Judas! Were you drunk when Ursula was taken, or have you spent your thirty pieces of silver on beer? Either way, I'm going to thrash you both like dogs. Now stand still and take what's coming to you!" Thomas bellowed. Quintana groaned and rubbed his chin but at least the blow had brought him to his senses.

"What are you talking about, you stupid son of a Persian whore? Someone must've tampered with our cups and if you don't believe me, look at Bos! It normally takes him a week of solid boozing to get like that," said Quintana, jerking his thumb at the still comatose Frisian.

The sound of drunken snoring prompted Thomas to look at Bos, who was lying face down in a pool of stale beer, but as he did so, Quintana crashed his fist into the Englishman's face. The punch set Thomas' ears ringing but he countered with a vicious jab that landed in his opponent's midriff and, as the Portugee bent double, he drove his knee into Quintana's nose.

The force of Thomas' blow sent Quintana tumbling backwards over the table and the impact also knocked Bos off his chair. The two men's flailing arms and legs smashed their collection of earthenware mugs into a thousand pieces and the cheap wooden furniture splintered into firewood.

"What, in the name of Persephone's pink pomegranates, is going on?" Bos spluttered, whereupon Quintana informed him that Ursula was missing and

Thomas had lost his mind.

"He says the stupid trollop's got herself kidnapped by Scaliger's men whilst we were blind drunk!" Quintana said as he wiped the blood from his nostrils. Bos' reaction to this accusation was characteristically ferocious and Thomas soon found himself reeling from a series of bone-crushing punches.

"No one tells me I can't take my drink!" Bos cried as he pummelled the Englishman's face and ribs. Thomas felt his lip split, and the taste of blood filled his mouth, but he managed to stay on his feet. In desperation, Thomas blocked Bos' next attack with his left arm and used his right to deliver a vicious uppercut that slammed into the Frisian's jaw. The Englishman's punch would have flattened any lesser man but Bos merely shook his shaggy head and spat a blackened tooth onto the rush-covered floor.

"You punch like my old mother," he sneered.

"And you groan like your mother when I'm ploughing her!" Thomas retorted. At this fresh insult, Bos growled and balled his fists to renew his assault. However, before the two pugilists could resume their bout, the inn's landlord came running over and he was accompanied by four burly men carrying heavy 'argument-settler' truncheons.

"Foreign pigs! Stop, or my sons will beat you good!" the landlord cried.

As the peacemakers struggled to separate the warring parties, Quintana tried to explain that the fight was only a minor disagreement between friends. Unfortunately the landlord refused to be mollified and he continued to demand payment for the damage they'd caused. This prompted Bos to argue that they'd all been poisoned by his bad beer.

"It's you who should pay us, you foul poisoner!" he bellowed, whereupon the barkeep turned puce with rage and threatened to call the watch unless the men produced some cash. Now it was Thomas' turn to direct his wrath towards their common enemy, and he promised to thrash the landlord until he'd learned how to keep better beer. However, before the Englishman could carry out his threat, Quintana put a calming hand on his shoulder and urged him to curb his anger.

"You can't help Ursula if we're all rotting in a Nuremberg gaol, so let's pay the scoundrel and go," he whispered. Thomas blinked as the madness left him. However, before he could beg the others' forgiveness, the irascible landlord repeated his demand for money.

With a grunt, Thomas tossed a handful of coins into the wreckage of broken chairs and splintered pottery, then marched towards the inn's door. As the others joined him, the innkeeper threatened them all with a week in the pillory if they ever tried to enter his establishment again, but the three men ignored him and stepped into the street.

Though there was an awkward silence as they walked away from the inn, eventually Thomas admitted that one of the tavern wenches must have slipped a sleeping draft into Bos and Quintana's drinks. He blamed the lingering effects of the mandrake root for scrambling his brains but the others insisted there was no need for any explanation. Instead, they apologised for not taking better care of Dracul's daughter.

"We might've guessed that Scaliger wouldn't let us resign from his service so easily but we can't return to Dracul without his precious princess. Remember he still holds Prometheus hostage," said Quintana.

"You're right, Portugee, that maniac will spend the

rest of his days sticking sharpened stakes up our Nubian comrade's arse if anything happens to his darling little girl," added Bos.

"At least I know where she is. The question is, will you help me free her?" Thomas asked and he explained that Dracul's daughter was being held prisoner in Scaliger's tower house near the Church of St Lorenz.

In the spirit of the renewed peace between them, Bos grinned and reminded Thomas of their vow to follow the man who'd escaped his own hanging all the way to Hell, if need's be. Quintana agreed that they ought to try and rescue Ursula at once, if they were to stand any chance of success, but he also sounded a note of caution.

"We'll need an army to break into a tower house," he said grimly but Thomas merely smiled.

"You're right and I think I know where to find one," he said and he strode off down the street, leaving the puzzled Bos and Quintana to follow.

# 12
## THE TOWER HOUSE

The victory of the nobles' Swabian League had brought some semblance of order to Southern Germany and though isolated bands of rebel peasants still roamed the countryside, as Thomas and his companions had found to their cost, the fragile peace had encouraged many people to spend Easter in the imperial capital.

With Holy Week now only ten days away, thousands of pious ploughmen and devout dairymaids had travelled to Nuremberg to thank God for their deliverance from the murderous Peasants' War and when Ursula's would-be rescuers left their inn they joined this growing throng.

Like fish caught in a rising tide, Thomas, Bos and Quintana were swept along the city's streets. However, when they reached the Lorenzer Platz, Thomas ignored Scaliger's tower on the far side of the square and went inside the church of St Lorenz.

As before, the bastion of Nuremberg's Lutheranism was packed with hundreds of eager disciples hoping to hear Spengler denounce the popish practices that were endangering their souls. Unfortunately, at this hour, the Moses of the New Covenant was absent from the pulpit so, instead of thrilling accounts of fire and brimstone, the congregation had to make do with an aged scholar explaining some dry point of doctrine.

Though everyone listened politely, most were thoroughly bored by the finer details of theology and the congregation seemed to breathe a collective sigh of relief when Thomas marched purposefully up the aisle, mounted the pulpit and elbowed the desiccated theologian aside. The determined look on the interloper's face silenced the few gasps from the crowd and Thomas' oratory soon held the entire church spell-bound.

"My friends, Our Saviour teaches that those who hunger and thirst after righteousness shall inherit the Kingdom of Heaven and I need the help of righteous people in a matter of the utmost importance. In recent months, your city has become a beacon of light for all those who love Christ but loathe the injustices of the Roman Church. Yet, even as I speak, there's a monstrous wickedness, hateful in the sight of God, taking place just yards from this House of The Lord!" Thomas cried and a murmur rippled through the congregation.

"Only yesterday, in this very church, I heard the learned Spengler denounce the tonsure and the veil. He spoke the truth when he said there's no sacrament in a practice that condemns God's children to lives of indolence in a monastery or convent, so I know that you good people will help my betrothed, who's being forced to enter a nunnery against her will!" Thomas added and the murmur of disapproval became louder.

"Like Abelard and Heloise, Dante and Beatrice, Romeo and Juliet, I'm to be parted from the woman I love through no fault of my own. She, who should be my bride, has been imprisoned by her wicked uncle in a tower that's in sight of this very church, so will you let this abomination continue? Or will you save this maiden from the cloister and let her enter the holy estate of matrimony, as all women should?" Thomas cried.

Those who remembered the pretty young novice being bundled out of their church the previous day answered with howls of indignation. Those who did not asked who would lead the armies of the righteous against the evil 'black crows' and Thomas was only too happy to accept this command. He declared that, like Joshua before the Walls of Jericho, he wouldn't rest until the fortress of God's enemies had been razed to the ground.

The crowd responded with even wilder cheering and, as their new Parzifal strode down the aisle to the door, people rushed to swear their allegiance to his cause. Though Bos and Quintana cursed Thomas for being an impetuous, lovesick fool who kept his wits in his codpiece, they, too, were swept up in the torrent of angry humanity that streamed out of the church.

"You idiot, Scaliger will cut the girl's throat before you can break down his door," Quintana hissed in Thomas' ear and Bos agreed that the defenders held all the advantages.

"Have you forgotten how we fought off the Brethren of the Ring besieging the watchtower? There were only four of us and Scaliger must have at least twenty men inside his fortress," the Frisian growled but Thomas insisted that Ursula's captors wouldn't confuse a religious riot with their private feud. Bos and Quintana remained unconvinced by this argument but it was too late to stop the angry mob.

Like the many headed, monstrous Hydra of Greek myth, the crowd slithered across the cobbled square and began to spit stones at the tower's grim walls. This barrage of rocks was accompanied by repeated demands for the captive nun to be released but it wasn't until every expensive pane of glass in the tower's ornate oriel window had been shattered that Scaliger appeared.

Leaning out of the ruined window's empty frame, he accused the angry multitude of being godless traitors who'd suffer the same fate as Muntzer, and the other defeated rebel leaders, unless they dispersed immediately.

"I'm a kinsman of His Imperial Majesty Charles V and he'll hang you all as *Bundschuh* scum unless you leave this place at once," he cried but a threat, particularly a threat from a pompous foreigner with ideas above his station, was not what the mob wanted to hear.

Some of the protesters started singing hymns, while others chanted slogans, and the din began to attract more and more people to the square. In reply to the mob's renewed storm of cobblestones and cat calls, the defenders hurled dead rats, the contents of chamber pots and other detritus to keep their enemies at bay.

The attack on the tower had now reached stalemate but this was the moment for which Thomas had been waiting. Whilst Scaliger tried to bully the increasingly agitated crowd, he showed Quintana and Bos the point, a few feet below the tower's battlements, where the roof of a neighbouring building joined the fortress's eastern wall. The ground floor of this rickety tenement appeared to be a haberdasher's shop and though Ursula's would-be rescuer insisted that this was the solution to their problems, the others failed to see how a purveyor of cotton and silks could help them free Dracul's daughter.

"Are you planning to knot together lengths of calico to make a rope?" Bos asked.

"If you are how will that help? A cloth merchant can't sell you a grappling hook," added Quintana but Thomas insisted he needed none of these items.

"All I have to do is sneak inside the shop and find the attic. There's bound to be a skylight leading to the roof and then I can crawl along its ridge to the tower's parapet. So long as the defenders keep watching the square, I reckon I can easily climb into Ursula's prison without being seen," said Thomas gleefully and the others had to admit that the plan had every chance of success.

The shop's proprietor, a balding man with a red face and large belly, was standing in the doorway of his emporium urging the crowd to teach the Italian papists a lesson. This unlikely evangelist was so busy shouting Lutheran slogans he didn't notice the three desperate burglars creep up behind him and, before he knew what was happening, Bos had clamped a huge hand over his face. The luckless haberdasher was bundled inside his shop and though he struggled like a pig in a sack he was quickly bound and gagged with strips of his own cloth.

"Stay here, keep the crowd focused on the tower and make sure no one follows me to the roof," Thomas whispered to Bos and Quintana but they wanted to go with him.

"You can't take on Scaliger's private army alone," Quintana hissed, yet Thomas insisted that one person was all that was needed to rescue Ursula and that the others would be of more help if they kept stoking the fires of the crowd's resentment. Bos began to grumble that Englishmen were more stubborn than a cardinal's mule but he joined Quintana by the door and, before his companions could change their mind, Thomas had disappeared up the stairs at the back of the shop.

The quiet inside the tenement seemed more frightening than the din outside and Thomas could hear his heart pounding as he made his way to the first landing. Here, a little to the left of the stairs, there was a half-open door and Thomas could see it was the entrance to the shop's living quarters.

If anyone happened to be looking through this door, they couldn't fail to spot the burglar crouched behind the stair's bannisters. Fortunately the excited chatter inside the room indicated that the household's women and servants were also watching the drama in the square.

Hardly daring to blink, Thomas pressed himself against the wall at the back of the staircase and began to inch his way upwards but luck was with him and he managed to pass the open door without being seen.

Moments later, Thomas had reached the building's attics, and he breathed a sigh of relief when he found that these rooms were deserted. Quickly finding a skylight, he climbed onto the roof and though he was more than fifty feet above the ground, he could hear the shouts from the street below quite clearly.

The defenders' continued refusal to agree to any of the Lutherans' requests had pushed the mob to the end of its tether and there were calls to fetch ladders, battering rams and even gunpowder, to force an entry. This was exactly what Thomas had hoped to hear and when he was certain that Scaliger's sentries were watching the square, he began to crawl along the roof's ridge.

The red earthenware tiles were old and rattled like bags of dry bones as Thomas eased his weight forward. With every clatter he paused, and braced himself for the crossbow bolt that would knock him from his perch like a wooden popinjay, but, far below, Bos and Quintana were doing exactly as he'd asked. Their repeated harangues continued to raise tensions in the square and the increasing danger from the mob held the sentries' attention. At last, Thomas reached the tower and, as silently as he could, he clambered over its parapet.

Panting with the effort of stealth, Thomas dropped onto the walkway behind the battlements at a point roughly halfway between the east and south turrets. The eastern turret, which faced away from the square, was unoccupied but the southern turret was manned by a sentry dressed in Scaliger's livery. The man wore an old fashioned, wide-brimmed, kettle helmet and, whilst this seemed to be the sentry's only armour, the man had a small arsenal of weapons.

Hanging from the man's belt, was both a rapier and a dagger, whilst to the sentry's left an unspanned arbalest, together with its windlass and quiver full of bolts, was propped against the turret's wall. Despite being armed with a powerful crossbow, the sentry was content to hurl nothing more deadly than gobs of spittle at the crowd below and he only realised that the tower's defences had been breached when Thomas' foot landed between his legs. The sentry howled in agony as his manhood was crushed against his own pelvic bone and he dropped to the turret's floor, clutching his groin.

Whilst the crippled sentry lay curled in a ball, opening and closing his mouth like a beached fish, Thomas relieved the man of his sword and dagger before tying him up.

Feeling better now he was armed, Thomas looked around for a way inside the tower and though he spotted a trapdoor halfway along the parapet, he also saw the sentry in the western turret desperately trying to span his own crossbow. Thomas didn't hesitate. Gripping his stolen dagger in one hand and shaking the rapier free of its scabbard with the other, he charged.

Cursing the patron saint of crossbowmen, the second sentry tossed the unspanned weapon to one side and, drawing his own sword and knife, ran to meet his attacker. The two men met in the middle of the parapet, and their long blades clashed with a shower of sparks, but after the heavy cat skinner swords favoured by German landsknechts, the slender Spanish rapier felt unusually light in the Englishman's hand.

At first, Thomas overcompensated for the weapon's unfamiliar weight but it didn't take him long to master the technique of lunge and parry. The trick, he discovered, was to employ both dagger and sword together, using one blade to block his opponent's thrust, then counterattack with the other.

Though the sentry was practised in this form of swordplay, he was more used to brawling in the backstreets of Verona. By contrast, the Englishman had learned his trade on the battlefield and Thomas' improvised method, combined with his stubborn refusal to give any ground whatsoever, unnerved his opponent.

It wasn't long before fear began to affect the sentry's judgement and when he made his first mistake, the point of Thomas' sword ripped a deep gash in the man's cheek. The pain from his lacerated face only added to the sentry's panic and his strokes became increasingly wild. His final flurry of blows ended in a desperate thrust that left his flank exposed and Thomas saw his chance.

With a cry of victory, the Englishman plunged his dagger deep into his opponent's unprotected side. The sentry gasped as the poignard's slender blade pierced his flesh and he slumped to his knees with blood spewing from his mouth.

Leaving the dying man to make his peace with God, Thomas scrambled through the trapdoor. The ladder below led to an attic directly beneath the tower's roof and though the only way out of this garret was a spiral stair in the far corner of the room, Thomas hesitated. If Scaliger had heard the sound of fighting on the parapet, he'd send men to investigate so Thomas froze and waited at the top of the stair like a cat beside a mouse hole.

After a minute, in which the only sounds to be heard were those of the defenders barricading the tower's entrance, Thomas told himself that "craven heart ne'er won fair Rosamunde" and began to descend the stone steps as quietly as he could. Clutching his sword and dagger ever more tightly, Thomas made his way to the next floor, where his way was blocked by another guard. This man was standing on a short landing in front of a small door. However, like the sentries in the turret, he was expecting any attack to come from below, so he had his back to the stairs that led to the roof.

With the rest of Scaliger's retainers defending the tower's entrance, Thomas reasoned that this man had to be guarding the chamber where Ursula was being held prisoner and, though the door was sure to be locked, he could see a large key hanging on a ring attached to the guard's belt. Like a cutpurse approaching a wealthy mark, Thomas took one careful step forward and then another whilst the guard continued to look down the stairs.

The guard's curiosity was his doom and he knew nothing of the intruder's presence until he felt the cold touch of steel against the back of his neck. Without waiting to be told, the terrified man raised his hands in surrender and spoke to his assailant in bad German.

"Please, spare me, I'm a humble man with a nagging wife and many children," the man stammered but Thomas assured him that he had no quarrel with henpecked husbands.

"Just open the door without making a sound and I'll let you live," Thomas hissed and he pressed the point of his dagger a little deeper into the guard's flesh to make sure he understood. Beads of sweat rolled down the guard's stubbled cheeks but he obediently took the key from his belt and turned it in the lock. There was a soft creak as the door swung open, but, before anyone could enter the room, a large jug flew through the doorway and hit the guard full in the face.

The terracotta pot splintered into a blizzard of razor-sharp shards and the guard was knocked backwards. Blinded by the blood pouring from his shattered face, the man tripped, smashed his head on the stone stairs as he fell and lay still. There was no time to see if the recumbent guard was dead, as the racket made by the exploding jar was bound to alert the rest of the garrison, and Thomas thought it prudent to make even more noise before entering the chamber.

"Ursula, it's me!" Thomas cried as he stepped cautiously into the room and, though he was relieved to see Dracul's daughter was standing a few feet from the door, the look on her face was terrifying. Ursula's eyes were full of vengeful fury and if she was surprised or grateful to see him she didn't show it. Instead, she treated her rescuer as if he was no more than a servant she'd sent to enquire about the weather.

"What's going on?" Ursula snapped and, as there was no time to chide the girl for her ingratitude, Thomas explained that he'd organised the mob to keep her captors busy whilst they made their escape.

"We must go, so I hope you have a head for heights," Thomas said as he bundled the girl through the door.

Though Ursula began to complain that she'd no head for stupid riddles, Thomas ignored her protests and propelled her up the stairs to the roof. They emerged onto the tower's parapet to see the trussed sentry, whom Thomas had emasculated earlier, struggling to free himself and the sight of the man rekindled Ursula's unbridled wrath.

"Bastard … swine… filthy son of Circassian sodomite! I'll teach you to try and dishonour a royal daughter of House of the *Drăculeşti!*" Ursula yelled and she stamped hard on the sentry's already badly bruised groin.

The stricken sentry must have passed out with pain, because he now lay motionless on the turret's floor, and before Ursula could inflict further punishment, Thomas had dragged the girl to the spot where he'd climbed over the battlements.

"That window is our doorway to freedom," he said and he pointed to the open skylight on the neighbouring building's roof. Ursula, however, remained unimpressed.

"Do you expect me to fly there? I'm not a stork," she said testily but Thomas insisted that the journey was not as difficult as it looked.

"Just crawl along the ridge and, for God's sake, hurry," he urged but Ursula's reply was to snatch the dagger from Thomas' hand and point it at her rescuer's throat.

For a moment, Thomas wasn't sure what the girl meant to do, as she had the look of someone who'd rather kill than face death, but then she seized the hem of her novice's habit and cut away all the cloth below her knees. Being a nun, Ursula wore no stockings or petticoats beneath her skirts and Thomas stared appreciatively at her smooth, shapely limbs.

"Now, I can climb," she said as she tossed the dagger and strips of cloth at the Englishman's feet.

Picking up the discarded items, Thomas watched Ursula scramble over the battlements and straddle the roof's ridge like an odalisque entertaining a fat Turkish bey but, despite the alterations to her habit, the cloth rode up to reveal even more of the girl's naked thighs. The sight made Thomas whimper with passion but his lustful thoughts were interrupted by the sound of someone climbing the ladder that led to the parapet.

Thrusting his dagger and the remains of Ursula's habit into his belt, Thomas sprinted back to the trapdoor just as a man's fingertips appeared at the edge of the opening. Without a second thought, he slammed the heavy door shut and the oak planks sliced through the exposed fingers like a cleaver cutting through sausages. There was a howl of pain, followed by a loud crash as whoever owned the severed digits fell off the ladder, but, for good measure, Thomas heaped the two lifeless sentries over the trapdoor to ensure it stayed shut.

Once he'd secured his line of retreat, Thomas ran back to the parapet and saw that Ursula was already halfway to the skylight. However, as he watched, one of the roof's worm-eaten rafters gave way.

With a cry of terror, the girl was pitched sideways and, having lost her balance, she began to slither down the steeply pitched roof along with an avalanche of broken tiles and splintered wood. Her fingers clawed at the slippery roof in a desperate attempt to slow her progress but it was her mutilated clothing that saved her. The frayed hem of her habit caught on an exposed nail and Ursula came to a halt barely a hand's span from the edge of the roof.

"Hang on, I'm coming!" Thomas yelled as he clambered over the parapet but, when he arrived at the edge of the ragged hole in the roof, he saw that Ursula was too far away to reach.

"In the name of St Andrew, what are you waiting for, you stupid English peasant? Get a rope and throw it to me!" Ursula cried and, as her words stung his soul, Thomas remembered the strips of cloth the girl had cut from her skirts. Retrieving the short lengths of fabric from his belt, Thomas knotted them into a crude rope and tossed one end to Ursula.

"Catch!" he cried but it took several attempts before the girl caught the lifeline. To add to their peril, Ursula was heavier than she looked and the cloth wound around Thomas' hand bit into his flesh like a hangman's noose. Ignoring the pain, Thomas pulled with all his might and, slowly, he hauled Ursula to safety. Once the girl was back on the roof, he guided her to the skylight and helped her clamber into the attic.

"By all the simpletons in a parliament of fools, couldn't you think of a better way to escape than crawling along a roof like a lizard?" Ursula said when they were both standing in the darkness of the shop's garret.

"Next time, I'll build a mechanical bird," Thomas snapped and, before Ursula could reply, he'd hurried her down the stairs. Thomas was surprised to find Quintana and Bos waiting for him in the shop but they insisted that they'd been forced to take shelter.

"Where in the name of Hyperion's sunburned backside have you been? Things are getting ugly out there," said Bos and he jerked his thumb in the direction of the square.

"The Frisian's right, you may have unleashed the Titans from Tartarus but they're not happy," said Quintana and, as he spoke, the tocsin bells began to sound across the city. Hearing the alarm, Thomas rushed to the shop's doorway and saw that the square outside now looked like a battlefield. Whilst he'd been inside the tower, hundreds more zealots had answered the call to defend God's Truth as they saw it and, like the *fähnleins* of the imperial army, the differing groups had gathered around different banners.

Those who carried simple flags, decorated with nothing more than verses from the bible, had vowed to free the imprisoned girl and drag her popish persecutors before the city council, or die in the attempt. By contrast, those who followed the intricately embroidered pictures of saints, felt it was their sacred duty to defend the Church of Rome.

The entire square was now filled with these rival groups, all waving their banners, blowing their horns and shouting their support for either Luther or Pope Clement, and it wouldn't be long before their battle of words and music became a war of fists and steel.

Even as Thomas and the others watched, scuffles broke out between those trying to batter down Scaliger's door and those trying to relieve the besieged garrison. However, before any of them could leave the shop, they heard the sound of horses' hooves galloping along the cobbled streets.

From somewhere on the far side of the square, the screaming began and in the next instant Nuremberg's city militia burst into the Lorenzer Platz like the wrath of God. There was a storm of bright flashes and loud bangs, as these guardians of municipal order discharged their pistols indiscriminately into the mob, and the surviving rioters' hymns of praise to The Almighty quickly turned into shrieks of panic.

With their pistols spent, the militiamen drew their swords and charged. The crowd tried to flee but, the press of so many people trying to squeeze into the narrow streets leading away from the ancient market square, prevented their efficient dispersal. Groups of armoured horsemen crashed into the knots of wailing citizens that had formed at the entrance to each street and the riders' sabres butchered human flesh without fear or favour.

Soon the square was littered with bloodied corpses, torn banners and severed limbs.

The carnage only served to increase Thomas and the others' desire to quit Nuremberg; unfortunately, with city's streets transformed into a gore-spattered shambles, their chances of escape seemed non-existent. Bos wondered if there was a cellar or attic in which they could hide, whilst Quintana suggested they should disguise themselves as washerwomen, but Thomas thought that water offered their only way out.

"With the streets in turmoil no one will be watching the river," he said and though Bos refused to believe that the city's water gates would be left open during a rebellion, Quintana agreed with Thomas.

"We must go this minute, because, if we're found with the girl, we'll be blamed for starting this riot and that means the scaffold, or worse," he said. On hearing the Portugee's words, Thomas hurriedly turned to the cloth merchant, who was still lying on the floor, looking like a rolled-up carpet, and gave the man a sharp kick in the ribs to attract his attention.

"Do you know how we can get to the river without being seen?" Thomas demanded and he pointed his sword at the shopkeeper's perspiring head. The hapless haberdasher glanced nervously at the bloodstained blade in the Englishman's hand and nodded, so Quintana quickly removed the man's gag.

After sucking in a great lungful of air, the merchant blurted out that an alley at the back of his shop led to a small wharf used by the tradesmen on this side of the river. Pausing only to stuff the gag back in the struggling shopkeeper's mouth, the four fugitives quickly found the door that led to the shop's courtyard and were soon in the alleyway beyond.

The narrow ginnel smelled of stale urine and stagnant mud. However, just as the cloth merchant had promised, it led to a stone quay. There were several small rowing boats tied to wooden posts set into the wharf's cobbles and though their owners had fled as soon as they'd heard the din of the riot, they'd had the good sense to take their oars with them. Cursing the boatmen's foresight, Thomas and the others clambered aboard the nearest vessel, cut its mooring rope and used their hands as paddles to row away from the dock.

The lack of proper oars, combined with the river's sluggish current, meant it took almost half an hour to reach Nuremberg's western water gate but, just as Thomas had predicted, with the city in uproar no one noticed a loose rowing boat drifting aimlessly downstream. Unfortunately, Bos' gloomy prognosis was also justified and every one of the city's gates had been closed as soon as the riot had begun.

The city of Nuremberg was encircled by massive double walls but, where the Pegnitz flowed in and out of the imperial capital, these cyclopean ramparts were carried over the water on broad stone arches. To prevent an attacking army entering by these culverts, an iron portcullis protected the outer arch but the inner span was guarded by nothing more than a wooden boom.

The winching mechanisms for these barriers were housed in two separate pairs of towers, which stood on either side of the river like the Pillars of Hercules, and the sentries had lowered their gates' defences as soon as the alarm bells had sounded. Though Bos groaned when he saw the heavily defended bastions, Quintana pointed to a patch of willow trees overhanging the water and suggested that they could hide there until the gates were eventually opened.

As the trees offered the only possible sanctuary, everyone in the boat began to paddle for the bank as hard as they could. However, once the little skiff had slipped silently under the willows' curtain of branches, Ursula began to voice her fears that even a casual search of the riverbanks would be certain to lead to their discovery. Though this was indeed a possibility Thomas tried to reassure the girl by saying that it would be nightfall in a few hours and that the militia would be kept busy by the riot until long after sunset.

"All we have to do is wait and we can swim to safety under cover of darkness," he said confidently.

In the absence of any alternative plan, the others agreed to be patient but lying silent and motionless in the bottom of the boat strained everyone's nerves. As darkness fell, a strange glow in the sky only increased the men's sense of foreboding but Ursula gave a little squeak of delight and she thanked God for sending them their means of salvation.

"Heaven be praised, the city's on fire," she whispered as the air became filled with the acrid smell of smoke. How, or why, the conflagration had started no one in the boat could tell but Thomas and the others were quick to take advantage of the situation. Realising that the flames would provide a new distraction for the city's watchmen, Thomas slipped over the boat's side and started swimming towards the water gate.

The oily water was bitterly cold, and smelled of the thousands of chamber pots emptied into the river every day, but this was no time to be squeamish. Anyone who wasn't fighting the fire would be hanging from a gibbet by dawn, so Thomas ignored the putrid corpse of a dead dog that floated past his face and focused on the water gate fifty yards away.

Though the boom under the first arch, which consisted of two tree trunks chained together like a thresher's flail, presented no obstacle to a relatively strong swimmer like Thomas, the iron grating under the second arch was an entirely different matter. A fully grown man could never hope to pass through the narrow spaces between the portcullis' metal bars, yet the rust and weed that encrusted its ancient ironwork offered some hope.

If the water gate's defences hadn't been repaired recently, there was a chance that the winter floods had made a larger hole in the portcullis somewhere beneath the water's surface. Thomas was not in the habit of praying but he offered a silent plea to Germany's river gods as he dived under the water.

It was impossible to see anything in the murky depths of the Pegnitz but the bars of the portcullis provided a useful series of handholds. By grasping the iron latticework firmly, Thomas was able to haul himself to the spikes at the bottom of the barrier and, though the entire structure was in good repair after all, he found to his great joy that the current had scoured a shallow trench in the soft mud directly below the grating.

Fighting the urge to breathe, Thomas wriggled through the narrow gap between the portcullis' spikes and the river bed before clambering back to the surface. Just as he felt as if his lungs were about to burst, he emerged into the chill night air, though for several minutes he could do nothing except grasp the iron grating and marvel at his good fortune.

When he'd recovered his strength, Thomas signalled for the others to join him and though they also negotiated the boom without difficulty they were confounded by the grating. Bos in particular couldn't work out how Thomas had crossed this insuperable barrier.

"What foul wizardry transported you to the other side of this damnable portcullis?" Bos demanded to know but Thomas merely laughed.

"It's simple, I used the bars as a ladder to climb down, there's a gap at the bottom," he whispered.

At this, Bos and Quintana moaned that they weren't mermaids or Leander reborn but Ursula gave a snort of disgust and disappeared beneath the surface of the foul-smelling river. Her rescuers waited anxiously for a moment, but she soon joined Thomas on the far side of the grating, and when she emerged she was smiling.

"I prayed to St Florian and he guided me through the perils of the deep!" she gasped happily.

# 13
## THE FORGER

Though they cursed Bos for his clumsiness, Thomas and Quintana took deep breaths and plunged back into the freezing river to help their comrade. The water was as black as a banker's heart, and neither man could see anything in the stygian darkness, but they could feel the eddies created by the drowning man as he thrashed his arms and legs in an effort to free himself.

Inch by inch, Thomas and Quintana groped their way towards the panic-crazed Frisian, and somehow they managed to grab hold of his flailing wrists, yet the harder they pulled the more immobile Bos seemed to become. Undaunted, the two men continued to wrestle with their struggling comrade until the agonies of suffocation forced them back to the surface.

"Take my knife, some of his clothes must be caught on the spikes so you cut him free whilst I pull," gasped Thomas. Quintana nodded and reached for the blade but it was Ursula who snatched the dagger from Thomas' outstretched hand.

"It would be better if I cut your friend loose whilst you both pull," she said firmly.

The men had no breath to argue, so, after refilling their lungs, the three angels of mercy returned to the bottom of the river. Worryingly, the water felt calmer as they descended and when they reached Bos they found that he'd stopped moving.

Unless they hurried, the merciless nixe would claim another victim, so Ursula hurriedly found the fold of Bos' breeches that had become entangled in the rusted spikes and cut away the offending cloth. As soon as Bos was freed from the grating's iron grasp, Thomas, Ursula and Quintana pulled the unconscious man to the surface but the Frisian remained unnervingly quiet as he emerged from the river's depths.

At least they were all outside the city's walls, so, as swiftly as they could, Thomas and the others hauled their lifeless comrade to the riverbank. Gasping with the effort, they dragged Bos out of the water, and after laying him face down on a mudflat, Thomas began to pummel the Frisian between his shoulder blades with all his might.

Sat astride Bos' back, the Englishman looked like a laundress beating a pile of washing on a large, flat stone but his repeated blows soon had the desired effect. As the foetid river water was forced from Bos' lungs, Thomas' efforts produced great paroxysms of violent coughing from his patient.

In his convulsions, the half-drowned Frisian contorted his massive frame and though Thomas was thrown backwards into the reeds, the tempest passed as quickly as it had come. Whilst Thomas extricated himself from the tangle of bulrushes, and Ursula said another prayer, Bos rolled onto his back and lay still. For several anxious minutes the only sign that the Frisian was still alive was the rise and fall of his, barrel-shaped chest but at last Ursula's prayer was answered and Bos opened his eyes.

"By the great, rusted anchor of St Clement, I was dead and you raised me from my watery tomb. For that, Englishman, you have my eternal thanks, yet if you ever make me dive into a river again, I'll rip off your arm and beat you to death with the wet end!" Bos roared.

"If you weren't the size of the fish that ate Jonah you wouldn't get stuck in a little ditch like the Pegnitz!" Thomas retorted but, before he could berate the Frisian further for his shameless lack of gratitude, Quintana told them both to be quiet before they attracted the attention of the city's nightwatch.

"Cease your mewling, the pair of you! We need to get out of here as soon as possible, so help me find a path that leads away from the river," he said and though the others grumbled that they needed rest, they joined the Portugee in his search.

By morning, the four filthy fugitives had found the road that led north and no one paid them the slightest heed as they walked back to their camp. Despite feeling utterly exhausted, the thirty mile journey was completed with remarkable speed but when they reached the wagon fort they discovered that news of the Nuremberg riot had arrived before them.

The rumours that a Protestant mob had tried to stop a young girl from entering Holy Orders had given Dracul much cause for concern, so, whilst Ursula was returned to her *seraglio*, her chaperones were ordered to appear before the Grand Master at once.

Unlike their previous meetings, when a relaxed Dracul had drunk *kahve* and reclined on a divan, dressed in a loose robe, for this audience Ursula's father was wearing his black armour and was seated on a black throne decorated with gilded dragons. Dracul's lieutenant, Radu, stood to the left his master and, curiously, Prometheus was standing on the right.

The Grand Master looked as inscrutable as one of the carved serpents decorating his chair and whilst Prometheus seemed to be confused by his presence, Radu had the air of a man who'd bribed all the jurors at the trial of his most hated enemy. By the look on Radu's face, Thomas guessed they'd all been summoned to answer for their failure to protect Ursula, yet no one spoke until Dracul had recited a prayer to the Archangel Michael, judge of the damned and slayer of dragons.

"There's been talk of fighting in the imperial capital whilst you were there, so, tell me, was my daughter the girl who tried to renounce her sacred vows?" Dracul asked coldly. In reply, Thomas was about to lie as boldly as he dared but something told him that, in this instance, the truth might serve him better.

"No dastard assassin or vile traitor could stop me from saving your daughter from your enemies," Thomas cried and he began the story of Ursula kidnap.

Like a bored king being told a well-known tale by his troubadour, Dracul listened to the Englishman's highly edited narrative with a face of lead. However, when Thomas named Scaliger as the man responsible for perpetrating this outrage, he leapt to his feet.

"That snake had the temerity to lay his vile hands on the sacred person of my daughter?" Dracul exclaimed furiously but Thomas was quick to assure him that his daughter's confession before the Holy Virgin's relics in the *Frauenkirche* had given her ample spiritual protection during her ordeal.

"Have no fear, My Lord, your daughter is still full of God's grace," said Thomas, whereupon Dracul threw back his head and laughed.

Those standing before the Grand Master found this

suddenly change in Dracul's mood highly disconcerting. They couldn't forget that this was a man who thoroughly enjoyed inflicting the worst tortures on those who'd failed him. However, instead of ordering their painful execution, Dracul congratulated Thomas and the others for their ingenuity in delivering his daughter from Scaliger. Radu, on the other hand, stubbornly refused to add his plaudits to those of his master.

Looking like a jilted bride at her sister's wedding, Dracul's lieutenant reminded everyone of the principal reason for the expedition to Nuremberg and demanded to know if Thomas had conceived a plan to prise the Holy Lance from the clutches of the godless Hapsburgs.

"I hope you have good news, because, whilst you were dallying in Nuremberg's inns, the Sultan's army has marched to Adrianople! Now King Louis of Hungary has declared that all the Christian princes of the east must join his crusade to oppose Suleiman. So, if the Draconist cause is to succeed, Lord Dracul must have the relic before Louis can raise his rival banner," said Radu, and he commanded the Englishman to speak before Dracul had him flogged, but Thomas ignored the note of triumph in the little man's voice and announced that he could easily cut the Gordian knot that tied the Lance of St Maurice and St Longinus to the Holy Roman Emperor.

"My Lord, since the city authorities have banned the public display of the imperial relics, only the emperor and visiting kings may set eyes on the Holy Lance but this is to our advantage. If the casket containing our prize is to remain suspended halfway between heaven and earth, all we have to do is smuggle a ladder into the Church of the Holy Spirit and what we seek will be ours," said Thomas and he added that it had been seeing Scaliger's badge of a ladder that had given him the idea. Unfortunately this good omen did not impress Radu and he was quick to pour scorn on the Englishman's plan.

"By the great wolf's head of the Dacians, do you take us for fools? The monks guarding the casket may be half-blind and senile but even old men can spot a thirty foot ladder in the midst of their own church!" Radu cried, yet Thomas insisted that nothing was out of reach for those who had the courage to attempt the impossible.

"Our ladder won't look like a ladder, it will be disguised as a carrying chair," he said and he described how a portable throne, identical to the ceremonial litters used by popes, bishops and the rebel chief Little Heinrich, could be adapted to their purpose. Radu began to repeat his objections but Dracul held up his hand for silence and demanded to know more.

Ignoring Radu's hostile glances, Thomas insisted that all the thieves needed to do, in order to possess the Holy Lance, was to disguise themselves as a powerful foreign monarch and his entourage. As befitting his royal status, their king could insist that he was carried inside the church in his litter before being left alone to pray. Once the monks had withdrawn, the thieves could erect the ladder, open the casket, retrieve the Holy Lance and reassemble the carrying chair within minutes.

"When the vigil is ended, the Holy Lance can be smuggled out of the city hidden inside a secret compartment built into the chair. Best of all, because the casket must remain closed by law until the next imperial coronation, there's no need to substitute a fake for the genuine relic," said Thomas and though Dracul seemed to approve of the scheme, he insisted that the thieves still needed the counterfeit lance.

"The Emperor Charles despises Luther, and all those who follow him, so he may order the monks to revive the ceremony of the *Heiltumsweisungen* this coming Eastertide. If there's no lance to be paraded through the city, my plans will become known at a time not of my choosing and that's something I wish to avoid. Besides, I've already sent for the man who will craft the imitation," said Dracul and Radu quickly seized on his master's mild chastisement of the Englishman.

In a voice as cold as a witch's teat, Dracul's lieutenant demanded to know why Nuremberg's city council, or the monks who guarded the Holy Lance, would open their doors to a bogus king in the first place. Thomas, however, had the perfect answer for this question.

"Our king won't be a sham, for there's one among us who has the blue blood of princes flowing through his veins. Moreover, neither Nuremberg's city fathers nor the monks of the Holy Spirit will be able to refuse a request from a king who's also the heir of St Maurice," said Thomas and he looked directly at Prometheus.

Before Radu, or Prometheus, could voice their objections, Thomas reminded everyone present that the Roman soldier who'd carried the Holy Lance from Egypt to The Alps had been a native of the same country that their Nubian comrade had been born to rule. For a moment there was a hushed silence in the tent but the spell was broken by Dracul, who gave a rapturous cry of joy and turned his face to Heaven.

"By all the company of angels, I praise God for His great wisdom and I give thanks unto The Lord that He has sent the Blessed Maurice Reborn to stand beside me as my ally. I also swear on the graves of my ancestors, Vlad Dracul the Elder, his son Vlad Dracula and his son Mihnea, my father, that I will not rest until I've been crowned king of Christ's New Jerusalem!" Dracul exclaimed but Radu cried out in protest.

"My Lord, do you really think this heathen slave can convince people he's the fabled Prester John?" Radu sneered but the words died on his lips as Prometheus sprang at the underling and clamped his huge hands around Radu's throat.

"I'm no heathen slave, I'm Djoel, son of Djoel, a prince of the royal blood, true heir to the Three Kingdoms of Nubia and my people had accepted the Lord Jesus Christ as their Saviour long before your ancestors learned that their shit stank!" Prometheus roared as his victim clawed and kicked the air. In desperation, Radu fumbled for his dagger but Prometheus pressed his thumbs deeper into the wretch's windpipe and the blade slipped from the little man's grasp.

Once Radu's rodent eyes began to bulge in their sockets, Dracul should have intervened yet, strangely, he did nothing except smile. For longer than was strictly prudent, the Grand Master savoured his lieutenant's suffering and he only asked for Prometheus to spare the man once Radu's face had turned a deathly shade of blue.

"Calm yourself, 'Djoel son of Djoel'. Radu's tongue is loose but he means well and, besides, I like the Englishman's plan. It's ingenious, daring and worthy of men like us who were born in the purple," said Dracul and Prometheus accepted this acknowledgment of his rank as an apology. However, even though the Nubian released Radu, it took almost a minute for Dracul's lieutenant to find his voice.

"You would go into battle served by men such as this My Lord?" Radu croaked but this was exactly what the Grand Master had in mind.

"It's my destiny to be served by kings, for I am the King of Kings! When I present the true Holy Lance to my army, all will know that Francis, King of France, is a vile traitor; Louis King of Hungary is a young fool and the Emperor Charles is a shameless usurper, whose claim to the imperial throne is as worthless as the lump of iron we shall place in his precious casket!" Dracul cried and he ordered that work on the carrying chair must begin without delay.

This seemed to be the signal for a valet to enter the tent, bow low, and announce that a stranger was at the camp's gate. The news transported Dracul to new heights of elation and he commanded Thomas to bring this honoured guest into his presence at once.

Hiding his confusion, Thomas obediently hurried to the wagon fort's entrance. Here he saw a man on horseback and his servant, who was driving a large, four-wheeled cart, were waiting to be admitted. The rider was dressed in a luxurious mantle, trimmed with expensive fur, and his face boasted fine, handsome features framed by a neatly trimmed beard and unfashionably long hair. Thomas guessed that the new arrival was the craftsman Dracul had commissioned to fashion the replica lance. However, his eyes opened wide with surprise when he heard the forger's name.

"I am Albrecht Dürer of Nuremberg and I must attend the Grand Master of the Order of the Dragon without delay," the rider said in a soft, cultured voice.

Though they'd never met, Thomas felt as if he knew the man as well as his own brother. His tutor, Cornelius Agrippa, had claimed that no library could be called complete unless it boasted copies of all Dürer's books, so Thomas had spent many hours studying the great artist's treatises on mathematics, geometry, architecture and military fortifications.

Leaving Dürer's servant to argue with the gate's sentry over where his master's cart should be parked, Thomas escorted the artist through the camp. His guest said little as they walked to Dracul's wheeled palace but Thomas couldn't help wondering why such a celebrated man would risk journeying through a forest full of bandits and outlaws to meet a deluded madman like Lord Dracul.

Though Thomas had no doubt that Dürer possessed the necessary skills to make an exact copy of the Holy Lance, he also knew that the artist's talents had brought him immense wealth and an enviable reputation. Finally, the torture of ignorance was too much to bear and Thomas made bold to enquire why Dürer had answered Dracul's summons.

"Forgive me for speaking boldly, My Lord, but what brings you to this lonely forest?" Thomas asked.

"The Grand Master sent a message asking me to perform a task that will bring rewards more valuable than gold and more lasting than fame," Dürer replied.

This cryptic remark explained nothing and, before Thomas could interrogate the artist further, they'd reached Dracul's quarters. Ushering his guest inside, Thomas noticed that the others, including Radu, had been dismissed, yet, to his delight, he was invited to stay.

"Forget Da Vinci and Michelangelo. With brush or pen this man's skill exceeds that of the Italian poltroons in ways beyond measure! More importantly, he's one of us," said Dracul and he ordered the artist to unlace his shirt. Without a word, Dürer dutifully exposed his shoulder to reveal the faded mark of the *Ouroboros* seared into his flesh.

"My ancestors came from Transylvania and their name was Ajtósi. The word means door in the Magyar tongue, which becomes Dürer in German," he said quietly.

"This is the best of omens, because Master Dürer will open a door to the entire east," said Dracul with a rare smile and he began to explain precisely what he expected of the artist.

In a hushed voice, the Grand Master of the Order of the Dragon told Dürer that he planned to raise a new army of crusaders to fight the Turks but he needed the Holy Lance of St Maurice and St Longinus to ensure a Christian victory. However, because the avaricious Hapsburg emperor had repeatedly refused all requests to allow other princes to carry the Holy Lance into battle, it would be necessary to steal it and conceal its theft by placing a fake lance in the casket where the genuine relic was kept.

"The Emperor chooses to live in Spain, and cares nothing for the east, yet he believes that if the Holy Lance leaves Nuremberg his House of Hapsburg will fall. The fool is so blinded by his own selfishness, he can't see that the real threat to his empire is from the Sultan!" Dracul cried and he ordered Dürer to do all he could to further the Draconist cause.

In addition to creating an exact copy of the Holy Lance, Dracul instructed the artist to write a letter of introduction to Martin Geuder, one of Nuremberg's most important civic officers and a man whom Dürer knew well, recommending Prince Djoel to the city council.

"You'll say that this noble Prince of Nubia is a baptised Christian who's been living in Venice since his defeat and exile by heathens in the pay of the Turks. You'll also say that this virtuous prince wishes to drive the infidels from his homeland and seeks God's blessing for his crusade," said Dracul, at which the artist bowed and agreed to do what had to be done.

"I'll undertake this important work gladly but I may need a month to complete such difficult tasks," Dürer replied but Dracul insisted that time was a luxury that they couldn't afford.

"You have two weeks. Any longer and Suleiman will be quenching his thirst for blood in the taverns of Buda and Pest by Michaelmas Day," said Dracul but he added that Dürer could have all the men and money he required. Again, the artist bowed his head as he said that he'd begin the work immediately.

Within hours of the artist's arrival, the camp was engulfed in a fog of sulphurous smoke and the sound of hammering filled the air as the Draconist camp was transformed into an alchemist's laboratory. Just as Dracul had instructed, Dürer had brought crucibles to smelt metal, as well as wax and sand to make moulds. His cart carried bricks and ironwork to build a small forge and there were plenty of charcoal burners in the surrounding forest to supply fuel.

Though he knew nothing of the goldsmith's art, Thomas volunteered to assist Dürer because he was eager to study the magic that transformed bars of metal into something of value and beauty.

The distinguished artist was happy to show off the skills he'd learned from his father and he instructed Thomas in several techniques used by gold and silversmiths. The eager pupil learned how to draw silver into wire and beat tiny pieces of gold into squares as large as a kerchief. However, though the apprentice displayed some skill, only the master had the genius to fashion the replica lance.

To guide his hand, Dürer referred to sketches he'd made in preparation for a painting of the imperial crown jewels. This previous work had been commissioned by Nuremberg's council but now these drawings allowed Dürer to forge the counterfeit relic for Dracul with remarkable speed.

The first task was to turn a bar of iron into a slender blade about the length of a man's forearm and shaped like the leaf of a willow tree. This was easily done but to make the metal look almost twenty centuries old was much harder. To recreate the patina of centuries, Dürer placed the blade in a series of bowls filled with vinegar, warm salt water and cold freshwater.

The blade spent twenty-four hours in each of these baths and whilst the metal was being cured like a pickled gherkin, Dürer turned his attention to the various adornments that commemorated the transformation of the pagan Spear of Destiny into the Holy Lance that had pierced Christ's side.

According to legend, after his victory at the Milvian Bridge, the Emperor, Constantine the Great, had cut a slot into the centre of the blade to hold a nail from the True Cross and fastened it in place with knotted silver wire. Seven centuries later Constantine's successor, the Holy Roman Emperor, Henry IV, had added a silver band bearing the inscription:

*CLAVUS DOMINI HEINRICUS + D GR A
TERCIUS ROMANO IMPERATOR AUG HOC
ARGENTUM IUSSIT FABRICARI AD
CONFIRMATIONE CLAVI LANCEE SANCTI
MAURICII + SANCTUS MAURICIUS*

Though the Latin was clumsy, its meaning was clear; the sliver of metal that formed the blade's spine was:

*The nail of The Lord, and Henry, by Grace of God sublime emperor of the Romans, ordered this piece of silver made for attachment of the nail to the Holy Lance of St Maurice*

Curiously, the addition of this extra sanctification hadn't been enough for another Holy Roman Emperor. Two hundred and fifty years after Henry's death, the Emperor, Charles IV, had ordered the centre of the blade to be wrapped in a thin sleeve of beaten gold, inscribed with words:

## LANCEA ET CLAVUS DOMINI

The words meant: *the lance and nail of Our Lord* and Dürer recreated all these adornments with such meticulous attention to detail, even the intricate knots in the silver wire were reproduced with perfect accuracy.

All the while, Thomas watched the master craftsman at work with increasing admiration. He could never hope to match Dürer's abilities but he helped where he could and he soon became so engrossed in their momentous task he forgot all about Ursula.

Even without the distraction of his labours, just catching a glimpse of the girl had become impossible because Dracul now watched over his daughter's honour even more jealously than before her trip to Nuremberg. Until she could be returned to her convent, the wagon in which she was confined was guarded so closely not even a prayer could enter.

Though Ursula was forced to endure days of idleness, Bos, Prometheus and Quintana worked as hard as Thomas at their allotted tasks. Under Prometheus' direction, the camp women transformed the Draconists' long coats, voluminous breeches and high boots into the flowing robes of Africa.

Meanwhile, Quintana composed more letters to Nuremberg's city council to further bolster Prince Djoel's credentials.

These letters purported to be from a Portuguese merchant, who'd become the High Chamberlain of Prince Djoel's exiled court, and they declared that the Heir of St Maurice and Rightful King of Nubia wished to found a great order of chivalry to rid his homeland of all infidels.

· In the effusive language of diplomacy, Quintana proclaimed that Prince Djoel had been greatly impressed by tales of the Hospitaller and Templar Knights, who'd fought to recover the Holy Land for Christ, and His Royal Highness hoped that his new order of chivalry would restore the Christian churches in Egypt and Libya as well as Nubia. Furthermore, in honour of Prince Djoel and St Maurice's shared Nubian ancestry, these warrior monks would be called the Order of the Holy Lance.

To ensure the success of Prince Djoel's crusade, Quintana's letter humbly asked Nuremberg's city fathers to allow The Order's founder, together with its first four initiates, to conduct the necessary vigil and ceremonies of knighthood in the chapel where the Holy Lance was kept.

Having read Quintana's letters, few people could doubt that the Light of the Gospels would cease to shine in Africa unless the exiled Prince Djoel was allowed to dedicate his new order of knights to the relic which ensured victory in battle. Bos, however, was one of those who doubted the Portugee's wisdom.

"Nuremberg's Lutheran burghers won't take kindly to anything that resembles popish idolatry," he cautioned, yet Quintana told the Frisian to set aside his fears.

"The letter our long-haired friend has penned would convince Luther himself that Prince Djoel is his most ardent convert," he said and he showed Bos what Dürer had written to Herr Geuder.

The letter Dürer had written stated that Prince Djoel had come to believe that both the Orthodox and Roman

Churches had fallen into error and had been abandoned by God. As a result of this belief, His Royal Highness had appointed a Lutheran chaplain so he could be sure that he, and the people of Nubia, would worship in a manner most pleasing to The Lord after their liberation. Bos perused this letter with keen interest but when he read the last line, he frowned.

"It says here that Djoel has appointed a Lutheran to be his chaplain but who's this cuckoo trying to enter our nest?" Bos said irritably, whereupon the Portugee burst out laughing.

"It's you, you flatulent Frisian fool!" Quintana cried.

Once the letters had been written, Dracul sent them to the imperial capital and, whilst the plotters waited for a reply, work began on building Prince Djoel's carrying chair. Dracul graciously donated his own throne and its conversion into a royal *sedia gestatoria* was well within the talents of the camp's carpenters and seamstresses. The chair's seat was reupholstered in red velvet, and its black frame covered with gold leaf, before the chair was fitted to a platform with iron rings at each corner.

These rings held the chair's carrying poles and they measured more than twenty feet in length so the litter could be slung between a pair of horses or carried on the shoulders of a dozen men. To prevent the poles from slipping through the platform's rings, several grooves had been cut into the wood, but a number of these notches seemed to serve no purpose other than decoration. This unnecessary embellishment concerned Bos deeply and he warned Thomas that taking excessive pride in one's work was a sin.

"It is written in the Book of Proverbs that pride goeth before destruction and a haughty spirit before a fall. Such vainglorious decoration will weaken the wood and those poles are likely to break," said Bos, whereupon Thomas insisted that the extra notches were essential and their purpose would become clear once they were inside the Church of the Holy Spirit.

The chair's final adornment was a splendid ornamental canopy, made from more red velvet and decorated with expensive gold brocade. This baldachin was supported by four gilded wooden rods that fitted into more iron rings attached to the chair's legs, back and arms. The canopy was an essential badge of royal, or episcopal, rank but it could be easily removed if it offended the city's Lutheran council. Finally, the secret compartment that would be used to smuggle the replica lance into the church, and the genuine relic out, was installed below the chair's seat.

Everything was ready as soon as was humanly possible and on the day when the pious celebrate the martyrdom of St Lambert, Dürer and the four prospective thieves presented the Grand Master of the Order of the Dragon with a rosewood box containing the replica lance. Like a priest blessing The Host before Holy Communion, Dracul opened the box with great reverence and gazed at the forgery with as much wonder as if he were looking at the original.

"If I didn't know otherwise, I'd swear this was the blade that touched the body of Our Lord and brought forth His water and blood," he whispered and, as Dürer bowed low to acknowledge the compliment, a thought struck Quintana.

"Why go to all the trouble of substituting this fake for the original? If it's good enough to fool the monks who guard the real Holy Lance, your army won't know the difference and will follow you just the same," he said but, once again, the Grand Master's rage was ignited by a few seemingly innocent words. In the space of a heartbeat,

Dracul was transformed from a humble penitent into a vengeful archangel and, when he spoke, his voice sounded like the whisper of death.

"If I don't carry the true Holy Lance into battle, The Lord God Almighty won't fight on my side. The war with Sultan Suleiman will be lost before it has even begun and all Christians will be doomed to live in Turkish slavery until the Day of Judgement. Now do you understand the importance of this relic? I hope you do, because if any of you attempt to deceive me, I'll have you all impaled so slowly it'll take you a month to die," Dracul hissed and the Portugee felt his bowels turn to water.

"Forgive me, My Lord, I didn't know what I was saying," Quintana managed to mumble. Dracul, however, had already turned his attention back to Dürer and his former good humour instantly returned. The Grand Master was not only fulsome in his praise for the replica relic, he congratulated the artist on the letter of introduction he'd written.

"This very morning, I received a most courteous reply from Nuremberg and Herr Geuder has granted everything for which we have asked. Not only has he given permission for Prince Djoel to pray before the Holy Lance, he states that any such a vigil must be conducted in a way that does not violate the city's ban on the public worship of relics!" Dracul said happily. The others looked at each other in confusion but Thomas quickly grasped the implication of this condition.

"You mean Nuremberg's illustrious city fathers have insisted that Prince Djoel seeks God's blessing and guidance in private?" Thomas said in surprise. He was scarcely able to believe this good fortune but, before any of the others could comment on the foolishness of the imperial capital's authorities, Dracul urged caution.

"The Lord, in His infinite wisdom, has rewarded our courage but we must hasten to press our advantage. Those who are to recover our prize must leave for Nuremberg at first light, whilst I go east to prepare for the Ritual of Rebirth," said the Grand Master and he explained that there was a great deal to be done before the Holy Lance could be revealed to his new army of warriors for Christ.

"You'll not go with us to Nuremberg, My Lord?" Dürer said in surprise and, in reply, Dracul told the artist that their parting, though necessary, would be brief.

"When you have the Holy Lance you must journey to Hungary and meet me on the Plain of Pannonia. Radu knows the place and he will guide you," replied the Dracul and he repeated that if Thomas or any of the others broke their oath by failing to bring the genuine relic with them, there'd be no place on earth safe from the Order of the Dragon's wrath.

# 14
## PRINCE DJOEL

As before, the speed with which the Draconists broke camp was astonishing. In the twilight hour before dawn, all the dome-shaped tents were dismantled and packed onto the carts that had formed the wagon fort's walls so, by sunrise, only a circle of muddy grass at the centre of the forest clearing showed that the camp had ever existed.

The long, serpentine column looked like the biblical Israelites crossing the wilderness as it headed south, yet their progress was surprisingly swift. With the arrival of April the weather had turned warm, the roads had ceased to be impassable quagmires and the Draconists reached the last crossroads before Nuremberg in just three days.

Where the road divided, Dracul separated his followers into two groups. The larger group, which included the Draconists' women, children and most of the men, would go with the Grand Master and make a new camp east of Buda, the Hungarian capital.

The smaller group, comprising of the thieves and two dozen riders under Radu's command, would continue to the imperial capital. Furthermore, to act as Prince Djoel's guide and interpreter, Dürer was ordered to travel with the Nubian's entourage, who were now disguised as fearsome desert warriors.

After staining their pale European skin with walnut juice, the Draconists assigned to Prince Djoel had wrapped strips of white linen around their heads to make turbans and their long riding coats had been quilted to look like the padded armour used by African horsemen. These clothes, together with curved sabres tucked into their broad sashes, and strings of brightly coloured woollen tassels tied to their horses' bridles, turned Dracul's Wallachian *hussars* into an escort fit for a prince of faraway Nubia.

In addition to his riders, the heir of St Maurice would be accompanied by Thomas, Bos, Quintana and Radu. These four men would be the first to be inducted into the 'Order of the Holy Lance' and in this mummery the apostate seminarian, Bos, would play the role of Prince Djoel's Lutheran chaplain, whilst Quintana would pretend to be the Portuguese merchant who'd become head of the Nubian court in exile.

To add substance to the illusion, Bos had dressed in a cleric's white surplice and black cap, whilst Quintana had donned the expensive silks and furs of a man high in royal favour. These costumes had been provided by Dracul's own wardrobe and the Grand Master found something particularly special for Thomas and Radu.

It had been decided that the Englishman and Dracul's lieutenant should play the captains of Prince Djoel's Praetorian Guard, so they, too, had stained their hands and faces with walnut juice. However, instead of dressing in the simple garb of desert horsemen, they wore expensive suits of Turkish armour. These exotic harnesses had been taken from two of the sultan's *sipahi* cavalrymen which Dracul had killed with his own hand.

The mix of mail and plate armour with which Thomas and Radu clad themselves, came complete with oriental helmets decorated with long spikes and mail visors that covered most of the wearer's face. Apart from adding further veracity to their deception, Thomas' visor would prevent anyone from recognising him as the man who'd led the mob that had saved an unwilling nun from a life of misery in the cloister.

Once the metamorphosis was complete, the desert riders said goodbye to their families and watched them join their comrades on the road that led east. Thomas also watched the Draconists' wagons trundle away and realised that he couldn't be sure if Ursula was with them.

As there was a strong possibility that the girl had already been returned to her convent, Thomas began to imagine himself riding to Ursula's nunnery and carrying off Christ's reluctant bride. However, his daydream was interrupted Quintana who announced that Prince Djoel was waiting for the captain of his guard to assume his post. With a grunt of irritation, Thomas put aside all thoughts of Ursula and hurried to join the procession.

The carrying chair had been slung between two of Dracul's sturdiest horses and Prometheus was already seated on his mobile throne. As befitting his princely rank, he wore a golden circlet around his head, though this diadem had been fashioned from polished brass rather than pure gold.

Besides his simple crown, Prometheus wore a voluminous robe of yellow linen, gathered at the waist by a red silk sash. His beard and hair had been curled with hot irons and this led Bos to remark that their companion resembled Belshazzar at his feast, but it was as Djoel II, Prince of Dotawo and Rightful Lord of Nubia's Three Kingdoms, that Prometheus gave the order to march.

Though the imperial capital had welcomed countless foreign embassies in the past, the visit of such a mysterious monarch had aroused unprecedented curiosity in Nuremberg's citizens. The news had also done much to unite the city divided by the recent riot and, by the time the Nubian prince and his party appeared on the horizon, a large crowd had gathered in front of the city's southern gate. The host of excited townsfolk lined both sides of the road for almost quarter of a mile and as the royal procession approached, they cheered as wildly as the people of Jerusalem had cheered Jesus.

In reply, Prince Djoel's herald sounded a long, silver trumpet and the party came to a halt at the far end of the wooden bridge over the city's moat. Besides the throng of unruly plebeians, fifty of Nuremberg's most worthy patricians waited to greet their royal guest and, once the fanfare had died away Dürer and Quintana, crossed the bridge to present Prince Djoel's diplomatic credentials.

The celebrated artist introduced Quintana, who looked magnificent in his luxurious ambassadorial robes, to each member of the imperial capital's council, the heads of Nuremberg's ancient families and the elders of the city's protestant churches. The wealthy noblemen and civic dignitaries had also dressed in their finest clothes and were mounted on sleek, richly caparisoned horses but the Lutheran preachers wore nothing but their plain black robes and went on foot.

Strangely, considering Prince Djoel's request to pray in Nuremberg's last Catholic monastery, the abbot of the Hospital of the Holy Spirit was nowhere to be seen but his absence was no accident. It was the council's avowed intent to establish Nuremberg as a free, Protestant city, so they meant to use Prince Djoel's visit to challenge both papal and imperial authority.

The defeat of the peasants' revolt had done nothing to deter the twenty-six civic fathers from openly questioning the rule of their absentee emperor. Therefore, in an extraordinary general meeting of the city council, they'd voted overwhelmingly in favour of opening Nuremberg's gates to this powerful foreign potentate and the task of helping Prince' Djoel establish his Order of the Holy Lance had been entrusted to Martin Geuder.

Herr Geuder was the magistrate responsible for supervising the city's religious buildings and his task had not been easy. The abbot of the Church and Hospital of the Holy Spirit was as stubborn as Balaam's ass and he'd refused to allow heretics to enter his church. In the end, Geuder had been forced to threaten the priest with the dissolution of his monastery unless he co-operated.

Faced with the final extinction of Holy Mother Church in Nuremberg, the abbot had agreed to the ceremony but he'd insisted that the casket containing the imperial relics must remain suspended in mid-air at all times and that the monks must be allowed to interrupt the crusaders' knightly vigil to say their own nightly offices of Vigils and Matins.

For once, Geuder was in complete agreement with the venerable abbot as he too considered the prohibition on lowering the reliquary to be a wise precaution. Prince Djoel might be an important guest but neither the abbot nor the magistrate was so foolish as to trust a complete stranger with the city's most precious possessions.

Few of those watching their civic and spiritual guardians greet Prince Djoel and his chamberlain were aware of the complex negotiations that had taken place prior to their arrival and they applauded loudly as Quintana offered his master's warmest greetings to all the citizens of Nuremberg.

"My Sovereign Lord, who begs nothing more than to be a humble pilgrim in your illustrious city, has asked me to extend to you his sincerest and most heartfelt hope that his visit will usher in a new era of lasting friendship and brotherhood between two great Christian peoples!" Quintana cried. In reply, Geuder declared that he was delighted to welcome His Most Noble Majesty, before saying, with unintentional irony, that he hoped Prince Djoel would find what he sought in Nuremberg.

"If St Maurice's heir seeks friends and allies, he will discover the people of this city are most anxious to join his quest to rid God's world of despots and heretics," Geuder cried and, with the diplomatic niceties completed, he invited Prince Djoel to attend a feast to be held in his honour at Nuremberg's castle.

Whenever important personages visited the principal city of the Holy Roman Emperor's German domains, they were lodged in the imperial fortress, which occupied a high crag on the northern side of Nuremberg, and Geuder was determined that his royal guest should be no exception. With a score of drummers and flag bearers leading the way, Geuder escorted Prince Djoel and his entourage across the city and, much to his satisfaction, the crowds lining the streets gave the foreign dignitaries a truly imperial welcome.

Even those who'd shown no interest in the Nubian prince's arrival stopped their chatter and put down their tools to see the living embodiment of St Maurice pass by. Little girls waved at this mysterious king, who waved politely back, whilst wide-eyed boys imagined themselves fighting the fearsome soldiers of his escort. Accompanied by the crowd's jubilant cries, the procession wound its way through Nuremberg and Thomas was relieved to see that most of the city had survived the riot he'd started.

The damage from the fire was limited to the area around the Lorenzer Platz, where the haberdasher's shop was among the dozen wooden buildings that had been burned to the ground, and as Thomas rode past the smoke-blackened walls of Scaliger's tower, he began to wonder what had happened to its owner. It seemed likely that Scaliger was either in a dungeon or his grave, but, after seeing the abandoned fortress, Thomas couldn't help thinking that the scheming spy had escaped.

From the Lorenzer Platz, Prince Djoel and his escorts made their way to the steep, serpentine street that led to the Nuremberg's castle and Thomas was surprised to find that the emperors' official residence formed only one part of the fortress's sprawling array of towers, chapels and ramparts. Besides the imperial palace, called the *Kaiserburg*, there was the old Burgrave's Castle and rising above them both was the *Kaiserstallung*. Though this massive building looked like a keep, it actually housed the imperial stables and public granaries.

Once Prince Djoel and his men had dismounted, the riders were taken to barracks near the colossal round tower of the Sinwellturm, though the Nubian prince together with his chamberlain, chaplain and captains of his guard, were shown to rooms close to the emperor's private chapel. Here, the visitors were left to prepare themselves for the forthcoming feast but there was barely time to wash the dirt from their faces before they were summoned to the castle's banqueting hall.

The great feast Geuder had arranged to welcome Nubia's exiled prince proved to be the hardest test yet for the plotters. Fortunately, despite becoming befuddled with drink, they all played their parts beautifully. As the wine flowed, Prometheus, who was overjoyed to be using his baptismal name of Djoel once more, told stirring tales of how his people had defended their homes against Eastern Africa's heathen tribes and his hosts wept when they heard how Christian Nubia had fallen.

Though Prince Djoel's ancestors had kept the dark forces of idolatry at bay for centuries, eventually a tribe called the Funj had succeeded in conquering all the Christian nations of the Upper Nile.

The kingdom of Dotawo had been the last to succumb to this pagan people from the marshes of the south and so, though the fabled Æthiops, who lived beyond the Mountains of the Moon, still worshipped in the name of Jesus, the Good News of The Gospels was no longer heard in Nubia.

The exiled prince's tale of woe was no lie and nor was the revelation that his father, also named Djoel, had died fighting the invaders when his son had been little more than a child. With his eyes full of tears, the younger Djoel related how most Nubians had lost the will to resist after his father's death and this had enabled the Funj to be victorious. In defeat, the young prince had been carried to safety by a band of loyal followers, who'd hidden Dotawo's heir in a remote desert monastery, but their numbers had been too few to drive out the Funj.

At first, Nubia's conquerors had been content to worship their pagan gods. However, after the Turks had subjugated neighbouring Egypt, the king of the Funj had accepted Islam in a desperate attempt to preserve his own independence.

With all the zeal of a convert, this tyrant had persecuted his Christian subjects and hunted the young Prince Djoel across the burning deserts of Nubia. Once the boy had grown to manhood, he'd continued his father's fight; until a traitor had revealed the prince's hiding place and he'd been forced to flee to Venice.

Though there was a great deal more to tell, Prometheus was careful not to destroy the heroic illusion he'd created by revealing the ignominy of his arrival in Venice. Whilst it was true that he'd fought the Funj invaders bravely, after his betrayal and capture he'd been sold as a slave to a Barbary corsair. Prometheus should've ended his days chained to the oar of a galley, yet Fate had intervened and he'd been freed during a fierce battle between the corsairs and a Venetian fleet.

As a Christian, Prometheus had been allowed to settle in Venice but, as no one had believed that he was an exiled prince, he'd been forced to eke out a living as a prize-fighter. In the ring, he'd been known as 'Prometheus the African Titan', yet he rarely discussed this episode in his life and, before anyone could enquire further, he'd stood to give a toast.

"I'm grateful to you and your city for giving me sanctuary but I cannot rest until the Turks, and their Funj allies have been destroyed. Only when all of Africa has accepted the Lord Jesus Christ as their saviour and returned to the Communion of Saints will my vow be fulfilled. This is the oath I took on the grave of my father, and this is the oath I shall swear before the Holy Lance, that was once carried by my forebear, St Maurice!" Prometheus cried and he drained his cup whilst his hosts' cheers echoed around the hall's rafters.

The feasting continued for many hours, during which time Prince Djoel, Bos and Quintana ate and drank their fill, but Thomas and Radu didn't partake of the splendid dishes and fine wines being served. In keeping with their roles of loyal captains of Prince Djoel's personal guard, the two men stood either side of their master's chair and watched the proceedings as impassively as the stone sphinxes that guarded the pyramids of Meroe.

Both men wore their suits of mail and hidden behind his helmet and visor, Thomas could listen to the various conversations. He was desperate for news of Scaliger and it wasn't long before Geuder began to boast of a great victory the city's Lutherans had won over a dastardly agent of the pope.

"Some rascally French bishop sent his mewling cats-paw to spy on us but, when he tried to force an innocent girl to enter a convent against her will, we soon sent him packing. I'll wager the pox-riddled papist won't stop running until he's on the other side of the Alps!" Geuder slurred. The strong Franconian wine was making Nuremberg's supervisor of religious affairs talk a little too freely but Prince Djoel, who professed that he also had no love for the Popes of Rome, was delighted to hear such news.

"Those who embrace Luther's teachings are blessed by God and when I'm restored to my kingdom, all his followers shall share in the wealth of Africa!" Prince Djoel declared and he reminded the city fathers that the legendary mines of Solomon were located within the borders of his realm. There and then, Prince Djoel decreed that only Nuremberg's merchants would be allowed to trade with his liberated subjects and only Lutheran priests would be allowed to preach in Nubia's restored churches.

These proclamations produced another round of boisterous cheering, whereupon His Noble Highness begged his hosts' permission to withdraw, as he was overcome with fatigue. The burghers repeated their thanks that such a mighty prince had chosen to grace their city with his presence but Dürer said his farewells. The artist wouldn't be among those initiated into the Order of the Holy Lance; however he promised to commemorate this historic event on a vast canvas that would later hang in Nuremberg's city hall.

As Prince Djoel and his retinue returned to their quarters, Thomas wondered if Dürer had made himself scarce in case their plot unravelled but he couldn't blame him for that. If their true purpose became known, they'd all die agonising deaths, yet even with thoughts of the rack and noose filling their minds, the thieves slept soundly. Most of the following day was spent in private meditation, and waiting for darkness to fall, because the ceremony that would inaugurate the Order of the Holy Lance could only begin once the sun had set.

In accordance with the ancient rules of chivalry, the initiates were bathed and dressed in the robes of squires preparing for knighthood. In homage to death, the men wore black shoes and hose. To represent purity, they put on plain white habits, and to proclaim they were of noble blood, yet humble in the sight of God, they donned red cloaks with the hoods pulled over their heads to hide their faces from the Devil. The squires' new spurs, broadswords and white shields, emblazoned with a yellow cross symbolising the desert sun, were a gift from Nuremberg's council and these would be carried by pages as the knights-elect proceeded to their vigil.

Though he was dressed as a warrior monk, Prince Djoel was still of royal rank, so the gilded litter was fetched to carry him to the ceremony. However, as a mark of his humility, the portable throne was now carried by eight Draconists on foot instead of being slung between two horses.

As His Most Noble Highness took his seat, Bos said a prayer and torches were lit so the procession became a river of light flowing from the imperial palace to the Church of the Holy Spirit.

The spectacle looked even more magnificent than Prince Djoel's entry into the city and it was watched by even larger crowds of happy, singing citizens. The religious strife of the last few months had been forgotten and for this one night the people of Nuremberg revelled in the sort of festival that had been abolished by their new spiritual guardians.

With so many people crowding the streets, it took an hour for the procession to reach the Church of the Holy Spirit but eventually the Nubian Prince and his escort arrived at Nuremberg's only remaining monastery. The abbot who'd reluctantly agreed to host the ten hour vigil stood on the steps of his church, and listened patiently as Herr Geuder introduced his guest, but if the priest still resented the bullying he'd suffered at the hands of his Lutheran enemies, he was Christian enough not show it.

"May I welcome St Maurice's heir to this House of God. Please enter in peace," said the abbot as the litter and ornaments of knighthood were carried inside.

Once the ceremonial swords, spurs and shields had been placed on the altar, and the litter set down, the servants withdrew, leaving their master to be attended by his four knights-elect. With heads bowed low, and hands clasped in prayer, Prince Djoel and the other initiates walked up the church's aisle in silence but when they reached the chancel's entrance they gasped in wonder. To mark the birth of the Order of the Holy Lance, hundreds of candles had been placed in a circle below the casket containing the imperial relics and their flickering light made it shine like the Star of Bethlehem.

"Is the Holy Lance inside there?" Quintana whispered as he gazed at the reliquary. His question was meant for Thomas but it was answered by the abbot, who was issuing a warning.

"Not only is the Holy Lance one of the Instruments of Our Lord's Passion, it has been carried by every Holy Roman Emperor since Charlemagne. Its value is therefore beyond measure, so I must insist that, during your vigil, no man enters the circle of light beneath the reliquary," said the abbot and he gestured towards the candles under the casket.

"Though I would dearly love to see the Holy Lance with my own eyes, I shall follow the example of my countryman St Maurice and obey the will of God with joy in my heart," Prince Djoel replied humbly and the abbot smiled at the mention of the Holy Roman Emperors' favourite saint.

"Indeed, Maurice is venerated by all those who know that serving Christ often requires the supreme sacrifice. The saint understood that his duty to God was to live as a soldier yet die as a man of peace and that is why he intercedes on behalf of all those who must lead armies in the search for an end to war," the abbot replied and he invited the men to kneel whilst a mass was said asking God to bestow his blessing on their quest.

As the rest of the monastery's monks filed into choir stalls, the crusaders knelt on the cold, marble floor and listened to the processional hymn that began the service. Within minutes, their knees began to ache with dull pain but, during the next two hours, Thomas and the others suffered the agony of mental as well as physical torture.

For what seemed like an eternity, the monks sang their psalms, and begged forgiveness for the sins of mankind, yet all the while, the thieves were thinking of how to break God's commandment not to steal.

At last the final blessing was said and, in accordance with their rule of keeping silent after the last prayers of the day, the monks neither spoke nor sang as they retired to their dormitory. All that remained was for the chapel's sacristan to start the water clock that counted off the hours until the monks returned to keep the next office.

This clock was kept in its own room to the right of the altar and was closed off from the rest of the apse by a heavy iron grill. The sacristan had to unlock a door in this cage to enter and reset the device, which looked like a huge pair of scales.

One end of this balance was positioned over of a wooden water butt and chains fastened to this end of the beam were also attached to a heavy brass bowl, which had sunk to the barrel's bottom. Above the opposite end of the balance, a large bell had been hung.

The sacristan retrieved the brass bowl, emptied it and placed it carefully on the water's surface so that it floated. However, the bowl had a tiny hole in its base so it would slowly refill with water; when the bowl sank, the other end of the beam would rise and strike the bell.

Once he'd reset the clock, the sacristan locked the cage before withdrawing to his cell and as Thomas watched him go, he realised this was the bell that had woken him whilst he was lying in his sickbed. He toyed with the idea of breaking into the cage to stop the clock but decided against it. Provided they worked swiftly, there was plenty of time for the thieves to complete their task before the monks came back.

"I reckon we have no more than an hour before the abbot returns to say Vigils," said Bos, echoing Thomas' own thoughts.

"Then we must proceed without delay," he said and others agreed that they should act before fatigue robbed them of their strength. With the fateful decision made, the men stripped off their stifling hoods and retrieved the carrying chair from the back of the church.

Ignoring the abbot's request to stay outside the circle of candles, the five men carried the portable throne, which was surprisingly heavy, to a point directly below the reliquary, but they hesitated before beginning the next phase of their operation. Only when they were all certain that no alarm had been raised did the thieves start to dismantle the chair.

Leaving his comrades to slide the carrying poles, together with the rods supporting the chair's canopy, out of their iron rings, Thomas fetched one of the swords from the altar and used it to cut the brocade from the canopy's red velvet cloth into a number of separate pieces. Whilst the others fitted the thinner rods into the extra 'decorative' notches cut into the chair's carrying poles, Thomas took some of the gilded rope and tied each rod firmly in place.

Once this had been done, the whole structure was lifted up and, using the rest of the brocade, lashed to the back of the chair. The result of the thieves' frantic labour was a ladder that reached to a point just below the top of the reliquary and even Radu had to admit that the Englishman's solution to the problem of reaching the Holy Lance was ingenious.

"By the great fangs of the Dacian Wolf, with a dozen of these devices I could storm the walls of Constantinople," said Dracul's lieutenant appreciatively. Bos, however, had much less faith in the flimsy and highly unstable structure.

"Are you insane, Englishman? That ludicrous construction will tip over the moment anyone tries to climb it," he said with a snort of disdain but Thomas insisted that the ladder would be perfectly stable if the others sat on the throne and used their combined weight as a counterbalance.

"The Englishman's right, not even God's grace could move a stubborn Frisian once he's sat on his fat arse," said Quintana. In reply, Bos ignored the insult and demanded to know who was going to climb the ladder.

"As I'm no angel, don't ask me to ascend to heaven by this death trap," he said, so Quintana volunteered Radu, who was easily the lightest of the five men in the church. However, Dracul's lieutenant pointed out that he was not tall enough to reach the casket even if he stood on the top rung of the ladder.

"God made me as I am and you as you are," he said bitterly and this prompted Bos to remark that Quintana should rise to the challenge.

"Seamen spend their lives climbing ladders, so the honour should go to the Portugee, who's always boasting about his time at sea," he said, yet it was Thomas who settled the matter by insisting that the task needed a thief as well as a sailor.

"The casket is certain to be locked and only you have the skills to open a lock without leaving a mark," he said and he produced a roll of cloth from beneath his robes. This parcel contained several metal hooks, which looked like the probes used by surgeons to dig bullets out of wounded flesh, but Quintana recognised them as a set of locksmith's tools.

"Where in the name of St Nicholas' beard did you get those?" he gasped, but, before Thomas could answer, Prometheus spoke. The Nubian had taken no part in the others' discussion about who should scale the ladder, instead he'd been keeping a close eye on the water clock and now the brass bowl was more than half full.

"I estimate that we've less than half an hour before the monks' return, so whoever is to climb the ladder had better make a start," he said, whereupon Quintana sighed and bowed to the inevitable. Whilst Thomas had been studying alchemy and Bos learning his catechism, the orphaned Portugee was being schooled by some of the best thieves in Lisbon, so he took the lock picks and began to undress.

As Quintana couldn't hope to climb the ladder dressed in his knightly robes, he stripped to his hose whilst Radu retrieved the replica lance from its secret compartment. The church was cold but the Portugee was sweating as he opened the rosewood box and took out the fake. Even though the blade was a forgery, its golden sleeve glittered in the candlelight and it looked hauntingly beautiful.

Without a word, Quintana wrapped the replica in the cloth containing the lock picks, tied the bundle around his waist and turned to the ladder. The distance to the casket was not all that great; however, if he fell, he'd most likely break his neck or dash out his brains on the unforgiving stone floor. With a shiver, Quintana put such thoughts from his mind, took a deep breath and began to climb.

Like a stilt walker at a country fair, Quintana grasped the ladder's upright poles, rather than its horizontal rungs, and he placed his feet as close to the bindings as he could. In this way his weight pushed the poles apart, tightening the knots and making the structure work for, instead of against, him but he still had to use all his strength to negotiate the considerable gap between each of the ladder's four rungs. The perspiration ran down the Portugee's back from the exertion, and his stomach tied itself in knots in anticipation of imminent disaster, but at last he made it to the top.

By standing on the highest rung of the makeshift ladder, Quintana could easily reach the casket's sloping lid. Unfortunately, just as Thomas had predicted, there was an enormous padlock protecting its contents. Cursing his luck, Quintana began to fumble for the lock picks but, as he did so, he realised that this was no ordinary padlock.

In place of a keyhole, there was a row of seven octagonal wheels set into the lock's hasp and the different faces of each wheel were marked with a different letter of the alphabet. To open the lock, the wheels had to be turned to spell out a word.

"Hurry, the abbot and his monks could return at any minute," Prometheus whispered loudly.

High above the Nubian's head, Quintana tried to quell the panic rising in his gorge, but it was an unequal fight, and he cried out in desperation.

"The damned casket's fastened by a coded lock and I've no idea of the password. Can any of you think of something?" Quintana wailed but the others' replies were of little help.

"I think you should be quiet before you raise the alarm," growled Prometheus

"Whatever you do, don't try and force the lock because that will betray the theft," added Radu.

"Just keep trying different words," suggested Bos.

"I've no skill in codes and ciphers, that's Thomas' affair. Let him try!" Quintana snapped.

"All right, come down but, for all our sakes, be quiet. The sacristan will be listening for the clock's bell," Thomas whispered and the Portugee didn't have to be told twice.

Whilst Quintana returned to earth, Thomas stripped off his own vestments and as soon as he'd been given the bag containing the fake lance, he took his place on the ladder. The Englishman was no sailor, and the ladder's rungs cut into the soles of his feet like a Spanish torturer's bastinado, but he gritted his teeth against the pain and struggled to the top. Once confronted with the lock, he forced his mind to ignore the discomfort and concentrate on unravelling the code.

The keyword had to be seven letters long, to match the seven wheels, but if the code was a random jumble of letters he could be in Nuremberg until the Second Coming and not guess the answer.

On the other hand, a complex code would be too hard for simple minded monks to remember, so the key had to be a single, significant word. Thomas' first thoughts were to try the names of the city's main churches but then he remembered that both SEBALD and LORENZ contained only six letters.

Undeterred, Thomas began to think of other saints who might have a special significance for Nuremberg and he suddenly realised that the man who'd brought the Holy Lance to Europe had seven letters to his name. Feverishly, he turned the wheels to spell M-A-U-R-I-C-E and tugged at the padlock but it remained firmly closed.

"By the bloodstained ball sack of the castrated Cronos, get a move on! The monks will be back any second," Bos hissed from below but this was the last thing that Thomas needed to hear. The note of urgency in his comrade's voice only served to wipe every rational thought from the Englishman's head and he replied by cursing the Frisian for doing nothing to help.

"Don't just stand there like a eunuch in a harem, at least try and fix the water clock so that damned bell doesn't ring," Thomas cried. Without thinking, he turned to see if there was any tangible sign of the monks' return and, as he did so, he began to lose his equilibrium. Instinctively Thomas tried to shift his weight to re-balance the ladder but his jerky movements caused the structure to sway even more violently and there could only be one outcome.

After a brief struggle with the uneven forces being imposed upon them, the lashings holding the ladder's vertical poles to the chair's frame snapped and the whole structure came clattering to the ground. The others gasped as they waited for Thomas to fall but the Englishman remained floating in the void, his feet kicking like a hanged man.

At the last moment, Thomas had managed to grasp the iron chain holding the casket but, as the others tried to think of a way to bring him down, the sound of the clock's alarm bell echoed around the empty church.

# 15
## THE HOLY LANCE

The water clock's bell was followed by another, fainter ringing, which came from the direction of the monks' dormitory. This, the thieves realised, was the sound of the sacristan rousing the other friars from their slumbers and the noise of the discordant clanging filled them terror.

"The monks will be back soon, so what are we going to do about Thomas?" Prometheus asked and he looked up at the Englishman, who was still dangling from the casket's chain and kicking his feet like a frog trying to swim across a pond.

"Get me down, I can't hold on much longer!" Thomas hissed. Unfortunately, the ladder was in ruins and there was no time to make even simple repairs.

"Climb on top of the casket. If you lie still, no one will be able to see you," Bos suggested and the sound of the monks' rhythmic chants drifting into the church ended the discussion. With fear fuelling his aching muscles, Thomas managed to haul himself onto the casket. However, once he'd reached this precarious position, he had to lie flat and grip the lid's sloping sides with his hands and knees to stop himself from sliding off.

Leaving Thomas to conceal himself as best he could, the others returned the carrying chair to the darkness at the back of the church.

Though a close inspection would reveal considerable damage to both the chair's frame and its canopy, a casual glance wouldn't arouse suspicion. When all was as it should be, Prince Djoel and his attendants replaced their hoods and resumed to their kneeling positions beneath the casket. It was only then that Bos realised that Thomas' absence had reduced the number of knights-elect by one.

"Wait, the Order of the Holy Lance is missing one of its initiates!" Bos cried and he dashed to a life-sized, wooden statue of St Luke, patron saint of doctors, which stood in a niche by the entrance to the church. The Evangelist was depicted kneeling in prayer, so Bos dragged the heavy image to the spot where Thomas should have been and threw the Englishman's discarded robe over its painted wooden head. In the candlelight, the covered statue might just pass for a man asking for God's blessing. Nevertheless, Bos prayed that the old abbot's eyes were not as sharp as they'd once been.

The decoy was finished just in time and as soon as the initiates had bowed their heads to resume their devotions, the first of the monks appeared at the top of the chapel's night stairs. The nave and chancel were instantly filled with plaintive singing and as the friars took their places in the choir stalls, the abbot walked over to the kneeling men. The priest knew better than to disturb those at prayer, so he merely pronounced the Pax Vobiscum and made the sign of the cross.

From his lofty perch Thomas watched this tableau, feeling like an angel hovering over an old man's deathbed, yet the increasing pain in his chest and loins brought him back to his senses. The two sides of the casket's sloping top formed a sharp ridge that dug into his ribs and groin like the 'Spanish Donkey' and Thomas began to understand why prisoners of the Inquisition feared that torture device more than any other.

To add to Thomas' woes, he had to remain perfectly still because the slightest movement might set the casket swinging. Any creak of the iron chain, or the casket's shadow creeping across the chancel's floor, was bound to alert the monks; yet keeping himself motionless presented new dangers.

The act of remaining as lifeless as a corpse took a surprising amount of energy and this effort, combined with the warm air rising from the hundreds of candles below, caused sweat to form on the end of Thomas' nose.

Whilst he was struggling to grasp the casket's polished sides, he could do nothing to wipe the annoying droplet away and eventually it fell. Thomas watched in silent agony as the drop of sweat sped towards the abbot's tonsured head, then, at the last second, the priest finished his blessing and turned to face the altar.

Alone in the shadows, Thomas breathed a sigh of relief as the drop of sweat hit the floor, yet he still had to endure another half-hour of turgid ritual.

In an effort to fight the numbing pain that was slowly seizing his entire body, he turned his thoughts back to the coded lock and wondered if the password protecting the sacred symbols of the German Reich might have something to do with the Holy Roman Emperors. One by one, Thomas tried to list all the imperial rulers he could think of: Otto ... Henry ... Frederick ... Charles!

The name Charles had seven letters and Thomas was convinced that he'd found the answer to the riddle. Unfortunately, the service wasn't over.

For the next half hour he had to remain perfectly still, with the key to the most priceless treasure in Christendom burning in his mind and the misery of cramp in his limbs. No inquisitor could've invented such exquisite torture but at last the abbot spoke the words of the dismissal and the monks retreated to their dormitory.

"Thomas, are you still there?" Quintana whispered once the monks had departed.

"I'm here and I think I've discovered the word that will unlock the casket!" Thomas replied.

In his excitement, the Englishman stretched his cramped and aching limbs but, as he did so, the casket started to sway alarmingly. Panic suddenly replaced his elation and, to prevent himself from falling, Thomas had to cling to the casket's chain for a second time. The iron links groaned in protest, until, after a few agonising seconds, the great silver reliquary came to rest once more.

As before, Thomas had to calm his pounding heart and quiet his trembling muscles before he could move. However, once the casket had settled into its former position, he managed to raise himself upright. Sitting astride the casket, he carefully turned the wheels of the padlock to spell the word CHARLES but when he tugged at the hasp, nothing happened.

Under his breath, Thomas groaned. He couldn't believe that he'd been wrong, because the man who currently occupied the throne of the Holy Roman Empire was Charles V. His antecedent, Charles IV, had added the relic's golden sleeve and the first man to wear the imperial crown was Charlemagne.

Though Thomas couldn't accept that these facts were a mere coincidence, as he tried to make sense of his miscalculation, he remembered that Roman Catholic monks always wrote in Latin.

To those who spent their lives in a monastery, the first emperor's name was not Charlemagne or even Charles the Great but Karolus Magnus and KAROLUS had the required seven letters. Trembling with exhilaration, Thomas turned the wheels to spell K-A-R-O-L-U-S and heard a faint click. Quelling the desire to whoop with joy, he removed the padlock and cautiously opened one side of the casket's sloping lid.

Inside were the imperial treasures and the hundreds of rubies, diamonds, emeralds and other precious stones which decorated each item seemed to glow like a myriad of fireflies. As his eyes grew accustomed to the shadows, Thomas could see a large bible with a cover of beaten gold, the imperial crown, sceptre and orb and several ceremonial swords. These included the sword of Otto IV in its gilded scabbard and the fabled blade that was once carried by both Attila the Hun and Charlemagne.

These priceless artefacts sat side by side with several smaller reliquaries, each of which had been carefully labelled. One gold vessel held a shaving from Christ's crib, whilst another contained one of the Baptist's teeth and a fragment of his robe. A third ornately decorated urn boasted a bone from the arm of St Anne and a fourth held a piece of the tablecloth used at the Last Supper.

Any one of these precious items was worth an emperor's ransom but Thomas was only interested in the cushion at the centre of the casket and the eighteen inches of dull iron nestling in its crimson velvet.

Hardly daring to breathe, he removed the cloth tied around his waist and unwrapped the forgery before reaching down and picking up the real Holy Lance. The genuine relic's metal felt colder to the touch than that of the fake but, when Thomas held the twin blades side by side, he couldn't really differentiate between them.

Having marvelled long enough at Dürer's skill, Thomas was about to place the forgery in the casket when he was interrupted by Radu.

"Do you have it?" Dracul's lieutenant whispered.

"Yes, I have the Holy Lance in my hand and whilst I make the exchange, you can think of a way to get me down from this harpies' perch," Thomas snapped but he was barely able to conceal his elation. He looked again at the two blades. They were absolutely identical and, for a moment, even he didn't know which was which.

"Will you get a move on, you're being slower than Methuselah's grandfather taking a piss!" Quintana said irritably but Thomas was too busy to chide the Portugee for his impatience.

After wrapping one of the blades inside his cloth bag, and tying it across his chest like a bandolier, he laid the other on the velvet cushion before closing the casket's lid and refastening the lock. With this done, Thomas looked down to see that Bos, Prometheus, Quintana and Radu were now standing directly underneath the casket and they were each holding a corner of the cloth from the carrying chair's canopy.

"As your precious ladder's broken, and we've no tools to mend it, this is the best we can do. So jump, unless you're afraid," said Radu, with an ill-disguised sneer, but Thomas refused to be goaded by a schoolboy insult.

"Are you mad? That rag will be my shroud," he cried, yet the others were adamant that they could catch him.

"Put your faith in God and all will be well," urged Bos.

"You flew from The Hornberg's tower and that was a great deal higher than your present eyrie," said Prometheus. Thomas wanted to remind the others that he'd spent weeks making a pair of artificial wings before attempting that desperate leap but, as there was nothing to be gained by waiting, he merely shouted a warning and launched himself into space.

A heartbeat later, Thomas felt soft velvet caress his cheek but this was followed by the unyielding hardness of the chapel's floor smashing into his spine. Though his precipitous fall had been slowed by the cloth, the force of the impact had wrenched Radu's corner from his grasp and Thomas hit the flagstones so hard the breath was driven from his body.

"You butter-fingered bastards couldn't catch the pox in a French brothel!" Thomas groaned once he'd recovered his wind. The others ignored his anguish, and demanded to see the Holy Lance, so, cursing the callousness of thieves, Thomas unwrapped the relic and held it up for everyone to examine.

"By all the tortured souls of the damned, it looks as if its edge could cut clean through bonds of Hell!" Prometheus declared.

"Are you sure this is the actual spear that was used at the Crucifixion? Because it looks like the fake," said Bos.

"It's supposed to look like the fake, you ignorant Lutheran clod," said Quintana, yet, as he stared at the relic, the madness of greed began to seize the Portugee's soul and he demanded to know why they shouldn't keep this powerful talisman for themselves.

"If this lump of iron makes any army invincible, why give it to someone else? Why shouldn't we use it to conquer our own kingdoms? Then we could all live in castles with a hundred horses in the stables, a hundred cooks in the kitchens and a hundred high-born whores in the beds," Quintana said in a strange voice that was a mix of indignation and excitement.

"What are you talking about? You couldn't plough more than one trollop at a time without resting for a week and, whilst you were snoring your head off, your starving peasants would slit your throat," said Bos.

In reply, Quintana insisted that he deserved limitless wealth and power just as much as any king or emperor and he began to rail against the injustice of birth which decreed that he should have nothing, whilst cruel tyrants enjoyed every luxury that the world had to offer.

This prompted Prometheus to remind the Portugee that all those who sat upon a throne were cursed.

"Have you forgotten the tale of Damocles? It teaches that all those who hold power over others can never sleep soundly. The Holy Lance once belonged to my countryman, and my people are held in bondage by heathen tyrants, but I'll not carry this relic into battle unless God wishes it," he said and Radu added that even Lord Dracul dared not wield the spear until his right to own it had been proved at the Ritual of Rebirth. Thomas was about to remark that he'd already touched the relic without incurring the wrath of God but he was silenced by Quintana's admission of defeat.

"So be it, we'll take this cursed thing to Dracul and let him risk damnation whilst we enjoy the many and magnificent rewards he's certain to grant us," he said sarcastically, so Thomas said nothing as he wrapped the cloth around the blade and hid the bundle in the carrying chair's secret compartment.

"Now we have what we came for, let's leave this place and the city before the monks return," Radu said excitedly, but Prometheus insisted that quitting the church to soon would be foolhardy in the extreme.

"That way destruction lies because our deception will quickly be discovered if we exit with unseemly haste. We must therefore continue with our vigil until dawn," he said firmly.

The others had to agree that, to avoid arousing suspicion, they ought to remain in the church until the Order of the Holy Lance had received God's blessing, so Bos returned to its niche the statue that had taken Thomas' place before joining the others at their prayers. The thieves remained on their knees until daybreak, when the monks returned to say Lauds, and once the office celebrating the dawn of a new day had finished, the ceremony of knighthood could begin.

To the accompaniment of more prayers and psalms, the abbot blessed the knight-elects' spurs, swords and shields, as they lay on the altar. Once this had been done, the initiates took Holy Communion before proceeding to the Ritual of the Accolade. This final step on the road to knighthood required the candidates to take the oath of loyalty to The Cross, before being touched on the shoulder with a ceremonial sword, but only a person of royal blood, or the Grand Master of their order, could perform this part of the ceremony.

Having been born in the purple, Prince Djoel was of the correct rank to officiate. However, as he approached the altar to receive his sword from the abbot, the priest held up his hand to halt the proceedings. At first Prometheus thought his disguise had been penetrated but the abbot was smiling.

"Your Highness, I must beg your pardon for my previous rudeness but I've spent the entire night in prayer and God has absolved me of the sin of pride with which I was gravely afflicted. In His mercy, He sent the Holy Spirit to remind me that the law forbidding the veneration of relics was passed by heretics and therefore is no law at all. Though the Lutheran apostates may cast me into prison, I'd be shirking my duty as a Christian if I didn't allow you to perform The Accolade with the relic that will bless your order and guarantee victory in your holy struggle," said the abbot and before Prometheus could protest, the priest had ordered the casket to be lowered.

From high above the chancel, came the sound of a windlass being turned and, as the casket began its ponderous descent, Prometheus was struck dumb by this sudden change of fortune. For his part, Quintana thought his pounding heart would burst, Bos and Radu felt their bowels turn to water and Thomas bit his lip until it bled.

Once the reliquary was three feet above the marble floor, the abbot gave a second signal and, with more clanking of chains, it shuddered to an abrupt halt. The sight filled the thieves with the terror of being discovered yet, somehow, they managed to stop themselves from rushing forward, seizing their weapons and slaughtering every monk in the church. Even when this emotion had passed, it took what remained of their will to remain motionless as the old priest turned the wheels of the coded padlock and opened the lid.

For what seemed like an age, the abbot peered at the relics through his rheumy eyes, then, to Thomas and the others' abject horror, he reached inside the casket and took out the cushion upon which the Holy Lance rested. With trembling hands, the abbot reverently lifted the relic towards the east and began to pray.

"Lord Father Almighty, maker of all things in Heaven and earth, we give thanks for this new day and for the continued possession of this, the most sacred reminder of Christ's Passion. May the power of the Holy Lance, once held by the Blessed Saints Longinus and Maurice, strengthen the hand of thy son, Djoel of Nubia and bring him victory in his great crusade against the godless heathens who deny the Truth of the Gospels and poison his homeland with their sacrilege," he intoned.

When the prayer was finished, a deacon sprinkled holy water over the knights-elect and the kneeling men silently prayed that the priest would replace the relic in the casket. The abbot did nothing of the kind. Instead, the monk turned to the Prince of Nubia and invited him to dub his crusaders with the weapon that had once touched the flesh of God Incarnate.

"I believe it's customary to use a sword for The Accolade but for the Knights of the Holy Lance, only the Holy Lance itself will suffice," he said and he held out the cushion for Prince Djoel to take hold of the relic.

Fearing he would suffer the same fate as Uzzah the Israelite, Prometheus hesitated until he remembered that the real Holy Lance was hidden inside the carrying chair's secret compartment. Yet, even with this knowledge, the Prince of Nubia's hand shook as he took the spearhead from its cushion and his voice almost cracked as he repeated the words of the chivalric oath:

> *Do all here swear:*
> *Never to do outrageous murder,*
> *To always flee treason and cruelty,*
> *To give mercy to him that asks it,*
> *To aid and comfort ladies, damsels*
> *and gentlewomen in their hour of sorrow or distress,*
> *To worship God and fight for His Truth,*
> *To succour and protect the clergy of His Holy Church,*
> *And always, upon pain of death,*
> *Fight no battle in wrongful quarrel?*

When the four initiates answered that they would, the Prince of Nubia and first Grand Master of the Order of the Holy Lance touched each man on both shoulders with the spear's tip.

"I dub thee Sir Matthew," Prince Djoel said to Bos and he named his other knights of the Holy Lance after the three remaining evangelists because, in his panic, these were the only names he could remember.

Once the knights had received their new titles, Prometheus returned the ancient spearhead to its cushion and the priest said a blessing before placing the blade inside the casket.

"The Holy Spirit is indeed with you, Your Highness, for as I replaced the Holy Lance I had the most extraordinary feeling. I felt that it had been made anew and, like our Saviour at The Resurrection, its power had increased beyond measure," he said happily and he ordered the casket to be raised.

"You're too kind, Father Abbot, yet I confess I feel weak, as if I've just recovered from a grave illness," croaked Prince Djoel as the rusty iron chain creaked and rattled overhead.

"You have, my son. You've been cleansed of all sin by the power of the Holy Lance, now go forth and smite God's enemies wherever you may find them," said the abbot and Prince Djoel, his mouth dry with the fear of imminent discovery, informed his new knights that they may withdraw.

With all due reverence, the abbot escorted the new Grand Master and his four Knights of the Holy Lance to the litter at the back of the church. However, as Prince Djoel sat on his portable throne, the priest noticed that the chair now lacked its canopy. Bos saw the quizzical look on the abbot's face and immediately explained that it had been deliberately removed.

"By this act, our most worthy Prince Djoel wishes it be known that he has turned away from all worldly vanity," said Bos.

As a further proof of the knights' new humility, the Frisian offered the valuable cloth to the abbot on condition that it was sold and the money used to help the poor, the sick and the old.

The abbot was delighted to accept such an expensive gift and he thanked his royal guest profusely as Prince Djoel's escort was summoned to carry His Most Noble Highness back to Nuremberg's castle. If the abbot wondered why the Nubian prince had been happy to sacrifice his baldachin to his vow of modesty, but not his throne, he kept his thoughts to himself and instead made the sign of the cross as a gesture of goodbye.

Though the return journey was more subdued than Prince Djoel's previous processions, the celebratory feast that marked the birth of the Order of the Holy Lance was just as lavish as before. The thieves had to endure a whole day and night of drunken revels before they could quit the city but, at dawn on the fourth day after their arrival in Nuremberg, the new Knights of the Holy Lance left for the mysterious East.

Once again, Prince Djoel was carried through the streets of Nuremberg on his gilded litter. However, with the Holy Lance hidden in a secret compartment beneath his princely posterior, this was the most nerve-wracking journey of all.

Each of the Knights of the Holy Lance knew the biblical story of Benjamin's silver cup, yet, whilst they feared that the success of their theft might be some part of an elaborate trap, all they heard were their hosts' cries of farewell. Much to their relief, they reached the city's gate without being unmasked and soon the towers of Nuremberg were safely behind them.

Pausing only to burn the cumbersome litter, and change into clothes better suited to hard riding, the Lance

Bearers and their escort spent the rest of the day galloping towards the Hungarian border. That night, the column camped in the open and they thanked God for their good fortune, until the heavens opened.

The unseasonal storm turned every road into a morass, so a journey that should have taken five days lasted ten. Frustrated by the constant delays, Radu promised to punish his men with vile tortures unless they made better progress but no one could do anything about the incessant rain.

"That piece of iron hidden beneath Thomas' shirt will be nothing but a pile of rust by the time it gets to Dracul," said Quintana as the men shivered through yet another downpour.

"At this rate, the Draconists would be better off putting their faith in a wooden ark instead of a metal spear," added Bos, who was trying to wring the worst of the water from his rain-drenched cloak.

"Perhaps God is trying to cleanse the world of the terrible blasphemy we've just committed," said Prometheus and though Thomas assured him that God had better things to do, nothing he said could relieve the Nubian's gloom.

The sodden column reached the Danube several days later than they'd hoped, yet, when the bridge at Esztergom came into view, the rain clouds cleared. The warmth of the early May sun improved everyone's humour and, once they'd crossed the river, Radu told his men that the end of their journey was in sight.

On hearing this, the riders forgot their aching backsides and spurred their horses to a gallop but, when they reached the hillside where Dracul and the other Draconists should have been encamped, they found nothing but a circle of trampled earth.

Though this patch of mud indicated that the other Draconists had abandoned the site only recently, and there was no sign of a fight, the riders feared for their families' safety so they dismounted and began to hunt for any clue that would explain what had happened.

After a brief search, one of the riders found a single word, POENARI, scratched onto a rock, whereupon Radu ordered his men to water their horses and prepare for another long ride. The Draconists obediently took their animals to a nearby stream but Thomas, Bos, Quintana and Prometheus refused to take another step until they'd been told what POENARI had to do with Dracul's disappearance.

Though Radu was surprised by the other Lance Bearers' ignorance, he patiently explained that Poenari was the hidden castle of the *Drăculeşti*, which now served the Order of the Dragon as their chief preceptory.

"Any man who bears the mark of the *Ouroboros* may seek refuge at Poenari and if our Grand Master is there, we must follow without delay. The castle lies in the mountains that divide Transylvania from Wallachia but we can be there in a few days, if we ride hard," he said. However, this knowledge did little to persuade Bos and Quintana to continue their service with the Order of the Dragon. The Portugee insisted that their agreement with Dracul required them to deliver the Holy Lance to this spot and no more.

In reply, Dracul's lieutenant reminded Quintana of his Draconist oath but this prompted Bos to declare that all vows made under the influence of a drug were null and void. These words did nothing to diffuse the situation and Radu's face became a gargoyle of fury as the Frisian declared that he too would go no further. Finally, Prometheus spoke.

"Have you forgotten the oath that we all swore on the sacred spear? As that vow was taken willingly we're bound to its terms, whether we like it or not, therefore we must use this relic of Christ's Passion to do God's work. If that means journeying to the ends of the earth, so be it," he said firmly.

The others could hardly believe that the Nubian had taken the ceremony of knighthood so seriously, yet, before they could convince him that the Order of the Holy Lance was a sham, Radu began threatening the mutineers with death.

"Hear me, you scabrous dogs, if you abandon the only Christian prince who can save the east, I'll have you impaled right here and take the Holy Lance to Lord Dracul myself!" Radu cried and he shouted an order to the rest of his men.

Immediately the Draconist riders at the stream left their horses and came running up the hill with their sabres drawn. Bos, Prometheus and Quintana drew their own swords but, before the first blow could be struck, Thomas pulled the Holy Lance from beneath his shirt and held it high above his head.

"All of you, put up your weapons! You see how I hold the Holy Lance without being struck by Heaven's thunderbolt? Do you need any further proof that God has chosen us all to carry this relic to Lord Dracul, wherever he may be?" Thomas cried.

The sight of the spear had the desired effect on the Draconists, who fell to their knees in prayer, and even Radu felt the madness of anger leave his soul. Once they'd realised that they too had little choice but to carry the relic to Poenari, Bos and Quintana also sheathed their swords and an hour later all the Knights of the Holy Lance were back in the saddle.

For three days, the lance-bearers had good, easy riding. The sun shone and the whole of the Pannonian Plain seemed to be at peace but the tranquillity did nothing to improve Bos and Quintana's humour. They remarked that the peasants tilling the soil and the shepherds tending their flocks would be better employed by preparing for war, yet it wasn't until the riders reached the Hungarian town of Lipova that the riders received their first news of the gathering storm.

Night had fallen and Radu's men were preparing their supper of black bread and dried horse-meat when a beggar appeared demanding alms. At first, the riders tried to shoo the foul-smelling pauper away but all of a sudden, the wretch stood upright, stripped off his filthy rags and pointed to the mark of the *Ouroboros* that had been burned into his shoulder.

No other introduction was necessary and the beggar was immediately taken to Radu, who was eating his meal with Thomas and the others. Dracul's lieutenant recognised the man and after greeting each other warmly, the beggar explained that he'd been ordered to wait for the riders and give them news.

"I am to impress on you the need for urgency because the Turkish army is now encamped at Philippopolis, which is only four days' march from the Danube," he said but Radu wanted to hear about Hungary's king.

"What tidings of Louis, has the boy raised his banner?" Radu asked, whereupon the beggar spat into the fire in disgust.

"He tried, and when no one answered the royal summons, he went hunting," said the beggar. Strangely, this news that the young Hungarian king had failed to attend his own muster had the same effect on Radu as aquavit on a dying man and Dracul's lieutenant leapt to his feet, spluttering in triumph.

"So, Louis would rather hunt deer than kill Turks? Is such a brazen poltroon fit to lead the armies of Christ?" Radu shouted, and the others had to admit that if Hungary's King couldn't command the respect of his own knights, he should stand aside. However, the beggarly spy insisted that Louis hadn't given up entirely.

"The King intends to call a new muster in three weeks' time, at the town on the Danube known as Mohacs, so Lord Dracul must raise his own standard before the vainglorious Louis or our cause is lost," he said earnestly and Radu promised that they'd deliver the Holy Lance to Poenari by then or die in the attempt. Ignoring Thomas and the others' protests, Dracul's lieutenant ordered his men to remount and the column continued its journey by the light of the moon.

By dawn, the Draconists had reached the road that ran parallel to the River Mures. However, after a few miles, Radu turned off this well-travelled highway and led his men into a narrow valley, where an almost invisible track began its journey over the mountains. As men and horses climbed higher, the steep hillsides' birches and rowans were replaced by larches and pines but soon even these hardy conifers had disappeared.

As the riders neared the top of the pass, not even the tough upland grasses could cling to the sheer slabs of naked rock that soared for hundreds of feet into the sky and the mountain took on the appearance of a giant's immense castle.

Surrounded by these natural ramparts, Thomas began to understand why some people believed that Transylvania's lonely peaks were home to evil spirits. Yet, for the moment, there was more to fear from the thin air and bitter wind which was as cold as a dead man's fingers.

It took several hours but at last the riders reached the summit and Radu was delighted to find that his secret path to Poenari was still unguarded. The lack of a watchtower on the frontier also came as a great relief to Radu's men, because every man who served Lord Dracul had been declared an outlaw by Wallachia's current ruler. However Thomas, Bos, Quintana and Prometheus failed to share the Draconists' joy.

To the recently ennobled Knights of the Holy Lance, Dracul's domain appeared to be a strange land and their sense of foreboding only increased as they descended the mountain. The narrow path followed an angry young river as it tumbled through a series of rocky gorges and once the dense forests of pine trees had returned, a strange noise, which sounded like the howling of an Irish banshee, filled the air.

"What, in the name of the Holy Virgin's milk, is that?" said Quintana, as the unearthly shrieks froze the blood in his veins, but Radu's explanation did little to settle his nerves.

"That is the cry of the wolf-dragon, the beast that devours all those who fail Lord Dracul," he said ominously.

# 16

## THE CASTLE OF POENARI

Before Radu could explain to Thomas and his comrades what a wolf-dragon might be, their destination appeared on the horizon, yet the sight of Poenari offered little comfort. The castle was situated at the end of a high, mountainous ridge and its tall, slender towers rose above the skyline like the bony fingers of a ghoul clawing its way out of a grave. As they drew nearer to the fortress, Radu gleefully added to his guests' unease by saying that Poenari had been built on the graves of those who'd dared to challenge the *Drăculești*.

"These stones were cemented in place with mortar made from the blood and bones of our enemies. Now these traitors serve their lawful masters for all eternity!" Radu cried.

According to Radu the first Castle of Poenari had been constructed centuries ago, to guard the narrow pass through the mountains, but it had fallen into ruin when a better road had been built further east. The ruins of the original fortress had remained abandoned and forgotten until Vlad Dracula had triumphed in his war with Wallachia's noble *boyars*.

After declaring an amnesty, Vlad Dracula had invited his former enemies to celebrate Easter at the great cathedral of Târgoviște. However, once the unsuspecting *boyars* had knelt in prayer, Vlad Dracula's men had burst in and arrested them all.

As punishment for murdering Vlad Dracula's father and brother, the luckless nobles and their families were loaded with chains and forced to walk barefoot to the ruins of Poenari. Here they were given a stark choice, rebuild the castle or suffer the dreadful death of impalement. Not surprisingly the prisoners had chosen the former and for years they'd laboured like the Israelites who'd built the pharaohs' pyramids.

When their clothes rotted off their backs, the wretched captives were forced to work naked and when they died, their bones were ground into powder to make cement. Even after Poenari was finished there was no mercy because the emaciated survivors were impaled anyway, in order to preserve the castle's dreadful secrets.

"It used to be said that Poenari was the castle of eternal night, because the sky was always black with crows feasting on human carrion," said Radu and Thomas began to understand why no honest traveller used this road over the mountains.

A mile from the castle, the main road met a track that snaked its way up the mountain's almost vertical slope. This track was as twisted as the lies of an unfaithful wife and so steep the riders had to dismount, hobble their horses and leave them to graze by the river's edge.

After posting men to guard their mounts, the rest of the column continued on foot and as they reached the summit of the ridge, the wolf-dragon roared again. This fearsome noise sounded like the screams of those who'd died so horribly beneath Poenari's walls, yet, whatever the truth of Radu's stories, Thomas and the others could appreciate why Dracul's ancestor had chosen this spot for his refuge.

The hidden stronghold of the *Drăculeşti* was a small, rectangular castle that overlooked the deep, wooded gorge cut by the river. Nothing could move along the only road through this untamed forest without Poenari's sentries knowing and its walls were surrounded on three sides by sheer cliffs. These vertiginous rocks meant the fortress could be defended by a handful of men and the only way in or out was along a treacherous path that followed the crest of the ridge.

Considering its location, it was hardly surprising that Poenari was not a large fortress but its ramparts were thick enough to withstand even the largest siege engines. The walls and towers had been built according to the eastern style, using flat, red bricks laid on stone foundations, but there were no visible battlements. The walkways on top of the castle's walls were covered by wooden galleries, which projected a few feet beyond the masonry, and Poenari's four round towers were capped by tall, conical roofs that looked like the pointed hoods worn by Spanish penitents during Holy Week.

Between the eastern and western towers, a square keep, with a pyramidal roof, rose above the walls and though colourful flags of welcome had been hung on either side of the castle's gate, Poenari looked no more approachable than a rabid dog. The entrance to the fortress was protected by a grim half-moon bastion, equipped with three menacing cannon, and a broad chasm, spanned by a narrow drawbridge, separated the castle rock from the rest of the ridge.

The ravine was over twenty feet deep and, as Dracul's guests tramped over the drawbridge, Radu told them how assassins from a rival clan had once thrown their host into the tangle of thorn bushes that filled the bottom of this dry moat.

"Lord Dracul only survived because he's been blessed by God and cannot be killed, except by sorcery," Radu declared proudly. Thomas, however, wasn't listening.

Ever since he'd first caught sight of Poenari, Thomas had been wondering if Dracul's daughter would be released from her seclusion to greet her father's guests. However, wherever Ursula was, she was not in the small, cramped courtyard that lay between the castle's gateway and the keep.

Though the sun was high in the sky, Poenari's walls cast a long shadow over the castle's inner ward, so it retained all the chill of a winter's night. Thomas and the others shivered as they entered this cobbled courtyard but there was no mistaking the warmth of Dracul's welcome. The Grand Master was waiting patiently by the keep's doorway and he was dressed in the fine silks and expensive furs befitting a Wallachian prince.

"My friends, I've hardly been able to contain myself these past few weeks. Do you have the Holy Lance with you?" he beamed as the weary travellers brushed the dust of the road from their clothes.

"We have it, My Lord," said Thomas and he began to fumble beneath his shirt for the cloth bag that contained the relic but Dracul ordered him to stop.

"Not here. Something this sacred must be treated with the proper respect, you will therefore follow me at once," he said excitedly, whereupon Bos and Quintana groaned and begged to be allowed an hour or two to rest and refresh themselves.

"Like a nun needs Holy Communion, my throat also craves bread and wine," said Quintana.

"Even a dog must eat and drink," added Bos, yet Dracul refused to obey the normal laws of hospitality.

"There'll be plenty of time for filling your stomachs later," their host said curtly and he insisted that Thomas, Bos, Quintana, Prometheus and Radu follow him along a narrow passage that led from the castle's entrance to a second, much larger, courtyard.

The passage linking the castle's two wards ran between Poenari's keep and its southern wall, so any attackers who breached the gate's defences would have to run the gauntlet of arquebusiers and crossbowmen stationed on these ramparts. However, bullets, boiling oil and crossbow bolts were not the only things that protected the second courtyard.

Halfway along the passage, there was a sturdy, iron grill set into the wall of the keep and this grating had been ingeniously constructed so that it could be raised like a portcullis or used as a gate to separate the first courtyard from the second. For the moment, the gate was closed, and there was no hint of any danger, until a dozen snarling, black mastiffs hurled themselves against its bars.

Instinctively, Dracul's guests stepped away from these slavering, baying hounds. Their host, nonetheless, merely laughed at his guests' discomfort before soothing the beasts like a widow cooing over a favourite grandchild.

"Just as Hades had Cerberus, his monstrous three headed cur, to guard his dismal realm, I have these dogs. They obey only me and, after they're released at sunset, any living thing they find in the courtyards will be torn apart," said Dracul but he assured his guests that they'd nothing to fear from his pets.

In spite of this promise, Thomas and the others couldn't stop themselves from imagining the hounds' razor sharp teeth ripping into their flesh. Yet, once they'd passed these canine sentinels, they entered the most pleasant part of Poenari.

The castle's second courtyard, which measured roughly two hundred yards across, consisted of a broad expanse of grass surrounding an outcrop of bare rock and sitting on top of this grey island, in a sea of green, was a large, circular building. The walls of this single storey, windowless structure were built of massive cyclopean stones, strengthened with huge baulks of timber, and its door was at the top of a flight of thirty stone steps.

The building looked much older than the rest of the castle but the only clue to its purpose was the tall, slender spire rising from the centre of its roof. This seemed to suggest that the edifice served as Poenari's chapel, but the strange tube of yellow and green linen flying from its top was not a banner belonging to any Christian church.

The cloth cylinder, which was at least eight feet long, had been embroidered to resemble a serpent's scales and one end was fixed to a painted, wooden head which had the features of both a wolf and a dragon. The head was hollow and inside were three long tongues of thin metal which vibrated whenever the wind blew.

It was this device that had caused the moaning sound which had unsettled Thomas and the others on their approach to Poenari, but Dracul pointed to the ancient standard of the Dacians and proudly declared that the mountain had long been a holy place for his ancestors, both pagan and Christian.

"The Hall of the Wolf-Dragon is so hallowed, only those who bear the sacred mark of the *Ouroboros* may enter and live," said the Grand Master and, with a flourish of his cloak, he began to climb the steps. Struggling to ignore their growing sense of reluctance, Thomas, Bos, Prometheus and Quintana followed.

At the top of the steps, two sentries, who were dressed in the same style of Turkish mail and spiked helmets that Thomas had worn in Nuremberg, guarded a pair of heavy oak doors. These gatekeepers carried Russian *bardiche* axes with long, curved blades that could slice through steel-clad flesh and bone at a single stroke. As Dracul approached, the guards opened the doors to admit their master but before the others could enter, they had to surrender their swords and daggers.

Once the hall's doors were closed, the only light inside came from candles but as soon as their eyes had become accustomed to the gloom, Thomas and the others gasped in wonder. The entire length of the building's circular wall was lined with alcoves and in each shadowy recess there was a living, breathing dragon.

From *basilisks* and *wyverns* to *lindworms* and *cockatrices*, all the mythical monsters of the Old World were tethered in these alcoves. There was even a winged serpent from the New World of the Americas, and each dragon was spewing clouds of smoke from its nostrils.

At the sight of these writhing, fire-breathing behemoths, Quintana cried out in alarm, Prometheus cursed himself for surrendering his sword so easily and Bos recited the prayer to banish evil. Thomas, however, realised that these monsters were nothing more than artful frescoes.

"Calm yourselves, it's the flickering shadows cast by the candles that give these painted beasts the semblance of life and the smoke they exhale is nothing more than incense," he whispered and he pointed to the smouldering tapers held in silver holders at the end of each dragon's snout. The fumes from these splints filled the Dragon Hall and the air was heavy with the pungent smell of exotic perfume.

Whilst the others recovered their composure, Dracul strolled to a pair of red velvet curtains at the far end of the hall and, after making the sign of the cross, pulled on a gilded rope. The curtains parted to reveal an altar, covered by a cloth of purple silk which had been embroidered with the symbol of the *Ouroboros*. Two braziers full of burning coals stood on either side of the altar and behind it was an ornate throne.

Though the throne was made of polished ebony, it looked as terrifying as a mythical Gorgon, because, like the grotesque daughters of Echidna, it was adorned with snakes. A serpent's body coiled around the chair's legs, and seven carved heads, which also spat smoke, sprouted from its back and arms.

"This is the *Balaur*, father of all dragons and guardian of my house," said Dracul and he instructed Thomas to place the Holy Lance on the altar protected by his serpent throne. Obediently, Thomas unwrapped the relic and laid it gently in the centre of the altar's purple cloth.

"Is this the Holy Lance carried by St Longinus and St Maurice? Is it the Spear of Destiny carried by the Emperors Constantine, Charlemagne and Otto?" Dracul asked in a breathless whisper and Thomas assured him that it was.

"This is the blade that I took from the casket that hangs in Nuremberg's Church of the Holy Spirit and may God strike me dead if I lie," he said solemnly but Dracul wasn't listening.

The Grand Master had walked to the altar and was stretching out his hand, as if to try and detect the relic's holiness. Yet Dracul also knew the Old Testament story of Uzzah and he was careful not to touch that which belonged to God alone. Even with these precautions, some sort of unseen power seemed to flow from the metal into Dracul's body and he appeared to shrivel like a miser corrupted by greed.

"I can sense the presence of God in this blade! The King of Hungary may be a young fool and the King of France may have sold his soul to the Sultan but if I have the Holy Lance, all Christian men will flock to my banner. Together, we shall drive the Turks back into the trackless wastes of Asia, and the House of *Drăculeşti* shall rule over a new Empire of the Romans for a thousand years!" Dracul croaked.

Standing in the shadows, the Grand Master's guests feared for their host's sanity but they dared not interrupt as Dracul declared that only the *Drăculeşti* were descended from both the Roman Emperors of the West, who'd first civilised the land of Dacia, and the Roman Emperors of the East who'd fought the pagan Goths on the banks of the Danube.

As his rambling oration continued, Dracul went on to accuse all the German Hapsburg emperors of being uncivilised brutes, the French Valois kings of being arrogant, narcissistic fops and the Turkish Ottoman sultans of being godless barbarians. Finally, the Grand Master insisted that only he had the right to wear the imperial diadem.

"The Ritual of Rebirth, which will prove that I'm the only true heir of Augustus, Constantine and Charlemagne, must be performed as soon as possible!" Dracul cried and he looked directly at Thomas. The Englishman felt a shiver of fear run down his spine, but, before he could answer, the Grand Master of the Order of the Dragon had declared that this ritual would be the crowning achievement of Thomas' occult career.

"You brought the *Graoully* out of the watery abyss to free you from your prison in Metz. You called upon the winged *Firedrake* to carry you over the walls of The Hornberg and now you will summon the greatest of all dragons, the one that will bring me back from the grave!" Dracul cried and Thomas began to tremble with terror.

The dramatic escapes that had so impressed the Order of the Dragon's Grand Master had all been accomplished without the help of any fabled beast, yet it was clear that nothing Thomas said would convince Dracul of this. The Grand Master was adrift in the ocean of his own words and in a voice that sounded like a preacher warning of the dangers of hell-fire, he reminded everyone in the hall that the Holy Lance was a power for evil as well as good.

"Because Holy Lance was the instrument of Christ's death, it is both blessed and cursed. Even Charlemagne, who brought the Gospels' light to the heathen Saxons, was struck down by God's anger and I too will face His wrath if I touch the Holy Lance before I've proved myself worthy. My test will be to follow the same path taken by Our Lord Jesus, so, though I must die, Thomas will summon the dragon that carries me through the Valley of Death to be reborn," said Dracul but his sorcerer, who'd at last found his voice, began to protest.

"Please, My Lord, what you ask isn't possible for any mortal!" Thomas cried but Dracul insisted that this was his sole reason for bringing the Englishman to Poenari.

"You're the only man who's proved that he can tame both dragons and the power of the Holy Lance. With my own eyes I saw you touch the hallowed blade as you placed it on the altar, yet you are unharmed. There can be no clearer sign that you're not only a great sorcerer, you're also blessed by The Almighty," he said and though Thomas repeated that only God could raise the dead, Dracul declared that Peter had restored Tabitha to life, whilst Paul had brought Eutychus back from the grave.

"But what if I fail?" Thomas said in desperation.

"You must not fail, because the fate of all Christendom depends on your success," Dracul replied and he compounded Thomas' misery by revealing that all the important princes of the east had been invited to Poenari to witness the Grand Master's resurrection.

"When those who've denied my right to rule see me conquer death, they'll flock to my banner. Therefore, if you refuse to obey me, Radu will see to it that you and your friends suffer all the torments of Tartarus before you die!" Dracul cried and he barked an order. Seconds later, Bos, Prometheus and Quintana were surrounded by armoured men wielding lethal *bardiche* axes, and without their swords they could do nothing except surrender, but Thomas was roused to anger.

"You Judas sired by Ephialtes and Tarpeia! These men have fulfilled their oath and brought you the greatest prize in Christendom and this is how you repay such loyalty?" Thomas shouted at Dracul but it was Radu who answered him.

"Calm yourself, Englishman. Nothing will happen to you or your companions, provided that Lord Dracul is restored to life," he sneered and he ordered the guards to escort the Grand Master's 'guests' to rooms in the castle's South Tower.

"By Satan's unholy shit-pot, watch what you're doing with those toothpicks!" Bos roared as four guards nervously prodded the giant Frisian with their axe blades.

"In my country, those who betray the laws of hospitality are flayed alive and fed to the jackals!" spat Prometheus as he too was ushered towards the Dragon Hall's entrance.

"I had a better welcome when I was robbed in a Sicilian brothel!" Quintana moaned.

In spite of their vehemence, Dracul ignored his guests' complaints and Thomas could only watch in frustrated rage as his struggling companions were bundled out of the Dragon Hall. When they were alone, Dracul turned to his hapless necromancer and filled his cup of desolation to overflowing.

"I've commanded all the Christian lords on the eastern frontier to assemble at Poenari by St Mary's Day. They may have ignored King Louis' summons but they'll dare not refuse me now I have the Holy Lance. On that day, you'll perform the Ritual of Rebirth and the Lords of the Danube shall witness my death and resurrection, just as Mary of Bethany beheld the Crucifixion and the risen Jesus," said Dracul. Inwardly Thomas groaned. He needed time to find a way out of his predicament but St Mary's Day was only a week away

"My Lord, I must have at least a month to prepare such powerful spells and enchantments," Thomas said feebly but Dracul refused to listen to his objections.

"You may have a room in the East Tower in which to work and your task will be easier if you have this," said the Grand Master and from beneath his cloak he withdrew an oilskin packet. Thomas knew at once what was wrapped inside the waterproof cloth; it was his copy of *The Munich Handbook of Demonic Magic*, which he'd tried to hide in the abandoned tomb.

As he undid the package, Thomas supposed that one of Dracul's men had followed him, and had seen him conceal the spell book in the burial mound, but he said nothing. Instead, as he examined the battered pages, he wondered if Dracul's spy, and the thief who'd ambushed him in the forest, had been one and the same person. Again Thomas thought it unwise to enquire further and he merely thanked Dracul for recovering the *grimoire*.

"My Lord, I'm grateful. My only thought was to keep the book's secrets hidden from our enemies," said Thomas but Dracul felt that the Englishman's carelessness needed rebuke.

"Your caution does you credit but your foresight should have told you that we would need the knowledge contained in this priceless volume for the Ritual of Rebirth," he said sternly.

"As ever, your wisdom is our salvation, My Lord and, now that the *grimoire* has been returned to me, nothing can prevent your triumph," said Thomas humbly, even though, as far as he knew, no one before or since Christ's Crucifixion had ever cheated death.

In spite of his misgivings, there was no point in Thomas trying to claim that *The Munich Handbook* couldn't help him resurrect a corpse because some of the book's spells really did promise to raise the dead. Fortunately, Thomas' feigned humility had convinced Dracul that his sorcerer was now contrite and he graciously gave him permission to withdraw.

Outside the Dragon Hall, Thomas was met by one of the castle's stewards, who took him to his appointed room in Poenari's east tower. With his mind in turmoil, Dracul's sorcerer climbed the stairs to what he imagined would be his prison yet Thomas was pleasantly surprised by the chamber's comforts.

Despite being part of the castle's fortifications, the circular room was furnished with a bed, table and chair. There was even a fireplace with a log fire burning in the grate. The room also boasted two slender windows and from one of these openings Thomas could look out over the vast forest which stretched from the castle all the way to the horizon. The other window offered a view across the larger courtyard to the Dragon Hall.

With a bow, the servant left the room and as soon as he was alone, Thomas placed the oilskin packet on the table but he didn't open it. Instead, he glanced around the chamber in an instinctive search for spies and eavesdroppers.

The recovery of *The Munich Handbook* had convinced him that Dracul must be having him watched at all times and this meant he'd have to take the most extreme care, if he was to leave the Castle of Poenari alive.

Whatever else happened, Dracul must believe that any ritual Thomas performed had genuine magical properties and though the room offered no obvious place for a spy to conceal himself, he had no way of knowing what hidden passages or secret chambers had been built into the tower's walls.

In case one of Dracul's men was watching his every move, Thomas decided he must follow the laws of magic to the letter and the first of these rules insisted that no spellbook could be opened until the occult forces that governed it were in proper alignment. This requirement protected the secrets contained in any *grimoire* because, although there was nothing to stop a layman from opening a book of spells and reading the pages, if the hour of the day was wrong, or if the proper preparations hadn't been made, any spell cast by the interloper simply wouldn't work.

If such failure was to be avoided, *The Munich Handbook* could only be opened during the second hour after sunset, so, whilst he waited for darkness to descend on the castle, Thomas scrubbed the table clean with a piece of coarse stone he'd prised from the wall. When the wood had been thoroughly scoured, he took a piece of charcoal from the ashes in the fireplace and drew a magic circle on the whitened planks.

The circle consisted of two rings inscribed with the alchemical symbols for the six planets and the name of the angel Tartys who ruled the second hour of the night. When this was done, Thomas took a candle from the sconce on the wall, lit it and dripped some of the melted wax around the edge of the circle. Beeswax, being the symbol of industry, was the substance most pleasing to all angels and by the time Thomas had finished his preparations, the proper hour had arrived.

Only now did Thomas take the *grimoire* out of its oilcloth wallet and place it in the centre of the circle he'd drawn on the table. Yet, even now Thomas refrained from opening the book of spells until he'd asked God and Hermes Thrice Blessed to grant him wisdom. Only when this was done could Thomas study the book's complex diagrams and incantations.

Though he no longer believed in the efficacy of magic, Thomas hoped that studying the elaborate futility of the spells in *The Munich Handbook* would at least help him think of a way to convince the lords of Wallachia that Dracul could cheat death. Unfortunately, as the night slipped by, his studies only served to convince him that he was doomed.

Either Dracul would die or Thomas would have to admit that he had no power over the supernatural, though it hardly mattered which. Whether he was a murderer or a fraud, he'd suffer the terrible death of impalement once he'd failed to revive Dracul.

After spending several hours in fruitless reading, Thomas became frustrated by his inability to prevent his grisly fate, and he slammed the useless book shut before hurling himself onto the bed. He was soon asleep but it wasn't long before he was woken by the sound of an argument in the courtyard outside.

One of the angry voices belonged to Radu, who was ordering a woman not to enter the East Tower, but this was followed by the sound of feet running up the stairs to the sorcerer's chamber. The slap of soft leather on stone was barely audible but to Thomas it sounded louder than any alarm bell and he leapt from his bed. Fearing the worst, he began to search his room for something to use as a weapon. However, before he could arm himself, the door crashed open.

Framed in the doorway was Ursula and she was no longer dressed as a nun. Instead of a coarse, woollen habit, an expensive gown of scarlet linen covered her body and her face wore the mask of Lyssa, pagan goddess of frenzied rage.

"Traitor! I know you plan to kill my father but I'll kill you first!" Ursula screamed and curling her fingers into talons she launched herself at her enemy. Thomas ducked instinctively, yet Ursula still managed to rake her nails down his face.

Cursing this maenad for her folly, Thomas wiped the blood from his lacerated cheeks. As he did so, Ursula kicked him hard in the most vulnerable part of any man's body. Thomas felt as if a barrel of gunpowder had exploded in his groin, and though he collapsed to the floor, howling in pain, Ursula showed him no mercy. In an instant she was sitting astride his chest and pummelling Thomas' head with her clenched fists.

"In the name of Ishtar's gates, will you let me explain? I want to save your father from himself!" Thomas cried as he tried to nurse his shattered loins with one hand and fend off Ursula's punches with the other.

"Don't speak in riddles, you cur suckled by Lilith's teat!" Ursula yelled and she continued to vent her anger on Thomas' skull until he could stand it no longer.

Ignoring the pain, Thomas braced his feet against the floor, arched his back and sent the harpy flying across the room. Before Ursula could recover, Thomas had hauled himself painfully to his feet, seized hold of the girl and thrown her onto the bed as if she was nothing but a sack of laundry.

"In England, I'd take you to the church steps and beat seven shades of sense into you!" Thomas cried as he tried to staunch the streams of blood flowing down his shredded face. Although his threat failed to cow the girl, she began to nurse her own bruises rather than inflict any more on her enemy.

"My father will have you killed, with every torture he can devise, for raising your hand to me," she hissed.

"No he won't. He's brought me all the way across Christendom to perform his Ritual of Rebirth, so he's hardly likely to dispose of me now," he replied. For a moment, Thomas stared at Ursula and though her eyes flashed red with rage, he wanted her more than he'd ever wanted any other woman. For her part, the girl seemed to sense Thomas' lust and the knowledge that he desired her only fuelled her anger.

"Don't play games! This obscene ceremony is a blasphemy and I'll do everything I can to prevent it, even if that means killing you! I'll put snakes in your bed, or I'll cut your throat whilst you sleep, I'll put poison in your wine, I'll ..." Ursula's voice trailed away as she failed to think of any more ways to confound an assassin but, in that same instant, Thomas solved the riddle of how to accomplish Dracul's death and resurrection.

"Listen to me, unless you want to spend the rest of your life rotting in a convent," Thomas snapped and he began to explain exactly how he planned to help Dracul rise from the dead without breaking the laws of man or

God. Though the plan that he outlined had only been in his mind for a few seconds, the girl listened intently and Thomas said a silent prayer of thanks when she reluctantly agreed to a truce.

"You're quite sure my father won't die," she said slowly and Thomas insisted there was no danger.

"I can fulfil your father's wishes without harming him but you must trust me," he said. Ursula's face betrayed her confusion but she knew she had no choice.

"Trust doesn't come easily to a *Drăculeşti*, yet, if you can open Hell's gates without releasing Satan, then so be it," she said and, without another word, she quit the room. Whether Ursula went directly to her father to report their conversation, Thomas didn't know, but, soon afterwards, a steward arrived and escorted him to Dracul's apartments in Poenari's keep.

The Grand Master of the Order of the Dragon was quietly eating his breakfast, a simple affair of black bread and goat's milk. However, on seeing Thomas' battered and bruised face, he angrily demanded to know what strange misfortune had befallen his sorcerer.

Nervously, Thomas explained that he'd been up all night battling with ferocious demons in an attempt to unlock the secrets of the grave and Dracul clapped his hands with delight on hearing this news.

"Your courage and devotion are admirable, Master Sorcerer. Did you succeed in learning what you needed to know?" Dracul asked eagerly. Thomas nodded and began to describe how the Saviour of Christendom should die.

"Death must not be caused by a fatal injury because no spell can reattach a severed head or plug a bullet hole through the heart. Even the hangman's noose may cause too much damage," Thomas said sternly and he prayed that Dracul wasn't planning on being crucified.

"Very well, but how exactly should I leave this life?" Dracul asked with no hint of fear in his voice.

"You must drink a special poison which I shall prepare," Thomas replied and he began to list all the items he would need. These included a rod made of alder wood, a live pig and a few ounces of orpiment, the mineral used by artists to make a yellow pigment and by poisoners to create arsenic.

# 17
## CANTARELLA

As every person of rank kept some means of secretly dispatching their enemies readily to hand, Thomas was not surprised that Dracul kept a supply of orpiment, the ore from which arsenic could be extracted, in his castle. Barely an hour after he'd made the request, Radu delivered a small block of this toxic yellow mineral to Thomas' chambers and Dracul's sorcerer began his diabolical work.

Though Dracul offered him servants and assistants, Thomas insisted on working alone, as he wished to ensure that no one discovered or even suspected the secret of his deception. He had absolutely no intention of administering a fatal dose of poison to a man who had more than a hundred bloodthirsty battle-hardened bodyguards to protect him; therefore he planned to give Dracul the distillation of arsenic that alchemists and poisoners called *cantarella*.

Provided Thomas calculated the dose properly, this diluted form of arsenic would give Dracul the appearance of death without proving fatal. The Grand Master's heartbeat and breathing would become so weak no physician would be able to detect the presence of life yet, after two or three hours, Dracul would revive. Though he'd wake feeling like he'd spent a month drinking with Satan's cup bearer, Dracul would live.

To begin with, Thomas ground a small piece of orpiment into coarse grains which he roasted in his fireplace to produce a silvery, metallic powder. The fumes produced by the heated granules were lethal so, though the draw of the fireplace carried the poisonous smoke away from Thomas' chamber, the jackdaws nesting among the chimney pots dropped from the sky like the quail that fed the Israelites.

Once the pure arsenic had been separated from its ore, Thomas mixed a pinch of the toxin into a bucket of swill. This he fed to an unfortunate pig and the animal promptly expired in a cacophony of strangulated squeals.

As soon as the pig was dead, Thomas opened its belly with a sharp knife and sprinkled more of the pure arsenic powder over its entrails. Now it was necessary for the carcase to putrefy.

To allow this to happen naturally would take several weeks, so he accelerated the process by placing the dead pig in one of the castle's outhouses and lighting a fire. The atmosphere inside the shed quickly became stifling and the pig's flesh began to decay in a few hours. By noon the next day, the stench of death and swarms of flies had transformed Dracul's already grim castle into a scene of Biblical apocalypse.

As the loathsome odours swirled around Poenari's walls and courtyards, the superstitious servants began to mutter that a magician of terrible power had come into their midst. The grooms and valets took to wearing their crucifixes over their shirts, whilst the serving wenches and scullery maids rubbed garlic on their breasts to ward off any incubus that might feast on their blood as they slept.

Even the South Tower, where Bos, Quintana and Prometheus had been lodged, wasn't high enough to rise above the great fog of putrescence and it wasn't long before Thomas' strange activities made life unbearable for its occupants.

"By the parboiled head of St Cecilia, what is that vile stink? Has the Black Plague returned or have Bos' Lutheran relatives come to stay?" said Quintana as he covered his face with a rag.

"That smell is not as vile as your popish mouth. Now shut up and deal," replied Bos.

"It's no good, I can't concentrate on primero whilst being slowly poisoned by these noxious vapours and I'll wager our English sorcerer is responsible," said Prometheus as he threw his cards on the table.

The others agreed that the time had come to put an end to the mysterious pestilence that now engulfed the top of the mountain so they left their chamber and went in search of Thomas.

Though Dracul's hostages were not allowed to leave Poenari, in accordance with their status as 'honoured guests', Bos, Quintana and Prometheus were free to wander the castle. However, they soon regretted leaving the tower as the smell in the enclosed courtyard was far worse than in their chamber.

"In the name of Moloch's murdered children, this foul air is more than a Moorish tanner could bear!" Prometheus cried.

"You're right Nubian, this filthy reek comes straight from the Devil's own backside and will most likely kill us all if we stay here," Bos added so, as it was clear that no good could come of remaining in the courtyard, the three men hurried back to their tower.

In fact, only the fumes from the heated orpiment were truly lethal and even the poison that Thomas was preparing would have no effect unless swallowed. However, in the foetid air of the pig's steamy sepulchre, the sorcerer knew nothing of his friends' fears and he continued to sprinkle more arsenic over the animal's rotting entrails. He did this every four hours, day and night, for three days, until the substance oozing from the rancid flesh had become *cantarella*.

Once Thomas was satisfied with the results of his labours, he collected the revolting liquid in a glass vial, which he stored in a little wooden box filled with straw. With the *cantarella* prepared, he ordered the pig's carcase to be burned, much to the relief of everyone in the castle, but there was a lot more to do before the Ritual of Rebirth could be performed.

Ignoring the puzzled stares of the servants, Thomas collected the rendered fat from the burning pig, mixed it with saltpetre purloined from Poenari's magazine and fashioned this strange tallow into several thick candles, each the size of a man's forearm. He also spent several hours scouring the castle's cellars for rats and mice.

As soon as he had a sack full of squeaking, wriggling vermin, Thomas retired to his room and gave strict orders that he must not be disturbed. The servants, who were now utterly convinced that Dracul's sorcerer was either mad or preparing a spell of such power he could unleash an army of demons at will, were only too happy to leave the Englishman alone.

With St Mary's Day drawing ever nearer, Thomas became so intent on his studies, he didn't notice the steady procession of Hungarian, Wallachian and Transylvanian lords making their way up the track to the castle. No fewer than four score of the most powerful men in Eastern Christendom, accompanied by their retinues, had made the difficult journey to Poenari and if these men knew of the *Drăculeşti's* reputation for enslaving their visitors, they chose to ignore it.

Perhaps these *boyars* feared the Turkish Sultan more than they feared the Order of the Dragon's Grand Master. Perhaps they hoped that Dracul could broker an alliance between the Danube's feuding families, or perhaps they were drawn to the Ritual of Rebirth by the mystic power of the Holy Lance.

Whatever the reason for their attendance, Dracul made sure that each guest was treated like the royalty they believed themselves to be and, within hours, the sounds of ribald celebration were echoing around the castle's grim walls. Throughout the day, and for most of the night, the keep's banqueting hall was filled with feasting noblemen and the castle's servants had to work tirelessly to satisfy the visitors' gargantuan appetites.

Whilst stewards served every type of game, fish and fowl, wenches filled wine cups so the guests could drink endless toasts and the only people in the castle excluded from these festivities were Thomas and his comrades. The Englishman was too busy to notice such an insult but the tantalising sights, sounds and smells of the visiting lords' carousing gave Bos, Prometheus and Quintana new cause to resent their confinement.

"Sweet Jesu, do I detect the aroma of roasted pork again?" Prometheus groaned as he toyed with the bowl of thin gruel and chunk of black bread that was supposed to suffice as the prisoners' supper.

"Surely everyone here is heartily sick of swine flesh," said Bos but Quintana thought that Dracul had a better reason for serving tender suckling pig and fine wines than the sin of gluttony.

"It's a test. Dracul knows that no Mohammedan will eat pork or let wine pass his lips, so if any man here refuses his hospitality, he must be a Turkish spy," said Quintana, who was standing at their chamber's window watching the Grand Master welcome another gaggle of diplomatic dignitaries.

With a groan, the Portugee began another tirade against the God that decreed he must dine off black bread and goat's cheese whilst others feasted on swan and peacock, but his familiar rant against life's unfairness ended abruptly in mid-sentence.

"What's the matter, are you ill?" Prometheus asked but the Portugee urged the others to come and see for themselves what had unnerved him.

"Look, it's Scaliger!" Quintana cried as his comrades joined him at the window and he pointed to the man in the black cloak who'd just appeared in the small courtyard by the castle's entrance.

"This can't be, a man as artful as Scaliger would never enter his enemy's fortress willingly," said Bos. However, there was no mistaking the new arrival's long beard or gouty limp.

"If Dracul has never met Scaliger, or seen his portrait, our Italian friend could easily pose an ambassador or chaplain to one of these warlords who now infest Poenari, and no one would suspect he's the Sultan's spy," said Quintana.

"That still doesn't explain why he'd risk life and limb coming here," said Prometheus, yet the Portugee was adamant that Scaliger had come for the Holy Lance.

"If Dracul's announced that he now has the relic, you can be sure that Scaliger will have heard about it and come to Poenari to steal the Holy Lance for the Turks, just as he'd always planned," he said, yet Prometheus scoffed at the idea that Scaliger could be so arrogant, or so foolish, as to believe that he alone could defeat the entire Order of the Dragon.

"Have you forgotten that this castle is garrisoned by a hundred Draconists all armed to the teeth and sworn to defend their Grand Master to the death?" Prometheus said. This prompted Quintana to insist that Scaliger wouldn't have walked into the dragon's lair without allies and he reminded the others that Dracul had many enemies, whilst the Sultan had many friends, on both sides of the Danube.

"Scaliger could easily have made pacts with all the Wallachian princes who are already in league with the Sultan. Now he's simply waiting for the moment to strike," said Quintana and the others had to admit that there was every chance that Dracul could be caught in his own web of lies.

"Even if Scaliger fails, Dracul will probably die during his foul ritual and if he does, the Draconists will tear the four of us to pieces," said Bos.

"And if Scaliger succeeds, he's hardly likely to forgive us for deserting him," added Prometheus.

"We're in more merda than a swineherd whose pigs have eaten nothing but bean pods for a month and I say we get out of here tonight," growled Quintana. The others needed no further persuasion and they began to discuss how they could break out of an impregnable castle that was perched on top of a mountain and guarded by a small army of fanatics.

Whilst Prometheus, Bos and Quintana plotted their escape, Thomas made his final preparations for the Ritual of Rebirth. His experiments on the luckless rats and mice had given him an idea of the dosage that would imbue a man with the semblance of death. However, to convince everyone that Lord Dracul had truly outwitted the Grim Reaper, he needed to prepare the Dragon Hall for its leading role in the charade.

To do this, Thomas dressed in a hooded black cloak and returned to the Dragon Hall carrying a long wooden staff and a jar of yellow paint, which he'd made by mixing more powdered orpiment with egg yolk.

Trying to look as menacing as possible, Dracul's sorcerer climbed the steps to the Dragon Hall and swept past the iron-faced guards. The deathly silence inside the darkened chamber was strangely comforting, yet, when Thomas saw Lord Dracul seated in infernal splendour on his *Balaur* throne, he felt his resolve evaporate.

The Grand Master, who was dressed in his sinister black armour, was surrounded by smoke wreathing from the throne's seven carved heads and this gave him the appearance of one of the demons he'd meet on his journey through Hell.

On seeing such a diabolical vision, Thomas hurriedly apologised for his intrusion and began to walk slowly backwards towards the Dragon Hall's door but Dracul ordered his sorcerer to stay.

"Welcome, Master Necromancer. I've been waiting for you, for I'm keen to know more of the Dark Arts you mean to employ to bring me back from The Abyss. Will you instruct me in the ways of The Left Hand Path?" Dracul said.

Curiously, the Grand Master spoke with something approaching humility but Thomas wasn't deceived. Dracul's presence made it clear that, for all his rhetoric, he didn't trust his new sorcerer and Thomas would have to follow the Ritual of Rebirth exactly as described in *The Munich Handbook* or risk being accused of treachery and attempted murder.

"I'd be honoured, My Lord," Thomas lied and he explained that he intended to summon *Volach*, the demonic lord who rode a monstrous two-headed serpent, and command this fiend to transport Dracul though Satan's realm.

In the hierarchy of Hell, *Volach* was a Great President who had dominion over snakes and dragons. Yet, once bound to the necromancer's will, this demon could be ordered to betray Satan and fetch any ghost from the Realm of Shades.

"*Volach* won't appear unless I draw three magic circles," Thomas added and he described how two of these rings would protect both Dracul and his sorcerer from the poisonous miasma that surrounded all creatures released from The Pit.

The third ring would cage *Volach* during the demon's brief visit to earth and *The Munich Handbook* gave strict instructions on the type of tools a sorcerer must use to draw these magic circles. A spell to raise a mighty Prince of Hell required an equally powerful wand, so, for the Ritual of Rebirth, the sorcerer's staff needed to be six feet long and fashioned from alder, as this wood had a strong resistance to decay.

To this wand, Thomas had to tie a brush made from the bristles of the pig he'd slaughtered and, once this had been done, he explained to the Grand Master the meaning of the symbols he was about to paint on the Dragon Hall's floor.

"In death, your body, My Lord, must lie on this altar so the first circle will protect your mortal remains whilst *Volach* leads your soul back to the light," said Thomas and he drew three concentric rings around the altar before writing the words of the spell that would raise Dracul from the dead.

In the outermost ring Thomas wrote:

HUNC CIRCULUM FACIO IN NOMINE DEI
PATRIS OMIPOTENTI QUI SOLO VERBO
UNIVERSA CREAVIT

In the middle ring he wrote:

HUNC CIRCULUM FACIO IN NOMINE
CHRISTI VIVI QUI HUMANUM GENUS HUMANO
SANGUINE REDEMIT

In the innermost ring he wrote:

HUNC CIRCULUM FACIO IN NOMINE
SPIRITUS PARACLITI QUIA APOSTOLORUM ET
PROPHETARUM CORDA SUA GRACIA
ILLUSTRAVIT

Between the words of these verses, he drew a Greek
cross, but, in the two halves of the circle on either side of
the altar, he drew the outline of a Latin cross and wrote:

PER HOC SIGNUM SANCTE CRUCIS GRACIA
DEI DEFENDANT AB OMNIS MALA.

"What does this mean?" the Grand Master asked and
though Thomas wondered if Dracul was pretending to be
ignorant of Latin so as to test him, he translated the spell:

*I make this circle in the name of God, The Almighty Father,*
*By whose word all things were created.*
*I make this circle in the name of the Living Christ made man,*
*Who hath redeemed all men through his most precious blood.*

*I make this circle in the name of the manifest Holy Spirit,
Who, through the Grace of God, shines in the hearts of the
apostles and the prophets.*

*May this holy sign and the Grace of God protect us all from the
evil that besets this world.*

These words seemed to renew Dracul's faith in his
own destiny, so he ordered his sorcerer to continue and
Thomas dipped his brush back into the poisonous yellow
paint. To complete the altar circle, Thomas had to draw
four symbols, to represent an ox, an eagle, a lion and a
man, at the cardinal points of the compass. On each of
these symbols, which stood for the four authors of the
gospels, he placed a small, glass vial but only one
contained *cantarella*.

The last thing Thomas wanted was for Dracul to
vomit up the poison before it could take effect, so only
the fourth vial held the noxious liquid. The other vials
contained nothing but strong wine made bitter by the
addition of wormwood, but the Grand Master was
ignorant of this fact.

Once he'd finished this circle, Thomas drew a second,
just far enough from the first so he could stand in its
centre and touch the altar with the tip of the wand held in
his outstretched hand. He connected the two circles with
a long, sinuous line, which represented the stars of Draco,
and Dracul recognised this device as the dragon
constellation which never sets below the horizon.

Inside the second circle Thomas sketched the outline
of an upside down letter T surrounded by a large
crescent. The inverted T represented the pagan tree of life
whilst the shape of the new moon had been used since
ancient times to represent the womb.

Around the edge of this circle, he wrote the names of the demons that would try and steal his soul during the ritual, and inside the T he wrote the names of the angels who'd protect him.

For the last circle, which had to be strong enough to hold *Volach*, Thomas drew a large double ring with the demon's seal and cipher inside. *Volach's* Seal consisted of a Greek cross surrounded by a plain circle and a symbol which looked like a dagger between each arm. Each of these daggers had its point touching the centre of the Greek cross.

To the right of the demon's seal, Thomas drew the cipher for *Volach's* name, which comprised a semicircle with two symbols that resembled the Greek letter ξ at each end of its base, and the double-barred Cross of Lorraine inside. Finally Thomas wrote V-O-L-A-C-H between the two outer rings of the circle and on each letter of *Volach's* name he placed one of the candles he'd made from saltpetre and pig fat.

Throughout these complex proceedings, Lord Dracul watched Thomas as carefully as a schoolmaster supervises a lazy pupil but he seemed more than satisfied with the results. The Grand Master even went so far as to congratulate his English sorcerer on his skill and ordered him to return to his chamber and rest for the remaining hours before the ceremony began.

Exhausted by the task of preparing the Dragon Hall, which had taken all night, Thomas gratefully returned to his tower and took to his bed. He slept until dusk the next day but he awoke feeling refreshed and excited. If he'd calculated correctly, Dracul would 'die' at midnight the following evening and a few hours later this second Lazarus would leave the stygian gloom of the Dragon Hall and emerge into in the new light of a golden dawn.

If his ruse succeeded Thomas would become the most celebrated magus in Christendom. However, as he revelled in the thought of kings and emperors trying to outbid each other for his services, he involuntarily touched the scratches on his face made by Ursula's surprisingly sharp fingernails.

The wounds, though slight, were still sore and served to remind Thomas that the girl was unlikely to forgive the man who'd poisoned her father, even if Dracul survived the Ritual of Rebirth. The thought that Ursula might be forever beyond his reach angered him and he cursed himself for being stupid enough to think he could tame a dragon's daughter.

Alone in the darkness, Thomas continued to ponder how a girl could love and hate her father in equal measures until his thoughts were interrupted by the sound of drunken laughter. Dracul's dissolute guests were spending their host's final hours feasting, yet, though was he irked by the noise of these lesser men taking their pleasure, their carousing gave him an idea.

There was no reason why he shouldn't use *The Munich Handbook* to summon Ursula to his bed and, even though he'd never yet cast a spell that worked, he'd lose nothing by trying. The fact that there were less than twenty-four hours before he had to perform Dracul's ritual didn't deter him because the second hour after sunset had begun and he reckoned this to be a good omen.

Quickly retrieving the *grimoire* from its wrapping, Thomas placed it in the reading circle he'd drawn earlier and turned to the section on erotic charms.

There were plenty of love spells from which to choose, in fact most of *The Munich Handbook* seemed to be devoted to finding either a woman or a horse without having to pay for either, but Thomas quickly dismissed those rites that required unobtainable ingredients. At this hour, and at such short notice, he had no chance of finding vellum made from the skin of a female dog or the heart of a snow-white dove.

If he were to have Ursula that night, Thomas needed the simplest of all enchantments and his heart sang as he found a spell that required nothing more than drawing the life-sized outline of a woman on the floor. This done, the sorcerer had to write the word TUBAL on the picture's head, REUCES on its right arm and SATAN on its left. Finally, the magician had to write his own name where the drawing's heart should be and to set the spell in motion he had to recite the words:

> *You are URSULA,*
> *Only daughter of MIRCEA also called DRACUL*
> *Of the House of DRACULESTI,*
> *May you SATAN and may you REUCES,*
> *Without delay so afflict her arms,*
> *That she can do nothing but desire to embrace me.*

This, it seemed, was all that was needed to make any maiden surrender to his charms but the book didn't say how long it would take for the magic to work. A spell that took days to be effective was of no use to Thomas but, in the absence of an alternative, he drew the diagram on the floor and said the simple incantation.

Once he'd cast the spell, all he could do was wait but he'd barely kicked off his shoes, and stretched himself out on his bed, before there was a knock at his door.

"Thomas, it's me, may I come in, or are you at prayer?" Ursula said softly.

Astonished by the sound of Ursula's voice, Thomas begged a minute to dress. Though his reason insisted that nothing, not even magic, could have brought the woman he desired to his room so quickly, he scrambled to his feet and pulled a shirt over his head.

Pausing only to scuff the love spell from the floorboards, he opened the door to see Ursula and she was looking more alluring than ever.

"You came," Thomas said hoarsely as he admired the girl's elegant gown and tight chemise, which was cut so low he could see a promise of what lay beneath. He wanted to reach out and touch the girl, to make sure she wasn't a phantom, but though the look in Ursula's eye suggested that she'd grown tired of her virtuous life, he stayed his hand.

"Did you send a message? I received none, I came because my father asked me to give you this," she said and she held out a roll of cheesecloth. Though Thomas was bewildered that his spell should make Dracul's daughter plight her troth with muslin, Ursula would say nothing more until he'd opened the package.

With a shrug, Thomas obeyed and unwrapped bundle; inside was a scarlet robe made from the finest silk and decorated with the symbol of the *Ouroboros* embroidered in gold thread. Though old, the robe must have cost a king's ransom when new and Ursula explained that it had been made for the first Dracul to wear during his initiation into the original Order of the Dragon.

"It's my father's wish that, you wear this sacred garment during the Ritual of Rebirth," she added but putting on clothes was the exact opposite of what Thomas had in mind.

For a moment he wondered where he'd gone wrong in preparing the love spell, then Ursula suggested that he ought to try the robe for size and he couldn't do that whilst he was wearing his baggy linen shirt.

"Here let me help you undress," she said and, as her fingers fumbled with the laces of his collar, Thomas felt his whole body harden with lust. When Ursula lifted the shirt over his head, his mouth became dry with desire and when she ran her fingers over the muscles of his chest. It was all he could do to control himself.

"You wear the dragon mark. Did the hot iron hurt terribly?" Ursula said breathlessly as she traced the scar on his shoulder with her fingertips and when Thomas flinched she gave a little gasp, as if the thought of pain excited her.

"If you asked me, I'd willingly endure any torment," he said and, taking hold of her hand, he touched her fingers to the scratch marks on his face. At this, Ursula blushed and lowered her eyes in embarrassment.

"I'm truly sorry about what happened before. I was angry and frightened. It's not natural for a man to want to die and the nuns taught me that refusing God's gift of life is a sin. They say suicides spend an eternity between Heaven and Hell and I couldn't bear the thought of my father roaming purgatory as an insubstantial shade," she replied humbly.

"You have my word your father won't die or even be harmed by my hand," Thomas said soothingly and he pulled the trembling girl into his arms. She gasped as he felt for the ribbons that secured her gown and she sighed with delight as the garment fell to the floor. Thomas silenced her feeble protests with a kiss and let one hand slip to her buttocks whilst the other snuffed out the room's single candle.

In the darkness, Ursula pressed her body against his and Thomas felt the soft curve of her breasts against his naked chest. She made no protest when he kissed her, so he took her gently in his arms and led her to the bed.

As if to make up for her previous violence, Ursula gave herself to him gladly. She revelled in the ecstasy of physical pleasure and whimpered with delight as she begged him to stop, and urged him to continue, in equal measures. The two lovers became so enraptured with each other they didn't hear the faint click as a hidden catch was released and a secret panel behind the room's fireplace swung silently open.

The night was warm, so Thomas hadn't lit the logs in the grate, and having pledged his soul to Aphrodite, he continued to lead Ursula along the secret paths of love unaware that a man in a long, hooded cloak had slipped into the room. Like the shadow of death, the stranger stood watching the star-crossed lovers but Thomas and Ursula remained utterly oblivious to the shade's presence until he spoke.

"I'm pained to see you like this, Thomas. As a scholar I thought you were above such animal desires," the intruder sneered. The shame of discovery caused Ursula to scream, yet the rage of frustrated lust gave Thomas strength and he leapt from the bed to confront the man he'd sworn to kill.

"Scaliger! Come a step closer and I'll show you just how much pain I can inflict on your pestilential person," Thomas cried but his uninvited guest held up his hand for silence. The moonlight filtering through the chamber's window gave Scaliger the look of a ghost but when he spoke his voice was as sharp and as sinister as an executioner's axe.

"I'm not known by the name of Scaliger in Poenari. Here I'm Francesco Bordone, chaplain to the noble Transylvanian House of Báthory," he said loftily.

"You can call yourself Adolphus the Talking Horse for all I care, just tell me what you're doing here before I call the guard," Thomas cried but he knew his threat was mere bluff. With Ursula naked in his bed, he could do nothing but listen to what Scaliger had to say.

"Did you think I'd stay away with Dracul boasting that he has Christendom's greatest relic? As the Turks are Lords of Jerusalem, the Holy Lance belongs to the Sultan and I intend to take it to him," he said but Thomas scoffed at the idea.

"You've made a grave mistake in coming here, because, when I reveal your true identity to Dracul, you'll be delivering your next lie from the top of a sharpened stake!" Thomas cried but now it was Scaliger's turn to remain defiant.

"I think not, because, if you reveal who I am, I'll be forced to tell Dracul that you've just deflowered his precious daughter! So if you and the girl want to live, you'll say nothing and keep to our original bargain. You'll ensure that Dracul's ritual fails so that the superstitious fools who put their faith in this madman will have to acknowledge Sultan Suleiman as their lawful overlord. Now put on some breeches, your vile nakedness sickens me to my stomach," said Scaliger. Thomas, however, refused to be cowed and he spat his defiance like a cobra battling a mongoose.

"The clothes of moral outrage don't suit such a verminous traitor like you! So listen to me, 'Bordone', or whatever your name is. I could snap your scrawny neck like a twig if I wanted and dead men can say nothing," Thomas snarled. This threat also missed its mark and Scaliger smiled knowingly before making his reply.

"If my body is found, or if I disappear, there are plenty of others secretly loyal to the Sultan who are already in Poenari. They'll denounce you, or kill you, it matters not. Half of Dracul's noble guests would choose Sultan

Suleiman over the *Drăculeşti*, or the Hapsburgs, and they'll gladly avenge my death. So, I repeat, if you want to live you'll make sure that Dracul dies ... permanently," he sneered and, having checkmated his former ally, Scaliger left the room by the same clandestine route he'd entered.

"What are we going to do?" Ursula sobbed as the secret door swung shut. In answer to her tears, Thomas could only curse himself for not having discovered the hidden passage during his previous search and, though he felt around the fireplace for the door's catch, he found nothing. Curiously, this failure only strengthened Thomas' resolve to quit Poenari and, as he pulled on his hose, he declared that if Ursula wanted to join him she'd better hurry.

"I'm leaving, if you want to come with me, you'd better get dressed," he said and there was no mistaking the note of urgency in his voice.

The girl opened her mouth to protest but she knew it was useless. Having lost her virtue, she had no value as a nun and having dishonoured her father, she had no value as a daughter. If she stayed in Poenari, she'd share the fate of all those who failed Lord Dracul, so she made the only decision she could. She hastily pulled on her clothes and followed Thomas into the stairway outside his bedchamber.

"We can't go into the courtyard because it's after dark and the dogs are on the loose," Ursula said nervously but Thomas had no intention of facing the hounds.

"Trust me," he whispered as he took Ursula's hand and led her to the covered walkway that ran along the top of the castle's walls. Moments later, they were climbing the stairs in the tower where his comrades had been quartered. However, when he opened the door, he was amazed to see the others surrounded by piles of straw.

"What in the name of Beelzebub's stinking buttocks are you lot doing? You look like the miller's daughter waiting for Rumpelstiltskin," he said, yet Bos, Prometheus and Quintana were just as surprised to see Thomas as he was to see them.

"We might ask you what you're doing with Dracul's daughter," said Bos, staring at Ursula.

"God's Hooks, Frisian, does the fornicating English bastard have to draw you a picture? What do you think he's been doing?" said Quintana.

Without going into the lurid details Bos required, Thomas quickly explained that Scaliger was in the castle and threatening to denounce them all unless they helped him thwart Dracul's plans to lead a new crusade against the Turks.

"We already know he's here, we saw him," Prometheus replied.

"And you didn't think to warn me?" Thomas said with ill-disguised annoyance.

"We were going to, when we'd finished making this," said Bos and he held up a length of plaited straw.

"Corn dolls! You know what my father will do to you, and me, if he thinks we've betrayed him, yet you waste time making decorations for a harvest festival?" Ursula cried in horror but Thomas understood exactly what his companions were trying to do.

# 18
## THE RAVINE

Once they'd seen Scaliger, Bos and the others had quickly realised that they'd no future as Draconists but they couldn't agree on a plan of escape. Fighting their way out of Dracul's fortress, or sneaking past the sentries wearing elaborate disguises, offered little chance of success. Nor could they hide in a cart that took away rubbish and night soil because the castle's waste was simply pitched over the walls.

Apart from the drawbridge, the only way in or out of Poenari was to fly or climb down the precipitous cliffs and, as there was neither the time nor the desire for Thomas to build them a flying machine, they'd resolved to do the latter.

To escape Poenari by climbing, the fugitives would need a rope and whilst their host had failed to provide enough bed linen to make one, the palliasses on which they slept were a different matter.

These crude mattresses were stuffed with straw rather than feathers and the dried stalks could easily be plaited into a rope. Using a long skein of this twisted straw, they could lower themselves into the ravine by the castle's entrance and then search for the secret path that would lead down the mountain to freedom.

"Are you sure there's a way out of the ravine?" Thomas asked, whereupon Quintana rolled his eyes and reminded them all of what Radu had said when they'd first arrived at Poenari.

"Don't you remember the story he told us? Assassins in the pay of his enemies threw Dracul into this chasm and left him to die, so, if he survived, he must've found a hidden way down the mountain. We can escape by the same route, once we have a rope long enough, so if you want to leave Dracul's house of death, sit down and give us a hand," he said but Ursula was still unsure.

"I may have been only a child, but in all the years I lived at Poenari I never heard of any secret path that led out of the ravine," she said but the others had already returned to their work.

With a shrug, Ursula sat down and picked up a handful of straw. However she soon regretted her decision. In a matter of minutes the coarse stalks had turned her delicate fingertips into bloodied lumps of raw meat. Nevertheless, she continued with her labours because she knew that the pain in her hands would be nothing compared to what she'd suffer if she failed to escape from her father's castle.

The prospect of being impaled focused everyone's attention and, though it took two more hours to finish the rope, Lady Fortune gave them all a crumb of hope. The straw had taken so long to plait, the sounds of carousing from the castle's keep had ceased, yet, even with all of Dracul's guests falling into a drunken stupor, there was no time to waste. The moment the rope was finished, Prometheus coiled it around his shoulder and walked to the room's door.

"Though there are sentries in the towers overlooking the entrance, Poenari is so remote the walkways are left unguarded at night," he said before he disappeared down the stairs and into the darkness. Reluctantly, the others followed and joined Prometheus in the covered gallery that connected the castle's watchtowers.

The Nubian's plan was simple. The gallery directly above the ravine projected a few feet beyond the wall, so, whilst the darkness hid them from view, they could lower the rope, climb down and look for the hidden path. The only problem that Prometheus could foresee was the presence of a sentry in Poenari's West Tower. To reach a suitable spot for lowering the rope, they would have to pass this guard.

The West Tower was a tall, circular turret that overlooked both the ravine and the drawbridge. An arched vault allowed the castle's sentries to pass from the southern to the western walls. However, apart from a ladder that led to the watchtower's upper floors, the vaulted chamber was empty.

"The sentry must be in one of the galleries above our heads. Do you think he'll spot us when we lower the rope?" Bos asked.

"We daren't risk it," Prometheus growled but, before he could climb the ladder to silence the sentry, a guttural voice called out. The men looked at each other in confusion, as the words meant nothing to them, but Ursula squeaked in alarm.

"He's wondering why his relief's early," she whispered.

"Then say something, before he calls for help," Thomas urged, so, in a louder whisper, Ursula told the sentry that she'd come from the kitchens with food and wine but her long skirts meant she couldn't carry the victuals up the ladder.

"Besides, if you want a little spice for your sausage, you'd better come here," she added with a flirtatious giggle and her words were immediately followed by the sound of a trapdoor being opened. Crouched in the shadows, the men heard the sound of leather boots on wooden rungs and held their breath. Seconds later, the guard reached the bottom of the ladder but, as he grinned greedily at Ursula, Prometheus pounced.

With the speed of a cobra, the Nubian whipped the straw rope he was carrying around his victim's neck and pulled with all his might. The sentry tried to scream, but no sound came from his crushed windpipe, and when he tried to claw his way free of the noose, Prometheus pulled the rope even tighter.

For a fraction of a second, the sentry felt the knife-sharp straw cutting into his throat before the bones in his neck snapped and he fell lifeless to the floor. For a moment, Prometheus stood panting by the sentry's corpse but, though the man had died with barely a sound, the dogs in the courtyard had sensed that something was wrong. The ever-watchful hounds erupted into a pandemonium of panicked barking; fortunately the fugitives' prayer, that the dogs' warnings would go unheeded, was answered.

The angry cries of the guards in the other parts of the castle soon quieted the restless hounds and, when all was silent once more, Prometheus dragged the dead sentry to one of the gallery's shuttered windows. For the powerful Nubian, it was the work of a moment to pitch the corpse into the night and the drop was so great nobody heard the body land on the rocks far below.

With the sentry gone, the fugitives' avenue of escape lay open and excitement replaced fear as they reached the walkway above the ravine. However, the only openings in this gallery's wooden walls were slits for the castle's crossbowmen and arquebusiers. Staring at the gallery's solid oak planks, Dracul's daughter felt her nerve evaporate and she declared that they'd more chance of escaping from a coffin.

"You fool! You've led us into a trap," Ursula hissed at Prometheus. In reply, the Nubian simply pointed to the machicolations which had been cut into the floor.

"We can use any one of these murder holes as a way out," he said gleefully. However, as he tied one end of the straw rope around a beam supporting the gallery's roof, Quintana took great delight in pointing out that Bos was much too big to fit through apertures meant for boiling oil and quicklime.

"We'll be here until next Michaelmas unless our fat Frisian friend loses some inches from his great bovine belly," he said, whereupon Bos raised his foot and brought it crashing down on the gallery's floor. The thin planks splintered as if they'd been hit by a culverin ball and the new hole was more than wide enough to accommodate his ample girth.

"There, an elephant could get through that," he said and this prompted Quintana to suggest that Bos should be the first pachyderm to lower himself into the abyss.

"Why do I have to go first?" Bos complained.

"Because, if the rope holds you, it'll hold anyone. Now, are you going to climb down or do we have to throw you down?" Quintana said.

Though Bos continued grumbling, he took hold of the rope, squeezed himself through the jagged hole in the floor and disappeared into the gloom. The straw creaked and groaned alarmingly, but the Frisian made it to the floor of the chasm safely and when he'd disappeared into the nearest thicket, Quintana followed.

Again the rope protested at such harsh treatment but the Portugee also reached the bottom of the ravine in one piece. Now it was Ursula's turn but she suddenly declared that her lacerated fingers made it impossible for her to climb down by herself.

"Plaiting that cursed straw cut my hands to ribbons," she moaned, so Prometheus hauled up the rope.

"Fear not, we'll lower you down," he said and whilst Thomas tied the rope around Ursula's waist, Prometheus took up the slack. When all was ready, he also took hold of the rope and before Ursula could change her mind she swung herself into the void. For a heartbeat, the girl remained suspended in space but, once the two men had braced themselves against her weight, they started to feed the rope through their hands. Inch by creaking inch, Ursula descended through the darkness and as soon as Prometheus felt the rope go slack he took his turn.

Now only Thomas was left inside the gallery and, peering through the hole in the floor, he watched Prometheus and Ursula disappear into the briars at the bottom of the ravine. Though Thomas couldn't believe that the sentries had failed to spot them, a glance along the darkened walkway confirmed that they hadn't been followed so he began his own descent.

Passing the castle's mouldering stones made Thomas feel like a bucket being lowered into an ancient well, and though the straw was difficult to grasp, he countered the pain by imagining Dracul's face once he'd discovered that his sorcerer had vanished into the aether. Yet, even as this thought entered his head, the rope snapped.

"Thomas!" Ursula squealed as she watched him fall fifteen feet into a gorse bush and she held her breath as the snake of twisted straw followed the fallen angel like the tail of a comet.

For a moment there was silence, and everyone feared the worst, but they soon heard the hushed cries of a man desperate to be released from an unwelcome embrace.

"By all the bastard sons of a Spanish pope, get me out of here!" Thomas croaked and though the others chided him for his clumsiness, they crawled through the thicket to help.

"You're making quite a habit of falling from high places," said Quintana as he and the others took hold of Thomas' ankles.

"Again, like Lucifer, you've been cast down for your pride, so pray for God's mercy," said Bos but Thomas could only stifle his cries of pain as he was pulled free of the briars.

"God's Wounds, those thorns tore at my flesh like the pitchforks of a thousand devils!" Thomas said when he'd been released from the bush. Unfortunately that wasn't the end of the fugitives' problems.

Just as Ursula had feared, there was no obvious way out of the ravine. However, though Quintana insisted that a secret path was supposed to be hidden, Prometheus suggested that it must be on the opposite side of the crag to the main track. Cursing the vengeful god who created thorn bushes, the escapers crawled to the northern end of the ravine to look for the secret path but all they found was another sheer precipice.

"By all the sulphurous pits in Lucifer's Infernal Kingdom, the path must be at the southern end of this Godforsaken abyss after all," groaned Bos, so the fugitives began to crawl back the way they'd come.

The first glow of dawn was beginning to brighten the eastern sky, so Thomas and the others had to slink on their bellies to avoid being seen from Poenari's towers, and by the time they'd reached the other end of the chasm, their faces and clothes had been shredded by the pitiless thorns. Yet their suffering was in vain because there was no sign of any path.

"We're caught like rats in a sewer," Ursula said in horror, but Prometheus was more hopeful and he pointed to the drawbridge, which was still raised.

"At least our absence hasn't been discovered. If we hurry, perhaps we can climb out of the ravine and use the main track down the mountain," he said but it was already too late. Thin shafts of sunlight were turning the castle's red roofs to gold and any attempt to scale the ravine's rain-polished walls would be spotted by Poenari's keen-eyed sentries.

All the fugitives could do was wait for night to return but at least there was a suitable thicket in which to hide. One particular jumble of briars would lie directly under the drawbridge when it was opened and there was just time to crawl beneath its branches before the clanking of heavy chains announced the beginning of a new day.

The drawbridge groaned like a man's guilty conscience as it was lowered and the next sound the fugitives heard was that of barking dogs. The men clenched their fists in anticipation of a hard fight but the dogs' yelps and growls drove Ursula to the point of hysteria. The girl began to shake uncontrollably, and Thomas had to clamp his hand over her mouth to stifle her cries of terror, but even his confidence vanished when he heard Radu's voice hailing them from above.

"Hear me, Master of Devils! I know you and your treacherous companions are hiding somewhere in the ravine, therefore let us end this charade without wasting any more time. Surrender, admit your folly and beg your Grand Master for forgiveness and he may yet be merciful. Persist in your deceitful ways and your end shall be most terrible!" Radu yelled, yet, in spite of his blood curdling threats, Thomas and the others made no reply.

"So be it!" Radu shouted and he ordered one of his men to fetch a lighted firebrand from the castle's kitchens. From their hiding place beneath the brambles, the fugitives wondered what Dracul's lieutenant intended to do but they still refused to show themselves. Finally Radu's patience was exhausted and he called out for a third time.

"I'll count to ten then I'll toss this lighted torch into the ravine. I hardly need remind you that it's high summer and the bushes in which you hide are tinder dry. So unless you wish to be roasted alive ..." Radu left the end of his sentence unfinished to add weight to his threat but he didn't have to begin counting. As soon as the fugitives smelled the smoke from their persecutor's torch, they scrambled out of the thicket and rose to their feet.

"All right, we give up," said Quintana bitterly.

Smiling in triumph, Radu ordered a long ladder to be lowered into the ravine but his air of victory vanished when he saw that Ursula was with the hated foreigners.

As the captives began clambering out of the chasm, Radu stared at the girl and his face had the expression of a cuckolded husband watching his faithless wife leave the another man's bedchamber, but when Ursula reached the drawbridge, Radu screamed at her with spiteful rage.

"You wicked strumpet, do you know what you've done?" Radu cried as Ursula joined the other prisoners but Dracul's daughter refused to be intimidated by her father's underling.

After smoothing her crumpled clothes and straightening her tousled hair, she looked at Radu with pure contempt and her gaze was as poisonous as that of the fabled *basilisk*.

"I've done nothing of which I'm ashamed. Can you say the same, little man?" Ursula said and though Radu's face turned puce with strangled fury there was no time for further talk.

The girl was bundled away by a dozen clucking maids and as she was ushered inside the castle, Ursula glanced over her shoulder to look directly at Thomas. The fear had returned to her eyes and, before he could shout any words of hope or encouragement, one of Radu's men smashed the wind from his body with a stout cudgel.

With a groan, Thomas sank to his knees, which was the signal for Radu's men to vent their anger on the others. Bos, Prometheus and Quintana were also beaten to the ground by a hailstorm of vicious blows from clubs and quarterstaffs but the assailants were careful not to cause their captives any permanent harm. Radu's purpose, at least for the time being, was merely to bludgeon his prisoners into submission and once iron shackles had been fastened around the captives' bruised wrists and battered ankles the beatings stopped.

"The pain you feel now is nothing compared to the agony you'll suffer for betraying your sacred oaths!" Radu cried and he ordered the four men to be thrown into the castle's strongest dungeon. Ignoring Thomas and the others' torrent of vitriolic curses, threats and protests, the Draconists hauled the struggling prisoners to their feet and pushed them through Poenari's narrow gateway.

With their manacles rattling like the breath of dying men, the prisoners were marched into the castle's keep and down a flight of stone steps. At the bottom of this staircase there was a large, vaulted chamber built of crumbling brick and from here a series of archways led to a labyrinth of darkened tunnels that disappeared into the bowels of the castle.

The prisoners had no time to wonder how many slaves had died hewing these sinister passageways out of the solid rock because they were quickly hurried along the largest of the tunnels to a heavy wooden door that was black with age. With his black rodent eyes shining in triumph, Radu slid back the door's bolts and the prisoners were pushed inside.

Though the dungeon was smaller than those Thomas had experienced in London and Metz, it was otherwise identical to the prisons in which he'd been previously incarcerated. Rusted chains hung from rings cemented into the damp walls, the floor's flagstones were covered with a thin layer of filthy straw and the only light came from a barred window set high in the wall opposite the cell door.

By standing on tiptoe, Thomas was able to peer out of this tiny opening but the view offered little comfort. Beyond the bars he could see nothing but the grass of the larger courtyard and the stones of the Dragon Hall so he turned away from the window and slumped to the straw. The others were also sitting dejectedly with their backs to the walls and each seemed to be resigned to their fate.

"Perhaps we should've stayed with that two-faced bastard, Scaliger, after all," said Quintana.

"It would've made no difference, except we'd be probably be sitting in a dungeon in Paris or Constantinople," said Dos.

"We're being punished for our sacrilege, we should've left the Holy Lance where it was," added Prometheus but Thomas refused to see divine retribution in their current predicament.

"If we're still alive, it's because Dracul needs us and if I can make him the ruler of a new Christian empire in the east, both he and God may yet forgive us," he said.

However, his words did nothing to dispel the gloom in the dungeon.

"I hope you're right, Thomas, because, if you're not, Dracul will have us all squatting on sharpened poles by sundown," said Quintana, yet sunset came and went and the prisoners remained in their dungeon. For the moment, their only torture was to be kept in near total darkness but at the fifth hour after dusk they heard the sound of their cell's door being unlocked. Seconds later, the dungeon was flooded with the light from a torch as Radu and a dozen Draconists entered.

"It's time, Englishman. You'll come with me and perform the Ritual of Rebirth at once or suffer a most disagreeable death," said Radu but Thomas sat motionless in the torchlight and refused to obey the command.

"Where's Ursula? I'll do nothing until I know she's safe," he said angrily. Thomas was determined not to betray his fears to Radu but Dracul's lieutenant merely laughed at his defiance and spat in the Englishman's face.

"The bitch-whore is unharmed, though remember this, you scabrous louse: if you fail, she'll die and her death will be on your conscience, if you have one," Radu sneered.

"What do you mean by that?" Thomas demanded but Radu would say no more. Instead, he ordered his men to remove Dracul's sorcerer from the cell by force and the guards didn't need to be told twice. All the men under Radu's command were veterans of the battle in the forest and the fight in Marburg, so, having seen their fellow Draconists killed by Thomas and his companions, they took great delight in inflicting as much pain as possible on the Englishman.

Reeling under a succession of vicious punches, Thomas was dragged to the vault beneath Poenari's keep where his chains and clothes were removed. Having been stripped naked, Thomas was doused with water and scrubbed clean, before being told to put on a fresh undershirt as well as the scarlet *Ouroboros* robe.

When he was properly dressed, Thomas was bundled outside into the warm, summer night and whilst his mind spun with the speed of his sudden restoration to Dracul's favour, he was taken to the top of the steps that led to the Dragon Hall. Still drunk with pain and bewilderment, Thomas struggled to stand unaided but the deafening clarion call from a score of unseen trumpets restored the Englishman to his wits.

The notes of the fanfare were still echoing around the castle when the courtyard in front of the Dragon Hall became ablaze with light. Fifty men carrying torches filed slowly around the foot of Poenari's walls, whilst another fifty formed an avenue of stars that stretched all the way from the castle's keep to the Dragon Hall. Minstrels began playing sombre music on lutes, drums and sackbuts and as the music grew louder, a cortège for the living dead began to walk with funereal solemnity along this avenue of torches.

At the head of this procession walked Dracul. He was bareheaded, barefoot and dressed only in a shroud of white linen. Behind him, there followed a hundred of the most powerful Christian nobles in Transylvania and Wallachia and they were all dressed for battle. The torchlight glinted off their steel armour and though Thomas didn't know their names, the cruel expressions on their faces identified them as ruthless men. These princes were absolute monarchs in their own petty fiefdoms and they'd only follow a king if he proved to be stronger than themselves.

The one dignitary not wearing a polished breastplate or plumed helmet was dressed in the black cloak and square cap of a scholar and he walked a little way behind the others because he needed the aid of a staff to take each painful step. Though Thomas instantly recognised Scaliger, before the Englishman could shout a warning to Dracul, who'd now reached the foot of the Dragon Hall's steps, he felt the point of a dagger pressing into the small of his back.

"Keep silent, you stinking piece of Saxon shit! If you utter one word about Lord Scaliger, your whore will die slowly and painfully," Radu hissed.

The revelation that Dracul's lieutenant was also in the pay of the Sultan was almost impossible to believe, and though the proof of Radu's treachery was the steel blade threatening to fillet his spine, Thomas was not of a mind to surrender meekly.

"What did Scaliger promise you, Dracul's throne? His daughter? Both? I warn you, Radu, if Ursula dies, I'll summon ten thousand demons so powerful they can make Scaliger and all those who follow him suffer unimaginable torments until the end of time," Thomas growled but Radu dismissed the feeble threat with a snort of derision.

"You couldn't summon enough piss to wet yourself! I was loyal to Dracul until Lord Scaliger revealed the duplicity of *Drăculeşti* women. Ursula had promised me that we'd be wed as soon as her father had defeated the Turkish Sultan but instead she gave herself to you. Now, you'll be the instrument of my revenge," he sneered and, though Thomas tried to speak, there was no time to argue as Dracul was beginning to mount the steps to the Dragon Hall.

As soon as the Grand Master had reached the top of the stone stairs, the fanfare of trumpets sounded for a second time and the flower of Danubian chivalry turned to look down the avenue of torches that led back to the Castle of Poenari's keep. The sound of the trumpets was replaced by the slow beat of drums and as another figure was marched across the courtyard, Thomas felt his soul cry out in agony.

The new arrival was Ursula. Like her father, she wore only a loose shift but she was not taking part in the Ritual of Rebirth willingly. She was shouting, cursing and struggling violently as four Draconists dragged her along the avenue of light towards the Dragon Hall.

As Ursula's cries grew louder, Thomas turned his head away in disgust, yet, as he did so, he noticed a pair of iron rings set into the stonework near the top of the steps. These rings were spaced about three feet apart and two ropes had been threaded through them. Once Ursula had been manhandled into position, her wrists were tied to these ropes and a gag stuffed in her mouth.

With her protests muffled, and the knots tied tight, the guards hauled Dracul's daughter off her feet until she was hanging ten feet above the ground. Once this had been done, two more Draconists rammed a sharpened stake in the earth directly below the pinioned girl.

As he watched this grotesque ceremony, Thomas realised that, if the ropes were cut, or the knots came loose, Ursula would fall onto the stake and be impaled, yet Dracul seemed to be delighted with the results of his men's labours. Whilst Ursula fought vainly against her bonds, her father addressed the crowd in the harsh tones of Cato addressing the Roman senate and he made no attempt to disguise the note of triumph in his voice.

"Behold! This woman was discovered in the act of fornication. Like all women, she's sinful, and like all sinners she must die, yet God is merciful. If I can pass into the Valley of Shadows, battle with the Angel of

Death and emerge victorious, her sin shall be redeemed and she will live. If I fail, she'll follow me to the grave!" Dracul cried. A great explosion of cheering erupted from the crowd and only Thomas seemed to show any sense of horror at Ursula's fate.

"My God, she's your daughter!" he croaked but Dracul insisted that he had no daughter.

"Until Ursula is cleansed of sin, she's dead to me, so, restore me to life and she'll be freed. Fail and she will die," Dracul whispered to his necromancer.

The callousness of these words stunned Thomas into silence but the crowd continued cheering as Dracul ordered the Holy Lance to be brought forth. Silently, the great wooden doors of the Dragon Hall swung open and five acolytes, each dressed in a long, white robe, emerged from the shadows.

The first of Dracul's disciples carried an ash pole seven feet long but each of the other four held a corner of the purple cloth that, until now, had covered the Dragon Hall's altar. In this way, the acolytes could carry the Holy Lance to their Grand Master without touching the sacred metal. However, when they presented the relic to Dracul, instead of picking up the blade, he stared at his sorcerer and the light of madness shone bright in his eyes.

"Before we begin, you must prove to me you're still blessed by God," he said to Thomas and he ordered his sorcerer to fit the Holy Lance to its new shaft.

Ignoring Dracul's demonic gaze, Thomas snatched the wooden rod from its bearer with one hand and retrieved the Holy Lance from the altar cloth with the other. Holding the two pieces high above his head he fitted them together and Dracul, who'd expected his sorcerer to be struck dead by a thunderbolt, could only stare in wonder as Thomas presented him with the restored spear.

"This is the blade that pierced Our Saviour's side, take it if you wish to conquer," Thomas declared angrily, and he offered the Holy Lance to the only man prepared to sacrifice his child to win the east for Christ, but the Grand Master hesitated.

"Not yet. I must still pass through the Vale of Death before I'm worthy to touch that which touched the flesh of God made man but the Ritual of Rebirth may now begin!" Dracul cried and he turned to face the crowd.

With Thomas standing behind him, the torchlight glinted off the Holy Lance's gold sleeve, giving the impression that a tongue of fire, sent by the Holy Spirit, had appeared above Dracul's head. There was a gasp of appreciation from the crowd in the courtyard below but the Grand Master raised his hand and everyone fell silent.

"Let all those who refuse to believe that I've been chosen by God to rule Christendom, behold the Holy Lance that wounded Christ's side at Calvary and know that by this sign I shall defeat all my enemies, including death!" he cried and the courtyard was filled with a fanfare loud enough to wake Lucifer himself.

The uproar numbed Thomas' senses and it was all he could do to carry the Holy Lance into the Dragon Hall. Once they'd passed from the light into the darkness, and the wooden doors had been slammed shut, the crowd's cheers were silenced. However the eerie quiet inside the hall seemed more terrible than the pandemonium outside.

Besides Dracul and his sorcerer, twelve princes from the most powerful families on the Danube, with Radu at their head, had also entered the Dragon Hall and they now stood in a semicircle in front of the marble altar. Whilst the noblemen prepared themselves for their role in the ceremony, Dracul knelt at the edge of the first magic circle and began to pray.

If Dracul was nervous at the prospect of his own impending death, he didn't show it and he addressed the men who would witness the Ritual of Rebirth in a voice as tranquil as a tomb.

"My brothers, you're the new apostles who shall proclaim my resurrection. Once I've returned from the grave, you shall go forth into the world and announce that, though Lord Dracul has suffered death, he has risen to lead all Christian men to glory," he said and he looked directly at Thomas.

When their eyes met, the Englishman felt as if his soul had been gripped by the cold hand of Satan. There was no longer any humanity in Dracul's expression, and his stare was that of a beast, but for all his madness, Thomas had to admire the man's courage. Even if his sorcerer had no faith in magic, Dracul was certain he'd win his battle with the Angel of Death.

"Work your enchantments well, Englishman," Dracul whispered and he lay down on the marble altar.

# 19

## THE DRAGON HALL

As he stared at Dracul's recumbent figure, Thomas felt his fingers grip the shaft of the Holy Lance more tightly. There was nothing to stop him from plunging the spear into Dracul's chest, and sending this monster to his grave forever, but murdering the Grand Master wouldn't solve Thomas' dilemma.

If Dracul died then he, Ursula and his companions in the dungeon would be slaughtered by the enraged Draconists but, on the other hand, if Dracul survived, then he, Ursula and the others would be killed by Scaliger and his allies.

There was only one possible course of action: Thomas had to convince everyone in the castle that Dracul had truly cheated death. If, somehow, he could make Dracul appear to emerge from the grave, then there was a chance that both the Grand Master's enemies and the Sultan's clandestine supporters would abandon Scaliger and join Dracul's crusade after all.

In the confusion that was bound to follow such a miracle, he could free Ursula and release the others before Radu could carry out any of his threats, so, clinging to this faint spark of hope, Thomas put all thoughts of peril from his mind and began the ancient Ritual of Rebirth.

"My Lords, this rite is the most dangerous that any magus may perform because, though Lord Dracul must die, he must not be embraced by the Angel of Death," Thomas said gravely.

After making the sign of the cross, Thomas pointed to the symbols he'd drawn around the altar and explained that this magic circle was a portal through which souls could enter and leave the Valley of Shades. However, before he could begin the spell that would separate Lord Dracul's spirit from his body, he had to banish the Dark Angel *Samael*, who conveyed the souls of the dead to the Underworld, from the Dragon Hall.

"Only then may Lord Dracul enter The Abyss in safety but, in order for him to return, I must also summon the vicious demon *Volach* and command this Great President of Hell to guide our master's soul back to the light. The laws of nature that govern this world do not apply in the worlds that exist beyond death. Therefore, though his journey may take aeons of celestial time, here it shall seem as if Lord Dracul has been gone for no more than a few hours. So, My Lord, are you ready?" Thomas asked.

"I'm ready," said Dracul and he crossed his arms over his chest to mimic the pose of the dead whilst Thomas stood in the second circle he'd drawn. Holding the Holy Lance as far down the shaft as he could, he lowered the spear slowly so that its tip hovered a few inches above Dracul's heart.

"I shall now banish *Samael*, the Angel of Death, who serves both the God of Light and the Lord of Darkness," said Thomas and he began the first incantation.

*By GOD the FATHER ALMIGHTY,*
*And by those angels he hath made,*
*And by those four beasts which uphold the world,*
*And by every good creation God hath made in heaven and earth,*
*I conjure you, SAMAEL,*
*That you should have not the power to remain in this place,*
*I conjure you, servants of the DEVIL, servants of SATAN,*
*Servants of THE ENEMY,*
*So that you may be banished from this place.*
*Author of sins,*
*Deceiver of souls,*
*Envious one,*
*Inveterate murderer,*
*Who sought the death of the immortal GOD made man,*
*In the name of Our Lord JESUS CHRIST*
*AUDI ET TIME ERGO!*
*Hear and be afraid,*
*For the angels and archangels press upon you to leave this place,*
*The martyrs and confessors press upon you to leave this place,*
*Now arise and be gone!*

"The Angel of Death and his cohorts have now departed but Lord Dracul's soul must also leave quickly, for *Samael* is powerful and he may return at any moment," said Thomas and, before the witnesses could demand proof that the hall had been cleansed of evil, he began the next part of the ritual.

Stepping out of his magic circle, Thomas stood in front of the first vial which he'd placed on his drawing of an ox. This symbol represented St Luke the Evangelist, patron of physicians, and though it contained only the harmless mix of wine and bitter herbs, Thomas reverently placed the tip of the Holy Lance on the vial before reciting another spell:

*In the name of the FATHER, SON and HOLY SPIRIT,*
*I cast out all demons, so that he who drinks from this bottle,*
*Might take up serpents yet suffer no injury,*
*And drink poison yet suffer no harm.*
*By the power of the Wondrous Lance,*
*Which touched the flesh of The Redeemer,*
*I command it!*

After speaking these words, Thomas picked up the vial, removed the stopper and placed the little bottle in Dracul's hand. The Grand Master hesitated for the briefest of moments before drinking the contents and, when nothing happened, he looked strangely annoyed that he wasn't writhing in agony.

"Take heart, My Lord, the spell won't take effect until after the final draught," Thomas whispered and Dracul nodded in understanding as his necromancer moved to the next vial. The second bottle stood on the drawing of an eagle, which represented St John the Evangelist, and here Thomas declared:

*Let the eagle that soared with CHRIST to Heaven,*
*Watch over MIRCEA DRACUL*
*Of the House of the Drăculeşti,*
*As he passes from this world into the next!*

Again, Thomas touched the top of the vial with the tip of the Holy Lance before he handed it to Dracul and again the Grand Master drank the contents without suffering any ill effects. Now, Thomas moved to the third bottle, which stood on the symbol of St Mark the Evangelist. This saint is also invoked by physicians in need of protection, and here the sorcerer intoned:

*The Lion of Judah will conquer, the Root of David will sprout,*
*And DRACUL of the Drăculeşti shall be reborn!*

After Dracul had consumed the third vial's contents, Thomas moved to the final bottle, which stood on the drawing of a man. This symbol represented St Matthew the Evangelist and here Thomas proclaimed:

*CHRIST conquers, CHRIST rules, CHRIST reigns!*
*May OUR SAVIOUR defend this pious servant of GOD,*
*from every fantasy and vexation of the DEVIL,*
*By the power of the Holy Lance,*
*I command it,*
*AGIOS, HYSKYROS,*
*ATHANATHOS, ELEYSON!*

The instant Dracul drained the fourth vial, he sat bolt upright and his face contorted into a mask of strangled pain, then in the space of a heartbeat, every muscle in his body suddenly lost its strength and he slumped back onto the altar. The breath of life left the Grand Master with a whisper but, as the empty vial fell from Dracul's fingers and shattered on the stone floor, Radu ran forward.

"You mustn't enter the circle, Dracul is under its protection and if you cross its boundaries the spell will be broken!" Thomas shouted but Radu ignored the warning and deliberately stepped over the painted lines. Dracul's once faithful lieutenant held a small piece of polished metal over his master's mouth and when it remained unclouded he placed his fingertips on either side of Dracul's neck.

"There's no breath or heartbeat; already the skin grows cold. Sweet Jesu, have mercy upon us, the Lord Dracul is really dead!" Radu cried.

Like Saul struck blind Dracul's lieutenant staggered out of the circle. However, before Radu could remember which side he was supposed to be on, Thomas had declared he was about to summon *Volach*, and that any further interruptions could prove fatal to them all. At this, two of the Danubian princes seized hold of Radu whilst Thomas lit a splint from one of the braziers of glowing coals by the altar.

Holding the lighted taper in one hand, and the Holy Lance in the other, Thomas entered the third of his magic circles, which was adorned with the candles he'd made from saltpetre and pig fat. Raising the Holy Lance high above his head, he began the final spell:

> *I address Lord VOLACH, Great President of Hell,*
> *Behold the instrument of CHRIST's Passion and hear me,*
> *In the name of the FATHER,*
> *I summon thee from the depths of The Abyss,*
> *In the name of the SON,*
> *I call upon thee to pass from darkness into light,*
> *In the name of the HOLY SPIRIT,*
> *I command thee to appear within this, thy Seal and Cipher,*
> *In the name of all the kings of Hell*
> *BAEL, PAIMON, BELETH PURSON, ASMODAY,*
> *BALAM, BELIAL,*
> *Thou, O VOLACH, wilt obey me!*

Once the words of the final spell had been spoken, Thomas lit each of the saltpetre candles, which instantly produced thick clouds of stinking, purple smoke. The noxious fumes quickly filled the hall and, as the sorcerer became enveloped in the foul-smelling fog, he screamed like a heretic feeling the first touch of the Holy Inquisition's flames.

"*Volach* is more powerful than I ever imagined and I may not be able to cage him within the circle! All of you, for the sake of your immortal souls, leave this place and do not return until I've defeated the thirty-eight legions of demons this fiend commands!" Thomas yelled.

In truth, there was more danger from being suffocated by the choking smoke than from diabolical monsters but the princes of Wallachia and Transylvania were not about to risk either. Dragging Radu between them, they retreated from the Dragon Hall as quickly as they could.

As soon as the pusillanimous princes had left, Thomas ran to the hall's entrance and barred the doors with a heavy oak beam before extinguishing the candles. He'd used the trick of mixing pig fat with saltpetre once before, and he hadn't dared hope it would work again, but it had. Everyone in the castle was now convinced that the Dragon Hall was under siege from an army of demons; all Thomas had to do was to wait for Dracul to recover.

Confident that the poison would soon lose its power, the sorcerer sat on the seven-headed-dragon throne and waited for the 'corpse' to show signs of life. However, an hour passed and Dracul remained as motionless as a carved effigy in a church.

After another hour had slipped by, Thomas began to fear that, despite his careful calculations, the *cantarella* had induced death rather than sleep and he couldn't stop himself from imagining what would happen if Dracul couldn't be revived. There was little doubt that the Draconists would skewer him like a spatchcock if their master was truly dead, yet, whatever happened, Thomas vowed to himself that he'd die with a blade in his hand rather than a sharpened stake between his legs.

"I swear, by Jehovah, the God of Battles, whether or not there's any divine power in this rusty old spear, I'll use it to kill as many of my enemies as possible before I too am laid in my grave," Thomas muttered grimly. Seconds later, his solemn oath was interrupted by a shout from outside the hall.

"Hear us, sorcerer, enough time has passed for Lord Dracul to revive. Show us that he's risen or face the consequences!"

The voice sounded like Radu and, in desperation, Thomas glanced at Dracul's corpse in the hope there'd been some change. Unfortunately, the Grand Master's limbs were still as stiff as a bishop's staff and his face was the colour of ancient parchment.

"You fools, if I open the doors now, *Volach* and his legion of the damned will be released into the world!" Thomas yelled but the time for bluff had passed and his warning was lost in the sound of a loud crash as something large and heavy was hurled against the Dragon Hall's doors. Seconds later, another thump echoed around the ancient stone walls and the dust shaken loose from the rafters fell like soft, grey snow.

"Cease this blasphemy! Lord Dracul is waking and, unless there's absolute silence, the spell will be broken!" Thomas lied. Again his warning was ignored and the solid oak doors seemed to bend under the impact of another mighty blow.

In desperation, Thomas ran to the altar and began to rub Dracul's chest in an attempt to stimulate the circulation of blood and other humours. The battering ram was making more than enough noise to wake the dead and then, as if in response to the rhythmic thumping from outside, the sorcerer felt warmth return to the cold flesh beneath his fingers.

There was just enough time for Thomas to give a great cry of triumph before Dracul's body became seized with convulsions and he was violently sick. Not even Bos during one of his week-long bouts of drinking could produce such enormous volumes of vomit, and Thomas was engulfed in so much bile it soaked through his robe to his undershirt, but worse was to follow. As soon as Dracul had finished emptying his stomach, he voided his bladder and bowels with equal force, and once his body could give out no more, he lay in a pool of his own ordure, howling like a new-born babe.

"Am I alive or am I still in Hell? I remember nothing. Perhaps Hell is nothing but nothingness for all eternity and that is its true horror," Dracul wailed, yet there was no time for Thomas to show mercy as the pounding of the battering ram was suddenly replaced by the sound of splintering wood.

"The memories will return but now you must show yourself to the crowd or no one will believe you've truly conquered death," Thomas said hurriedly and he hauled the reeking Dracul to his feet. A heartbeat later, Radu and a dozen heavily armed princes of the Danube burst into the Dragon Hall.

"Surrender, vile assassin!" Radu shouted but, though he pointed his sabre at Thomas, he let the blade fall to the floor when he saw Dracul standing before the altar. The Order of the Dragon's Grand Master was dazed, naked, covered in filth and shaking with febrile cold but he was unmistakeably alive.

"Behold the Man!" Thomas cried and he propelled the tottering Grand Master towards the hall's entrance.

The steel wall of armoured men parted, and some even fell to their knees, as the second Lazarus left the Dragon Hall to receive the acclamations of his disciples. However, if Thomas had imagined that the resurrected Dracul would appear bathed in the light of a golden dawn he was disappointed. The morning was cold, grey and damp and the weather, combined with the purging effects of the *cantarella*, made Dracul look less like a chivalrous crusader and more like a drunken beggar who'd been fished out of a cesspit.

In spite of his appearance, the Grand Master had the strength to lift his arms and, as he gave thanks to God for his deliverance, the rain began to fall. The summer shower was short, yet it was sufficient to wash most of the dirt from Dracul's body and when the sun finally emerged, the crowd began to believe that Lord Dracul had been re-baptised by God himself.

"No assassin can kill me, I'm immortal and I shall build a third Roman Empire that will endure for ten thousand years. Where's the Holy Lance? From now on it must never leave my side!" Dracul cried. The pain in his voice and the stoop in his limbs had vanished and he was once more the hero chosen by God to lead the Christian armies of the east in a new crusade.

"The Holy Lance is here, My Lord. Now give the order to release your daughter!" Thomas urged as he pressed the spear's shaft into Dracul's hand.

The Grand Master nodded and strode purposefully to the parapet at the top of the steps but his order to free Ursula was drowned in a loud cheer. The adulation seemed to drive any thoughts of his daughter from Dracul's mind and he began to promise the crowd that all those who swore loyalty to the *Drăculeşti* would inherit the entire earth.

"By the power of the Holy Lance, I've conquered the world of the dead and by the power of the Holy Lance, you will conquer the world of the living!" Dracul cried and another storm of wild acclaim swept through the castle's courtyard.

As the clamour continued, Thomas peered over the stairway's parapet, and was horrified to see that Ursula was still hanging from her bonds. Worryingly, her body looked so limp and lifeless, he couldn't tell if she was dead or unconscious.

"My Lord, your daughter is at the point of death. You must free her!" Thomas repeated but, again, before Dracul could order Ursula's release, he was interrupted. This time, it was the man wearing a black scholar's gown who stepped forward and began to harangue the crowd.

"You've all been tricked by the liar, Dracul, and his fraudulent necromancer. The real spear of St Longinus still lies in a Nuremberg church, this I know because I've seen it!" Scaliger cried and there was a loud rasp of metal as every nobleman and Draconist in the courtyard drew his sword. Dracul's allies began to shout that the blasphemer must be cut down but, in reply, Scaliger's supporters formed a protective cordon around the Sultan's spy. The two sides stood shouting insults at each other until Scaliger held up his hands for calm.

"Everyone here has taken an oath to observe Lord Dracul's truce, so, even though he's a cheat and a charlatan, put up your weapons and listen to the message I bring from the Sultan of Sultans, Khan of Khans, Lawgiver, Lord of the Universe, Lord of the Ottomans and of all the lands of the East, Suleiman the Magnificent!" Scaliger cried. Some of the crowd gasped in awe at the list of the Sultan's titles, whilst others cursed Suleiman's name as a hated enemy, but when the cries of outrage and adulation had died away, Scaliger continued.

"The Great Suleiman knows of Dracul's feeble rebellion against his lawful overlord, yet he'll forgive every man who renews his oath of loyalty. In return, Suleiman offers you his protection, for he's a pious man who respects all Christians as a fellow People of the Book!" Scaliger cried.

In reply, Dracul gave a great shout of anger and, in a voice that sounded like the crack of doom, he declared that Scaliger was the enemy of all those who had faith in the Lord Jesus.

"Hear me, and mark my words well, this man who slanders me is a worse traitor than Judas who betrayed his God or Brutus who betrayed his friend!" Dracul bellowed but Scaliger ignored the outburst and announced that any resistance to the Turkish army was now utterly futile.

"Already Suleiman's *janissaries* have crossed the River Drava and the milksop King of Hungary was too busy ploughing his Hapsburg whore to fight. Whilst those who garrisoned Louis' castles and patrolled his borders now lie in cold earth, their king lies in silken sheets! What's more I can give you further proof that your cause is unjust and doomed. Not only is the spear in Dracul's hand a fake, the so-called miracle of his rebirth is nothing but a mountebank's trick!" Scaliger shrieked and he declared that every apothecary in Italy knew how to give a man the semblance of death by using *cantarella*. At this, the first whisper of disbelief rippled through the crowd but Dracul wasn't beaten.

"I swear this is the real Holy Lance, taken from under the noses of the usurper Hapsburgs by men loyal to me! Through its power I've cheated death and, just as it brought me back from the grave, so it shall revive my kin!" Dracul bellowed and his voice sounded so commanding, those in the courtyard were powerless to prevent what happened next.

Before anyone could stop him, Dracul had run down the hall's steps, snatched a sword from one of his men and sliced through the ropes that held his daughter suspended over the sharpened stake. The crowd gasped as Ursula fell and Thomas cried out in horror as Dracul's daughter was pierced through her heart.

Though every noble in Poenari had ordered unimaginably savage punishments to be inflicted on their slaves, serfs and captured enemies, Dracul's senseless slaughter of his own flesh shocked them all to the very depths of their souls.

Yet for all their profound disgust, the noble princes of the Danube could only watch in sickened silence as a ghastly red stain spread across the white linen of Ursula's gown. Even Scaliger was struck dumb but somehow Dracul found the strength to speak.

"In the name of God, I command *Samael*, Angel of Death, to open the gates of The Underworld and by the power of the Risen Christ, I command *Volach* to bring Ursula of the *Drăculești* back from the edge of The Pit!" Dracul cried and he touched Ursula's corpse with the point of the Holy Lance.

Nothing happened. Ursula's corpse hung from the stake like a broken doll and the Grand Master of the Order of the Dragon could only stare in utter bewilderment at the body his lifeless child.

"Thomas, do something, say a spell, restore her to life this instant!" Dracul hissed to his necromancer, who was still standing at the top of the stone steps that led to the Dragon Hall.

"I can't. I warned you, for the spell to work, death has to be accomplished through poison because no mortal man can restore life to a body with a stake driven through its heart!" Thomas shouted angrily and Dracul gave out a long shriek of anguish that came straight from the deepest circle of Hell.

"Deceiver!" Dracul screamed and he threw the Holy

Lance at Thomas, who ducked as the blade flashed past his head. The relic bounced off an iron stud in the Dragon Hall's oak doors and clattered to the floor. However, as the spear left Dracul's hand, a deafening shout of victory came from Scaliger's allies and they charged at the astonished Draconists.

The civil war Dracul had risked everything to avoid, now broke out in his own castle and, as the two sides joined in battle, the competing merits of the *Drăculeşti*, Hungarian and Turkish claims to Wallachia's throne were swept away in an avalanche of private hatred.

No quarter was asked or given as feuds that were centuries old erupted into an orgy of slaughter and though both Dracul and Scaliger became lost in the mêlée, one man remained detached from the butchery. Crouched behind the parapet at the top of the steps to the Dragon Hall, Thomas tried to channel the rage he felt over Ursula's death into action. He knew that he could only escape her fate by fighting his way out of Poenari, so he tore off his robe and snatched up the sword dropped by Radu. However, before he plunged into the fray, he also picked up the Holy Lance.

Though the spear's ancient metal was much too old and frail to be of any use in a battle, Thomas pulled the wooden shaft out of its socket and wrapped the blade in a piece of cloth torn from his discarded robe. Even if the relic lacked the power to revive the dead, it might still buy his life, so he hid the treasure beneath his undershirt and ran down the steps. Seconds later, Thomas was cutting his way through the mass of men that filled the courtyard.

In the swirling maelstrom of warriors fighting for their lives, no one noticed another half-crazed loon dressed in nothing except a shirt that still reeked of Dracul's piss and vomit. However, those who ignored the Englishman made a fatal mistake, because Thomas blamed Scaliger, Dracul and all their allies for Ursula's death. Enraged by his sorrow, he revelled in the joy of slicing through the ranks of her murderers, no matter which side commanded their loyalties.

Step by step, he cut his way towards the narrow passage that led to the castle's main gate and he bellowed like an angry bull as he felt his blade strike hard steel and soft flesh in equal measure. With a cry of inhuman rage, Thomas crushed the skull of one of Scaliger's men before slashing open the neck of a Draconist and as warm blood spattered his face, he saw Dracul surrounded by a dozen of his Danubian rivals.

The great Lord Dracul, who, less than an hour ago, had survived being poisoned by a foul concoction of arsenic and rotten pig entrails, was still naked, but the fire of the berserker's madness had been rekindled in his eyes.

From somewhere Dracul had acquired one of the curved *bardiche* axes used by the Dragon Hall's guards and, like Thomas, he had all the strength of grief in his arms. Several of the braver Danubian princes who challenged him were quickly cut down by the axe's enormous blade; yet, in the end, Dracul's foes were too numerous.

From nowhere, a crossbow bolt struck Dracul in the belly and whilst he tried to wrench the steel-tipped dart from his bleeding gut, a cowardly sword-cut from behind severed both his hamstrings.

Howling like a wolf in pain, Dracul fell to his knees and a storm of metal broke over his head as a dozen men armed with sabres, axes and spears fought to have the honour of killing the last Grand Master of the Order of the Dragon. The man who'd hoped to cheat death opened his mouth to protest at the injustice of being killed for a second time but, before any words could pass his lips, a spear point burst from Dracul's chest and a sabre smote off his head.

On the other side of the courtyard, Thomas had no time to glory in Dracul's death because he'd seen Radu sprinting towards the passage that led away from the larger courtyard. Without thinking, Thomas yelled a foul curse and ordered Radu to stand and fight.

In reply, Dracul's treacherous lieutenant barked an order, whereupon a scarred brute armed with a long, curved sword moved to block Thomas' way whilst Radu continued to flee down the passage.

"You and your coven of witches will never leave Poenari alive," the Draconist growled and he lunged at Thomas with his sabre but the Englishman was not to be denied vengeance.

Sidestepping his opponent's powerful, though clumsy blow, Thomas eviscerated his attacker with a deft slash that ripped open the man's belly and, whilst the Draconist vainly tried to stuff his own entrails back inside his body, he resumed his pursuit of Radu. Thomas reached the entrance to the passage in just a few strides but he had to stop when he saw his quarry standing in front of the cage that held Dracul's dogs.

With a wicked grin, Radu slid back the bolt and swung the cage door open so that it blocked off the entrance to the small courtyard but set the dogs free to attack his hated enemy.

Just as he had hoped, the infuriated mastiffs came bounding out of their confinement and Radu laughed in anticipation of seeing Thomas ripped to pieces. Yet, to his utter astonishment, the baying hounds ignored the Englishman and instead ran towards the sound of the battle in the larger courtyard.

"More diabolical witchcraft? Have you no shame!" Radu cried as he watched the hellish mastiffs disappear into the mêlée.

"You still doubt my power?" Thomas replied, even though he knew it was the scent of the late Lord Dracul clinging to his vomit-stained shirt that had saved him rather than any spell.

Whatever the truth of the matter, the sorcerer's apparent invulnerability convinced Radu that discretion was the better part of valour. He therefore ran off to take his revenge on Bos, Quintana and Prometheus, who were still incarcerated in Poenari's dungeon. Thomas followed but he was delayed by having to open the cage door and he emerged from the passage to see Radu disappearing inside Poenari's keep.

"Shoot the witch!" Radu ordered as he pushed past one of his men, who was standing by the keep's open door, nervously holding an arquebus against his hip.

The dullard nodded and put a match to the gun's touch-hole, but the terror of shooting a sorcerer made the man's hand shake so much his shot went wild. The Draconist disappeared behind a cloud of smoke and, before he could reload or bar the door, Thomas had crossed the courtyard and run him through.

Leaping over the man's corpse, Thomas entered the castle's keep and bounded down the steps that led to the dungeons. He sprinted through the warren of tunnels as fast he could and found Radu, sabre drawn, standing in front of the cell where Bos, Prometheus and Quintana were imprisoned.

The tunnel was filled with light from a lantern that was hanging from a nail in the wall and, though the prisoners shouted that they were alive, Thomas would have to deal with Radu before they could be freed.

"You know I could kill with a single magic word but, if you reveal the entrance to the secret path down the mountain, I'll let you live," Thomas promised. However, despite the look of fear on Radu's face, there was no surrender in his eyes.

"You may have power over poisons and dumb animals but I shall live to see you and your foul witch-familiars suffer a living death, chained to the oars of a Turkish galley!" Radu spat and he lunged at his enemy, putting all the hatred of a wronged lover behind his blow. Thomas easily turned the blade but his opponent quickly launched another ferocious attack.

Sharpened steel whipped around Thomas' head, until the Englishman felt as if he was being besieged by swarms of angry wasps, and the air in the tunnel became so stifling that sweat began to pour down his face. Instinctively Thomas wiped his stinging eyes with his sleeve but, as he did so, Radu slashed at his opponent's skull. The wide, looping stroke opened a long gash in Thomas' forehead and he cried out in pain as he felt a stream of hot blood mingle with the cold perspiration running down his cheeks.

Sensing that his enemy was weakening, Radu launched another furious assault and, with his eyes full of gore, Thomas was forced to give ground. Eventually his retreat was blocked by one of the sturdy wooden posts that supported the tunnel's roof.

Blinded by his own blood, and pinned against this immovable truss, Thomas had to parry his opponent's sabre strokes by pure instinct, yet his enemy's cry of victory gave him one chance to end the duel.

"Die, you scum-sucking spawn of Satan!" Radu cried but his shout warned Thomas that his enemy was closing in for the kill and he rolled to one side.

The cutting edge of Radu's sabre missed Thomas' head by the breadth of a harlot's virtue and buried itself in the ancient wood with a sickening thud. Scarcely able to believe his own foolish error, Radu began to curse the Fickle Fates that protected the hateful Englishman but, although he pulled at his sword with all the strength of panic in his muscles, his blade remained firmly trapped in the age-blackened wood.

Whilst Radu was trying to wrench his weapon free, Thomas quickly wiped the blood from his eyes and brought his own sword smashing down on the sabre's crossguard. Radu's blade was splintered in two by the sheer force of the Englishman's blow and, as the severed pieces of metal clattered to the floor, Thomas placed the point of his sword over his enemy's heart.

"You're a dead man, Radu! Yet, I say again, if you tell me how to get out of this infernal fortress, I'll let you live," Thomas repeated and at last Radu nodded his head. Dracul's traitorous lieutenant knew he was beaten and he raised his empty hands in surrender.

"There was a secret tunnel that led from the ravine down the mountain but, after it was destroyed by an earthquake, Dracul ordered another to be cut. The new entrance is hidden in the castle's powder magazine, now, if you have a shred of honour in your Saxon bones, keep to our bargain and let me go free," he said.

"You have my thanks but you will never have my forgiveness for sending Ursula to her grave and for that dastardly crime their can only be one penalty, death!" Thomas cried and he plunged his sword deep into his enemy's chest.

"You foul forked tongued, bastard son of Judas, you promised to spare me ..." Radu gurgled as he sank slowly to his knees.

"I lied," Thomas said and he ripped his sword from Radu's body with a sickening scrape of sharpened metal against bone.

"Then you'll perish by the dragon's breath!" Radu hissed but those were his last words. Blood-flecked spittle frothed at the corner of Radu's mouth and his eyes rolled back into his grinning skull.

# 20
## THE TUNNEL

With Radu and Dracul dead, Thomas felt that Ursula's murder had been avenged, at least in part, but the sounds of slaughter drifting through the tunnels meant there was no time to rest. The shouts of the victors, followed by the screams of the vanquished, declared that the Battle of Poenari had reached the keep and the prisoners inside the cell cried out for news.

"In the name of St Lawrence's roasted rump, will someone tell me what's going on?" Quintana bellowed from behind the dungeon's door, so Thomas quickly explained that Ursula, Radu and Dracul had perished but the fighting was far from over.

"What concern of ours is this war between the allies of Dracul and Scaliger? Let those godless foreign devils slaughter each other and, whilst they do, so we can make our escape," said Prometheus.

"You don't understand, if the Draconists triumph, they'll blame us for Dracul's death and we shall be impaled. On the other hand, if Scaliger wins, anyone who bears the mark of the *Ouroboros* will be executed immediately," Thomas said grimly.

"Then get us out of this dungeon, or have you forgotten that we all carry that foul brand burned into our flesh?" Bos cried.

The memory of Dracul's hot irons spurred Thomas into action. He grabbed the bunch of keys hanging from Radu's belt, opened the cell door and as soon the others' chains lay in the straw, he told everyone to follow him.

"The entrance to the secret path is in the castle's powder magazine, not in the ravine, after all," he said breathlessly and he unhooked the lantern from its nail outside the cell door.

As the others were too confused to argue, they let Thomas lead them through the labyrinth of darkened passageways and it didn't take them long to find a locked door that smelled like the entrance to a privy.

"That reek isn't piss, it's gunpowder," said Thomas eagerly and he fumbled for the keys he'd taken from Radu's corpse. The door swung open with a loud creak and the Englishman led his comrades into a long gallery with dozens of barrels stacked around its walls.

"By all the catamites in a papal bedchamber, this must be it," said Bos and, once Thomas had locked the door behind them, the men began sweeping aside the rushes that covered the cellar's floor in the hope of revealing the hidden exit.

"For is it not written in St Matthew's Holy Gospel, knock and the door shall be opened!" The Frisian added triumphantly but after searching for several minutes, all they'd found were solid flagstones.

With a growing sense of desperation the four men began feeling along the courses of brickwork for concealed latches but here they found nothing except crumbling mortar. Eventually Prometheus threw up his hands and cursed Thomas for a fool.

"You should've asked Radu how to find this tunnel's entrance before you turned him into worm's meat," the Nubian grumbled.

"Forgive me, but a desperate duel to the death is hardly the place to make polite enquiries," Thomas protested but as he, Bos and Prometheus continued to argue Quintana noticed that there was something strange about the way the kegs were stored.

The barrels stored along the walls on either side of the magazine's doorway had been placed vertically, end-on-end, but those stacked against the wall facing the door were on their sides. These horizontal kegs were arranged in a pyramid, with wedges at each end to prevent them from rolling away, but if these blocks were removed, the pyramid would collapse.

"It's the perfect camouflage, because anyone who wants to leave the castle in a hurry need only knock out those wedges to reveal the entrance to the hidden tunnel," said Quintana.

"What's more, here's the key to this diabolical lock," said Prometheus and he grabbed a broaching mallet that was hanging from a hook on the wall.

With one mighty swing, the Nubian knocked out the first of the wooden wedges and the stack of kegs obediently collapsed with a rumble that sounded as loud as thunder in the cellar's confined space. Even before Prometheus had removed the second wedge, enough of the barrels had rolled away to reveal a large circular slab, that measured at least six feet across, and it was decorated with an gargantuan carving of the *Ouroboros*.

The symbol of the snake being strangled by its own tail was surrounded by a Latin inscription but the words had become so faint with age Thomas had to hold up his lantern to read them.

## CAVETE DRACONIS SPIRACULUM

"Beware the dragon's breath. That's what Radu said as he died, yet I'm the man who can tame dragons!" Thomas laughed. Quintana, however, urged the Englishman to be less proud of his reputation and more careful of his candle's naked flame.

"Dragons be damned, we're in a room full of gunpowder and a careless spark from your lantern will blow us all straight up Satan's shit-hole," he hissed. Unfortunately, his warning was lost as the sounds of men running through the tunnels that connected Poenari's cellars became louder.

"Find the catch that opens this door or we're all dead!" Bos cried but, as the slab seemed to be held in place by nothing more than its own weight, Thomas and the others put their shoulders against the carving of the *Ouroboros* and pushed.

With a tortured groan, the slab rotated on a hidden pivot to reveal a flight of downward sloping steps. This stairway disappeared into the darkness and as the four men peered into the gloom they felt as if they were staring into the mouth of an unholy sepulchre.

To add to their discomfort the stench of decay that rushed from the tunnel's mouth made Thomas and the others retch, yet, before they could recover, the cellar's rotten, rat-gnawed door burst asunder and a dozen armoured knights clattered into the room. The swords in their hands were stained with blood and they demanded that the witches submit to God's mercy or die.

"The traitor Dracul is dead, so surrender, you loathsome servants of Lucifer, or suffer the same fate as your foul master!" cried one of the knights but Thomas spat his defiance.

"From The Abyss we came and to The Abyss we shall return," he hissed. However, as Thomas held his lantern up to the tunnel's entrance and prepared to take his leave, the whole cellar was filled with a blinding light that roared out of the tunnel's mouth like the breath of a dragon.

Though the tongue of brilliant blue flame swept through the vault so quickly no one was badly burned, the effect on the knights was devastating. The metal-clad men became paralysed with terror and their fear turned to panic when Thomas declared that he was the sorcerer who'd tamed both the *Graoully* of Metz and the *Firedrake* of The Hornberg.

"I'm Thomas Devilstone, Master of all Dragons, and I've summoned the fire-breathing, seven-headed *Balaur* that guards Poenari!" Thomas proclaimed. In their dazed state, the knights would have believed anything about their enemy's castle of evil and they ran for their lives.

"Was that truly the dragon's breath?" Prometheus asked once their foes had disappeared down the darkened passage that led back to the castle's keep.

"That was no dragon, it was the wrath of God," snapped Bos as he extinguished the last smouldering hairs in his beard.

"More likely it was firedamp and I should've known better. The mines of my homeland are full of it," Thomas muttered as he patted out a spark that had added an extra hole to his ragged undershirt.

"Didn't you hear me telling you to be careful with that lantern? Now look what you've done!" Quintana wailed and he pointed to one of the piles of rushes that the men had created during their search for the hidden door. The tinder-dry stalks had been set alight by the fireball and the flames were already licking one of the barrels of gunpowder.

With a cry of horror, the four men began stamping on the burning rushes but their attempts to put out the fire only succeeded in sending showers of sparks swirling into the air. This blizzard of glowing embers ignited more fires where they fell and soon the whole cellar was ablaze.

"It's no good, we'll have to take our chances in the tunnel or we'll be blown straight through the Gates of Hell!" Prometheus shouted. The others didn't have to be told that it was madness to spend too long fighting a fire in a powder magazine, so they followed the Nubian into the tunnel and the light from the burning cellar was soon behind them.

The darkness and smell of rotting sewage that filled the cavern threatened to rob the men of their wits but they dared not take the lantern with them for fear of igniting another pocket of firedamp. Fighting their growing sense of dread, as well as the overwhelming desire to be sick, Thomas and the others began feeling their way down the flight of slippery stone stairs. Each step was like walking on ice and the slime-covered walls offered no hand holds.

It was only a matter of time before someone missed their footing and Thomas was the first to be pitched headlong into the darkness.

The Englishman collided with Bos and the Frisian clattered into Quintana, who knocked Prometheus off his feet just as the stairway reached its steepest point. The four men slithered down the remaining steps like fish swept over a flooded weir but they landed at the bottom of the stairway having suffered little more than grazed knees and bruised elbows.

There was still no light to see by, yet the path seemed level and Prometheus thought that they must be near the tunnel's exit.

"Come on, I'm a creature of the sun, not the night," he said and he set off through the gloom. Like sinners lost in the darkness of their own ignorance, the others followed as best they could but, after the tunnel had taken one more turn, they were halted by a wall of cold, featureless granite.

With a pitiful moan, Quintana declared that Poenari would become their tomb after all, and Thomas cursed the idleness of builders who failed to complete their work, but Bos reasoned that, if the entrance to the passage was sealed with a slab of rock, the same might be true of its exit.

"Like Our Lord in the Holy Sepulchre, if we wish to be reborn we must roll away the stone," he said and he began to feel for a crack that might mark the edge of a door. After several minutes of anxious groping, Bos gave a cry of triumph and urged the others to help him.

Once again, the four men had to don the mantle of Sisyphus but, after much sweating and cursing, the stubborn wall of rock moved. A heartbeat later, there was a screech of protest and the monolith fell away from the tunnel's exit.

With a shout of relief, the men crawled through the opening to find themselves in the ruins of an ancient burial chamber. Centuries of storms had washed away the tomb's earthen walls but the massive capstone and its equally large, supporting uprights remained.

The structure was surrounded by lush grass and a grove of pine trees. However, whilst this part of the forest was as untroubled as a saint's conscience, a glance around the glade showed that the men had emerged from the tunnel only halfway down the northern side of the mountain. As Thomas and the others knew that their enemies would renew the pursuit once they'd had overcome their fears, they hastily re-blocked the tunnel before they allowed themselves to rest.

"As I'm not a mole or a mountain goat, I must rest before we go on," said Bos and he threw himself onto the soft turf.

"Five minutes, no more. Someone is sure to follow us soon and I'll wager they'll not be friendly," said Prometheus as he filled his lungs with fresh, clean air.

"Are Dracul and his daughter really dead?" Quintana asked as he glanced nervously back up the mountainside and the others instinctively followed his gaze.

By peering through the trees, the four men could just make out the Castle of Poenari on top of its pinnacle of bare rock and, though they all shivered at the thought of their narrow escape, Thomas confirmed that at least one of their enemies would trouble them no more.

"Dracul and his Order of the Dragon are destroyed," he said and, if Quintana still had any doubt, Thomas pointed to the cloud of smoke rising from behind the castle's walls. The others looked at the black, oily smudge spreading across the sky and, as each man silently thanked God for his reprieve, Thomas told them about the battle in the courtyard, Dracul's last moments and Ursula's dreadful end.

"Poenari is truly evil. May God wipe it from the face of the earth, just as he destroyed Sodom and Gomorrah," said Bos yet, even as he spoke, his words were lost in the sound of an enormous explosion erupting from the mountain's peak.

Instinctively, all four men leapt for the shelter of the ruined tomb and, as the noise of the explosion rolled down the valley like a thunder-storm, they pressed themselves into its earthen floor. Though the echoes of this deafening blast soon died away, the roar of the *Balaur* was instantly replaced by a hellish tattoo of crashes and thumps as colossal chunks of broken stone and fractured masonry smashed into the glade.

Where these cyclopean boulders fell, they splintered branches and sent up huge fountains of earth but the tomb's granite roof protected Thomas and the others from certain death. This brutal bombardment also ceased as quickly as it had begun, yet, when the four men emerged, blinking, into the sunlight, they couldn't believe their eyes.

"Behold the Wrath of The Lord thy God," said Bos, and he pointed to Poenari's summit.

The explosion had reduced Dracul's castle to a shattered ruin. Most of the northern wall had disappeared and, where the Dragon Hall had once stood, there was now nothing but an enormous gash in the rock. It was as if the *Balaur* had indeed risen from its lair and chewed the entire top off the mountain.

"The fire we started must have exploded the gunpowder in the castle's magazine," Quintana gasped unnecessarily.

"At least both Scaliger and Dracul are now being judged by St Peter," said Prometheus as he tried to shake the ringing from his ears and Bos added that The Almighty would always punish those who worshipped idols and false gods.

"Do we need any further proof that venerating relics is a sin? What Thomas took from Nuremberg and brought here isn't the Holy Lance, it's the Devil's lance! We should all fall to our knees and thank the Lord Jesus for burying that cursed object under whatever's left of Poenari," he said but, instead of bowing his head in prayer, Thomas grinned sheepishly and produced a tattered bundle of rags from beneath his shirt.

"I'm afraid I still have it," he said and he unwrapped the roll of cloth to reveal the Holy Lance. Bos and Prometheus could only stare at the object for which Dracul had given both his life, and the life of his daughter, but Quintana asked the question that was in all their minds.

"Is this the real spear that was present at Golgotha? I thought Scaliger said it was still in Nuremberg," he said, whereupon Thomas snorted with indignation and insisted that he had the genuine relic.

"Scaliger probably saw the fake we left behind and, even if he wasn't fooled, he wouldn't hesitate to lie if it persuaded people to abandon Dracul's crusade. Besides, if Scaliger didn't believe the real Holy Lance was at Poenari, why did he come here?" Thomas said and, though Quintana and Bos remained unconvinced by his arguments, Prometheus was sure that their survival was proof they had the real spear.

"We're the only men marked with the *Ouroboros* to survive the Order of the Dragon's destruction. Dracul's dead because he claimed that he was the equal of Our Lord Jesus and Scaliger's dead because he made an unholy alliance with the Turks. God struck them down for their unpardonable sins but the Holy Lance protected us because we can still use its power to win back the east for Christ," he said earnestly.

"Are you saying that we should use the Holy Lance to help you reclaim your throne?" Thomas asked cautiously.

"If you are, you'll be alone, for I've no desire to visit the Torrid Zone," said Bos and even Prometheus shook his head.

"I don't believe that it's my destiny to carry the Lance of St Maurice back to Nubia, at least not yet. The Turks advancing on the Danube are much closer to hand and they must be defeated before I can return to my kingdom. Until that day comes, I daren't touch the Holy Lance lest my people share the fate of Dracul and his Draconists," he said.

"The Nubian's right, too many lives have been lost for the sake of this old spear. I say we bury it or throw it in the nearest river," said Bos but Quintana warned that their decision shouldn't be made in haste.

"The iron may be worth nothing but the precious metals must have some value," he said, looking at the gold sleeve and silver wire that decorated the blade with greed in his eyes, but Prometheus insisted that it would be the worst blasphemy to hide or damage the relic.

"Our continued existence on this earth is a clear sign that God wishes us to take the Holy Lance to King Louis of Hungary, because he's now the only Christian monarch who can turn back the tide of Suleiman's *janissaries*. Will you abandon Christ in His hour of greatest need? Or will you join me in finishing our holy task?" Prometheus said firmly and he reminded his comrades that the King was holding a new muster at Mohacs in just a few days' time.

Though the Nubian's proposal was discussed for some time, eventually they all agreed that the Holy Lance should be handed over to the Hungarian King as soon as possible and even Quintana consented to accompany the Devil's lance to Mohacs.

"Though I hope Louis has deep pockets, because I shall expect a very handsome reward for saving his realm," he said.

"Then it's agreed, we all ride to Mohacs and see if we can turn this piece of scrap iron into Hungarian gold for us and a Christian victory for God," said Thomas.

"At last, a practical application for your alchemy, Master Sorcerer!" said Quintana, yet the jest only reminded Thomas that he'd left *The Munich Handbook of Demonic Magic* in the castle.

The *grimoire* that contained Leonardo da Vinci's irreplaceable notes and drawings must have been burned to ashes in the funeral pyre of Poenari but, though Thomas' soul groaned in agony at the thought of his own carelessness, there was no time to mourn the loss of this priceless book. It would take a week of hard riding to reach Mohacs and the men's most pressing task was to find horses.

Fortunately, Prometheus remembered the ponies they'd left grazing by the river when they'd first arrived at Poenari and a quick search located both the animals and a shack containing the necessary saddles and bridles.

What had happened to the men set to guard these horses, Thomas and the others neither knew nor cared, they were simply happy that they wouldn't have to walk to Mohacs. It took less than ten minutes for the men to saddle four of the healthiest looking beasts and by sunset they had left the Castle of Poenari far behind.

For three days, the Lance Bearers had pleasant riding but Lady Fortune's wheel soon turned and when they reached the Pannonian Plain, they found that the once bustling farms and villages, through which they'd passed just a few weeks ago, were now deserted. Houses both great and small stood empty, market squares and churches were silent and even the wayside taverns had been abandoned by their innkeepers.

The closer the travellers came to Mohacs, the fewer people they saw and by the time they were less than a day's journey from their destination, even the fields and meadows were devoid of all living things.

"I'm so famished, I could eat the bark of a tree," said Bos irritably.

"We'll be lucky to find a the bark of a dog in this wasteland," said Quintana and whilst Thomas agreed that Louis' foraging parties must've stolen everything edible days ago, Prometheus pointed out that it could've been Suleiman's *janissaries* who'd eaten every cow and chicken for miles around.

Fuelled by the red mist of hunger, the argument over who'd picked the bones of Hungary clean continued until Bos noticed a line of horsemen half a mile to the north. These riders were following the crest of a low hill and, though they were too far away to be identified with any certainty, the Frisian was convinced that they must be Hungarian militia.

"They can't be Turks, because you never see a Turk until his dagger's sticking out of your chest, so if those fools are sitting up there like targets at an archery contest, they're either not very bright or not very skilled in the arts of war," he said, but, a moment later, the patrol wheeled off the hill and galloped towards the road.

There was no possibility of their weary mounts outpacing fresh horses, nor was there anywhere to hide on the treeless plain, so the Lance Bearers were forced to wait anxiously for the patrol to arrive.

"From where did you steal these horses? Answer before I have you flogged and hanged," the patrol's captain demanded yet, despite the man's threats, the four travellers breathed a sigh of relief.

The captain was evidently no Turk, as he wore expensive European half-armour that covered his chest and thighs. Moreover, the sign of the cross was painted on both his breastplate and his Italian-style *burgonet* helmet. He also spoke with a heavy German accent and was armed with the type of cat skinner sword that was favoured by *landsknechts*.

Though the captain's men were less well-armed, Thomas knew that it was customary for Hungary's kings to hire German, Italian and Balkan mercenaries to strengthen their armies of feudal knights and peasant levies. He also had no doubt that a professional soldier would appreciate the value of intelligence, so he informed the captain that he had information that could turn the tide of the war.

"If you serve your God and King faithfully, take us to Louis of Hungary without delay," said Thomas, however the captain was not a man who was used to taking orders from beggars. He eyed the paupers suspiciously, yet, whilst his reason told him to hang them all as horse thieves, there was something in Thomas' bearing that made him believe his story.

"The Archbishop is the one who must decide your fate but I warn you, if you're lying, you'll be dancing with the Devil by nightfall," the captain said gruffly and he ordered the travellers to surrender their swords.

Before Prometheus could demand that this German lick-spittle showed more respect to those who had the power to save Christendom, Thomas had handed over his weapon and if the captain was surprised that only one of the travellers was armed, he didn't show it. Instead, he ordered his men to escort the mysterious beggars to the Hungarian camp without delay.

Mohacs owed its existence to a Roman fort, which had been built to guard a ferry crossing over the Danube. Unfortunately, in later centuries, a new road linking the Caesars' eastern and western empires had been constructed to avoid the malarial swamps that surrounded the town. As a result, in the ten centuries since the last Roman legionary marched away, the once prosperous settlement of Mohacs had been reduced to a collection of crude wooden huts clustered around a fortified church and a muddy market square.

The Hungarian army was camped a few miles to the south of Mohacs on the edge of a wide flood plain. This flat, open countryside, which was interrupted by nothing more than a few clumps of scrubby trees and an occasional stream, stretched away to the south for several miles until the land began to rise to form a low ridge. The stifling summer heat made the grassy heath shimmer like water and, as Thomas approached the camp, he silently congratulated the king for choosing his ground well.

The left flank of Louis' army was protected by a broad expanse of marsh, which formed the west bank of the River Danube, whilst the firm ground to the front of the Hungarian lines offered plenty of room for both cavalry and pike squares to manoeuvre. A further advantage of the terrain was the lack of cover, which meant the Turks couldn't advance without being spotted by Louis' patrols, and it was a mark of the King's confidence that there was no wagon fort protecting his camp.

Despite the failure of Louis' first muster, at least 25,000 men had answered his second summons. However, whilst this was a large army by European standards, it was nowhere near the size of host that the Sultan of a vast empire could put into the field. There were rumours that more than 50,000 Turks were advancing on Mohacs but, if the men in the Hungarian camp were troubled by such hearsay, they preferred to keep their thoughts to themselves.

As Thomas and his comrades rode past the lines of snow-white linen tents, they saw no fear in the soldiers' eyes. Instead, whether they were sun-bronzed serfs more used to ploughs than pikes, or battle-scarred mercenaries skilled in the profession of arms, each man was making his preparations for the forthcoming battle with an air of calm efficiency.

Everywhere that Thomas looked, he saw halberdiers and swordsmen sharpening their weapons, pikemen their practising drill and gunners their mixing powder. Yet, in spite of all these martial activities, the gaily coloured flags, fanfares of trumpets and beating of drums gave the camp the mood of a St Bartholomew's Day fair.

"This is the tent of Tomori Pál, Archbishop of Kalocsa. I will announce you," grunted the German captain when they'd arrived at the centre of the camp and moments later, Thomas and the others were being ushered inside the priest's sparsely furnished quarters. There were no rugs or mats on the floor, just bare grass, and the only comforts were a cot, a folding table, a chair and a wooden frame holding a full harness of fluted, golden armour.

The panoply's gilded plates looked magnificent, if a little old-fashioned, and were a strange contrast to the plain monk's habit that Tomori was wearing. Though he'd been born to live the life of an obscure country nobleman, war had changed Tomori's destiny and the name of Hungary's most famous archbishop was now so well known, it was almost impossible to separate the truth from over-embellished legend.

Some said that Tomori had become a monk after the death of his wife and that he'd only accepted an archbishopric at the personal insistence of the previous King of Hungary. Others maintained that Tomori had vowed to wear only a soldier's armour or a monk's garb until the Sultan had been defeated. Whatever the truth of these stories, three years ago, this warrior-monk had defeated the Turks in a great battle fought near the Serbian city of Sirmium.

Unusually for a Catholic prelate, Tomori wore a neatly trimmed beard and though he was in his early fifties, his eyes burned with the zeal for battle normally found in much younger men. These warrior's eyes, combined with his long, thin nose and high cheek bones, gave the Archbishop the appearance of a majestic bird of prey and he fell upon the new arrivals like a hungry falcon swoops on a pigeon.

Before Thomas could speak, Tomori had demanded news of John Zápolya's Transylvanian army and cursed the tardiness of the man who was supposed to bring 10,000 battle-hardened veterans to Mohacs more than a week ago.

"Yet, even as Our Lord forgave Peter for his weakness, I'll forgive John, if he joins us in time to smash Suleiman!" Tomori declared. Though Thomas, who'd never heard of anyone called Zápolya, had admit that he had no news of the Archbishop's hoped for reinforcements, even as he begged Tomori's pardon he offered a promise of salvation.

"Take heart, My Lord Archbishop, for we bear a gift for the King of Hungary that will ensure his glorious victory," he said brightly but this was not what Tomori wanted to hear.

"In the name of Heaven, Louis needs men who can fight, not grubby pedlars touting worthless trinkets!" he snapped but Thomas countered by declaring that his filthy garb was meant to conceal the value of what he carried from thieves.

"As this gift is from the Holy Roman Emperor, Charles of Hapsburg, it's beyond any price," Thomas explained yet, as he removed the cloth bundle from beneath his shirt, the Archbishop snorted with impatience and demanded to know why Charles had sent a pile of rags instead of cannonballs. In reply, Thomas simply unwrapped the Holy Lance and Tomori's expression of annoyance turned to confusion.

"Do my eyes deceive me? As a boy I saw this relic of Christ's Passion paraded through Nuremberg, so how does it come to be here? I thought that every emperor swears he'll never let the Holy Lance leave the soil of his empire," he said suspiciously but Thomas had expected such a question and he told the Archbishop that, as soon as His Imperial Highness had heard that Sultan Suleiman had invaded Hungary, he'd spent many hours in prayer until God had revealed His wishes.

"The Almighty told Charles that he must not abandon Christ's Church in the east, yet the Emperor couldn't send the Holy Lance to Mohacs openly for fear of breaking his coronation oath. His Imperial Highness therefore decided to send the relic in secret and he hopes that, once the Turks have been crushed by its power, the Holy Lance will be returned to Nuremberg with all speed," he said and, though there wasn't a word of truth in Thomas' story, the Archbishop believed him.

"God be praised that, even at this late hour, Charles of Hapsburg has come to his senses! So, come, we shall take this treasure to the King as soon as we've dressed in attire that's more appropriate for a royal audience," said Tomori happily.

Whilst Tomori put on his golden armour, Thomas and the others washed and dressed in clothes better suited to imperial emissaries. In the absence of a proper reliquary, the Holy Lance was placed in a small wooden chest used to store communion wafers and Tomori summoned a dozen of his most pious monks to carry it to the King.

As was to be expected, Louis' tent was more comfortably furnished than that of his Archbishop.

Carpets covered the floor, tapestries hung from the walls and, to complete the illusion of regal power, the young King of Hungary greeted his guests seated on a gilded throne flanked by a dozen courtiers.

The nineteen-year-old monarch was dressed in fashionable silks and furs which complimented his handsome features and athletic frame. His broad shoulders and well-formed limbs looked well able to wield a full-sized sword, so, even though his beard had yet to reach the full growth of a man in his prime, Louis looked every inch the paladin.

"Your Majesty, I bring wonderful news. His Imperial Highness, the Emperor Charles, has at last sent us something to guarantee our victory over Suleiman," said Tomori, whereupon the King sniffed with disgust and remarked that his brother-in-law hadn't sent so much as a letter in reply to his repeated requests for men and money. Undaunted, Tomori ordered his monks to open the chest and Louis gasped in surprise when he saw what it contained.

"Is this the same blade which pierced Our Saviour's side?" Louis said breathlessly and Tomori said that it was.

"This sacred spear was carried by St Longinus at the moment of Our Saviour's death and by St Maurice on the day of his martyrdom. It was with the Emperor Constantine the Great when he won his great victory over Maxentius and his pagan army at the Battle of the Milvian Bridge and with Charlemagne when he defeated the heathen Saxons. Thanks to Our Lord's sacrifice, this relic protects all Christ's faithful soldiers, from the humblest pikeman to the most exalted emperor, and its presence here means that God has seen fit to bless our holy crusade," said the Archbishop. For a moment there was silence and the King crossed himself before he spoke.

"If it's God's will, I too shall carry this weapon into battle, just as Constantine and Charlemagne did before me, and like them, I shall take the light of Christ's Gospel into the lands made dark by our enemies. Have a new shaft fitted immediately and fetch my armour. Our men must see this wondrous relic at once," said Louis.

"Perhaps they'd be happier to see 50,000 *landsknechts* marching to their aid," said Quintana under his breath. Fortunately, no one heard him.

# 21
## MOHACS

At noon, the trumpets sounded and Louis' army of noble knights, professional mercenaries and peasant levies gathered around a wooden rostrum in the centre of the open space that served the camp as a parade ground. Thomas and the others were ordered to stand at the foot of this platform and, whilst they waited for the king and his Archbishop to appear, Quintana repeated his concerns that the Hungarian army had too many aristocrats and not enough guns.

"Remember the slaughter of Pavia? For all their steel armour and cast-iron pedigrees, the French knights were no match for our guns," he muttered but his words were lost in another clarion call of trumpets.

Once the fanfare had died away, an expectant hush descended upon the crowd. Moments later, Louis and Tomori emerged from the royal tent and began walking towards the dais with all the solemnity of those about to be shriven, yet both men were dressed for battle, not confession. The king was clad in an exquisite suit of black armour inlaid with gold and his helmet was crowned with a plume of pink ostrich feathers.

Likewise Archbishop Tomori wore his distinctive panoply of fluted, gilded armour; though the plumes of feathers adorning his helmet were the purest white.

Together, the two men looked like the archangels Gabriel and Michael. However, instead of carrying flaming swords, the king's hands were clasped together tightly in prayer and Tomori held a long spear with its blade wrapped in a cloth made of expensive purple silk.

The Archbishop carried this spear out in front of him, like a processional cross, and once he'd joined the King on the dais, he instructed the whole army to kneel. After pronouncing a blessing, Tomori removed the weapon's silken wrapping to reveal the Holy Lance and the sight of the relic produced loud gasps of astonishment from the assembled soldiers.

Though the ancient spear had been fitted with yet another new shaft, there was no mistaking the iron blade, with its gold sleeve, which Tomori was showing to his wide-eyed men. Strangely, the Archbishop seemed to have no belief in the curse, which had terrified Scaliger as much as Dracul, and when he spoke, he lifted the Holy Lance high above his head so that everyone present could bear witness to the munificence of the Lord God.

"Fifteen centuries ago, Our Saviour suffered death upon the cross and, at the very moment the spirit of The Son began its journey back to The Father, the blind centurion Longinus pierced Christ's flesh with this blade. As soon as the spear's tip opened the last wound of The Passion, blood and water flowed from Our Lord's body and the sight in Longinus' clouded eyes was restored. By this miracle, God showed that His Son could conquer death and, henceforth, all those whom God has chosen to carry the Holy Lance have triumphed over their enemies!" Tomori cried.

The soldiers gave a loud hurrah in reply but Tomori called for silence and began to say a Holy Mass that would absolve every man in the Christian army of his sins. Each of the new crusaders listened patiently to the words of The Eucharist and, once the men's souls had been cleansed, Tomori placed the Holy Lance in the outstretched hands of their King. Now it was Louis' turn to kindle the fires of war in the hearts of those who'd sworn to fight for the Prince of Peace.

"Suleiman's rule over the Christians of the east is an abomination in the sight of God but we shall free our Brothers in Christ from the Sultan's slavery. The presence of the Holy Lance in our midst is proof that we march with God's blessing and by its power we shall scatter our adversary's armies!" Louis cried and, just as the Wallachian princes had cheered Dracul, so the Hungarians, Poles, Croats, Serbs, Bosnians, Moravians and Bohemians of Louis' army cheered their King to the Vault of Heaven. Even the normally cynical German and Italian mercenaries joined in the prayers of thanks for this evidence of God's favour, until Louis begged for quiet.

"But what of those who brought us the instrument of our salvation, shall they go unrewarded?" Louis asked rhetorically and he pointed to Thomas, Bos, Prometheus and Quintana, who were standing in front of the dais like pawns on a chessboard.

Before any of the reluctant heroes could protest, Tomori's monks had ushered them onto the rostrum, whereupon Louis announced that, in recognition of the perils these men had faced in bringing the Holy Lance to Mohacs, they'd each be invested with the Order of St George. This, Louis added, was Hungary's most ancient order of chivalry, yet those about to be honoured could barely stifle their cries of disbelief.

"By all the saints, was ever one man invested with both the Order of St George and the Order of the Dragon?" Bos whispered as the incredulous men were instructed to kneel.

"To say nothing of the Order of the Holy Lance," Prometheus muttered as he remembered how they'd invented their own order of knighthood to swindle the abbot of Nuremberg out of his precious relic. Thomas was about to remark that joining the ranks of Hungarian chivalry seemed to be a lot less painful than becoming Draconists but Louis had begun the short ceremony of investiture and he fell silent.

"It's a peculiarity of the Order of St George that its members wear no special robes or insignia. Instead they may write the words of the order's oath on whatever they may choose," said the King and, drawing his sword, he touched each man lightly on the shoulder with its tip.

"Say after me these words: in truth I will do justice to this fraternal society," the Archbishop ordered. However, though Thomas and the others repeated the words of yet another order of chivalry's vow, they felt no more noble than before.

"You're now Knights of St George and in further recognition of the great services you've performed, you shall join my personal guard," Louis said with pride. Quintana, however, inwardly groaned.

All the Portugee wanted was a purse stuffed with golden guilders, a fast horse and directions home. Unfortunately, before he could decline this latest honour, Louis had dismissed both his new Knights of St George and the rest of his army. Quintana and the others gratefully retreated to the tent they'd been allotted but, once they were alone, the exasperated Portugee exploded with rage.

"Was ever a man so cursed? Three times in as many months I've been elevated to the rank of knight, yet I'm still as poor as a pork butcher in Jerusalem! What use is a knighthood? Can a man eat chivalry? Can he drink honour? I say we go back to this boy king and tell him that unless we see some cold, hard cash, we'll take his blessed spear back to Nuremberg," he said bitterly but Bos and Prometheus urged patience.

"God has brought us here to punish those who'd deny Christ and, whether our rewards lie on Earth or in Heaven, Our Redeemer will not abandon us," Bos said sternly and Prometheus added that the greatest prize in life was to die in the service of The Lord.

On hearing this, Quintana cursed his companions for being pious fools, though Thomas offered the Portugee a small crumb of comfort.

"Suleiman's richer than Croesus, so his tent's bound to be stuffed with gold, and once he's been defeated, we can help ourselves," he said, yet Quintana refused to be mollified.

"How long do you think Louis' slow-witted farmers, antiquated, armoured knights and mercenaries of very doubtful loyalty will last against 50,000 fanatical Turks all willing to die for their God?" Quintana asked but, before anyone could answer, a chorus of trumpets sounding the alarm sent them all scurrying from their tent.

The flat, treeless countryside beyond the Hungarians' camp had been baked a dull brown by the fierce summer sun, yet, though most of the sky remained as blue as the Madonna's robe, a long, hazy cloud had formed above the low ridge at the southern edge of the plain. This cloud seemed to hang in the vault of heaven like a priest's promise of salvation but it had not been created by the power of God or Nature.

The strange miasma had been made by the smoke from hundreds of Turkish campfires, yet, though the sight of their enemy caused consternation in the Hungarian ranks, it was too late in the day for either side to attack. After posting sentries, the King's captains ordered the remainder of their men to rest, so the four recently ennobled Knights of St George joined the ebbing tide of soldiery returning to their tents.

The hot humours of war coursing through their veins made sleep impossible, yet, whilst Bos, Prometheus and Thomas spent the hours discussing how they'd spend their plundered gold, Quintana didn't speak a word. It was strange to see the usually loquacious Portugee sitting in glum silence but the first crack of thunder miraculously restored his voice.

As heavy rain began to beat on their tent, Quintana proposed that they should slip away whilst the sentries took shelter, but Prometheus was appalled and insisted that fleeing from a battle was the worst dishonour. Bos added that no man could run from God's purpose, whilst Thomas maintained that trying to leave the camp now would be madness.

"This storm won't last long and, once it's passed, both sides will be sure to send out patrols to look for prisoners to interrogate. Even if you evade the Turks, if you're found outside our camp by the Hungarians you'll be hanged as a deserter," he said.

"Besides, the safest place in any fight is next to the most important man on the field and here that will be the Hungarian King Louis," added Bos.

At first Quintana refused to accept this logic, but, after the others had reminded the Portugee that they'd be among the 2,000 noble bodyguards surrounding Louis as he rode into battle, he threw up his hands in surrender.

"By the Madonna's milk! I swear you fools would be lost without me but, if I die at Mohacs, I'll be back to haunt you. Now, while we wait to be sliced in two by Turkish scimitars, what about a little primero?" he said.

From the pouch that hung at his belt, Quintana produced his pack of cards and by morning, the tally showed that the Portugee had won a hundred florins from each of the others. However, as none of them had any money, he graciously wrote off their debts when the trumpets sounded the call to battle.

Crawling from their tent, the four men emerged to see their comrades running in all directions but, even though the disparate elements of Louis' army had been together for less than a month, everyone found his place with remarkable speed. The snaking lines of pikemen from Hungary and Poland hurried to join the arquebusiers from Italy and the German halberdiers and, goaded by the sergeants' canes, these streams of humanity quickly became the two massive pike squares that formed the centre of the Christian host.

Each square was made up of 3,000 men carrying eighteen foot-long pikes, surrounded by two rows of troops armed with arquebuses, halberds or double-handed swords. When lowered, the pikes protected the gunners from attack yet, whilst this made a pike square as impregnable as a fortress, it was just as unwieldy. Now the air became filled with sergeants' curses as they laboured to dress their companies' ranks and files.

Whilst the infantry shuffled into their allotted places, the 12,000 horsemen of Louis' cavalry galloped away to their positions on the army's wings.

As the King's most experienced commander, Archbishop Tomori had been given overall charge of the Christian forces at Mohacs and the warrior-priest had decided to create a breakwater of tempered steel upon which the waves of advancing Turks would break.

The Archbishop's plan was to anchor his left wing on the treacherous marsh that lay at the eastern edge of the plain. He therefore sent his *hussars* and *stradiots* to guard this position as these lightly armed horsemen could advance through the bog if necessary.

By contrast, the armoured knights needed firm ground so, as the open grassland on the opposite flank was much better suited to iron-clad nobles wielding lances and broadswords, the Archbishop placed these heavy horsemen on the right of the pike squares.

The fifty cannon that had been brought to Mohacs were sited in front of the infantry but the 2,000 horsemen of Louis' personal guard, including the four new Knights of St George, were placed behind the pike squares and divided into two companies: one to act as a reserve and one to protect the King.

Most of the men who'd sworn to defend their sovereign with their lives wore full armour and carried a shield emblazoned with a complex coat of arms. Intricate heraldic designs were the proof of a pedigree extending all the way back to the children of Noah, but Thomas and his comrades had neither the funds nor the lineage to acquire such equipment.

Luckily, a sutler willing to extend credit to the King's new favourites had provided them with the gaudy, slashed doublets and striped hose, favoured by German mercenaries. The trader had also furnished them with the long, curved sabres preferred by Balkan *hussars*. Louis himself had presented each of those who'd brought the Holy Lance to Mohacs with a fine horse but, though they had an excellent view of the battlefield astride their new mounts, the Turks were nowhere to be seen.

"In the name of Julius Caesar's ghost, where, are they?" Bos grumbled as he scanned the empty plain for signs of activity.

"Maybe the Holy Lance has worked its magic after all and Suleiman has gone home to his *seraglio*," Thomas replied, yet Archbishop Tomori didn't share the Englishman's optimism and he kept the Christian army in the field all morning.

After several hours, the grey clouds that had brought the previous night's thunderstorm cleared and when the strong August sun reached its zenith, peasant women from the camp brought food and water. Full bellies did much to raise the spirits of Louis' men, and they continued to wait patiently for their enemies, but it was well after noon before the faint sound of drums announced that the Turks were finally on the move.

"This is good, our enemies must march during the heat of the day and no man fights well when he's tired and thirsty," said Prometheus as the first *janissaries* and *sipahis* crested the ridge on the far side of the plain.

"If they charge, our cannon will simply cut them down," Thomas added cheerfully but Bos pointed to the Turkish left.

"Do you see those camels being unloaded? The infidels mean to make camp so, if we attack, we'll catch them whilst they're disorganised," he said but, as they watched, the main body of the Turkish army began to descend from the ridge and form battle lines. The flood of men filling the plain was as relentless as an incoming tide but Tomori's men stood firm.

To crush his enemies, Suleiman had brought two armies to the field of Mohacs. The Army of Rumelia was recruited from the recently conquered Christian territories of Greece and the Balkans but the Army of Anatolia was drawn from the Turkish heartlands in Asia Minor. Both forces were a mix of *janissary* slave-soldiers and *azab* peasant-levies, who fought on foot, but the *sipahi* and *akinji* were mounted on good horses.

Like the Christian *hussars* and *stradiots*, the *akinji* were unarmoured skirmishers but the *sipahis* were the equivalent of Christendom's knights. Dressed entirely in chainmail, these noble warriors carried round shields, heavy swords and lances as long as their bloodlines.

The geography of Mohacs didn't allow the Sultan's two armies to march side by side so the troops assembling on the southern edge of the plain were the Rumelians. Suleiman sent all of this army's 20,000 horsemen to face Tomori's knights and gave them orders to protect the 10,000 elite *janissaries* as they took up a position opposite the Hungarian pike squares.

The Anatolians, when they arrived, would fill the gap between the Rumelian army and the River Danube. In the meantime, the Turkish infantry's exposed right flank would be covered by the Sultan's numerous cannon. Some of Suleiman's 150 guns were placed directly in front of the Rumelian *janissaries* but others were sited on the ridge behind the Turkish lines so they could fire over their comrades' heads.

The Rumelian infantry were still dressing their ranks when, with a fanfare of trumpets, Suleiman sent a company of his *akinjis* galloping across the plain to probe the Hungarian right. A lesser leader would've been taken in by this feint but Tomori ordered his knights to stand fast and sent a squadron of Louis' bodyguard to chase the Turkish horsemen away.

"If they've any sense, they'll keep going and not stop until they reach the Alps," said Quintana ruefully. However, whilst the Portugee said a silent prayer of thanks that he'd been ordered to remain with the Hungarian King, his comrades became infected with the bizarre madness of war.

When Bos and Prometheus saw that the Hungarians had routed the *akinji* patrol, they began yelling blood-curdling cries of victory and demanded that they, too, be allowed to attack. Even Thomas felt the thrill of battle seize his soul but his eager shouts were lost in the roars of the Hungarian cannon.

Accompanied by a hellish cacophony of ballistic screams, the bone-smashing iron balls slammed into the ranks of the Rumelian *janissaries* and *sipahis* half a mile away but the Hungarians' enemies were so numerous, the cannonade caused no more disruption than a pinch of salt dropped into a nest of poisonous spiders.

Oblivious to their losses, the Turkish captains continued to deploy their men. However Tomori was convinced that he still held the initiative and he ordered his armoured knights to drive the rest of the Rumelian cavalry from the field before they could organise.

Once again, the King's bodyguard was ordered to stand fast, so, like eunuchs in a harem, Thomas and the others had to watch in frustration as Tomori's noblemen spurred their steeds to the charge. The ground began to shake as hundreds of tons of polished steel and sweating horseflesh thundered across the open plain but this deafening sound was obliterated by the even louder tattoo of Turkish guns.

Scores of men and their mounts were disembowelled or beheaded by the murderous salvo that pulverised Tomori's knights. However the nobly born horsemen of Hungary never wavered and the Rumelians had no choice but to lower their lances, spur their own steeds and meet their enemies head on.

Like their aristocratic opponents, the Turkish *sipahis* had been schooled in the arts of war since childhood, yet they'd no time to close their ranks properly and their counter charge lacked proper cohesion. By contrast, the Hùngarian knights were still riding knee to knee as they smashed into the Rumelians like a colossal, iron hammer.

The fight soon became hidden behind the clouds of dust kicked up by the hooves of nearly 30,000 horses, so everyone else on the plain could only listen to the sounds of the slaughter and pray that their god would grant them victory. The butchery continued until a stream of Rumelians galloping away from the battlefield proclaimed another defeat for the Turkish Sultan.

The rest of the Hungarian army gave a loud cheer as a messenger carrying news of Tomori's victory reached their lines and, once the breathless, blood-spattered rider had presented the Archbishop's compliments to his King, he urged Louis to attack the Turkish centre before Sultan Suleiman's Anatolian reinforcements could arrive.

"God be praised, victory is ours!" Louis cried and, holding the Holy Lance high above his head, he gave the order for the whole of his army to advance.

The dashing *hussars* and *stradiots* on the Hungarian left obediently surged forward to exploit the gap between the Rumelian infantry holding the Turkish centre and the marsh but Louis led his personal guard to the right in an attempt to help Tomori mop up the Rumelian horsemen.

As the Christian cavalry galloped away, the Hungarian infantry's drums struck up the beat and, like a pair of giant porcupines, the cumbersome pike squares began to move. These masses of men and metal had only one ambition, and that was to trample whatever was left of the Turkish army into the dust of Mohacs, but though their resolve was firm, their progress was slow.

The defeated *sipahis* and *akinjis* were fleeing the battlefield so quickly many of Louis' guard began to fear that they'd be too late to join in the victory but the battle was far from over, because Tomori was now leading his men against the Turkish artillery on the ridge.

If the Archbishop's knights could cut down the Sultan's gunners, they could fall on the Rumelian infantry from the rear whilst the rest of the Hungarians engaged the *janissaries*' front.

Inexperienced though he was, Louis could see that if he also attacked the Rumelian infantry, the Sultan's best troops would be surrounded and not even *janissaries* could withstand being assaulted from all sides.

"For Father, Son and Holy Spirit!" Louis cried and, pointing the Holy Lance at the enemy lines, he ordered his men to charge. To add to the Rumelians' woes, the arquebusiers in the advancing pike squares loosed a lethal volley yet, though scores of Turks were struck down by the hail of Hungarian bullets, the Sultan's best troops didn't return fire.

All *janissaries* were chosen from the first-born sons of conquered Christians, yet, though they'd been enslaved and sent to the Sultan as tribute, these highly disciplined, well trained and fanatically loyal slave-soldiers belonged to an elite corps. As a mark of their exalted rank, they wore flamboyant clothes but, whilst their tall hats crowned with feathers, brightly coloured jackets and voluminous pantaloons looked more decorative than practical, there was nothing ornamental about their halberds, swords and arquebuses.

Every *janissary* was as skilled with a firearm as he was with a blade, yet it was their insane courage that allowed these men to wait until the last possible moment before touching their matches to their fire-pans.

The *janissaries'* fortitude meant that their fusillade tore into the Hungarian pike squares like the teeth of a giant saw and hundreds of their enemies died as their faces were shredded, their limbs broken and their bellies ripped open by the storm of Turkish lead.

Incredibly, this grisly winnowing of the Hungarians did nothing to slow their advance and, before either side could fire another volley, battle was joined. Moreover, as the first *janissaries* were skewered by Hungarian pikes or cleaved in two by German halberds, Louis' horsemen smashed into the Turkish infantry's exposed flank.

Though Thomas and his comrades had never fought on horseback, their mounts knew exactly what to do. With nostrils flaring and manes flying, the horses carried their riders into the thick of the battle and, when Thomas saw a man wearing a tall hat in front of him, he slashed with his sabre. The blade sliced through the *janissary's* neck with ease but, though his headless enemy disappeared beneath his horse's thundering hooves, Thomas was immediately confronted by two more Rumelian foot soldiers.

These Turks were armed with arquebuses, and they each aimed at their enemy's chest, but the first gun misfired and Thomas replied with a well-timed sword cut that caught the helpless arquebusier squarely in the face. The Englishman's sword neatly detached the man's jaw from his skull and, whilst the bloodied bone went spinning through the air, there was a loud bang as the second arquebusier fired.

The hastily aimed ball struck Thomas' horse in its shoulder and, though the beast wasn't badly wounded, it reared up on its hind legs with a terrifying whinny. Undaunted, the *janissary* hurriedly grasped his gun's muzzle, so as to smash the wooden butt into the animal's exposed belly, but, in that same instant, Thomas turned his mount and plunged his sabre into the Turk's chest. The *janissary* screamed and, as the man's cries of agony became a gurgle of death, Thomas heard a familiar voice yelling a warning.

"They're back, those Rumelian horsemen have returned!" Quintana shouted and he gestured wildly towards the enemy cavalry who'd somehow rallied after being routed by Tomori.

Through the fog of dust and gun smoke, Thomas glimpsed the Rumelians galloping towards the Hungarians. Seconds later, they crashed into Tomori's knights and this time the advantage was with the *sipahis*.

The Turks' lances struck with such force, the ground became littered with Christian knights who'd been knocked from their saddles and those who survived the bone-breaking falls were either crushed beneath their horses' hooves or swiftly dispatched by the *azabs'* knives.

These Turkish foot soldiers darted between the rearing horses like hounds among a herd of terrified deer. Shouting great whoops of victory, the *azabs* pounced on the fallen knights and there was no thought of ransom or mercy as they plunged their long daggers into the eye-slits of helmets or between the plates of armour.

Within minutes, the battlefield had become a bloody shambles and, whilst the Christian knights were being systematically butchered by the Rumelian *azabs*, the first companies of Sultan Suleiman's Anatolian Army appeared on the top of the ridge.

The arrival of 30,000 fresh Turkish troops instantly turned the tide of battle in Suleiman's favour and his mail-clad Anatolian *sipahis* smashed into the unarmoured *hussars* and *stradiots* on the Hungarian left with the force of a thunderstorm.

Though the Christian horsemen fought bravely, their swords were turned by the Turks' mail and in the face of superior numbers, they were forced to flee.

With both of his army's cavalry formations on the verge of defeat, Louis, his bodyguard and the pikemen still battling in the centre, were in danger of being surrounded but the King refused to surrender. Holding the Holy Lance in one hand, and wielding his broadsword with the other, Louis cut down his enemies with the skill of Samson dispatching Philistines, yet the Turkish net continued to close around him.

"My Lord, the battle is lost!" Thomas yelled but his cry of alarm came too late.

Even as he spoke, a mass of *janissaries* began to surround Louis with a hedge of sharpened steel and it seemed as if the King must fall, or be taken prisoner. Yet, before the Turks could strike Louis down, a man wearing golden armour cut his way through the press of men and grabbed the bridle of the King's horse.

A cloud of acrid smoke drifting across the battlefield momentarily hid the Archbishop's attempt to rescue his sovereign and, before Thomas could ride to their aid, Bos, Prometheus and Quintana had appeared at the Englishman's side. Seconds later, the smoke cleared to reveal Louis and Tomori riding for their lives, which prompted the others to curse the King for abandoning the fight. Thomas, however, was quick to remind his comrades of their oath.

"Our sworn duty is to protect Louis so let's follow him!" Thomas cried and he spurred his horse towards the wall of Turks who stood between him and safety. For the *janissaries*, the Archbishop's golden armour made a good target, and they were so intent on trying to shoot him down they failed to notice the four desperate men who fell upon their rear, but when these furies emerged into the open, there was no sign of Tomori or Louis.

Thomas, Bos, Prometheus and Quintana, who were simultaneously Knights of the Dragon, St George and the Holy Lance, were among the few Christians who escaped the disaster of Mohacs.

Most of Louis' men remained trapped in the vice formed by the Sultan's Rumelian and Anatolian armies and the *janissaries* showed their enemies no mercy. Suleiman's slave-soldiers turned every gun they had on the remnants of Louis' pike squares and poured volley after volley into their thinning ranks until the last embers of the once great Kingdom of Hungary had been completely extinguished.

"This isn't a battle any more, it's a massacre!" Bos cried, as he, Thomas, Prometheus and Quintana joined the surviving Christian horsemen who were galloping as fast they could towards their camp.

"Shut up and ride, or we'll suffer the same fate!" Quintana snapped but columns of thick, black smoke were already rising from the rows of Hungarian tents.

With their only avenue of retreat now blocked, Thomas and his comrades quickly realised that their last hope was to hide in the tall reeds at the edge of the marsh, so, they joined the other survivors in their headlong flight to the river.

Though Thomas and the others expected to be struck down by Turkish bullets at any moment, they reached the marsh safely yet there was no time to rest. As soon as they'd reached the soft ground, they abandoned their horses, dropped onto their bellies and began to crawl through the mud. Like eels searching for the safety of the sea, the men slithered through the stinking slime until they were lost in the forests of bulrushes.

Unfortunately, their torment had only just begun. Though the Turks were much too busy plundering the Hungarian camp to search the marshes, Thomas and the other survivors were forced to lie half-submerged in the cloying, bone-chilling mud for what seemed like an eternity. Hour after hour, the plaintive cries of the wounded and the terrified screams of the dying assailed their senses and, even after the sun had set, there was no respite because the entire Turkish army remained encamped on the plain of Mohacs.

The Sultan couldn't believe that the once mighty Kingdom of Hungary could only muster 25,000 men to oppose him and he was convinced that there must be a much larger Christian force waiting to block his advance on Louis' capital. Only when his scouts had confirmed that the road to Buda lay open did Suleiman give the order to march, yet his men were so numerous it was two days before the last Turk left Mohacs.

All that time, the pitiful remnants of Louis' army lay hidden in the stinking bog, with each man hardly daring to breathe in case he was spotted by an *akinji* patrol. Hundreds succumbed to the cold, hunger or their wounds and it was only when the skies became dark with crows feasting on human carrion that the few dozen men left alive risked crawling from their refuge. Like shipwrecked sailors cast ashore, these wretches hauled themselves onto firmer ground and though the plain was now deserted, the sight of a new hill at the centre of the battlefield filled everyone with terror.

At first the survivors thought that Suleiman had buried his dead in a huge mound, just as the Greeks had done after Marathon, but when they went to investigate, they saw that this monument wasn't made of earth or stone. Instead, as a warning to all those who refused to accept the Sultan's rule, Suleiman's men had heaped the decapitated bodies of their prisoners into a grisly pyramid and left the corpses to putrefy.

Those of Louis' army who'd survived the Battle of Mohacs felt consumed by rage as they gazed at this loathsome trophy. Yet they could do nothing except leave the crows to their banquet and there was no comradeship in defeat. Like chaff in the wind, the survivors simply drifted away.

With nowhere else to go, Thomas, Bos, Prometheus and Quintana decided to walk back to Mohacs, in the vain hope they'd find something to eat in the village. However, when they reached the small river beyond the ruined Hungarian camp, what little remained of their appetites quickly evaporated.

The stream's sluggish waters were now clogged with mangled, broken corpses and each bloody cadaver had been stripped naked by looters. Worse still, most of each body's flesh had already been chewed away by rats or packs of scavenging, feral dogs, yet, somehow, Prometheus managed to recognise the remains of the young Hungarian King.

"The curse was true. Louis wasn't destined to carry the Holy Lance so God struck him down," he said bitterly.

"There's no such thing as a curse, or how could I have held the Holy Lance in my hand?" countered Thomas.

"For once, the Englishman's right. Relics have no power for good or evil and that's the truth of it," added Bos, whereupon Prometheus rounded on the Frisian.

"Has it occurred to you that what we gave Louis wasn't the genuine relic? Maybe our famous sorcerer got confused and brought the forgery to Mohacs by mistake," he snapped but Thomas vehemently denied this foul slur on his reputation.

"Of course it's the real thing! I know it was dark ..." he began. Yet, he couldn't finish his sentence because there was a chance that he hadn't swapped the relics after all.

To restore his good name, Thomas tried to insist that Louis must have dropped the spear whilst trying to cross the river and he began to search in the mud for the missing Holy Lance.

Reluctantly, the others joined him but it wasn't long before everyone realised that they laboured in vain. After an hour, even Prometheus refused to help Thomas root through the piles of putrid corpses to find something that was probably a forgery and Quintana declared that they must move on.

"Forget it, Thomas. Real or not, some thieving *azab* will have picked it up and sold it by now. If it was the true spear, let the godless wretch suffer in Hell for his sacrilege and if it was fake let the scoundrel be damned for his greed," said Quintana and the others agreed that no purpose could be served by remaining in Mohacs.

The only question left to answer was where they should go. However, whilst Bos and Prometheus were in favour of returning to Italy, to rejoin the imperial legions fighting the French, Quintana declared that he was heartily sick of the martial life.

"I'm fed up with risking my neck for a measly four guilders a month, there must be an easier way for men of wit and courage to earn a crust," he said and he was astonished to see Thomas looking at him with a smile.

"Perhaps there is. I once read a book that told of vast riches buried in Italy," he said, and he explained that after the barbarian, Alaric the Goth, had sacked the ancient city of Rome, he'd buried his plunder in a hidden vault that had never been found, but the others chided Thomas for his credulity.

"Such tales of buried treasure are just stories to be told by bards after their noble masters have feasted," said Prometheus with a snort of feigned disinterest.

"And it's written in the Gospel of Matthew that man must not store up treasures on earth," added Bos.

"If you ask me, any barbarian king worthy of the name would've spent all his money on whores and wine in a week," said Quintana but Thomas was adamant that he knew how to find the lost treasure of Alaric the Goth.

"Say what you like, all I need is a copy of a Latin manuscript which was entrusted to the Jews of Apulia many years ago, so I'm going to Italy. My only question is: are you coming with me?"

## THE END

*Thomas' adventures continue in The Devil's Pearl find out more at www.thedevilstonechronicles.com.*

# ABOUT THE AUTHOR

Richard Anderton is married with four children and he works full time as a freelance writer. Though he contributes articles to newspapers and magazines on a wide variety of subjects, he has a particular interest in Medieval and Tudor history.

He lives close to the ancestral castle of the real Devilstone family, which inspired his first novel *The Devil's Band*, and *The Devil's Lance* is his second book featuring the fictitious dispossessed knight, alchemist, and soldier-of-fortune Thomas Devilstone.

Read more about the history behind the books, and Richard's other non-fiction history posts, on Facebook at: *www.facebook.com/thedevilstonechronicles*

You can also follow Richard on Twitter *@andertonTDC*

Made in the USA
Charleston, SC
02 November 2016